On a distant frontier, in a time long past,
in an ancient world filled with exotic
splendor and awesome dangers, a bold
adventurer set forth on a path of vengeance
and a quest for truth . . .

THE WALKING DRUM

Inspired by an inner drive as powerful as the beating of
the walking drums which set the rhythms for the mighty
merchant caravans of his day, young Kerbouchard is the
son of a fearless corsair. His father is betrayed and
sold into slavery by a corrupt baron who also kills
Kerbouchard's mother and destroys their home. Determined to find and rescue his father Kerbouchard em-
barks on a journey of enormous challenge, one that will
change his life forever.

Filled with all the rich historical detail, riveting drama
and robust characters that are trademarks of every Louis
L'Amour novel, here is a world-class adventure.

LOUIS L'AMOUR

THE WALKING DRUM

BANTAM BOOKS
TORONTO · NEW YORK · LONDON · SYDNEY · AUCKLAND

THE WALKING DRUM
Bantam Hardcover edition/June 1984
2nd printing . . . June 1984
Bantam paperback edition/May 1985

Library of Congress Cataloging in Publication Data
L'Amour, Louis, 1908–
The walking drum.

I. Title.
PZ3523.A446W27 1984   813'.52   83-25703
ISBN 0-552-24923-1

Published simultaneously in the United States and Canada

PRINTED IN THE UNITED STATES OF AMERICA

O   0 9 8 7

To Lou and Emily Wolfe

NORWAY

♦ Novgorod

BALTIC SEA

RUSSIA

Lubeck

SAXONY

SLAVS

Leipzig

Germany

BAVARIA

HOLY ROMAN EMPIRE

Danube R.

MAGYARS

Buda

Kiev

Dnieper R.

Volpno-Dobolak

Dniester R.

Bug R.

PETCHENEGS

Venice

Florence

Italy

Rome

DALMATIA

ADRIATIC SEA

BLACK SEA

BYZANTINE EMPIRE

Constantinople

MACEDONIA

KINGDOM

Palermo

SICILY

SICILY

GREECE

Megara

Athens

Troy

Iconium

Melitus

Thera

Rhodes

Malta

MEDITERRANEAN SEA

CRETE

MEDIEVAL EUROPE A.D. 1176

Almus Sentius

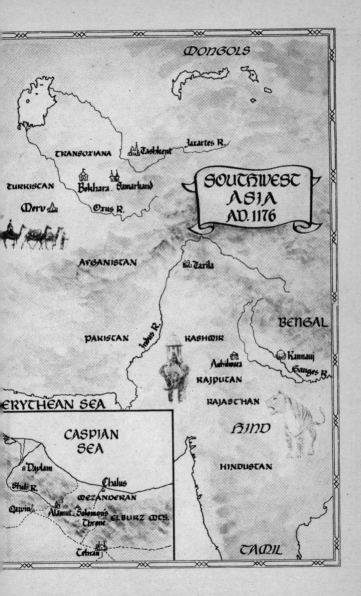

1

Nothing moved but the wind and only a few last, lingering drops of rain, only a blowing of water off the ruined wall. Listening, I heard no other sound. My imagination was creating foes where none existed.

Only hours ago death had visited this place. This heap of charred ruins had been my home, and a night ago I had lain staring into the darkness of the ceiling, dreaming as always of lands beyond the sea.

Now my mother lay in a shallow grave, dug by my own hands, and my home was a ruin where rainwater gathered in the hollows of the ancient stone floor, a floor put down by my ancestors before memory began.

Already dawn was suggesting itself to the sky. Waiting an instant longer, my knife held low in my fist, I told myself, "I will have that gold or kill any who comes between it and me."

Fire no longer smoldered among the fallen roof beams, for rain had damped it out, leaving the smell of charred wood when it has become wet, and the smell of death.

Darting from the shadows to the well coping, I ran my hand down inside the mouth of the well, counting down the cold stones.

Two . . . three . . . four . . . *five*!

With the point of my fine Damascus dagger, I worked at the mortar. Despite the damp chill, perspiration beaded my brow. At any time the men of Tournemine might return.

The stone loosened. Working it free with my fingers, I lifted it to the well coping. Sheathing my knife, I ran my

1

fingers into the hole, feeling for the box my father had
hidden there. They touched wood. Gently, carefully, I
drew it from the hole, a small box of strange-smelling
wood. Then from behind me, a soft footfall!

Turning, I saw that a dark figure loomed before me.
So large a man could only be Taillefeur, lieutenant to the
Baron de Tournemine, a veteran of mercenary wars.

"So!" Taillefeur was pleased. "I was right! The old
wolf hid treasure, and the cub has returned for it."

"It is nothing," I lied, "some trifles my father left
me."

"Let me have those trifles"—Taillefeur extended his
hand—"and you can be on your way. Let Tournemine
hunt his own children."

The night was cold. The wind chilled my body beneath the rain-soaked clothing. Nearby a large drop fell
into a puddle with a faint *plop*.

Among those who stopped at the house of my father
over the years had been a lean and savage man with a
knife-scarred, pockmarked skin. Grasping my arm with
fingers that bit into my flesh like claws, he grinned a
lopsided grin and advised, "Trust to your wits, boy, and to
your good right hand."

He had emptied his glass, leering. "And if you've a
good left and some gold, that helps, too!"

My left—my left hand rested upon the stone I had
removed from the well coping.

Boy I might be, but I was tall and strong as a man,
dark as an Arab from the sun, for I was not long from the
fishing banks beyond Iceland where I had gone with men
from the isle of Brehat.

"If I give you the box," I said as I gripped the stone
tighter, "you will let me go?"

"You are nothing to me. Give me the box."

He reached a hand to receive it, and I swung the
stone.

Too late, Taillefeur threw up his arm to ward off the
blow. He saved himself a crushed skull, but the blow
felled him in his tracks.

Leaping over his body, I fled to the moors, and for the second time in a few hours the moors were my saving.

What boy does not know the land of his boyhood? Every cave, every dolmen, every dip in the land and hole in the hedges, and all that lonely, rockbound coast for miles.

There I had played and imagined myself in wars, and there I could run, dodge, and elude. As I had run that afternoon to evade the men of Tournemine, so I ran now.

Behind me Taillefeur staggered to his feet. He got up and, groggy from my blow, staggered into the wall. I heard him curse. He must have glimpsed me running, because he gave a great shout and started after me.

Dodging into a hollow choked with brush, I scrambled through a tunnellike passage known to wolves and boys, and as the storm clouds were scattering like sheep to feed on the meadow of the sky, I came again to the cove.

The ship was there. The crew was ashore filling casks with water, and when they saw me coming, two of them drew swords and a third nocked an arrow to his bowstring, looking beyond to see if I was accompanied.

It was a squat, ill-painted vessel with a slanting mast and a single bank of oars, nothing like the sleek black ships of my father, who was a corsair.

The two who held swords advanced, looking fiercer when they realized I was but a boy, and alone.

"I would speak with your captain," I said.

They indicated a squat man, running somewhat to fat, in a dirty red cloak. His skin was swarthy, his eyes deep-sunk and furtive. I liked not the look of him and would have withdrawn had not the men of Tournemine been behind me, and searching.

"A boy!" He spoke impatiently.

"But a tall boy," one of them assured him, "and a strong lad, too!"

"Where do you sail?" I asked.

"Where the wind takes us." He eyed me with no favor, yet with a measuring quality in his glance.

"To Cyprus, perhaps? Or Sicily?"

He gave me quick attention, for such places were known to few but wandering merchants or Crusaders. But we upon this coast of Brittany were born to the sea. We were descendants of the Veneti, those Celtic seafaring men who, with their Druid priests, refused tribute to Rome and defied the legions of Julius Caesar.

"What do you know of Cyprus?" he sneered.

"My father may be there. I seek him."

"It is a far place. What would a father of yours be doing there?"

"My father," I said proudly, "is Kerbouchard!"

They were astonished, as I expected, for the ships of Kerbouchard harried the coasts, attacking the ships of many nations, trading beyond the farthest seas. My father's name was legend.

"Your voyage would be useless. By the time you came to Cyprus, he would have sailed."

There were lessons I had yet to learn, and one was not to talk too much. "His ship has been sunk, and my father has been killed or sold into slavery. I must find him."

The captain seemed relieved, for no man wishes to incur the displeasure of Kerbouchard, and he knew what he planned to do. Tall I was, and broader of shoulder than all but two of his crew.

"Ah? If you sail, will you work or pay?"

"If the price be not too great, I will pay."

The men of the crew edged nearer, and I wished for a sword. Yet what choice remained? I must escape with them or face the dogs of Tournemine.

"I could offer a piece of gold," I suggested.

"You would eat that much!" he said contemptuously, but his hard little eyes sharpened.

"Two pieces?"

"Where would a boy lay his hands upon gold?"

His sudden gesture took me by surprise, and before I could move to resist, I had been seized and thrown to the ground. Despite my struggles, the box was torn from my shirt and broken open. Bright gold spilled upon the sand,

and some of the coins rolled, setting off a greedy scramble.

The captain took the gold from their reluctant fingers to be divided among the crew. "Take him aboard," he commanded. "He has paid his way, but he shall work also or taste the whip."

My knife was jerked from its sheath by a moonfaced man with unkempt hair, who belted it. Him I would not forget. Damascus blades were hard to come by, and this was a gift from my father.

"You've learned something," the captain said, maliciously. "Never show your money before strangers. But do your work, and you shall live to see Sicily. I know a Turk there who will pay a pretty price for such a handsome lad." He grinned at me. "Although you may not long be a lad after he lays hands upon you."

Bruised and battered I was, but when my foot touched the deck a thrill went along my spine. Yet when taken to my place at the slaves' bench, and seeing the filth in which I must work, I tried to fight. That men could exist in such evil conditions seemed impossible, although there was little cleanliness in the houses along our coast, other than in my father's house.

He had traveled in Moslem lands in Africa and Spain, and brought to our house not only their rich fabrics but their way of living and their love of hot baths.

Shackled to my oar, I looked about me with distaste. How long I could endure this I had no idea, yet a time would come when I would learn how much a man can endure and yet survive. The condition of these galley slaves was abject, and I pitied them, and myself as well. Their backs bore evidence of what happened when their overseer walked along the benches with his whip.

Our craft demanded two men to each oar, and shackled beside me was a burly, red-haired ruffian. "You fought little," he said with contempt. "Have the Celts grown so weak?"

I spat blood. "The ship goes to Sicily, where I wish to go. Besides," I added, "death awaits me ashore."

His hard laugh told me that, whatever the whip had

done to the others, he still possessed spirit and strength. "If they get there!" he said cynically. "This lot knows little of fighting and less of seafaring. It will be a God's wonder if they do not drown all of us."

Red Mark he was called. "Have a care," he warned. "That brute on the runway is quick with the lash. Bend to your work, or he will have the hide off."

"My name is Kerbouchard," I said, and the saying of it made me sit a little straighter.

"It is a name with a sound to it," he admitted.

A little pompously, for I was young, I told him who my father was. "Men of my family were captains among the Veneti when they fought Caesar, and it is said there was a Kerbouchard among the monks who welcomed the Vikings when they first came to Iceland."

"A ship does not sail with yesterday's wind," Red Mark replied. "I know what Breton corsairing men have done, but what of *you*?"

"Ask me that question five years from now. I shall have an answer for you then."

Four years had gone since my father set forth on his voyage of trading and raiding, for piracy was a business of all ships when opportunity offered. The men of Brittany had been corsairs as long as ships had sailed on the deep waters.

As for myself, I had but returned from a voyage with the men of Brehat to the fishing grounds in the far west. Those months at sea had put muscles in my arms and shoulders and taught me how to live and work with men.

Returning home, I found our horses stolen, our flocks driven off, and that two of my father's oldest retainers had been set upon and murdered near Brignogan.

When my father was at home Tournemine trembled in his castle, for my father would have hung Tournemine by his heels from his own battlements. Yet try as I might, I could raise no men against him. Frightened they were, and cautioned, "Wait until your father returns."

When next Tournemine came, my mother and I met him at our gate with four strong men beside us, and two with arrows ready. We were too eager for his taste, so he threatened only, demanding tribute and promising to burn our place about our ears.

"Come when you will," my mother spoke proudly. "Soon Kerbouchard will be here to greet you."

His was a taunting laugh. "Think you I have not heard? He was killed fighting the Moors off the shores of Cyprus!"

This I repeated to Red Mark in whispers, and told how one day I had returned to find my mother murdered and my home in flames.

Mad with grief, I had sprung from behind a hedge and flung myself at Tournemine; only a quick move had saved his life. As it was, my blade laid open his cheek, showering him with blood. Astonished by the suddenness of my attack, his men failed to react, and I escaped, although my freedom proved to be short-lived.

Our galley sailed south, and over the next weeks I saw what Red Mark spoke was truth. These were not seamen. They blundered and wasted the wind. Fearful of losing sight of the shore they endangered themselves needlessly. Avoiding large ships, they preyed upon fishing boats and small villages, even murdering shepherds to steal sheep from the hill pastures.

The captain was called Walther, but of the crew we saw only Mesha, the brute who walked the runway with his lash.

On my mother's side, I descended from a long line of Druids, and I myself had received the training. From my earliest days I had been instructed in the ritual, so secret it was never written. All was learned by rote, for Druids were known for their fantastic memories, trained from birth.

Among the Celts a Druid took precedence over kings. The Druids were priests of a sort, but wise men, magicians and advisers to kings, keepers of the sacred knowledge. During my long days at the oar, I drowned my misery by

repeating in my mind the ancient runes, the ritual and the
sagas of our people, remembering as well our knowledge
of wind, water, and the flight of birds.

Each pull upon the oar brought me nearer to Sicily
and my father—if he lived. If he was indeed dead, I must
know, and if it was aid he needed, I must be strong to
help him.

Outside, the hull rustled the waters, scant inches
from our naked bodies. Red Mark and I teamed well, each
learning to spare the other.

Our captors were a mixed bag of ruffians, none of
them men of the sea. Each night they anchored, lying
often a whole day through, loafing and drinking. The
fishermen of Brehat with whom I sailed the cold outer
seas were daring men, not such petty rascals as these.
With those fishermen I had followed the gray geese from
Malin Head in Scotia beyond the green land to unknown
shores.

Navigation I knew well, and not only by stars but by
the sea's currents, the blowing of winds, the flight of
birds, and the fish. These things I kept to myself and
bided my time.

"Together," Red Mark said one day, "we might be
free."

For days we edged along the coasts of France and
then of Spain. Off the coast of Africa we attacked and
captured a small Arab merchantman.

Red Mark was contemptuous. "Cowards! They attack
nothing that is not helpless! Even Walther, for all his big
shoulders and loud mouth, is a coward."

An Arab prisoner from the captured ship was put at
an oar ahead of me, and the man beside him was a Moor
also. Knowing a few words of the language, I exchanged
greetings, and thinking to learn their tongue, I began to
listen and to practice. The few words learned before had
come from an escaped prisoner of the Moors, a seaman on
my father's vessel.

A night came when we turned back along the coast of Spain. One of the crew was a renegade, a thief driven from his village, and he offered to guide Walther to it. The galley was short of bread and meat, and the village, sparsely armed. Leaving guards, the crew took their weapons and went ashore.

An hour before dawn they staggered back drunk, dragging behind them a few miserable women and girls, leaving the village to hold the torch of its burning against the sky.

Red Mark ground his teeth and swore, memory lying cold upon him. His own village had been taken in just this way while he lay in a drunken sleep.

The crew no sooner staggered aboard than they cast off, fearful of reprisal. The sail was partly lifted, and the galley made slight headway upon the dark water, but with the rising sun, an offshore breeze filled the sail. With the wheel lashed the crew lay about in a drunken stupor while we rested on our oars, whispering among ourselves.

The wind freshened, and the vessel moved out upon the sea. Red Mark grinned at me. "This will put water into their knees! The lousy bunch of coasters!"

They sprawled on the deck like dead men, their bodies moving slightly with the roll of the galley.

There was a slight movement as one of the village women worked herself from under a man's heavy arm. She moved with infinite caution, and we, who could see but little of the deck, held our breath in hope for her. We who were in chains watched her who was free, wondering what she would do and hoping she would do something.

Her face was bruised and swollen from blows. She got to her feet, then drew his knife ever so gently from its scabbard, then she knelt beside the man and drew back the sheepskin jacket.

Ah, but this one knew where a man's heart lay! She lifted the knife high, then plunged it down.

His knees jerked, then relaxed slowly. She cast the knife away and went to the rail. She looked once toward the shore, not too distant yet, then dove over.

"She's drowning herself!" I protested.

"Maybe . . . yet it might be she will make it."

We peered past our oars and watched the sunlight flash upon her arms as she swam.

We never knew. The offshore breeze strengthened, and the galley moved out upon the sunlit water.

I wanted to believe she made the shore. The galley was five, perhaps six miles off the shore, but she was a strong-built wench with courage.

The deeper roll of the vessel started a cask moving. It banged against a bulwark, then rolled among us. Eagerly, the slaves bashed in the head of the cask and passed along their cups for the strong red wine.

Ah! There was a draft fit for men! The strong wine ran down my parched gullet, warming the muscles of my throat and setting my heart to pounding. It was a true wine, a man's wine, filled with authority.

We emptied the cask among us and tossed it over the side. Never had I been one for strong drink, but it was this or something which made me realize the wind that blew the vessel seaward might be a fresh wind for my fortunes.

With satisfaction I felt the roll become deeper, the wind stronger. Behind us the shoreline vanished.

A few drops of rain fell. One of the crew wiped a hand across his face and sat up. He stared stupidly at the sky, where clouds were now appearing, then a look of alarm flashed across his face and he leaped to his feet so suddenly he almost lost balance and fell. He grasped the bulwark and stared, aghast, at the deep-rolling sea beginning to be flecked with whitecaps.

He shouted, then he ran to Walther and shook him awake. Walther, angry at being suddenly awakened, struck out viciously. Then as the import of the man's words penetrated his awareness, he staggered to his feet. The crew scrambled up, too, staggering and falling and staring wildly at the empty sea.

They were far at sea; a storm was blowing up, and they had no idea in which direction lay the land.

Walther stared at the horizons. The sky was becoming overcast. No sun was visible.

"Now look!" Red Mark was pleased. "He has lost the land and has no idea which way to turn!"

Walther came along the runway among the slaves. Some of them must have been awake and would have noticed the vessel's course. He wished to ask, but dared not. He feared they might deliberately give him a wrong answer.

The galley wallowed in the sea, yet he dared give no order, for the direction chosen might easily take them further to sea. He glanced at Red Mark whom he knew to be a seafaring man, but the big Saxon's face showed him nothing.

At last he turned to me. I was younger than any other aboard but had come from a coast where all boys grow up knowing the ways of the sea.

"Which way did the wind take us?" he asked. "Where lies the land?"

My chance had come even sooner than I had dared hope.

"Tell me . . . *quickly!*"

"No."

The veins in his neck swelled. He gestured for Mesha and the whip. "We'll have it from you or your back in ribbons!" he threatened. "I'll—"

"If that whip touches me, I shall die before I speak one word. Death is better than this." I paused. "But you can make me pilot."

"*What?*"

Without the strong wine I might have lacked the nerve, but I think not, for I was my father's son.

Leaning on my oar, I said, "Why waste me here? Had I been pilot you would have no worries now. *I* would not have drunk wine. Why waste a Kerbouchard at an oar?"

Angrily, he turned his back and strode away, and when I looked around, Red Mark was grinning. "Now why didn't I think of that? But if you become pilot, will you forget us?"

"I shall forget nothing. I must wait my chance."

The clouds grew darker, and wind lay strong upon the sea. Waves crested and spat angry spray. The galley rolled heavily and shipped a small sea over the bow, the water rushing back and gurgling in the scuppers. Walther's face had turned green, and the crewmen were shaking in their wet breeches.

Walther walked back to me. "You shall try, and if you fail, you shall be hung head down from the bows until you die."

He turned to Mesha. "Strike the shackles."

When the chains fell from me, I stood and stretched wide my arms. It was good to be free. Then I turned upon the round-faced oaf who had stolen my knife. "Give me the blade!" I said.

He laughed scornfully. "Give you—? By the Gods, I'll—"

I kicked him viciously on the kneecap, and when he howled in anguish and bent to grasp his knee, I doubled my fist and struck down like a hammer on his kidney. He screamed and went to the deck on his knees. Reaching down, I took the knife from his belt.

"You will need a slave to take my place," I said. "There he is!"

Walther stared at me, hatred ugly in his small eyes. I knew then he would never be content until I lay dead at his feet.

"Take us to shore," he said sullenly, and walked from me. However, a few minutes later the moonfaced man was shackled in my place.

2

No man upon that deck was my friend, nor would I long survive unless I proved they could not do without me.

Returning to the coast presented no problem. No doubt several of those still in chains could have done as well. It was my good fortune to have spoken first, a lesson to be remembered.

Much debris littered the deck after their carousing, and once the galley was on course, I began cleaning up. Nor had I chosen a course that would take us immediately to the coast; I used every device to make it seem difficult.

Standing by the bulwark, I consulted the water, then I looked at the clouds. Then I wet my finger and held it up to get the direction of the wind, although it was obvious enough. Pacing the deck, I suddenly acted as if a decision had been made, and taking the tiller from the man on watch, I used my own hands to guide the ship.

Later, I relinquished the tiller to a crewman and went about making the place shipshape. Walther watched me suspiciously but approved.

When land was again in sight, I held myself ready, prepared to fight rather than return to the oar, but my arguments must have impressed Walther, for he left me alone.

There were sixteen oars to a side and two men to each oar. There was a deck forward and a deck aft, with narrow decks along the bulwarks above the heads of the galley slaves. Down the center where Mesha walked, it was open to the sky, and as he walked, his head was above the level of the deck. Constructed for coastal trade, she had cargo space fore and aft and more beneath Mesha's walk. She was slow and clumsy but seaworthy.

Aside from the slaves, sixty-two men made up the crew, and the number made it necessary to be constantly raiding to renew supplies. Originally, the vessel had probably been handled by no more than twelve men aside from slaves. Walther and his men feared to attack unless the advantage was obviously on their side. Several times they ventured close to a strong craft, but each time they sheared off and abandoned the attack.

Working about the deck, cleaning up, mending rigging, and maneuvering the craft, I began to plan.

Red Mark must be freed.

The Moors on the seat before Red Mark were good men, and there was another Moor near the stern whom I had not seen before. He was a strong, agile-looking man, unbroken by either Mesha's lash or the labor. He was a narrow-faced man with intensely black eyes and a hard, decisive look about him.

Contriving to drop some rope yarns near him, I bent to retrieve them and whispered, "You have a friend."

"By Allah," he said wryly, "I can use one! I am Selim."

Walking away, I felt Mesha's eyes upon me. He could have heard nothing but was suspicious by nature. He liked me not, nor I him, and the memory of his lash lay hot within my skull.

Young though I was, I knew the dangers a coward can offer, for his fear will often drive him to kill more quickly than if he were a brave man. Walther and his crew were cowards, and whatever must be done must be with care, for among them were a few good fighting men.

The crew liked me not at all. Occasionally, they vented their fury with words, but I ventured no replies, biding my time. I think they feared me because of my sudden rise and my decisive move against the man who had taken my knife. They feared what they did not understand.

Twice, they captured fisher boats, attacking lustily with swinging swords when the odds were seven or eight to one. And then, off the Mediterranean coast of Spain, they made a grand capture, and the fault was mine.

The sky had been blue that morning, and the air breathless, the sea smooth as glass. While busy splicing a line, I felt a sudden dampness. Suddenly, we were shrouded in fog, moving like a ghost ship through the mist.

A few minutes before the fog closed down I had glimpsed a merchantman sailing a course parallel to our own. Now, after a few minutes within the fog, I heard a faint creaking as of rigging, the slap of a loose sail, and a gurgle of water about a hull.

For what happened I have only myself to blame. I hated Walther and all his bloody, misbegotten crew, yet there was in me the blood of corsairs.

Walther came to stand beside me. "You heard something?"

"A ship," I said, "and not one of your scrawny fish boats but a fat, rich merchantman out of Alexandria or Palermo."

The glitter of greed was in his eyes. He touched his fat lips with his tongue. "They would be strong," he muttered, "we could not—"

"Why not?" I spoke with contempt for such fears. "Only one man was on deck when the fog closed in, and half the crew may be asleep. There was a storm last night, and they would be tired. Before they could organize resistance it would be over."

For once greed overcame caution. Grabbing a crewman, he sent him for others, and at his order I began to edge the vessel closer. Fifty men gathered along the bulwarks, keeping themselves out of sight.

Water slapped her hull, rigging creaked. We shipped our starboard oars, and the watchman on their deck came quickly to his ship's side, alarmed by the sound.

He saw us; his mouth opened to scream a warning, but an arrow transfixed his throat, and then our men were scrambling over their side. There was shouting then, a clash of arms, a scream of mortal agony.

That was the moment I had chosen to shear off and

escape, but the chance was lost in the instant of birth, for Walther was beside me, a sword point in my ribs as if he had guessed my intent. I dared make no move.

The surprise attack had been a complete success. The merchantman's crew awakened only to die; moreover, the ship was well-found, with a rich cargo of silk and cinnamon. There was gold and silver coin . . . and a girl.

She struggled to the ship's side, the prisoner of Cervon, a huge Gaul, the largest man in our crew. Beside her an older man pleaded and argued with the Gaul. Her eyes, wide with terror, looked across the rails of the two ships into mine. She could have been no more than sixteen and was very beautiful. Her eyes met mine, pleading and frightened.

"Stop him," I protested to Walther.

"He captured her. She is his."

There was envy in his tone, for he hated to see such a girl in the arms of another. It was an envy to be used.

"You would waste such a girl? That is no shepherd's daughter! Would you throw away a fortune for a moment in the scuppers? Can't you see? This girl is worth more than all the loot combined! Think what her family would pay!"

Greed won where any other argument would have failed. The Gaul was pressing her against the bulwark and fending off the older man with one hand. Even at this distance it could be seen that her flesh was soft and her dress woven with threads of gold.

A fortune-hungry and jealous man, Walther seized the chance. "Stop!" he shouted to the Gaul. "Bring her here, and the man as well!"

The older man spotted Walther and leaned over the rail of their ship. "We can pay, and pay handsomely if the girl is unharmed."

Cervon hesitated, angry, but found no sympathy, for envy as well as the idea of profit had turned the crew against him. Angrily, he swung her over the side and dropped her to our deck, where we were lashed alongside.

He left the man to find his own way, and went away, disgruntled and furious.

Already our crew was looting the vessel of both cargo and supplies. Bales and barrels came over the side, as the men stripped the vessel hurriedly, for fear a warship might intervene before the looting was complete.

The girl threw a glance my way and spoke to the older man beside her who also looked my way. Knowing I had spoken for her gave her more hope than the moment deserved. Yet I smiled at her, and she smiled in return.

When all attention was diverted by the stripping of the prize, I spoke softly to her, in Arabic. "Friend," I said.

The fog thinned, and our crew hurriedly abandoned the captured ship.

Ignoring the complaints of Cervon, Walther turned to the man. "Who are you? What can you pay?"

The man was not so old as at first he had seemed. He was well setup, a man of military bearing, gray of hair but clear of eye, and obviously accustomed to command. He had formed a quick estimate of Walther, and expected no mercy from the others.

"She is the daughter of ibn-Sharaz, of Palermo, a wealthy man, and one with power."

"She has not the Moorish look," Walther grumbled. "I think you lie."

"Her mother was Circassian, blonde as your northern girls. Treat her gently. If she is harmed, fifty ships will hunt you down."

"Fifty ships? For a slip of a girl?"

The man was brusque. "Fifty ships for the daughter of ibn-Sharaz, friend and adviser to William of Sicily!"

Walther paled. He had none of the sea rover's disdain for landlubber princes, although even a corsair might hesitate at the name of William of Sicily, descendant of Norman conquerors, his ships upon every sea, his spies in every port.

"Such a man can pay," Walther admitted, but speaking as much to advise his crew as to acknowledge the fact.

"Take us safely to any port in Spain, and you will be paid well and what you have done forgotten."

Of the first I was convinced, of the second I was not. This man and his kind were not likely to forgive such an injury, and I remembered the story my father had told me of the young Julius Caesar, taken by pirates. He promised to return after his ransom was paid, and hang them every one, and they laughed. Yet he did return, and he did hang them, and this man was of such a kind.

Walther strode off to discuss the matter with the crew, and the man spoke to me. "You have helped us. I value such aid."

"My word carries small weight here. Until recently I was chained to an oar. They neither like nor trust me."

"They listened to you."

"They are ruled by greed and envy. Each wanted her for himself, and hence was willing to listen when I suggested ransom."

"Remain our friend, and I shall replace the weight of your chains with an equal weight of gold."

When one is young, one does not think of gold but only of the light in a maiden's eyes. Yet a time would come when I would discover that one might have both—if one had wit.

Never had I seen such a girl. Our northern girls were stronger but their skin less fine from exposure to sun and wind, and they lacked garments such as she wore on this day. My father's house had been filled with treasures looted from eastern ships, and often he had spoken of the life in Moorish Spain where I longed to go.

Our northern castles were cold, drafty halls with narrow windows and few comforts, their floors scattered with straw and the accumulated refuse of months. My father had brought from Moorish Spain a love of beauty and cleanliness. So, accustomed to my own home, I could not abide the ill-smelling castles of nobles who had little but weapons and pride.

The old Crusaders learned a little, but merchants and minstrels had picked up the Moorish habit of bathing, changing their clothing instead of allowing it to wear out and drop off. Occasionally, travelers brought books to their homes. But books of any kind were rare in the land of the Franks, and the few available were eagerly read— but read only in private for fear the church might disapprove.

My father, not an educated man in the sense I was later to understand, was intelligent and observant, and like most of Brittany at the time was pagan rather than Christian. Christianity, for which my father had the greatest respect, had discarded much that was good along with the bad. The baths had been symbols of paganism, so baths and bathing were condemned, and few people bathed in Europe for nearly a thousand years. Books had been thrown out on the theory that if they repeated what the Bible said, they were unnecessary, and if they said what was not in the Bible, they were untrue.

Travel, ever an enlightening influence, had revealed to my father a more agreeable way of life. He had learned to appreciate the seasoned and carefully prepared food of the Mediterranean countries as well as their silken garments. The first rugs seen in Armorica were brought home by rovers of the seas, and many of the first books, also. Two of those brought to our house were Latin; another was in Arabic.

The first of the Latin books was Vegetius on the tactics of the Roman legion, and during that long voyage to Iceland and beyond, I read and reread it. The second book in Latin was the *Illustrious Lives*, by Plutarch.

The book in Arabic was on astronomy, and from this I learned much of navigation unknown in northern Europe. At various places in the volume were quotations from the Koran, and these I memorized.

Zorca, our Greek servant, had traveled up the Nile, had seen the pyramids, great temples, and all manner of strange animals. How much I could believe I did not know, but I loved his tales of Trebizond, the Black Sea, and the Greek isles.

The girl cast me a glance and said, "I am Aziza."

"And I am Kerbouchard, Mathurin Kerbouchard."

"It has a bold sound."

"My father was Jean Kerbouchard. It was also the name of an ancestor who fought Caesar."

The man glanced at me, his curiosity aroused. "What know you of Caesar?"

"He was an enemy of my people, but I have read of him in a book by Plutarch." Easing the tiller, I added, "Caesar attempted to destroy my people because they refused tribute."

Walther strode aft. "We go to a cove near Málaga." He drew from his tunic a chart from the vessel we had looted, and showed it to me, indicating a place on the shore. "Can you take us to that place?"

"I can."

"Do so, and when the ransom is paid you shall have a share."

Aziza's eyes were on me. Was she wondering if I would betray her for that reward?

Had she known my mind she would have been unworried, for there was no wealth anywhere that meant half so much as a glance from her eyes or the shape of her body beneath her thin clothing.

But I was young then.

3

When darkness came I was awakened and returned to my place by the steering oar. Near the bulwark huddled the two captives.

His name, I discovered, was Redwan, and he was a warrior as well as a statesman, a man of consequence. He slept now, snoring slightly. There was no sound from Aziza, and I suspected she was awake.

"Look to your steering," Walther advised. "We must not be discovered. Find the cove, and when shore is sighted, awaken me.

"Attempt no foolishness, for the Gaul is awake and so are the men of Finnveden. One sight of betrayal, and you will be killed."

Nor did I doubt his words, for the three men of Finnveden were cold and dangerous men, not so cowardly as the others, but morose and silent, vicious in any kind of a fight and without a thought for any but themselves. I suspected I should have to face them one day.

The sea was dark, the waters glassy. No oars were in use, only the sail to give us steerage way, for we wanted no sound to bring attention upon us.

There were no stars. Water rustled along the hull, phosphorescent ripples rolling back from the bow. The sky was heavily overcast with a hint of rain. Timbers creaked as the galley moved in a slow roll through the dark water. Here and there a slave muttered in his sleep, or murmured some half-forgotten name. Metal chinked upon metal as weapons touched in the night, for the men slept fully armed.

She came to me so quietly I scarcely realized her presence but for the perfume. Her hand touched my arm. "You must help us, Kerbouchard! *Please!*"

Her fear gave me strength, for when is one not the stronger through being needed?

Yet she stirred me in other ways, for along our Breton shores there were no such girls as this. Often they were lovely but never so soft and delicate as this.

"I shall do what I can."

"Already you have helped. It was you who stopped— that man."

"Your companion is a Moor?"

"A Norman. He was a great captain among them when he fought against us, but now he has become an ally."

Her nearness was disturbing, for I knew little of women, yet most of my fear was that she should be seen near me and our nearness misunderstood. Such a suspicion might be enough to throw her to the crew, so when she returned to her place near the bulwark I was relieved.

My experience with women had been slight, with little time for conversation. There had been a few meetings with girls on the moors who had a way of becoming lost where I was accustomed to wander alone.

Of course, there had been a time when a fine caravan camped atop the cliffs, and a young woman came alone to the beach to search for shells. She found more than she bargained for, which she seemed to appreciate and endure with fortitude, even to the extent of taking an active interest in the proceedings.

She was quite a beautiful young woman, the widow, I discovered, of a merchant in Angers. This I learned later at the inn where they stopped for the night.

She had come alone to the beach where I lay sunning myself on the warm sand, and her search for shells brought her closer and closer until I began to suspect that her interest in marine life might be more extensive than at first appeared.

When she discovered that I was awake, a conversation developed, so naturally I told her of the cave behind the dunes. Intrigued by the mystery of it, she wished to see the cave, but what she found there was obviously no mystery.

The boom of a not too distant surf interrupted my thoughts, and my call awakened Walther who came aft, rubbing sleep from his eyes. The dark line of the shore appeared, and one of the men of Finnveden took his place in the bow to conn us in.

The cove was a mere cutback in the shoreline, partly screened by a bluff, and no place to lie with southerly or easterly winds. We could dimly make out the white sands, which lay deserted and still.

A change had come over the galley. Once committed to demand ransom for the prisoners, the ship's company was alert. Armed men came aft, and others scattered themselves along the bulwark. From now until we were safely at sea, this guard would stand twenty-four hours a day.

The lure of a strange, shadowed shore was upon me. I listened to the whisper of the sea upon the sand, the creaking of the ship itself, the lap of water against the hull, and the *chock*, *chuck* sound from the trailing oars.

What destiny awaited me here? What girls might lure and laugh and leave me? What fortune might come? What mystery? In the strange and perfumed night I felt a stirring within me, a longing to be ashore, to go walking alone up through the trees that lay beyond the beach.

Walther came aft again with Eric, the eldest of the Finnvedens, Cervon the Gaul, and others.

Redwan was standing, Aziza beside him. Walther stared threateningly at him, but Redwan was not one to be intimidated by casual freebooters. "We shall send three men to Málaga," Walther advised him, "if they do not return, you will be put to death, and the girl, too, in time."

Redwan drew a ring from his finger. "Your men will live if they do as I say and if they convey this to Hisham ibn-Bashar, in Málaga. Tell him I insist upon secrecy and immediate payment."

"Secrecy?"

"Would you want a dozen galleys to descend upon you? Of course, there must be secrecy."

Walther accepted that, but it caused me to wonder. It seemed to me that Redwan might have another need for secrecy, some reason that might concern either Aziza or himself.

Walther hesitated, and I watched him with irritated contempt. He was a petty man accustomed to dealing with paltry sums and people of no significance. He had no idea what ransom to ask, nor did Eric or Cervon.

"I shall demand one . . ." he seemed to gain courage, "I shall demand three thousand dinars!" The figure exploded from him; he was frightened by his own boldness.

Redwan laughed harshly, irritably. "You are a fool, and you would make a fool of me! Do you think I am some rascally merchant that you'd demand a slave's ransom?"

There had been talk of ransom over the wine in my father's house. "Ten thousand," I interrupted, "would be the price I would ask, and it would be so small only because it could be so quickly collected and delivered."

Redwan was amused. "Walther, you would do well to resign your position to this man. He's more fitted to be a pirate than any of you."

Walther gave me an ugly look. He liked none of it, for his men were listening. Cervon had been startled by the demand for three thousand, but now that Redwan had accepted the idea of ten thousand Cervon was staring angrily at Walther.

"So be it then," Walther said, his little eyes bright with malice, "and you shall go to collect it, you, Eric, and Cervon."

The Gaul shook his heavy head. "I shall stay." He looked past Walther at Aziza. "Let the brothers go."

"It is better so," Eric agreed.

Redwan was pleased. "You will have no trouble. Hisham ibn-Bashar is skilled in such matters. He is an old man but quick-witted. Explain the situation, and he will do what is needed."

From clothing captured with the looted ship, I found that which suited me admirably, and I dressed as a Moorish gentleman of fashion. There was also a sword, a fine weapon, and one which I well knew how to use.

When I returned to the deck Aziza's surprised gasp was ample reward for my efforts. Even Walther was startled.

It was a temptation when I stood at last before him, a temptation to cut him down on his own deck. Long had I hated him for the brutal way he had robbed and enslaved me, forcing me to slave for his lot of yapping mongrels. When the time came, they would pay and have cause to repent their treatment of me.

Yet my major objective must never be forgotten: to find my way to Cyprus and free my father if he was imprisoned, and to learn of his fate whatever it might be.

Together then we could return to pay our respects to the Baron de Tournemine.

Yet here, now, lay the land of my dreams. Here were the cities of Granada, Seville, Toldeo, and Córdoba. How long had I dreamed, waking and sleeping, of such cities? For I wanted a life wider and deeper than my own Breton shores could offer. To make my way in a larger world, to see more, to learn more, to be more. This was my dream.

Even now I was learning, I was becoming. The clothing I now wore was far better than any I had ever possessed, and with envy I had observed the elegance with which Redwan carried himself. To such things must I pay attention, for I had much to learn.

Daylight was strong upon the water when we landed on the beach. Seeing my reflection in a patch of still water just back from the shore, I was suddenly aware that I need fear comparison to no man. I was taller than when I came to the galley, and infinitely stronger. The months of laboring at an oar added inches to my chest and shoulders, rounding my arms with muscle.

In the black full trousers, black boots of the finest cordovan leather, a smoke-blue turban of silk, a cloak of

dark blue wool worn over a white silk shirt and a dark blue
sash, I looked quite the Moorish dandy. Under the cloak I
wore a waist-length brocaded jacket of gold and blue.
Beside me the Finnvedens were shabby, grubby-looking
men in their leather jerkins.

Appearances count for little, and I knew I must shape
the character of the man I wished to be into something of
worth. Among the Moors I must be slow to act, observing
their behavior with care, and so learn how to conduct
myself.

My Arabic was good, if simple. It was unlikely I
would be called upon to carry on discussions of philosophy,
so the Arabic I knew would be sufficient. My Latin, if it
came to that, was excellent. Here and there I had picked
up a smattering of a dozen tongues or their argot, the
slang of waterfront and marketplace. Much of this had
come from my father's crew who were men of many
countries, or from those aboard the galley.

It was good to feel the earth beneath my feet again,
but one thing I understood. In my present garb I could
not come walking into Málaga like any peasant or herder
of sheep. I must have a horse, as a gentleman would.

We climbed the hill from the shore and stood at the
edge of a coast road if such it could be called.

Suddenly, I knew this was a beginning for me. I was
the one with the knowledge, and here I must take
command. The Finnvedens were my guards as well as
captors. Although I had become pilot, I had no authority
over the crew. I was still a captive, a slave. Yet Redwan's
message had been given to me, and I would negotiate.

Much of command is the ability to take command.

Eric interrupted my thinking. "Are we to stand here
in the sun? Let us be off!"

"Wait!"

They stopped, half angry, for my word had been a
command. "There is a caravan coming."

They listened, heard it, and squatted beside the road,
irritated at being stopped. I remained where I was. They
would appear to be menials; I, the master.

Three riders rode ahead, each dressed in the habiliments of wealth and fashion. Behind them rode twenty soldiers, a train of pack mules, and, I noticed with satisfaction, several spare horses.

Stepping boldly into the road, I lifted my hand.

Six soldiers, moving at some unheard command, detached themselves in groups of three and swept down upon me, swinging in a wide circle and closing in around me with drawn scimitars. It was a pretty maneuver.

Of the three who commanded here, one was young, not more than twenty-five, but haughty of face and manner. He wore a neatly trimmed black mustache and pointed beard; there was a lithe, easy movement about him that indicated trained muscles, but in his features there were lines of cruelty. I decided I did not like him.

He who rode in the center was much older, with a white full beard and a manner both dignified and noble. The third man was stocky of body and powerfully built. This one was obviously a soldier.

"Greetings, Eminence! I ask your consideration."

He with the haughty face spoke first. "Who are you? What do you do here?"

"Oh, Commander of the Faithful, I am but a poor student bound for Córdoba. Our ship was taken by the infidel. I go to Málaga to have speech with Hisham ibn-Bashar on a matter of greatest importance."

"I think you lie."

The older man studied me with shrewd, appraising eyes, yet not without humor. He was richly clad, obviously a person of importance.

"This matter of importance," the old man said. "What is it?"

"A message, Auspicious One, for the ears of Hisham alone."

"Give us the message," the young man demanded. "We will judge its importance."

"I have a trust," I replied.

Before the sharp-featured young man could reply, the older man spoke to the soldier beside him. "Duban, mount

these men. When we arrive in Málaga, do you go with
him to Hisham. I would have a report of this from him."

The Finnvedens made a hard thing of riding, but I
had known the saddles of my father's horses since birth,
and while they struggled to maintain their seats, I listened
attentively.

The hawk-featured young man was a military commander of importance, called ibn-Haram. It was a name I
felt I should have reason to remember, and I liked him
not at all.

We rode slowly, affording me ample time to see what
lay before and around me, and I was amazed. Never had I
seen a city or anything more than the villages along my
native coast, nor were those villages beautiful, but mere
collections of hovels, squat houses, and narrow streets
often filled with refuse.

We passed under the great gate at Málaga and wound
through narrow streets. Above us towered the walls of
houses, their high windows screened by alabaster. Often
behind those screens I caught a suggestion of movement.
These might be the Moorish beauties of whom I had
heard.

We next passed through a bazaar where booths offered all manner of strange things for sale. Carpets from
Isfahan, pearls from Basra, enameled leather from Córdoba,
linens from Salamanca, silks from Granada, woolens from
Segovia, the blades and armor from Seville or Toledo.
Surely, there could not be in the world another city so
crowded, so filled with the world's goods! I said as much,
and Duban laughed.

"Fool! See Córdoba! See Córdoba and die! One street
is ten miles long and lighted from end to end! There is
more light there by night than here by day! It has thousands of fountains, scores of magnificent buildings!

"It has been said there are sixty thousand shops in
Córdoba! But before you speak of cities, see Baghdad! See
Damascus and Alexandria, and there be those who speak
of even greater cities farther away to the east.

"This . . . ?" he shrugged. "It is well enough, I suppose."

Duban indicated a narrow street that turned off to the right, and led the way. The Finnvedens followed us, muttering irritably at their galled behinds and chafed thighs, sore from unaccustomed riding. "Who was the old one you were escorting?" I asked Duban.

"Abu-Abdallah, a friend to the Caliph."

We drew up at a heavy door of oak, bound with straps of iron and iron hinges. On either side was a narrow slit for the use of defenders.

The door swung open as Duban spoke, and we entered. Immediately, the hot street was left behind. We rode a dozen steps alongside a colonnade bordering a patio. Palm trees grew there, and vines trailed from the garden walls. The air was miraculously cool and pleasant. We dismounted, and a slave took our horses.

Duban turned to the Finnvedens. "Remain here," he said, but they began to grumble, so I suggested that I take Eric with me.

Duban glanced at the ill-smelling pirate and shrugged, then led the way along a shadowed passage. A Nubian slave met us and conducted us to a cool, thickly carpeted room. On the far side sat a plump, bearded man with a round, shrewd face and intensely black eyes.

He was neither young nor old, and when our eyes met I felt a premonition that this was a man important to me, and not only for the immediate problem.

He glanced from me to the Finnveden and then came to his feet in one swift, fluid movement. There were muscles beneath that fat.

"Welcome! Duban, you come too rarely to my miserable house!" He bowed. "May your shadow never grow less!" Eric stood glowering, liking none of this, for with no effort on my part the situation had moved beyond control of the Finnvedens, and I intended it to remain so. That they were suspicious of me I knew, and rightly so, for I meant to have the better of that pack of thieves, and not only for myself but for that courageous village woman whom I had seen dive overboard and swim off toward the shores of Spain.

"This one has, he says, a message for Hisham ibn-Bashar." He added with what seemed a warning, "I was escorting Abu Abdallah when we came upon him beside the road. Ibn-Haram was with us."

"Ah?"

Never had I heard so much expression in a word. I stepped forward. The ring of Redwan was upon my hand, the distinctive seal turned inward, and now with a gesture as of greeting I opened my palm toward him. It was a natural movement, and I doubted even Duban noticed its significance. Yet light fell upon it right as Hisham's gaze touched it.

"You may speak," he said, "what concerns me concerns my friend."

"It is a matter of ransom, a matter of ten thousand dinars. It is a matter, also, of the daughter of ibn-Sharaz."

Duban dropped his hand to his scimitar and moved to face both myself and the Finnveden.

"I must speak carefully"—I was using the Arabic—"for I am a prisoner also. This man and those outside were sent to guard me, to kill me if I betray them."

"A lie!" Duban scoffed.

"Wait!" Hisham lifted a hand. He asked several questions then, enough to tell him I knew those of whom we spoke. Had I mentioned them in the presence of ibn-Haram?

"He said nothing," Duban admitted. "It was most fortunate."

Here was some intrigue, and it was obvious they did not want known the captivity of Count Redwan. It was equally obvious that the two were friends to Redwan and enemies to that hawk-faced ibn-Haram, which suited me.

"What is done," I suggested, "had best be done quickly. Ibn-Haram was suspicious and might return, discover the ship, and make inquiries."

Hisham agreed. "Will your captain honor the ransom? Will he release the captives if paid?"

"I believe I can impress him that he must. Redwan has worried him by suggesting he would incur the wrath of William of Sicily, but believe me, Your Eminence, Walther is not to be trusted, only frightened."

"And if you return, what will happen to you?"

Briefly, I explained my position aboard the vessel. "I shall have to return aboard, but shall stay no longer than Cádiz."

Hisham hesitated momentarily. "Duban and I must talk of this alone. As you may have surmised, this affair has ramifications far beyond a matter of ransom. You and your men will be fed, and we will make a decision."

At his handclap a huge Negro appeared and led us to a room far back in the building. Little traveled though I was, the reactions of Eric amused me. At sea he and his brothers were the boldest of that motley crew, but here his boldness was gone, and he stayed close to me, unsure of where even to put his feet. He was a stocky man with small, suspicious eyes and sparse blond hair.

"They will get the gold," I told him, "and we shall be returning to the ship tonight."

"Ten thousand dinars! It is a great sum."

It could do me no harm to remind him. "Walther asked for but three thousand," I said.

"Walther is a fool," Eric said sullenly.

After we had eaten, we were shown to a chamber where we might rest, and lying awake on the cushions provided, I stared at the ceiling, listened to the sound of the fountain, and wished I could have taken more time to look about. This was the sort of house of which my father had spoken, and magnificent beyond anything I had imagined.

Now I had thinking to do. First, Aziza must be freed, and Redwan also. Then I must somehow influence Walther to proceed to Cádiz. If he did so, and I knew the crew would be bursting with eagerness to spend their gold where they could get its value, then I would plot to free Red Mark, Selim, and the others.

To get my money back would not be enough. They

had taken months of my life, and for this they would pay. For who is content to get only his capital back from an investment? There must be profit also.

Cádiz had many advantages. It was one of the oldest ports in the world, called Gades before it was Cádiz, and Phoenician ships had made it a major port before the time of he who is called the Christ.

If my father, a noted corsair, had been slain off Cyprus there would be some knowledge of it in Cádiz. Long ago my father had taught me to seek information where seamen gathered, for their talk was ever of daring and death, of the far lands and strange seas. There would certainly be talk of Kerbouchard.

Freedom first, then money. Freedom without money would simply make me a slave of another kind, a slave to a need for food, for shelter.

It was full dark when the Negro came. "Quickly!" he whispered, "there is no time."

Duban awaited us in a small, stone-flagged room. He was dressed in black, and handed each of us a black cloak. He glanced at my sword. "Can you use that?"

"Well enough," I said.

"Ibn-Haram is a man greedy for power, with many followers. He does not wish Count Redwan or Aziza to arrive here, so you may have need of a sword.

"If Aziza's marriage is completed, it will unite a powerful family of Córdoba with one equally strong in Sicily, and the plans of ibn-Haram will be ruined. He is desperate."

Horses awaited us, and a guard of armed men. Two leather bags were thrown across my saddle, and Durban himself carried two more.

The alley down which we rode was unpaved, so the hooves of our horses made no sound. A sally port was opened as we approached and closed silently when we had passed through.

Duban explained as we rode some of the trouble presently existing in Moorish Spain.

Aba Ya-cub Yusuf was in power, but many remained loyal to the Almoravids, although they had been deprived of power years ago by the Berber dynasty of the Almohads. Agents of the Almoravids moved among the friends of Yusuf, and no man could be sure who was friend or enemy. Old tribal feuds carried over from Arabia or North Africa still smoldered, for the Arab does not quickly forget.

The internecine struggles in Spain meant nothing to me, and I wished to keep my head on my shoulders, not lopped off because of some feud that was no concern of mine. My allegiance was to my father, myself, and my future, if any.

Only our saddles creaked in the night, only the wind stirred. Soon we could smell the sea, a freshness on the wind, a certain lightness in the sky.

Around me the soldiers loosened their swords in their scabbards, and there was a sitting straighter in the saddle, a readiness for combat.

The smell of fight was in my nostrils also, for I was young, and youth expects to live forever. Youth has not yet discovered that death recognizes no age limits. Death had brushed my shoulders many times in the past months, but it remained something that happened to others.

"Ride to the shore," Duban whispered. "Two of my men will remain with the horses. We—"

They came suddenly from the darkness, a rushing wall of mounted men. We had only a flash of warning before they were upon us, the pound of hooves, the sound of tearing earth, a clash of swords.

4

Scarcely had my feet touched ground before they were upon us, knocking me backward into the brush. As I scrambled from the brush, sword in hand, I was attacked by a huge bearded fellow in a coat of mail, who swung a wicked blow at my head. More from the impetus of my rush than skill, I went to one knee and thrust blindly upward, my point taking him in the armpit below his uplifted blade.

He screamed, and his falling ax but narrowly missed my skull. He screamed again and jerked free, reaching for the knife he carried, but my following slash laid open his throat from side to side, and he staggered off, clutching it with both hands.

Someone sprang upon me from behind, and tripping over a body, I fell, throwing the man from me. My outstretched hand dropped upon a sack of gold, and with rare presence of mind, I grasped it, rolling over into the brush. My attacker's descending blow with a battle-ax caught in the limbs above me, and my thrust entered his belly.

The unexpected onslaught had found me fighting blindly and without skill, with no thought but to survive. Around me all was a confusion of plunging horses and fighting men, clanging steel and the cries of the wounded.

The sack of gold brought me to my senses, for this was no fight of mine. Swiftly, I searched about for the other sacks and found them. They were of leather, strongly made to carry gold, and I gathered them to me.

The fighting had moved off some thirty or forty yards

where Duban and his men had gathered. Of the Finnvedens I saw nothing and cared less.

Grasping around for the last sack of gold, I found it, but along with it were a face and another reaching hand. In the next moment the man was up and striking at me, but I butted him in the face, feeling his nose crunch, and then I struck him with my fist as the old Greeks were wont to do. He fell, and groping for my sword, I recovered it and crawled into the brush, taking the gold with me.

The battle waged furiously for several minutes while I fought to catch my breath, then the fighting broke off, and there was a rattle of retreating hooves.

I remained still. Nearby a man moaned, but I made no move. In this group I was a man without friends. I was alone. Also, I was thinking, unless this gold reached the ship, there would be no freedom for Redwan and Aziza.

My clothing, which I had worn with pride, was smeared with dirt, blood, and leaves, but I seemed unhurt, a fact due more to luck than skill.

An hour passed. Soon it would be growing light. How many others might be lying about waiting for the light, I could not know.

Considering the gold, I thought how easily it might be concealed, and after the confusion when all had left the scene I might find an abandoned horse and ride away with ten thousand dinars. It was a princely sum to one in my condition, but there was a matter of self-respect. And of course, there was Aziza.

Honor can be a troublesome thing, but if one has it one does not lightly yield it.

Now, without the aid of Duban, I must negotiate the release of Aziza and Redwan.

One of the sacks had been slashed by a sword, and I bound it together as best I could, and retrieving the few coins from the leaves, I stowed them in my pockets. Then, with utmost care, I eased myself through the brush and down the slope. Several minutes later I found myself at the edge of the sand.

Beyond the sand the sea curled its foaming lips upon
the shore. Nearby I heard movement, somebody who
stumbled and almost fell. Hastily, I buried the sacks of
gold, then I emerged, sword in hand.

The walker was Eric, and with him one of his brothers.

His nose was broken and one of his eyes swollen shut.
So he must have been the one I had butted in the darkness!
Taking hold of his wounded brother, we three staggered
to the beach and hallooed the ship.

After some hesitation while the Finnvedens sat upon
the sand, a boat shoved off from the ship. Walther was in
it. He did not look pleased, just sweating and evil. It was
gold he wanted, and not us. "The dinars? Where are
they?"

Keeping a sword's length from him, I made no move
to sheathe my weapon. "The girl? Where is she? And
Redwan?"

"They are well," he said impatiently, "but where is
the gold? Is that what you bring back to me? Naught but
blood and trouble?"

"I have the gold. Bring them to the beach."

He stared at me, his eyes mean with feeling. "Who
do you serve? Me or them?"

"I serve myself," I replied coolly, "but it was the
bargain. They must be freed."

"You speak of gold, but what proof have I?"

Reaching into the pocket behind my sash, I showed
him several coins. "There is a sample of it, but you must
be quick, for soldiers are coming!"

"Bring the gold to the ship, and we will free the
prisoners."

I was very young, but not that young. I smiled
mockingly. "When the prisoners are ashore you shall have
the gold."

He did not like my words, and he liked me less. Nor
was he pleased by this new independence of mine. He
stared a moment, sullen with anger, then he went to the
boat, taking the Finnvedens with him. I remained alone
upon the shore.

They seemed to take a long time. The sun arose behind somber clouds, and finally the boat came with Redwan and Aziza in it. The giant Cervon was there, as well as a dozen others, armed and ready.

As we moved back from the beach, I explained what had happened. "You are not safe," I warned Redwan. "When they have the gold they will try to kill you and take back Aziza."

Cervon was coming toward us, and two others were closing in. It was she they wanted, of course. They would kill Redwan, and me also, and tumble her there upon the beach.

My plan had been to have Duban there with a line of fighting men. Instead, I was alone. Yet I had a memory.

A memory of a broken box upon the sand and men scrambling for gold.

"Wait here," I said to Redwan, "I will get the gold."

They started after me, but they stopped when I began to climb the steep slope. Up there an arrow or a stone from a sling would bring me down, and they were a lazy lot.

"I shall be quick," I said, "but you must be ready." I did not look at Redwan, but my speech was for him. "The men who fought last night will return in force."

Digging out the sacks, I took them to the steep edge, then returned for the rest. I threw two sacks down the hill, but the third I deliberately threw against a sharp rock. The sack split, scattering the bright, bright gold.

Men cried out and rushed forward, scrambling for the gold coins. Redwan caught Aziza by the hand and fled.

Sword in hand, I started down the hill, but suddenly Cervon saw the girl fleeing, and with a shout he started after her, others following.

Walther shouted and followed after them. One man let fly an arrow that struck Redwan's helmet. He fell.

He staggered up, shouting at Aziza to keep going, but Cervon was rapidly overtaking her until I cut through the trees. He caught at her dress, and the flimsy material tore in his hand.

Catching his arm, I flung it aside. He grabbed at his
sword, but I was having none of that and ran him through
the body. He fell, the great bloody mass of him, and Aziza
paused.

"Run!" I gasped hoarsely. "Into the trees!"

Redwan caught up Cervon's sword. "Into the trees!" I
repeated. "Hurry!"

They started, but then there was a great rush of feet
from down the slope, and something struck me hard behind the ear. I grasped my sword and turned to face them,
but then a wave of darkness swept over me and I fell.

When I awakened it was to movement. The earth was
moving, or I was in a litter. My skull throbbed heavily.
The surface upon which I lay rose and fell.

The sea. I was at sea again.

It was late dusk, the sky overcast. I was lying on the
afterdeck and could hear the slow, measured beat of the
oars. A toe prodded me. "Get up!"

Walther . . . he was alive, then.

Staggering to my feet, I lurched against the bulwark.
My eyes opened . . . *Aziza?*

My head throbbed like an enormous drum. Walther
was staring at me. "She got away! It was your doing!"

Our Breton gods had not given me a quick brain for
no reason. I had the sense to act amazed. "I got the gold
for you! Was not that the bargain?"

He was furious, hating me more than ever. He had
never intended for the girl to be freed, yet he had intended,
I am sure, that Cervon was to die.

"I don't understand!" I protested. "I was chasing her
when I was hit! How could she have escaped from us all?"

"You did not see the Moors?"

The rush of feet I remembered had been the ship's
crew, but the shouts and the charge had been the Moors,
but whose? Were they the men of Duban? Or of ibn-Haram?

Had Aziza escaped our ship only to fall into their

hands? It was an ugly thought. Yet, would they harm her? Would she not be a valuable hostage?

"I was pursuing them when something hit me."

"You were trying to escape."

"What? And leave the reward you promised?"

That stopped him, bottling up his doubts, for what man would run away from a promise of gold? "You will get nothing," he said irritably. "You are a fool."

Who is the wise man and who the fool? The question has puzzled philosophers. "Perhaps the gold you keep from me will buy you pain in the bazaars of Cádiz, pain left to you by some cheap wench."

"Cádiz? Who spoke of Cádiz?"

"Where else? When one has gold where else to go but where there are the finest women, the best wines, the luxuries of the earth?"

Four men, I learned, had been slain in the charge, and one of the Finnvedens had died earlier. Another had been killed by an arrow after they had gotten into the boat, and of course, Cervon was dead. They did not suspect that it was I who killed him.

The sword had been taken from me, and my dagger as well, but they needed me now, and I would have both weapons back one day.

The roll of the ship was sickening to me. My mouth tasted evil, and my head throbbed. What struck me was probably a stone from a sling. Well, we Celts are noted for our hard heads. And with that thought I drifted into sleep.

Rain awakened me. A hard dash of rain, then another. I staggered to the bulwark. Walther was nearby, revealed in a flash of lightning. "Get busy!" he shouted. "Do something!"

"In this storm? With all the gold you have, I would be snugged down in some port with a loaf and a bottle of wine."

The seas were crested with white. I got a hand on the steering oar. We were headed west, which was right for Cádiz, so I tried as best I might to hold that course. Then, as the sky was gray with arriving day, he came to me, his fat jowls glistening with rain. "I like not the weather," he grumbled. "Take us to Cádiz."

The lush beauty of Málaga had spoiled me for the dirt of the galley and the greasy faces of the crew. They hated me and I them, and it was but a matter of time until I escaped or they killed me.

Yet chained to their oars were Selim and Red Mark, among others, and to them I had promised release. How long ago it seemed.

Cádiz . . . it was my port of destiny. Somehow, some way I would seek payment from Walther, and somehow I would escape and be my own man once more.

And I knew how—if only I could make it happen.

Wild the wind and dark the rolling sea, yet not so dark as the waves within my mind. Walther must pay, and my old companions of the oars must be freed.

Then, the wide world would be mine! I would be off to find my father, off to seek what fortune there was for me, and somewhere, somewither, a lass.

5

My eyes opened on despair. The galley was silent; water lapped lazily against the hull, but I was a prisoner. The crew, except for a few to guard the slaves and myself, had gone ashore to Cádiz.

All my plans had come to nothing, and I lay still, trying to think my way out of the situation. Sitting up, I looked down the line of sleeping slaves. Only Selim was awake. Our eyes met.

Here was a man who knew hope. His eyes burned with the hot fire of eagerness, and it was I who had given him hope. Yet what could I do against four armed men?

From the granite and green of the Armorican hills of Brittany, from her lonely moors and shores, her menhirs and dolmens, the world outside had seemed a place of bright romance where I would stride heroically among my enemies. And here I sat a prisoner to a pack of petty thieves on a stinking ship.

Was I, the son of Kerbouchard the Corsair, to stand for this?

One of the four was a Finnveden with no cause to like me, with a bow and arrow at his hand. His arrow would transfix my guts before I could even stand erect.

To be reckless is not to be brave, it is only to be a fool.

Caution always, but when a man acts he should act suddenly and with decision.

The others slept, but what could I do against the Finnveden?

What was it the pockmarked sailor had told me long ago? "Trust to your wits, boy."

Perhaps I had no wits, but that stupid ox with the bow . . . I might think myself wiser than he, but what price wisdom with an arrow in the guts?

"They are having their fun ashore," I suggested. "It is a pity Walther would not allow us a bottle of wine."

The Finnveden did not reply. He did not ask the question I hoped for, so I suggested, "He could at least have given us a bottle from the stores."

The Finnveden was alert. "What stores?"

"He will be having plenty of wine ashore. Why did he forget to tell us we might help ourselves from what lies below?"

"There's wine below?"

"Of course. It is stored under the arms chest where Walther sleeps."

His piglike eyes searched mine. He was a man sadly lacking in faith in his fellow man. He trusted me not at all.

Selim was listening, understanding our talk.

It needed time for the Finnveden to make up his mind. He was a heavy-shouldered, hairy man, uncertain of temper as an old bear with a sore tooth. Finally, he awakened the others, and they whispered together. Suddenly, they came over to me, knocked me sprawling, and bound me, hand and foot. There was a trick my father had taught me, to take a deep breath and to distend the muscles while being bound. With the slack gained when one exhales and relaxes the muscles, one can do much.

The time was not yet . . .

They went below, under the afterdeck, and then came tumbling back to the deck clutching the wine I had seen Walther hide. They began to work the corks loose with their teeth and to drink.

One waved a bottle over me, laughing contemptuously when wine splashed in my face.

The sun rose higher. Walther and the others would be waking up in the bordellos ashore. Suppose a relief was sent before these had drunk enough?

Closing my eyes, I let the sun warm my muscles. Bound though I was, I could yet enjoy this pleasure, for I am one that from his earliest days has loved the physical delights: the warmth of the sun, the drinking of cold, clear water, the taste of salt spray, the damp feel of fog upon the flesh, and the touch of a woman's hands.

Lying upon my back, I could feel the gentle movement of the deck beneath me, the creak of resting oars, the muttering of sleeping slaves, the clank of a chain as one moved restlessly in his sleep.

Drunken laughter came to my ears, a welcome sound.

The crew might return at any moment, but one could not fret over what might be. One does what one can, solving problems as they appear. I heard a soft snore.

The Finnveden was asleep. The others conversed in a desultory fashion, nursing the last bottle of wine. For them it was a lazy, easy time. They were in port, the vessel lay at anchor.

There was slack in my bonds, but pitifully little, yet by shrinking myself as small as possible, rolling my shoulders inward and bringing my arms as close together as possible, I gained a little room in which to work.

As they talked, I worked my fingers around until I could pluck at the knots. By the time another man was asleep, my hands were free.

Impatient of delay and fearing the return of the crew, I worked swiftly to free my ankles. A sword lay beside the sleeping guard. Carefully, I got to my feet. Selim was watching, his eyes hard and bright.

Measuring the distance to the sword, I started toward it. One of the guards turned and looked straight into my eyes.

Shocked, he was for the moment immobile, then as he started to rise, I kicked him. It was a style of fighting we in Brittany had long known where the feet were used as well as the hands. My kick was sharp, accurate, and it caught him under the chin, snapping his head back as if it were hinged. I seized the sword as the other guard grabbed for it.

The razor-sharp edge of the scimitar swept up, slitting his clothing and slicing through his chin as if it were butter. He fell, trying to scream from a throat already choking with blood.

Selim cried out, and I spun about to see the Finnveden fumbling with his bow and an arrow, still befuddled by sleep and wine.

It was too far to jump. Tossing the sword up, I caught the blade in my fingers and threw it like a javelin. His bow came up, arrow lining on me, but in the instant he would have let go, the thrown blade struck home and sank deep.

The struggle had been swift, silent, almost noiseless. Glancing shoreward, I saw no boats upon the bay. Sunlight sparkled on the water, but nothing moved. Quickly, I bound the sleeping guard and then ran to the armorer's chest for tools.

With a bar I ripped away the hasps that bound Selim, and then we crossed to Red Mark. Slaves caught at our garments, begging to be freed, but Red Mark came first. In part because he was my friend, but still more because I needed another strong man beside me to enforce discipline necessary to our survival.

Suddenly, as Selim and Red Mark were freed, my plan matured, and I knew what I must do.

As the men came on deck, I caught Red Mark's arm. "I want the galley cleaned, stem to stern."

"What?" He was incredulous. "We must escape!"

"Look at them! Look at yourself! If you go into Cádiz like this, you will be known for what you are, and you will be enslaved again.

"Listen to me! I know what I do! First, we will clean the galley, then we will clean ourselves. There is clothing, bales of it, from the goods we have taken. Each of us will have an outfit, each will have gold, then you shall hear what I have in mind.

"But no wine! No drinking of anything more than water. Trust me!"

With a careful watch kept for any approaching boat,

the slaves worked swiftly. The galley was given a thorough cleaning, and the decks were sluiced down with salt water hoisted by buckets from the bay.

Selim and another man, on my orders, went below to calculate the value of the cargo. He had just returned to the deck with his report when we saw a returning boat. Instantly, the slaves returned to their stations. Two others took their places as guards.

The boat bumped alongside, and a man on board called out. When there was no response the man swore. "Sleeping!" he said angrily. "Wait until Walther hears of this!"

Over the side they came, and into our hands. The surprise was complete. One elected to fight, and Red Mark's sword spitted him like a pheasant over a fire. Two others were seized, thrown down, and bound. One of the slaves raised up and put an arrow into the neck of the boatman.

The ship was ours so swiftly that it worried me, yet the crew had been a bunch of louts. The wonder was they had even thought of relieving the guards. Half drunk, the returning crewmen had no warning, no readiness for what took place.

The rest of my plan remained, yet each moment was an invitation to disaster. Why not forget what I planned, divide the money, and let each go his way?

The Moors of Cádiz would not be friendly to escaped slaves, and Walther would certainly enlist their aid in our recapture.

"Use your wits," the pockmarked one had said.

Moreover, I had a score to settle. If my plan worked, I could send each slave on his way a modestly rich man, and I should have taught Walther a needed lesson.

"You are in charge," I told Red Mark. "I shall take Selim and go ashore. If any of the crew return, make prisoners of them."

What I needed now was a beggar, a beggar with a certain face.

6

Once ashore I left the waterfront and proceeded to the narrow streets of the city. The plan was one that must be quickly completed, and it was not the Moslem habit to hurry in such matters.

Delay could mean disaster. Again, I hesitated. Why not simply free the slaves and allow them to make their own way out of the country? Were they my responsibility?

They were not, yet well I knew that, freed and with gold to spend, they would be lured by the fleshpots of Cádiz, would attract attention, and in no time be discovered as escaped slaves and be in chains again.

My clothing had been carefully brushed and cleaned so that once again I looked the young man of fashion. The scimitar was mine again, and I had recovered my knife, yet to accomplish my purpose I appeared too young. What was needed was an assistant of age and dignity whose appearance would command respect.

Selim, who accompanied me, was at once too fierce in appearance and too piratical to inspire trust.

Cádiz in this year of 1176 was one of the great ports of the world, and to her bazaars came merchants with silks, spices, camphor and pearls, frankincense and ivory. The wools of England, the furs of Scandinavia, the wines of France, the carpets of the Levant were here and exhibited for sale.

Among the crowds were men of all nations and every manner of dress. Merchants mingled with pirates, soldiers, slave dealers, and scholars. Long had Cádiz been famous for shipping and trade. My old tutor, of Greek-Arab family, told me of a manuscript, left by Eudoxus, which described finding the prow of a ship from Cádiz floating in the sea off the coast of East Africa, and that long before Christ.

A beggar tugged at my sleeve. "Alms! Alms! For the love of Allah!"

It was a lean hawk's face into which I gazed, piercing eyes and a beak of a nose, a face ancient with evil and shadowed by cunning, yet there was something more, a touch of wicked humor, was it?

"Oh, Father of Lice," I said, "what claim have you for alms? You look to be a thief and a son of thieves!"

His shrewd old eyes held a gleam of satanic amusement. "A thousand pardons, Noble One! Pity, for my poverty and weakness! Alms, for the love of Allah!"

The face, the manner . . . now if he were clean?

"Conveyor of Vermin," I said, "I give no alms, but if you would have a gold piece, then we shall talk. A gold piece," I added, "or an edge of steel if you betray me."

"A gold piece?" His eyes gleamed maliciously. "For a gold piece I would smuggle you into the finest harem in all of Spain! For a gold piece I might—ah, I know just the wench! A devil she is, a fiend out of Hell, but wise in the ways of pleasure, and she has a—"

"I said nothing of women. Follow me."

Outside a public bath we paused. A muscular Negro with huge gold rings in his ears stood there. Gesturing to the beggar, I said, "Take this bag of fleas and dip it, scour it, clip it, and comb it. I would have it resemble a gentleman!"

"By Allah." The slave spat into the dust. "Am I a djinn, to perform miracles?"

The beggar leered at him. "O Master! With so many baths in Cádiz why bring me to this, which houses this stench in the nostrils of humanity? Why must I, in my old years, be forced to listen to this Shadow of Ignorance?"

"Enough!" I spoke harshly, for we Kerbouchards know the way of command. "Get him inside. Burn that hive of corruption he wears for clothing. I shall return in less than the hour with fresh clothing!"

When at last he stood before me—his beard trimmed, his hair clipped and combed, dressed as befitted a man of dignity and means—he looked a noble if a crafty man, and such a one as I wanted.

His name, and I have no doubt the rascal lied, was Shir Ali, from Damascus, a merchant in his time and later a dervish, who had fallen on evil days.

"You are a merchant again," I told him, "freshly arrived from Aleppo to dispose of a cargo and galley with all possible speed. The cargo is of spices and silk in bales. Dispose of it well, Shir Ali, dispose of it this afternoon, and you shall be amply rewarded.

"If there is a false move or I am betrayed in any way, I shall"—I put my hand upon the knife—"empty your guts into the dust!"

Selim leaned toward him. "And I will slice you to ribbons and feed you to the dogs!"

At a small shop we drank wine together, and I showed him the cargo manifest and measured the ship with words. He glanced at the manifest and nodded. "Excellent! In a week's time—"

"You have four hours," I said. "I am your impatient nephew from Palermo, whose inheritance this is, and I must leave at once for Toledo. You abhor haste, but with such an impatient youth, what can one do? Besides, there is a girl—"

He raved, he protested it could not be done. We would lose money! We would be cheated! It might be done in two days but—

"It is a pirate ship," I told him coolly. "The crew is in town getting drunk. You will sell it now . . . today."

His glance was unbelieving, then he shrugged. "You have courage," he said, "or you are a fool."

"My blade cuts both ways, so be quick."

Merchant he undoubtedly had been; thief he had probably been, but he had a way with him, did Shir Ali.

At every step I feared to come face to face with Walther or one of the crew, yet the old beggar would not hasten. "You have chosen well," he said, "for a beggar sees much that others do not. We know who is honest and who the cheat, who has the gold and who talks only into the wind." Suddenly, he stopped before a small booth, a mere stall in the bazaar, and he began to wail and tear his hair.

"Ruined!" he cried. "I shall be ruined! To sell now? This I cannot do! It is a sin against Allah to sell a ship at such a time!

"Think, Nephew! The ship itself is a treasure, but the bales of silk! Only let me hold it! Let me bargain! There are men who would pay roundly for such a vessel!"

Ben Salom, the old Jewish man who kept the stall, scented a bargain. "What troubles you, friend?"

Shir Ali wailed louder and a small crowd gathered, then he burst into a torrent of expostulation and malediction. His dear brother, the best of brothers, was dead! His ship, which lay in the harbor, must be sold, and this beardless youth, this lad beside him, he must be on his way to Toledo before the sun had set.

Argument and explanation followed, and Shir Ali told of the richness of the silk, the aroma of the spices. My beggar showed himself a man of imagination, even of poetry.

He wailed; he berated his bad fortune, the evil of the times, the sin of selling now when so much might be gained by waiting.

Suddenly, he broke off. "Come! Come, my nephew, I know just the man! For such a cargo he will pay—"

"Hold!" Ben Salom put up a hand. "Wait! Perhaps you need go no further. No doubt the ship is old. The silk has probably been long in her hull. The spices may have spoiled, but still . . ."

Shir Ali drew himself up, looking on Ben Salom with disdain. "What? *You* speak of buying? Where would you get a hundred thousand dinars? Where, indeed?"

"Who speaks of a hundred thousand dinars? It is the mouthing of fools . . . yet, let us not be hasty. Of a verity, Allah has sent you to me. Come inside."

Shir Ali pulled away. "Who speaks of Allah? What have we to do with you? There is no time to waste! The ship must be sold before nightfall, so how can I waste time in idle talk?"

Yet after much argument and many protests, we allowed ourselves to be led inside and seated cross-legged on the floor cushions while Shir Ali protested of wasted time. Several times he made as if to rise only to be pushed down again.

Ben Salom took the list and studied it, muttering the while and counting on his fingers. Shir Ali, Selim, and I accepted the wine he offered, and waited.

The shop was humble, but no man can long be in the streets without knowing what goes on in any city. There is a league of beggars, and what they do not know nobody knows.

The merchant summoned a boy and sent him hurrying from the shop, and in a matter of minutes he returned with two old, bearded men. Putting their heads together, they consulted the list, arguing and protesting.

Shir Ali got suddenly to his feet. "Enough! Enough of this!"

We were at the door when Ben Salom stopped us. "Take us to this ship. If it is as you say, we will buy."

"The ship also?"

"And the ship."

Now came the time of greatest anxiety. What if Walther had returned? Or what if he returned while we were aboard? A pitched battle would surely take place in which the port officials might well interfere. Yet the risk must be taken.

All was quiet as we approached the ship. The sun was warm; water lapped lazily against the hull. The merchants studied the vessel, their faces revealing nothing.

Taking a chance that they would understand, I spoke

to Selim in the Frankish tongue. "I think we waste time. It would be better to sell in Málaga or Valencia."

Ben Salom spoke anxiously to the man beside him, and Shir Ali glanced at me slyly, guessing my intent.

We were met at the bulwark by Red Mark and a dozen armed slaves. While Shir Ali and Selim showed the merchants the vessel, we waited anxiously, watching the shore.

Now was the dangerous hour. If we did not complete our sale before—along the shore a party of men were strolling, vaguely familiar.

Red Mark followed my gaze. "I think we are in trouble," he said.

"Walther is one of them," I added.

"What will we do?"

The big Saxon was frightened. Bold man that he was, the prospect of finding himself again in chains was a terrible thing.

"There are but five or six," I told him quietly. "We will take them."

"What about *them*?" His thumb indicated the buyers.

"They will be getting a bargain, and we will let them talk us down a little further."

Selim caught my signal. "Get them below," I whispered. "Show them the silk, open a cask of cinnamon. Keep them busy."

The former slaves resumed their places except for a picked lot of twelve who crouched along the bulwarks in readiness. Four others stood ready with their bows in case any tried to escape.

We heard the beat of oars, the bump of the boat alongside. Sweat trickled down my face and neck. I tried to wet my lips, but my tongue was dry. An attempt to swallow required a real effort. I went to the side of the ship that they might see me.

"Where is the Finnveden?" Walther demanded.

"Asleep. They found your store of wine."

That would anger him, and angry men are not cautious. "The fools! I'll show—"

He grabbed a line and came up the side like a cat, the others following. Yet, as he threw a leg over the rail, something caught his eye and he hesitated.

"What is it?" Alarm shadowed his face. "What—"

Too late he saw his danger as I leaped to seize him. An instant he hesitated whether to run or fight, and it was to his credit that he started to draw his sword.

Coward he might be, and bully he undoubtedly was, but cornered he was a powerful and dangerous man. He threw himself at me, and I retreated, trying to keep him off me.

There was a clash of arms, a choking cry, then my blade nicked his arm, drawing blood. He drew back suddenly, and before he could come at me, Red Mark's arm slipped across his throat and jerked him backward, off-balance.

Quickly, the fight was over, and the prisoners were bound with a sailor's speed and skill, all taken alive but one man. His would not be the first body to be found afloat in the harbor of Cádiz.

Attracted by the scuffle, Ben Salom came on deck. His eyes searched but found nothing amiss. "There is trouble?"

"Some rebellious slaves," I said.

Walther tried to shout, but Red Mark struck him in the stomach.

"You said nothing of slaves," Ben Salom protested.

"They go with the ship." I pointed at Walther. "But beware of that one, a wily rogue and a very great liar, but a taste of the lash and he will work well."

Ben Salom glanced at me. "You are young," he said, "but you speak with the voice of command."

"The ship is my inheritance," I replied.

All were silent. Undoubtedly, something here did not seem right. "I spoke quickly in the matter of the slaves, but I am sure it was my uncle's intention."

Ben Salom plucked at his beard. "We fear trouble! All is not well here."

"That is for you to decide. The galley is yours for a price, and these strong slaves with it."

"We must think. It is sudden."

Turning away, I said to Red Mark, "Bring their boat alongside. These men are leaving. We can catch the wind for Málaga."

"Wait!" Shir Ali cried. "I am sure Allah has brought wisdom to my friends. They will wish to buy."

Ben Salom began to wag his head, and I said, "To the boat. We sail for Málaga. After all, it was my uncle who wished to sell in Cádiz."

"Now, now," Ben Salom protested. "It is true your offer is good, but we just—"

"Cash," I said, "and within the hour. There will be no further talk."

"All right," Ben Salom spoke reluctantly. "We will buy."

"You," I said, "will remain aboard until the others return with the money."

An hour and ten minutes later, with darkness falling, I stood upon the streets of Cádiz with more money than I had ever seen in my life.

At the last I could have pitied Walther until I recalled the girl who swam ashore.

Red Mark was gone. To Selim I extended my hand. "Go with Allah," I said.

He hesitated. "But if we went together? You have freed me. I would serve you and only you."

"Go, then, to Málaga, ask discreetly of the maid Aziza and of Count Redwan. Learn if she is safe. Serve her if you can, and spend your money wisely."

We parted, and I walked up the narrow street, noticing the ragged beggar who drew hastily into an alleyway as I drew near.

First, I must inquire for my father, and if there was no knowledge of him, I would proceed to Córdoba where there would be records of all that happened in the Mediterranean. The caliph was a watchful man.

Too much time has passed, yet together my father

and I must return to our own Armorica and our vengeance against the Baron de Tournemine.

Meanwhile, the baron carried the scar I had left on his cheek, a memento of what was to follow.

It came to me then that I would send a message.

7

The old town of Cádiz stood atop a cliff, its harbor opening toward the western sea, and there were buildings that remained from ancient times. Some, it was said, built by the Phoenicians, others by the Romans or Visigoths.

Pausing on the dark street, I drew my cloak about me, for there was dampness in the wind from the sea. Selim had told me of an inn on a cliff above the sea, the Inn of the White Horse.

It was a place known to men who follow the sea, and I might come upon some news of my father there. There was in me an urge to be off, to be away from Cádiz. What if one of the slaves, celebrating his freedom, talked too much?

The tavern's common room was low-raftered and shadowed but crowded by men from all the ports: from Alexandria, Venice, Aleppo, and Constantinople. The tables were long and lined with benches. I found an empty place and ordered a tuna fried in olive oil, a loaf, and a bottle.

Across from me was a lean and one-eyed sailor with a savage face. He lingered unhappily over an empty glass.

"It is dry weather ashore," I said, "fill your glass." I pushed the bottle toward him.

He filled, then lifted, his glass. "*Yol bolsun!*" he said.

"Your language is strange," I said.

"My people were born on the steppes, far to the east and north. The words are a greeting, but sometimes a toast. They mean 'May there be a road!' "

"I shall drink to that," I said, and we drank together.

"Long ago," I said, "a Greek told me of the steppes, of far grass plains where fierce warriors rode, and of a land still farther called Cathay."

"He was a knowing man. You travel far?"

"As far as necessary."

"I am Abaka Khan, a king among my people." He smiled with sudden humor. "A small king, but still a king."

"I am Mathurin," I said, "with another name better left unspoken for the time."

"A man's name is his own."

"You are far from home."

"Ah." He shrugged, looked into his empty glass, and I refilled it.

"You look upon a man," he said, "who has been a king and a slave, a warrior and a sailor, a fugitive and a rescuer."

"I have been nothing," I said, "but there is tomorrow."

A voice was raised in drunken argument. "Dead! I tell you Kerbouchard is dead!"

"I do not believe it," another said.

"There will never be another Kerbouchard."

"I will not believe he is dead," the second man insisted stubbornly.

"He lay upon his back, eyes wide open to the sun. I say it who saw him, a gaping hole in his chest and blood staining red the water about him."

"When I was young," I prompted, "I heard tales of this Kerbouchard."

"Whatever was said was less than the truth," the second man said. "I say it, who sailed with him! Oh, a good man! A fair man! An extra share for all when Kerbouchard commanded."

Eating my tuna and bread, I listened to the fine talk, the home from the sea talk of ships and men and fights and blood and loot and women and the sound of oars and flapping sails. Among it all, again and again, the name of Kerbouchard. The Turk watched me, and suddenly he said, "I knew him, too, and that other name of yours? I believe I know it."

"Do not speak it here."

"A name is a name"—he shrugged—"only some names have a ring to them, like Kerbouchard!"

"He was trapped in a cove when the sun rose," a man was saying, "and there were five vessels. They closed in from both sides, shearing his oars and boarding him. They swept his deck with arrows, then with the sword."

"He lives," the second man insisted. "A lion is not to be slain by jackals."

"Do you call Abd-al-Ala a jackal?"

Ordering another bottle, I glanced across the room and saw a beggar in a corner by the door, a beggar with the money to buy a bottle. Where had I seen him before?

He did not look my way, yet I was sure he had been. Suddenly the room seemed close. Tasting my wine, I saw a door open at the side, and a slave came in, followed by a breath of cool night air.

Abaka Khan's eyes followed mine when I again glanced at the beggar. "It is a thing I could do for you," he suggested, "small payment for the wine."

"When I give wine there is no payment." Some men had arisen cutting off the beggar's view of me. "Take the bottle," I said, "and *yol bolsun!*"

Swiftly, I was gone, taking the door through which the slave entered.

A moment for the door to open and close, another to let my eyes adjust. A narrow alley that debouched upon a steep hill above the harbor. From whom was I escaping? I knew not, but I knew the smell of trouble.

It was time to leave Cádiz. What I needed now was a horse.

Down the hill I went to where the harbor waters were, and a wall. Following the wall, I found a narrow gate and a guard whose attention was distracted by a coin.

Scattered outside were merchants and travelers awaiting daybreak and the opening gates. Several fires were

still burning, and I crossed to one of them, then paused to
study the faces for those which seemed honest. Loosening
my sword and dagger, I went up to the fire. Two men
were there, a graybeard and a smooth-faced young man.
They looked up at me.

"You have horses," I said, "and I need one."

"You travel late."

"If I do not travel late, I may not travel at all."

"Horses are never cheap."

Over a cup of mint tea we talked of many things, and
bargained here and there. Perhaps I bargained well, for I
remembered Shir Ali and things he had said. Would I
ever see him again? Or Abaka Khan? How many are the
lives we meet and pass!

An hour before daylight I rode from their camp astride
a dapple-gray. The horse was a Barb, a fine animal, almost
black.

When the money from the ship's sale was divided I
found myself with five hundred gold dinars, and sewn into
my garments by my own hand were two fine emeralds,
two rubies, a blue sapphire, and three small diamonds.

Buying the Barb, I bought also a bow and a quiver of
arrows. Yet traveling alone was foolhardy, and I hoped to
attach myself to some group who wished to add to their
strength.

The beggar worried me. That he had followed me
from the port there was no doubt. He had been nearby
when I bade good-bye to Selim . . . why? Who was he?
Did he act upon his own, or was he serving someone else?

From the shelter of brush on a hillside I watched the
day's travel begin. My concealment was excellent and
gave me opportunity to observe those who were upon the
road.

A merchant passed with ten camels and several
mounted men, then a dozen soldiers in spiked helmets
and coats of mail rode by.

A cart came along drawn by oxen and guarded by two
mounted men, then came a motley, rough-seeming group.
Two of these detached themselves from the others and

took shelter on the hillside right below me, hiding themselves there. They settled down to observing the passersby.

Suddenly their talked stilled. A new party of travelers appeared, a tall man in black riding a richly caparisoned mule, with three retainers also on mules. All were armed, yet they lacked the bearing of fighting men. There were two pack mules also, yet the interest of the watchers below centered less upon their burdens than upon the man in black.

"It is John. It is John of Seville!"

When the small group had gone on along the narrow road, one of the two observers mounted and rode over the hill, passing close enough for me to see him well—a squat, powerful man with a greasy skin and uncombed hair. He was heavily armed.

The second man remained a little longer, then went down to the high road to follow John of Seville.

The Greek who was my tutor had talked of John. He was a converted Jew who worked with Raymond of Toledo in translating Arab classics into Latin and Castilian. He was a famous scholar and a man of influence.

My father was a man who respected knowledge, and our home had been a stopping place for travelers. Over the wine at night there had been much good talk of scholars and seekers after truth. My father's interest had been whetted by his travels as well as his occasional contact with the wise men of Alexandria, Rome, Athens, and Moorish Spain.

My father was dead.

Hating the thought, I had almost come to accept it. Yet the man who would not believe Kerbouchard was dead had more faith than I.

It was his faith against the knowledge of the other, yet did that man actually know Kerbouchard? He had spoken of seeing my father lying dead, and what could I place in the balance against that?

If he was dead, then I must return to Armorica and crush the Baron de Tournemine by myself, this man who destroyed my home and killed my mother and our retainers, this man must die.

There was no law to punish him, nor anyone but myself to see him pay for his crimes. I, Mathurin Kerbouchard, who was alone, I would see Tournemine die by my own blade.

Alone I was, but he who stands alone is often the strongest. By standing alone he becomes stronger and remains strong.

It was well that I felt so, for I was indeed alone. Trusting in my strong right arm and my wits might all be very well, but I had so much to learn and knew not if either the arm or the wit was sufficient.

The world into which I had been born was a world in turmoil. With the collapse of the Roman empire, the luxury and elegance of the world died also. Cities fell to ruin; aqueducts went dry, and unprotected fields returned to weeds and eventually to grass. For several hundred years Europe was a dangerous place in which to travel, infested by brigands or the ignorant, half-savage peasantry who slaughtered travelers and appropriated their belongings.

Warlike monks raided caravans or demanded tribute from villages. Often they fought with the nobles who were no more than titled brigands such as Tournemine.

Few men in Christian Europe could read or write, fewer even appreciated the importance of knowledge. The Christian countries had become dark seas of ignorance and superstition with only here and there a light of learning to provide a fitful glow.

After the deluge of blood and victory that carried the Arabs across Asia and North Africa into Spain and Sicily, there came a flood of enlightenment. From Alexandria came translations of the Greek classics, followed by the music, art, and medical knowledge of the Greeks, the Persians, and the Arabs.

Persian and Indian scholars found a warm welcome at the courts of the caliphs, and when the Umayyads were succeeded by the Abbasids, Arab civilization entered its golden age.

In Europe books were few and priceless. Peter de Nemours, Bishop of Paris, on his departure for the Crusades presented to the Abbey St. Victor his "great library," consisting of just eighteen volumes.

At the same time the Caliph al-Hakam, in Córdoba, possessed a library of four hundred thousand volumes.

Within my home, thanks to my father's travels, the atmosphere was different. We were not Christian and so were uninfluenced by the monks, for much of Brittany was still pagan.

Traveling monks as well as others were always welcome in our home and many a lively discussion took place around our table, so I knew of John of Seville and Raymond of Toledo.

Now I had seen him, but unless I was mistaken he was about to be robbed, murdered, or both. It was no business of mine, and I would do well to stay out of it, yet I knew I could not.

The sun was warm upon the hills, and I followed the road cheerfully. My Barb was an intelligent animal, and I held him back to conserve his energy for what might lie ahead. Yet as night drew near I began to close the gap, fearing I might be too far behind to help if an attack did come.

Before me lay a dense and wind-barbered forest, dark and tangled. A dim path led off into the woods, and it seemed to offer a cutoff that might put me ahead of John's party.

Turning quickly, I followed it, my sword ready for instant use. I went down a grassy slope and into the trail once more. Glancing back, I glimpsed three men staring after me. Had they meant to intercept me?

Drawing up beside the way, I let the party of John of Seville overtake me. As they drew near, they bunched as if for defense, although I was a man alone.

"Greetings, O Father of Wisdom! May your shadow never grow less!"

He was an oldish man with gray hair and a keen, inquisitive face, high cheekbones, and an aquiline nose.

"You speak Arabic but with a strange accent. What are you? Who are you?"

"A man who travels, who would give you warning."

"Warning of what?"

"There is a party of men before you and another coming up behind, and I believe they mean you harm."

Those who accompanied him were but a fat old man and two boys, although one of the boys was tall and strong.

"They mean to rob us?"

"It is my belief."

He pondered the answer, obviously uncertain what course to adopt.

"The man behind who watches us? We can wait for him and kill him. It would be one the less."

"Is it so easy then, to kill?"

"I prefer killing to being killed. One may talk of peace only with those who are peaceful. To talk of peace with him who holds a drawn sword is foolish unless one is unarmed, then one must talk very fast, indeed."

"We will seize him. Perhaps we can learn their plan."

At a curve in the road we drew off to one side, concealing ourselves in the brush. John and the fat man prepared to block the trail. Yet then there was a time of waiting, and John looked over at me. "You are Frankish?"

"A Celt. From Armorica, in Brittany."

"I know of it. You are a landless man?"

"My home was taken from me. I seek my father who was lost at sea."

"And now?"

"I go to Córdoba to see the library there."

He looked at me more thoughtfully. "Do you read, then?"

"Latin," I said, "and some Arabic."

"But there are few books in your country."

So I spoke of the books I had read, and we talked until the boy across the road hissed a warning.

The oncoming rider was walking his horse, approaching the curve carelessly, sure that his quarry was far ahead. Rounding the curve, he beheld John of Seville on foot beside his horse, apparently working at the saddle. He glanced sharply about and, seeing nothing, rode up to John, his hand on his sword hilt.

The boy was silent as I myself, and we had him before he could move. The tall boy slid a forearm across his throat, pulling him back. Together they fell from the horse. Coolly, I drew my scimitar. "Hold him a little to your left," I told the boy. "No reason to get blood on your tunic."

The prisoner stared at me, alarm in his eyes.

John nudged him with a toe. "You and the others? What is your plan?"

"You speak in riddles. I am only a traveler."

He was a surly rogue and a tough one, yet I believed him to have no more loyalty than most of his lot.

"What of the band ahead?"

"I know of no band."

"You lie," I said. "I heard your words as you planned. Keep a knife at his throat," I told the boy, "and should we be attacked, cut it at once. Cut deep," I advised, "I have seen men with heads half cut off who were not dead."

"Why not kill him now?" the fat man suggested.

"No!" The thief was frightened. "I owe them nothing. Let me go free, and I will tell."

The plan was not to attack us on the road but wait until we reached an inn that lay ahead. It was a logical stopping place. A small caravan of merchants was to stop also, and they would attack both at once.

"But they are strong, and there are several!"

"And one of them is our brother," said the captive. "All will drink wine, and when they sleep—"

With the men of the caravan asleep from drugged wine, they would kill them all. As yet they knew nothing of me, but I doubted my presence would cause them to alter their plans. Binding our prisoner's hands to the saddle, we started on. Clouds gathered, and there was a change in the air.

John of Seville glanced at me. "You have saved my life," he said quietly.

"Wait. Perhaps I have only made you aware of death. We do not yet know what the night may bring."

8

From the hill we could overlook the squat outlines of the walled inn, if such it might be called. In the courtyard there were camels and horses from the merchants' caravan. Four mail-clad soldiers were turning in at the gate, but nothing could be seen of the rough-looking band that had preceded us.

It lay in the open with no concealment nearby, but if a man within were to open the gates, it would prove a close and desperate place in which to fight.

Hassan, the tall boy of our own group, would fight well, of that I was sure. John of Seville, although no longer a young man, looked in good condition, and I could not doubt his resolution. As we entered the wooden gates wind whipped at our clothing, and a few spattering drops of rain began to fall. It would be a dark night.

We stripped the saddles from our mounts. The air in the stables was close but smelled of fresh hay. The camels seemed well fed and strong, and I commented on this to Hassan.

He gave them a contemptuous glance. *"Jamal!"* he said, shrugging. "Fit only to carry burdens. You should see our riding camels, the *batiniyah* or *Umaniyah* of my country!"

He told me of famous racing camels known to travel a hundred miles a day, often for several days in succession.

A big, dark soldier came in, and indicating an empty stall, he said, "Leave it. An important man comes."

He studied me with a slight frown, as if he found something familiar in my face. He hesitated as if to say something further, then changed his mind and walked away.

Inside the inn, John of Seville was seated cross-legged on the floor. Before him was a haunch of lamb from which he was shredding meat. He indicated I was to join him. The lamb was young, freshly roasted, and excellent. There was rice and a jug of wine.

Hassan joined us, full of talk of camels and the desert, pleased that I was interested, and eager to tell of the desert camel and its ways. Knowing that someday this might be important, I listened with all my attention.

John of Seville had little to say, but he did comment that one of the mailed soldiers had come to inquire about our prisoner and wished the prisoner turned over to him. Now this soldier came to us again. It was not the soldier to whom I had spoken in the stable, but his interest was in me. "You joined the party outside Cádiz?"

With my dagger I cut a thin slice of the lamb. "I travel to Córdoba to study."

"You can read?"

Putting my tongue in my cheek, I said, "I would learn better to read the Koran."

"You are a believer?" he asked doubtfully.

" 'Those who believed,' " I quoted from the Koran, " 'left their homes and strove for the cause of Allah—those are believers in truth.' "

Impressed, the soldier went away. John poured wine from the jug, and I detected the ghost of a smile on his lips. "Have you heard," he asked gently, "about the Devil quoting Scripture for his own ends?"

"The Devil survives," I replied.

"Is survival, then, the first thing? Is there not something else?"

"Honor first, then victory, but if a man is to learn, first he must live."

"You would be wise," he agreed, "to go to Córdoba or to Toledo. The best of all things is to learn. Money can be lost or stolen, health and strength may fail, but what you have committed to your mind is yours forever."

Of course. Had not my small knowledge of navigation freed me from chains? Had not my knowledge of Arabic taken me to Málaga, and thence to Cádiz?

It had done more. Already, because of the little I had learned, my life was richer, my appreciation of all things greater. Yes, I would go to Córdoba. Was not my father dead? Had not his ship been sunk?

As for Aziza, I knew not where she might be found, nor how to help her. Many forces were at work of which I understood nothing, and a blunder might do harm. Christian warred against Christian here, and Moslem against Moslem, Arab against Berber.

Aziza might have been carried off by her friends, and my inquiries might lead to her discovery by her enemies.

One of the mail-clad soldiers seated himself near us, another lay down near the merchant. It seemed unreasonable for men traveling together to scatter out, to sleep away from each other. The men from the caravan were already asleep.

When I had finished eating I went to the yard to bathe my hands and face. The wind blew stronger, and the sky was a sea of wind-tossed clouds. Lightning played weird shadow games over the far hills, and the trees bent before the angry wind. It was a night for evil to be abroad.

Often I walked the moors among the standing stones, the ancient stones of my people. What, I wondered, would John of Seville think if he knew that within my skull there reposed the sacred knowledge of the Druids?

Ages ago they had laid down their rules for clear thinking, for argument and discussion, the lore of the sea, sky, and stars, for many secret things also that savored of magic to the uninitiated.

Yet nothing in my native land compared with these cities of Spain. Paris, I had been told, was scarcely better than the filthiest of villages with refuse thrown into the street, carcasses of animals left decaying where they had fallen, and hogs belonging to the monks of St. Anthony wandering through the fashionable quarters of the city. Mud was so deep at times that women had to be carried through the streets on the backs of porters. Glass was almost unknown; windows were covered with oiled paper.

Again I thought of the ancient beliefs of my people. In Christianity I found much good, but judging by its effect upon the lands in which they were supreme, the Moslem religion seemed the most successful. Yet it might not always be so.

What was I to believe? I was a man of nature. The feel of a good sword in my hand, a horse between my knees, or of a ship's steering oar—in these I could believe. These answered to something within me.

The swing of a gull's wing across the sky, the lift of a far blue-shrouded shore, the warmth of the sun, the cold of a winter night, the salty taste of brine or sweat, the warm, wonderful feeling of a woman in the arms. In these I believed.

There was no doubt that Mohammed was a wise man. Did he not marry a widow owning many camels? Such a man is worth listening to.

Returning to the inn, I took my robes and lay in a corner near the wall and not far from John of Seville. Under cover of my robes I drew my scimitar.

Hassan was seeming to nod, but Hassan was a Bedouin from the desert and would be ready.

The long room where we were had but one entrance, that from the court. Our position would enable our blades to present a formidable wall of defense, yet something about the room disturbed me.

A soldier lay near me, seeming asleep. Watching, I detected a subtle, too careful movement of his hand. It was not the fumbling movement of a sleeping man but the slow, careful movement of a man trying not to be noticed.

My heart began to beat slowly, heavily. Suppose, just suppose, the soldiers were not what they seemed? Reaching out, I tugged the robe of John of Seville. His eyes opened and met mine, but he moved never a muscle.

Shaping the words with my lips, I said, "The soldiers are thieves."

There was instant comprehension. His head moved

but slightly, his eyes rapidly taking in the positions of the soldiers. One was within backstabbing reach of Hassan; another lay near the giant Negro who guarded the fat merchant. Each soldier was so placed as to kill a strong fighting man on signal.

My eyes fell to the knuckles of the nearest soldier. A flicker of firelight revealed his grip upon his sword. The time was now.

Lying in the deepest shadows, I was beyond the eyes of any of them. With a catlike movement I came to my feet, sword in hand. My left gathered the robe with which I had been covered. At that instant I heard, from the courtyard, a sound that was of neither the wind nor the rain.

A step took me from the shadows. My blade touched Hassan lightly. He looked up, and my point indicated the soldier near the Negro.

A foot scuffed on the cobbles outside, and the soldier started to rise. Flicking the robe at him, I let go, and it enveloped him in its folds. Stepping forward, I stamped down hard on his knuckles.

As I attacked the soldier nearest Hassan, he drew back his sword and threw it like a javelin at the soldier nearest the Negro. As that soldier had started to rise, the sword caught him across the bridge of the nose, drenching him in blood. Hassan followed his sword, retrieving it.

John was on his feet, and as the soldier nearest the door reached to unbar it, John hurled a stool. Missing the soldier, it rebounded with force, and the soldier leaped back to avoid it. John struck upward to his kidney with a dagger.

Instantly, the inn was a place of madness. The fat man who rode with John of Seville proved better than expected, and seeing us fighting the soldiers, he threw himself on the one remaining.

A weight of bodies crashed against the door the attackers expected to find unbarred, but the Negro waited there with a heavy woodsman's ax.

Around us there was a sudden silence. The man I

enveloped in my robe was taken. Of the four soldiers John of Seville had slain one, his fat assistant another, and Hassan disabled a third. As suddenly as it had begun the fighting was over.

Outside, men were battering at the door. Moving a bench, I placed it across and just inside the door, leaving room for it to swing wide.

"If we leave them outside, they will steal our horses and ride away," I explained. "Lift the bar!"

The door slammed open, and men charged into the room, two of them sprawling over the bench, a third tripping over the legs of the fallen men. A fourth died from the ax, Hassan accounted for a fifth. Leaping through the door, I rushed for the stables.

At the inn our men were disposing of the brigands, but within the stable all seemed still, then came a rustle of movement.

A man stood with his back to the wall at the end of the stable. He had been saddling the horse of John of Seville. As John had ridden a mule, his horse had been led throughout the day and was in fine shape. A splendid sorrel it was, with fine limbs and every evidence of speed and staying power.

The brigand held a sword, but his face was in shadow. My point lifted, ready for a thrust. Within the inn, lights were lit, and the rays fell through the stable window and across my opponent's face. It was the man who had robbed and enslaved me. It was Walther.

And I knew that I could kill him.

Mine was the stronger arm, the better blade. He had robbed me, sneered at me, insulted me.

"You!" he said. "I should have slit your belly that first day! I should have killed you rather than make you pilot. I knew it then."

"You can try to kill me now."

"You are too lucky. I shall not fight you."

"Coward!"

He shrugged, watching me from under heavy brows.

"Who is not a coward sometimes? You will let me go. You robbed me of my ship—"

"How did you get that ship?"

"—and you sold me as a slave." He leered at me. "I escaped before I could be chained. As for you, you have done enough."

Angrily, I glared at him. He was a treacherous, cowardly man. Had he stood in my place, he would have killed me, but it was not in me to simply run him through.

"Get out! But drop your sword before you come near me, or I shall dirty my blade in your fat belly!"

The sword fell, then he darted past me into the courtyard. Somebody shouted from the inn, then I heard a rattle of retreating hoofbeats.

A sentimental fool . . . such an act would kill me someday . . . one's enemies are better dead.

Or was that true? Did not a man's enemies make a sharper, more decisive man of him?

Remembering the scoundrel he was, I should have cut him down, then quartered him to be sure of his death, but with him at the point of my sword I no longer hated him. He was beneath contempt.

Hassan was at the door. "Did someone escape?"

"A thief, a coward and a thief who will suffer more alive than in dying."

9

Dawn dappled the tawny hills with alternating sunshine and shadow. One by one the travelers emerged from the inn, gathered their belongings, and departed. The little world of the inn where we who until the night before had been strangers, who shared battle and blood together, now shattered like fragile glass. Again we would be strangers to recall only at intervals the events of this night.

Today, I rode beside John of Seville who believed himself in my debt for the warning given. As we rode, he explained much that was to prove important in the months to come, much that was to bear upon my own future.

We in Brittany knew too little of the world outside— our news coming only from passing travelers or men who returned from the sea, occasionally from a merchant caravan traveling the remnants of the old Roman roads to the great markets and fairs in the towns.

As he talked, our world of ship, shore, and fishing began to seem small indeed, for he spoke of kings, castles, and Crusades, of ideas and the men who pursued them.

My father had returned from the sea with tales of swift attacks and bloody retreats, of faraway shores and strange beliefs, of silks, ivory and pearl, of battles and sudden death. These stories colored my youth, and I longed for such adventures myself.

Little did I know of kings and courts, or the means by which men became kings. Well I knew that Henry II was wedded to Eleanor of Aquitaine, and that Henry claimed our land for fief as he claimed much of the land of the Franks.

Of Louis VII, so-called Louis the Young, I knew little, but of Manuel Comnenus, ruler of the Byzantine Empire, the Roman Empire of the East, I knew nothing at all. Nor did I know this land through which we rode, but as we traveled John explained much that had set the stage for the situation that presently existed.

In 1130 Abd-al-Mumin had become leader of the rising power of the Almohads or Unitarians, and ten years later had begun a career of conquest, defeating the Almoravids in 1144. A year later his armies invaded Spain, and in the five years that followed he reduced all Spain to his control.

Torn by strife, Spain had existed under a variety of rulers, then came a handsome youth of twenty-one, Abd-al-Rahman III, and in a few short years he defeated his enemies both Christian and Moslem and welded Moorish Spain into one empire, building Córdoba into the greatest center of intellectual activity in the western world.

Tolerant to all creeds, especially Christians and Jews, known as People of the Book because they, too, followed the Old Testament, Abd-al-Rahman welcomed scholars from everywhere.

Moslem fleets commanded the Mediterranean; Moslem armies were victorious in Europe, in Africa, and in Asia. Moslem rulers controlled lands from far south of the Indus to past Samarkand, from the Atlantic coasts of Africa to the deepest reaches of the Sahara.

Later, when al-Hakam became caliph in Córdoba, there came to power both a scholar and a lover of books. More inclined to a life of study than to rule, he resigned many of his powers to a prime minister, a slave named Giafar-al-Asklabi.

From all corners of the world al-Hakam gathered books by the greatest of scholars. His agents ransacked the libraries and book marts of Baghdad, Samarkand, Damascus, Tashkent, Bokhara, Cairo, Constantinople, and Alexandria for books. Those which could not be bought were copied. He had been known to pay a thousand pieces of gold for a single manuscript.

At Seville, Toledo, and Córdoba he gathered scholars to translate these books into Arabic and Latin. The books of Rome and Carthage . . . John assured me Carthage had the greatest libraries of the ancient world and vast collections of records from her commercial colonies established in many lands.

Al-Hakam passed on, but the library remained. There were, John assured me, seventy public libraries in Córdoba to say nothing of the great libraries in private homes. The love of learning was of first importance, the poet and scholar ranked with the general and the statesman. Nor were these latter respected unless they, too, were poets and scholars.

Yet Abd-al-Mumin was a savage warrior who suspected all books but the Koran. "He destroyed the Idol of Cádiz," John said. "You may have seen the ruins in the harbor."

No man knew the origin of the huge figure. Built upon a series of columns one hundred and eighty feet high, the platform had been surmounted by a gigantic figure of a man, done in bronze. The right arm of the figure stretched toward the Straits of Gibraltar, and held a key. The entire statue was plated with gold and could be seen at a great distance by all ships approaching Cádiz from the open Atlantic.

Of unknown antiquity, the Idol of Cádiz, as it was known to the Arabs, may have been of Phoenician origin. It was said that Cádiz was founded by them in 1100 B.C. But what of the ancient Iberians who preceded them? Despite the hatred of orthodox Moslems for all idols—the Koran forbade representation of the human figure—the huge statue had survived nearly five hundred years of Moslem control. The Romans and the Goths had left it untouched, even though it was believed to be of solid gold, and the Vikings had tended to avoid the city fearful of the power of the colossal image. Then, in 1145 it was destroyed by Abd-al-Mumin. It was discovered the idol was of bronze, and not gold.

"Who could have built it?" I wondered.

"No man knows," John assured me, "only that it was very ancient. Some have said the Phoenicians built it, but they came for commerce and had no reason to expend enormous sums in a town like any other coastal village.

"Others believe it was built by the ancient Iberians who are said to have had a great civilization and fine literature.

"The figure held a key . . . to what? Its hand stretched out toward the empty sea . . . toward what? Someday divers may go down and find some clue near the base of the figure. Until then we shall not know."

My thoughts, I knew, would be forever haunted by the mystery of the colossal figure, an image of what? Reaching out toward what mystery? Who built it? When? Why? What lock awaited that gigantic key?

"Are there records," I asked, "of wars and battles? I wish to find knowledge of my father's death—if he is dead."

"Recorded? I doubt it. He was a corsair, and there have been many such. Many die whose valor is forever unknown."

The next day, traveling alone, I crossed the ancient stone bridge over the Guadalquivir, a bridge built by Romans. On the right stood the Great Mosque, one of the holiest places in the Moslem world. "See it," John advised, "it is an amazing sight."

The bazaars and streets teemed with people of every race and color. Strange sights met my eyes; strange scents tingled my nostrils; strange women walked veiled or unveiled along the busy streets, women with undulating hips and dark, expressive eyes.

Dusty though I was, and tired from travel, the expressions in their eyes told me they found me not unhandsome, and I sat the straighter because of it. What man does not like the attention of women?

A narrow street opened on my left, shadowed and cool. Turning my mount, I walked him into that haven of stillness, away from the crowd. Immediately, I was lost to the noise and confusion behind, yet where the street might take me I had no idea. Yet when I turned a corner, there was an open gate.

It was a corner where another street entered, and that one passed on into a maze of buildings, but before me lay the open gate, a stable where horses fed, and a glimpse beyond of trees, green grass, and a fountain. To the left and on the far side stood a colonnade of graceful Moorish arches.

Without thinking, I walked my horse into the gate and drew up, his shod hooves making a clatter against the stone walls. For a moment I sat there, drinking in the coolness and the beauty.

A movement drew my eyes, and I saw a tall old man beneath the arches. "You have peace," I said.

"Do the young respect peace?" He spoke gently, walking toward me. "I believed the young looked only for movement, for action."

"There is a time for peace and a time for war. From the hot plains of Andalusia to your court is a movement into paradise. I am sorry to have disturbed you." I bowed. "May your shadow never grow less."

"You have come far?"

"From Cádiz. Before that, the sea."

"How did you come to this place?"

"The street invited, your gate was open, there was a sound of water splashing, a smell of gardens. If you have traveled, you know how welcome are such sounds."

"Why do you come to Córdoba?"

"To study. I am very young, and not very wise, so where else would one come if not to Córdoba?"

"Your sword is not enough?"

"A sword is never enough. The mind is also a weapon, but like the sword it must be honed and kept sharp."

"Why do you wish to learn? Do you seek power? Riches?"

"What I shall seek tomorrow, I do not know. Today, I seek only to know. My mind asks questions for which I have no answers. Within me there is a loneliness for knowledge. I would know what is thought by wise men and what is believed in other lands, far from here. I would open the dark and empty avenues of my mind to the brightness of a new sun and populate it with ideas."

"Please get down. My house is yours."

He was old, but a man of fine bearing, his clothing worn but of quality. He shook his head as I moved to remove the bridle and saddle.

"A slave will care for him, and it will be done at once. Please come in."

He led me along the gallery to a small room where there were rugs, cushions, and a low table. In an alcove there was a tub, and water falling.

"Refresh yourself, and then we shall talk."

Alone in the shadowed room, I disrobed and bathed, then dusted my clothing. As I settled my scimitar into place, I heard a girl singing, a fine, sweet, haunting refrain. Pausing, I listened.

This—this was what made life: a moment of quiet, the water falling in the fountain, the girl's voice . . . a moment of captured beauty. He who is truly wise will never permit such moments to escape.

Who was she? Did she sing for love or the longing for love?

It was not necessary that I know her, for she was romance, and romance is so often in a garden, behind a wall, along a twilit street.

Opening the door, I stepped into the passage, and beyond the colonnade, sunlight fell across a garden where hibiscus, rose, and jasmine grew. A few minutes I stood there, letting the last of the tension flow from me.

The gate by which I had entered was closed, and it was barred from within.

10

Over a pilaf my host explained that his name was ibn-Tuwais, and that he was an Arab of the Quraysh, the tribe of the Prophet. He had been both a soldier and an official of the caliph.

"I have known many Franks, and was for a time a prisoner in Palermo."

"My father often spoke of the place."

"He is dead?"

"So it has been said, but perhaps the man lied, or was mistaken."

Many times stories are told merely to make the teller seem important, and how many times had men said they had themselves seen things of which they had but heard?

"What are your plans?"

"To remain here, to study, to learn, to listen for news. It has been said that all news comes to Córdoba."

"My roof is yours. I have no son, and kismet has brought you to me. In the meanwhile, I am not without sources of information. I shall seek news of your father. His was a name well known on the sea, and there will be stories."

"You must forgive me. I cannot share your home unless I am permitted to pay. It is a custom among my people."

Tuwais bowed. "Once I might have taken offense, but I am a poor man. You see a house of wealth, and so it was under the old caliphs, but the Berbers have offered me no position.

"Your company will please me, for in my youth I

made great talk with the scholars of Baghdad and Damascus. Moreover, I have a few books, some of them very fine, very rare."

He arose. "An old man's advice? Speak little, listen much. In Córdoba there is beauty and there is wisdom, but there is blood, also."

That night I read myself to sleep with the *Chronology of Ancient Nations* by al-Biruni, reading also from the *Almagest* of Ptolemy.

My thoughts turned to Aziza. Where was she? Did she fare well? Was she with her friends? Her beauty was a memory that would not be forgotten.

During the days that followed, I read, walked in the streets to learn my way, and listened to the spoken tongues, learning more of Arabic and something of Berber.

It was now more than four hundred years since the Moors had conquered Spain. Their invasion of France had been repelled by Charles Martel.

The corrupt empire of the Visigoths had collapsed before the first attack by a small band of Moslems led by Tarik, a veteran soldier. The Visigoth Empire had been a mixture of peoples and languages, many of them inherited from bygone years. The Iberians, Phoenicians, and many others left their mark. The Phoenicians were a Semitic people, settled in many places along the coast, opening trading establishments and sending their ships into the Atlantic. Their ships and those from Carthage, which had once been a Phoenician colony, sailed around Africa, went to the Scilly Isles for tin, sailed the coasts of Brittany and into the North Sea. As each mariner was jealous of his sources for raw materials and trade goods, we shall probably never know the true extent of their voyages.

The Greeks, the Romans, the Vandals, and the Goths had all invaded Spain, and left their mark upon it. Invading armies then, as well as now, left behind them an outbreak of pregnancy, destroying forever the myth of a pure race.

Never did I tire of roaming the streets, one of which, as Duban the soldier had told me, was ten miles long and lighted from end to end. The banks of the Guadalquivir were lined with houses of marble, with mosques and gardens. Water was brought to the city through leaden pipes, so everywhere there were fountains, flowers, trees, and vines.

It was said there were fifty thousand fine dwellings in Córdoba, and as many lesser ones. There were seven hundred mosques where the faithful worshiped, and nine hundred public baths. And this at a time when Christians forbade bathing as a heathen custom, when monks and nuns boasted of their filthiness as evidence of sanctity. One nun of the time boasted that at the age of sixty she had washed no part of her body but her fingertips when going to take the mass.

There were thousands of shops, with streets devoted to workers in metal, leather, and silk; it was said there were one hundred and thirty thousand weavers working with silk or wool.

Upon a side street I discovered a lean, fierce man who taught the art of the scimitar and dagger, and each day I went there to work with him. My long hours at the oar as well as a boyhood of running, wrestling, and climbing rocks had given me uncommon strength and agility. My teacher suggested another, a huge wrestler from India, a man of enormous skill, now growing old. He spoke Arabic fluently, and between bouts we talked much of his native land and those that intervened.

As black-haired as any Arab, my hair was curly and my skin only a little lighter than most of theirs. Now I cultivated a black mustache and could easily have passed for an Arab or Berber. In my new clothing, with my height, I drew attention upon the streets where I spent my time, learning the ways of the city, listening to the bargaining, the gossip, debate, and argument.

As yet I had chosen no school, yet each night I read myself to sleep with the writings of al-Farabi on Aristotle, and I was learning much. Among other things I learned that one could attain to no position unless one was adept at extemporaneous poetry, and poetry of all kinds was appreciated by men in the street as well as by the leaders in the brilliant intellectual and artistic life for which Córdoba was famous.

Knowing no one, I often sat alone in one of the coffeehouses that were springing up in the cities of Moslem Spain.

At first, when coffee became known, it was pressed into cakes and sold as a delicacy; later it was made into an infusion and drunk. It was said to be inspiring to the mind, a contribution to thought. The coffeehouses became the haunts of intellectuals and poets.

Coffee was a product of Africa but soon crossed the Red Sea into Arabia. Ibn-Tuwais, with whom I often talked the hours away, had been a friend of a learned man who told him of an ancient time when a ship a day had sailed from the Red Sea ports of Egypt such as Myos Hormus and Berenice, sailing to the faraway cities of India, Ceylon, and China. These vessels often brought cargoes of tea, and this, too, had become a favorite beverage. Unknown in Christian Europe, it had first been used for medicinal purposes, but was now drunk for pleasure.

Neither drink was known in Frankish lands, but seated in the coffeehouses, I drank of each at various times, twirling my mustache and listening with attention to that headier draught, the wine of the intellect, that sweet and bitter juice distilled from the vine of thought and the tree of man's experience.

Averroës, one of the great intellects of Islam, was qadi of Córdoba at the time. Maimonides, a Jew and a great scholar, had lived there and visited from time to time, or so it was said.

The tea and coffee houses were alive with argument, and there were Persians from Jundi Shapur, Greeks from Alexandria, Syrians from Aleppo mingling with Arabs from Damascus and Baghdad.

In one of the coffeehouses I frequented, Abul Kasim Khalaf, known to the Franks as Albucasis, was an occa-

sional visitor. Famous as a surgeon, he was even better
known as a poet and wit. The botanist ibn-Beytar was his
friend, and many an hour I sat, my back to them, but
hungrily gathering every word. In this way my education
progressed, but also I was learning more of the Arabic
language. From time to time they mentioned books, and
these I hastened to find for myself that I might learn from
them. Into every aspect of learning I threw myself with all
the hunger of the starved.

Each day I lingered in the bazaars, moving from place
to place to talk to merchants from foreign lands, and each
I asked for news of Kerbouchard.

Many knew nothing; others assured me he was dead,
but still I could not accept it.

Of Redwan and Aziza I heard nothing, although there
was much talk of politics.

Well-supplied with money from the selling of the
galley, I purchased fine garments, becoming very much
the elegant young man of fashion. I sat many an hour,
usually engrossed in some manuscript or book purchased
in the street of the booksellers.

And then one day I saw the most beautiful woman I
had ever seen.

She had come to the coffeehouse with Averroës himself,
he whose correct name was ibn-Rushd. They seated themselves opposite me one day when sunshine fell across the
door, leaving all within shadowed and still. It was an hour
when few were about, the place empty but for them and
myself. There were low tables before us, and we sat
cross-legged behind them on leather cushions.

A slave brought them tea and sweetmeats, a sweet-
meat called *natif.* She sat so she faced me, and from time
to time she lifted her long dark lashes and looked directly
at me, as she could not avoid doing. When she turned to
speak to Averroës I glimpsed her beautiful profile and the
length of her lashes. She was divinely beautiful, but are
there not many divinely beautiful women when one is
young and the sap of life flows swiftly in the veins? Yet
this one . . . she was superb!

"It is good to see you, Valaba," Averroës said.

Valaba? Like her namesake of one hundred years earlier, Valaba had made her home a rendezvous for the brilliant, for the poets, philosophers, and students of science. It was a period of enormous achievement, one of the great eras in the history of science. Not since the Athens of Pericles had there been such intellectual excitement, and the home of Valaba, as well as those of several other such women, had become a focal point for the exchange of ideas.

"When I was in Sicily," she was saying, "Prince William told me of Viking ships that had sailed to an island in the northern seas, and this must be Ultima Thule."

"Ah, yes," Averroës acknowledged, "a Greek named Phytheas is said to have sailed there."

She was very beautiful, and he who would be her lover must not be laggard. Glancing across my cup, I said, "If you will permit? I have visited the place."

Her dark eyes were cool. No doubt many young men had aspired to know her, and to know her better. Well, let them have aspirations. Where they aspired, I would achieve.

Averroës looked up with interest. "Ah? You are a man of the sea?"

"Briefly, and perhaps again. The land of which you speak is not the furthest land. There are lands beyond, and still others beyond those."

"You have been to Thule?"

"Long ago, from the shores of Armorica. Our boats fish in seas beyond the ice land where the seas are thick with fog, and sometimes with floating ice, but teem with fish. When the fog is gone and the skies are clear, one can often see, further to the westward, another land."

"And you were there, too?" In the tone of Valaba was a touch of sarcasm.

"I was there also. It is a land of rocky shores, great forests, and a shore that stretches away to both south and north."

"The Vikings spoke of a green land," Averroës said doubtfully.

"This is another, but of which my people have long known. The Norsemen went there from GreenLand and IceLand to get timbers to build their ships, or for masts. Sometimes they landed to dry their fish or to hunt."

"This land has been explored?"

"Who would wish to? It is a land of dense forests and savage men who have nothing to trade but furs or skins. The men who sail there look only for fish."

"You are not an Arab?"

"I am Mathurin Kerbouchard, a traveler and a student."

Averroës smiled. "Are not we all? Travelers and students?" He sipped his tea. "What do you do in Córdoba?"

"I have come to learn, and having found no school, I learn from books."

"You are a poet?" Valaba asked.

"I have not the gift."

Averroës chuckled. "Need that stop you? How many have the gift? There may be a million people in Córdoba, and all of them write poetry, yet not more than three dozen have even a modest gift."

They returned to their conversation, and I, to my reading, for I was beginning the great *Canon* of Avicenna, which was in many volumes and more than a million words on the practice of medicine.

When they left my eyes followed them, watching the slim and graceful Valaba. Had she guessed what was in my mind, she would have laughed at me. Which disturbed me none at all.

Who was I, a barbarian from the northern lands, to even know such a woman? I, a landless man, a wanderer, a casual student?

She was cool, aloof, beautiful, and wealthy. She was a young lady with the brains and judgment of men. Yet my time would come.

Ambition was strong within me. I wanted to see, to become, but, most of all, to understand. Much that here was taken for granted was new to me, and I found it best to tread lightly in all conversation unless I wished to make a fool of myself. Yet I was learning, and the ways of the city were becoming my ways.

The wider my knowledge became the more I realized my ignorance. It is only the ignorant who can be positive, only the ignorant who can become fanatics, for the more I learned the more I became aware that there are shadings and relationships in all things.

My Druid discipline had not only trained my memory but conditioned my mind to the quick grasp of ideas, of essential points. Most of what I read, I retained.

In knowledge lay not only power but freedom from fear, for generally speaking one only fears what one does not understand.

It was a time when all knowledge lay open to him who would seek it, and a physician was often an astronomer, a geographer, a philosopher, and a mathematician. There were several hundred volumes in the library of ibn-Tuwais. These books I read from and studied.

Here and there I began to make acquaintances. Mahmoud was such a one. A tall young man of twenty-four, vain of his pointed beard and mustaches. He was much of a dandy, but keen of wit and a ready hand with a blade. We met by chance in the Garden of Abdallah near the Guadalquivir.

It was shadowed and cool. Great trees created islands of shadow on the stone flags, and there I often sat with a glass of golden Jerez at hand and a book before me.

A shadow fell upon my page, and glancing up, I saw Mahmoud for the first time. "Ah? A student and a drinker of wine? Have you no respect for the Koran?"

It was a time for caution, for under the reign of Yusuf there were fanatics in Córdoba. Yet the stranger's eyes seemed friendly.

"If the Prophet had read Avicenna upon a hot day, he might have accepted a glass. Anyway," I added slyly, "he had never tasted the wine of Jerez."

He sat down. "I am Mahmoud, a student of the law, occasionally a drinker of wine."

"And I am Kerbouchard."

There in the shadow of a great tree we talked of what young men talk about when their world is filled with ideas and the excitement of learning. We talked of war and women, of ships, camels, weapons, and Avicenna, of religion and philosophy, of politics and buried treasure, but most of all we talked of Córdoba.

We ate figs, small cakes, and drank wine, talking the sun out of the sky and the moon into it. We talked of the faults of Caesar and the death of Alexander, and he spoke of Fez and Marrakesh and the great desert to the south of those cities.

It was the beginning of a friendship, my first in the land of the Moors.

Of course, there were John of Seville, whose name was often mentioned, and old ibn-Tuwais, whose name was not.

My gold disappeared, and I sold the sapphire. It bought leisure and time to study and roaming the streets at night with Mahmoud, and it bought much else.

Startling ideas appeared in a book newly come to Córdoba, a book written at the oasis of Merv by al-Khazini and called *The Book of the Balance of Wisdom*. It was an excellent account of the hydrostatics and mechanics of the time, but it also advanced the theory of gravity, and that air has weight.

We argued the subject furiously and were becoming quite angry when a girl passed by on a camel. We forgot gravity, and the weight of the air became as nothing.

Mahmoud leaped to his feet. "Did you see her? Did you see how she looked at me?"

"You?" His friend Haroun scoffed. "It was at Kerbouchard she looked! I have noticed this before. All the girls look at Kerbouchard!"

Mahmoud snorted. "That dog of an unbeliever? That stench in the nostrils of humanity? It was at *me* she looked!"

The camel had stopped in the hot, dusty street nearby. Four soldiers were escort for the girl on the camel, tough, surly-looking men, yet something about her drew my attention, and her eyes were meeting mine over her veil. It was not an illusion, not a vanity.

It was hot in the street, and a fresh sherbet had just been put before me. On impulse I picked up the sherbet and crossed to the camel in four quick steps.

The place where we sat in the garden adjoined the bazaar, and the attention of the guards was momentarily distracted by the confusion and the crowd.

"Light of the World"—I spoke softly—"accept this small tribute from your slave. Its coolness will speak my thoughts clearer than anything I can say."

She took the sherbet, and our fingers touched. Over her veil her eyes smiled, and her lips said, "Thank you . . . *Mathurin!*"

And then the four soldiers closed about me.

11

"**M**ove, animal!" A bearded soldier pushed me. "Get from here!"

Angered, I seized his arm with a wrestling trick and threw him over my shoulder and into the dust.

From behind came a yell of delight as Mahmoud and Haroun rushed to the fray.

The soldiers had closed in swiftly, but my months of training and the strength brought from the galley had left me ready.

Smashing a closed fist into one man's teeth, I struck to the belly of another soldier. Unaccustomed to blows, they staggered back, startled and hurt. Instantly, I stepped back and drew my blade.

It was hot in the dusty street, the noises from the bazaar were suddenly stilled. The soldier I had thrown to the ground was getting to his feet, and his face where it was not covered with beard was pale as death. He whom I had struck in the belly was still gasping for breath, but the others drew their swords.

Out of the hot, still afternoon death had come. Sweat trickled down my cheeks as they started for me, trained fighting men, iron-muscled and tough. Even as I faced them, my friends came alongside me.

"Do you take the center one, Infidel," Mahmoud said. "Haroun and I will have the others!"

A soldier spat blood from split lips. "Children!" He sneered. "I'll open your bellies to the flies!"

He lunged, but I parried the blade. My own point darted, flicking a spot of blood from his upper arm.

88

As the soldier shifted ground, a voice spoke clearly. "At noon, in the Court of Oranges!"

It was the girl on the camel, and as she spoke she struck the camel, and it started to move.

The soldier I had struck grabbed wildly at the camel, but the girl had started the animal into the crowded bazaar, scattering people in all directions. The soldiers tried to break off the fight, but I suddenly realized the girl had been their prisoner, and was escaping. With a quick turn of the wrist, I parried the blade and thrust. The soldier, attempting to break off and pursue the girl, took the full thrust of my blade and fell, screaming his agony.

From up the street there was a rush of feet, and Mahmoud caught at me. "Quick! Away!"

With a slash at the nearest soldier I fled after Mahmoud and Haroun who had darted down an alleyway into a street beyond. On the far side of that street Mahmoud leaped to a wall, rolled over, and dropped on the far side, Haroun and I following upon his heels.

There was a chorus of screams, excited more than frightened, and the shrill angry cries of an offended eunuch. We dashed across the gardens, twisting our way among a dozen or more pretty and scantily clad women. Mahmoud paused long enough under an apricot tree to seize one plump and pretty girl and squeeze her, kissing her swiftly before we threw ourselves over the far wall and into a narrow, shadowed alley.

We ducked and darted through stables and ancient buildings to emerge at last in another bazaar. Instantly, we ceased to run but walked sedately among the booths and shops, stopping finally to order *natif* and coffee. As we sat there several soldiers rushed through the bazaar, glaring about them.

Haroun looked across the small table at me, chuckling. He was a short, stocky man, this Haroun, one of the best fencers at the academy where we studied the art. "Do you know who those soldiers were?"

"No."

"They were the men of ibn-Haram."

Ibn-Haram? So then, the girl was Aziza. No wonder she had seemed familiar. Aziza . . . *here*?

They were looking at me. "You know who is ibn-Haram?"

"I have heard of him. Who has not?"

"He is a dangerous enemy, and the right hand of Yusuf."

What had she said? "At noon, in the Court of Oranges."

Unwittingly, my interference had given her a chance to escape, but had she any place to go?

Had the soldiers heard her speak of the Court of Oranges? My friends said nothing, so they might not have heard, and the soldiers were concentrating on me.

If they heard or remembered, the Court of Oranges could be a trap. But on what day? And at what time? No matter, Aziza would come, and I would be there to meet her.

"Take my advice and stay off the streets for a few days. You killed that man, I believe."

There was something in his eyes I had not seen before. Was it jealousy? Calculation?

When it was dark, we went our ways, and I carefully, along dark streets and empty alleys.

Ibn-Tuwais was seated over a bowl of fruit and a glass of tea when I entered. "You are in trouble?" he asked.

My face was flushed from hurry, and my manner must have reflected my mood. So for the first time I told him of Málaga, the fight on the shore, and the disappearance of Aziza and Count Redwan.

"She will have friends," he said. "I have an idea where she might go."

"And Redwan?"

"There is talk . . . he is a prisoner, I believe, in Zaragoza." Ibn-Tuwais chose a piece of fruit. "You have made a powerful enemy, but a man may be judged by who his enemies are, and their power."

"What would you advise?"

"Wait, and as your friend advised, stay off the streets and out of sight."

Wait . . . that, indeed, I must do, and every day, in the Court of Oranges.

The twelfth century was a time of restlessness in Europe. New ideas were creeping in, shaking the foundations of old beliefs. The second Crusade was history, but Crusaders had returned astonished at what they had seen and no longer content with their cold, drafty castles.

More than one hundred years had passed since William the Conqueror and his Normans invaded England, and now Henry II was consolidating his control over Ireland and Wales while putting down the last feudal revolt. At a small town named Oxford, a university with a tradition from an earlier time had been founded. Elsewhere Adelard of Bath and Robert of Chester, students of Arabic science, were offering their knowledge to a limited circle of students.

In Germany, Frederick I, so-called Barbarossa (Red-Beard), founded the Holy Roman Empire, and on his fifth expedition into Italy had been defeated by the Lombard towns at Legnano.

In China, the Northern Sung dynasty, with its great age of landscape painting, had come to an end, although landscape painting did not. Compositions of majestic breadth and exquisite detail, with a sparing use of line as well as interesting contrasts of light and shadow, had been created by Tuan Yuan, Kuo Hsi, Li Kung-lin, and Mi Fei, among others. In China the great historians, essayists, poets, and scientists were often statesmen as well.

The Southern Sung fought a reluctant war with the restless tribes to the north.

In 1161 explosives were used by Yu Tun-wen in defeating the Chin.

In ceramic art the magnificent Sung white was created and the Southern Sung artists were turning away from the beetling, picturesque crags and mountains to misty lakes, hills, and trees of softer landscapes.

In India, Mohammed of Ghur had begun the con-

quest of Hindustan, and Arab vessels were trading down
the east coast of Africa as they had done for as long as men
could remember. Their ships had sailed to China, explored the last islands of Indonesia, and returned with
cargoes to Red Sea and Persian Gulf ports.

Merchants and travelers from all the world came to
Córdoba, drawn by the wealth and brilliance of its society.
This society centered about the homes of a dozen beautiful
women who held court in Córdoba, gathering about them
the creative intelligence of the Arab world.

Córdoba was where I wished to remain, yet much
would depend on what happened when I met Aziza again.
Ibn-Haram was not a man to be crossed with impunity.
He would quickly decide that the fight in the bazaar was
not the accident it appeared to be but a plot to free Aziza.
He would not rest until he discovered who had been
involved.

Somehow I must meet Aziza and help her return to
her friends. Any attempt to do so could mean my death,
and in a quarrel that was not my own.

Was I a fool to become involved because of a girl I
had scarcely met?

Aziza had escaped into the city. She undoubtedly had
friends to help her, but she had wished to meet with me,
a risk she seemed willing to accept.

Restlessly, I paced the garden at the home of ibn-
Tuwais. The Court of Oranges and the mosque were familiar to me, but in the event one of the soldiers had overheard
her, I must be prepared to escape quickly.

"*At noon in the Court of Oranges!*" The words sang
in my ears, beat a rhythm in my blood.

Had Mahmoud and Haroun escaped? They might
have been picked up after leaving me, but if so, I had no
word of it. Nor did I trust Mahmoud. We had been
acquaintances, talking together, drinking coffee together.
He was, I knew, a man of intense vanity, and he had
declared it was he at whom Aziza had looked, to discover
otherwise might have been a blow. Nor would an aspiring
young man wish to cross ibn-Haram, who, if he aided him,

might confer favors. There had been something in his eyes I did not trust. I said as much to ibn-Tuwais.

The old man nodded. "Trust your instincts. Life teaches us much of which we are not aware. Our senses perceive things that do not impinge upon our awareness, but they lie dormant within us and affect our recognition of people and conditions. But you must be patient. In impatience there is danger."

He was right, of course, but patience is never the easiest of virtues, and outside these walls events were moving forward that could mean recapture for Aziza and death for me.

When at last I lay down to sleep, I did not expect to sleep, but weariness lay heavily upon me, and sleep I did. My last thoughts were of a man with a scarred face. *Wit and a sword*, he had said. It was a time for wit, but for caution also.

Worst of all, I might have to abandon Córdoba, my enchanted city. It was, with Constantinople and Baghdad, one of the three intellectual centers of the world, yet I think that with reservations, for I have begun to learn something of India and the far land sometimes called Cathay. What lies there? Surely, from the few books I have found their cities must be as great as these, or greater.

Córdoba, I had learned, came to its true greatness under Abd-erl-Rahman III and his successor, al-Hakam II from 961 to 976 A.D., and under the dictatorship, if such it can be called, of Ali Mansur from 977 to 1002. Miles of streets had been paved and lighted; there were many parks, bazaars, and bookshops. It was a city where I loved to roam, and I was only beginning to learn its ways.

What of the queenly Valaba? Of her my thoughts were guilty ones, for was I not in love with Aziza? Or was I?

No matter, if she needed my help, she would have it, but I must move with utmost caution. After all, Valaba was but a beautiful woman with whom I had exchanged a word or two. By now she had forgotten me, although my

vanity shied at the thought. Or was it something else than
vanity? Some affinity, perhaps, of which we were both
aware?

Long before daylight I finally fell asleep, while wind
stirred the vine leaves and wafted over me the scents of
jasmine and rose mingled with the coolness from the
fountains.

Would it be today? Would Aziza meet me in the
Court of Oranges?

Would love await me there? Or adventure and death?

12

At noon in the Court of Oranges the sun was hot. The air was heavy with the scent of flowers and lazy with the sound of running water. At noon in the Court of Oranges there was a shuffling of feet as the white-robed thousands moved slowly into the mosque. Above them the palms cast slender shadows over the orange trees, and golden fruit shone through the glossy leaves like the Golden Apples of legend.

There were four great basins in the Court of Oranges and water tumbled into them with a pleasant, sleepy sound. The air hung still and hot, thick with the scent of jasmine and rose, and along the walls were hibiscus, great soft red flowers beside others of pale gold or white.

On the north side of the Court was a minaret, one hundred and eight feet tall, so beautiful it might have been dreamed rather than constructed by the hands of men. Stately, beautiful, and created of stone intricately woven with threads of gold in fantastic tracery. At noon in the Court of Oranges I moved along with the shuffling throng, one of them but not of them, for my mind was not on things devout, nor my eyes upon the ground.

Here and there people stood about in groups or waited alone, muttering prayers or soaking up the hot, sultry beauty of the place. And among them might be Aziza.

Also among them might be the spies or the soldiers of ibn-Haram, for I knew what might be expected of that cold-faced soldier.

During my weeks of listening to the idle talk of the bazaars, I had overheard a good bit of gossip about ibn-

Haram. Skilled in intrigue, merciless to his enemies, he
was utterly without scruple, a strong, dangerous, intelligent man, inordinately ambitious and a supporter of the
caliph. It was whispered that he aspired to the caliphate
himself.

Against him and against Yusuf was arrayed an army of
quiet but determined people, some of whom were support-
ers of the Umayyad dynasty, long out of power, and others
linked to the Almoravids. In addition to these were those
who belonged to no party: the poets, philosophers, and
men of intellect who feared the ignorance, the bigotry,
and destructive policies of Yusuf. So far the caliph had
interfered little with such groups, but many believed their
time was short.

Of these Count Redwan was one. He had long been
an antagonist of the Almohads, and it was his plan to bring
the daughter of ibn-Sharaz to Córdoba and unite her in
marriage to a descendant of the Umayyads. Then, with the
power of William of Sicily behind them, they would seek
the caliphate once more.

It was a bold plan and might well succeed, for William had strong friends in Africa, and even more friends
among the pirates of Almería with their great wealth and
many ships.

Ibn-Haram no doubt intended to hold Aziza as hostage to keep ibn-Sharaz and William II out of the picture.

Feet shuffled softly in the Court of Oranges, and
easing from the crowd, I stood in the shade of the orange
trees, inhaling the perfume of the blossoms and watching
the crowd from under my brows, my head lowered.

Aziza was no fool. In all of Spain, perhaps in all of
Europe, there was no place so easy to lose oneself as here,
at this hour.

A gentle hand touched my sleeve, and it was she.

Her dark eyes looked into mine, and I wanted to take
her in my arms, to forget the place, the time, the danger.

"Do not look at me like that!" she protested, in a
whisper. "You frighten me!" But if the look in her eyes

was fear, I could wish that all women would be so frightened.

"How else could I look at you? You are beautiful!"

"We cannot stay here."

"Where is Redwan?"

"I do not know. He is a prisoner. I know not where."

Soldiers appeared at the outer gate. There were four . . . six . . . eight.

Not seeming to hurry, I took Aziza's arm and stepped into the shuffling throng. Within the temple was a long vista of arches and columns, shadowed and still but for the rustling of garments.

Across the mosque was a door, a very small door not often used, but one I had located before this, recognizing its possibilities. Escaping the crowd, we slipped through the door to the small garden beyond. Across it, then out in a public park.

We moved sedately then, yet I was thinking as we walked. It was unlikely my connection with ibn-Tuwais was known. Mahmoud knew of it, and Haroun, but if I could get there, horses would be available, and I had scouted several escape routes through the alleys of the city.

Past the stalls of sellers of incense, past the merchants of silk, past the astrologers and seers, we turned a corner into an empty, high-walled street where nothing moved but the wind, nothing loitered but the shadows.

Ibn-Tuwais greeted us and led us into the house. "You need explain nothing. This house was built in a time of trouble."

We followed to an inner chamber. He turned sharply in an alcove and leaned hard against the wall. The wall swung soundlessly inward, revealing a dark, narrow stair. "It has been used before this." He handed me a candle. "You will find food and wine."

When Aziza had taken the candle and gone down the stairs, the old man whispered, "It was near here where she disappeared, and they have begun a search of the entire quarter. You must remain until the search is completed.

"But"—he had started to walk away—"if anything happens to me there is a passage behind the wall. It opens in the same way and leads beyond the walls. When you leave the passage ride to the Castle of Othman. It is a ruin inhabited only by owls. You may hide there until you can escape."

"How can we ride?"

"The passage is for horses. It was made for sorties by cavalry. There is an entrance from within our stable, and your horses have already been taken below. There is food for them and for you, and a spring flows through a channel there. If necessary, you could remain hidden for weeks, but I would not advise it."

He paused, then his eyes hardened. "You are not a Moslem, but you have a lady in your care, a very important lady. If it should chance that she is harmed in any way, it would mean both your lives."

"Hers too?"

"Hers most of all. She would be killed, without question. Guard yourself, and her as well."

He hesitated again. "If circumstances permit you to return, my house is yours, always."

"At the Castle of Othman? There is a place to hide?"

His detail of the ruin was quick, explicit, and with military efficiency. "Quickly now! You must go!"

The door closed behind me, and I descended the steep stairs in darkness. Aziza had removed her veil and was placing food and wine upon the low table.

Above us there was a dull sound like the slam of a heavy door, only louder. I drew my sword and turned to face the stair.

Nothing.

Had I brought trouble to ibn-Tuwais? What had happened?

Aziza pointed to the table. "Eat," she said. "We must be ready when night comes."

We ate in silence. Of what she thought I know not,

but I was brooding about the old man up there. Had I brought torture and death to one I so admired and loved? Yet I could not return to help. To reveal myself now would prove what might be only suspected.

Packs lay upon the floor, for it seems ibn-Tuwais had considered everything. He knew what I was about, and where his sympathies lay. After all, he too was an enemy of Yusuf.

Upon a low table were piles of books. Ibn-Tuwais had expected trouble and had moved his precious library here. In Paris such books might buy a province, or a bishopric. The packs themselves contained food and four books. Obviously, he wished me to have them.

"Sleep," I told Aziza, "for with night we must go."

When she lay down I covered her with a robe. It had been early afternoon when we reached the house of ibn-Tuwais. Say four hours of waiting, another hour to travel the passage to a place beyond the wall, and we could emerge in darkness.

From the stack of books I chose one, a translation from far-off Cathay, *Essays of the Dream Pool* by Shen Kua.

A long time later when the candle's length indicated the time had passed, I replaced the book among the others. Someday, perhaps, I would complete it.

Aziza awakened at my touch and, rising, took up a fresh candle and lighted it. Shouldering the packs, I followed her along the passage.

The horses stood waiting, saddled and ready in their underground stable. Mounting, we rode through the passage toward the outer walls of the city.

The top cleared my head by only a few inches, some of it carved from solid rock. Several times we rode through small pools of water, and once for several hundred yards we rode along a stream of clear, cold water.

The passage ended abruptly. We faced a slab of rock; beside it was a lever of bronze. The work here looked like no work of Moor, Goth, or Phoenician, nor had I seen its

like before. I thought of the Idol of Cádiz . . . by the same
hands, perhaps?

Dismounting, I lay hold of the lever. An instant I
paused, and then I pulled down.

Nothing happened.

Our eyes met in the candlelight. Suppose it would
not open? Were we trapped, then?

Waiting an instant, I mustered all my strength, swinging my weight on the lever. Slowly, sluggishly, it yielded.
The great slab of rock swung slowly inward, stiff with age
and untold years of disuse.

There was a rush of cool night air, of damp vegetation,
a sound of trickling water.

Stepping outside, sword in hand, I found myself in a
narrow gorge, above me the stars. Only a few feet further
along, our trickle of water flowed into a larger stream.

Searching, I found the other lever, artfully concealed
in a crack of the rock. Aziza emerged, and I swung the
lever down and the door closed, more easily this time,
merging perfectly with natural cracks in the rock. Marking
the place in my mind, I concealed the lever and all signs
of the movement of the door.

Mounting, we walked our horses down the rocky bed
of the stream, and after riding for some distance we left
the water for an ancient trail, then rode along a lane used
by workers going to and from the fields. Far off, we
believed we could already see the tower of the Castle of
Othman.

Built long ago, already a relic when the first Visigoths
came to Spain, it may have dated from the Romans or
even the ancient Iberians. Destroyed and rebuilt several
times, it had become a place of ill omen, and few cared to
risk the dangers that seemed a part of it.

We rode in silence, depressed by our fears for ibn-
Tuwais. He might be put to torture or slain. To have
returned would only prove that he had aided us, leading
to his certain death, and what he had done for us would be
wasted.

How long could we maintain ourselves at the Castle

of Othman? How long before some passerby stumbled upon us or glimpsed some movement among the ruins?

Yet when we fled the castle, where could we go? For me alone it would be simple enough, yet one did not wander the countryside with a beautiful girl without causing talk, and in no case without a guard of horsemen.

Dawn still lingered beyond the horizon when we rode up the slope to the tower, and a huge old tower it was. There was little else, a ragged battlement, moonlight falling over the broken walls. A lonely, haunted place it was, forgotten upon its hill, a place with the smell of death upon it.

We walked our horses into the open gate and drew rein in the courtyard. It was dark and still when our echoing hoofbeats ceased. A bat fluttered by my head, and an owl spoke inquiringly into the shadows.

We had come to our hiding place, two ghosts to join our companion ghosts, yet my fears were for discovery, not things of the night. We who lived upon the lonely Armorican moors were accustomed to werewolves, vampires, and *tursts*.

"Mathurin," Aziza whispered, "I am afraid!"

Stepping down from the saddle, I lifted my hands to her. "The darkness is a friend to the pursued, Aziza, and where we are, love can be. Here we shall stay."

13

At dawn, in the Castle of Othman, the sun was bright. The ghosts, if such there were, had fled with the shadows. Water bubbled in the ancient fountain, but where gardens had been, lay a tangle of rank grass, unpruned shrubbery, and trees. Bark fallen from the trees lay on the grass, and over all was a carpet of leaves.

The wall had been breached in some forgotten battle, and the stones lay awry, often covered with vines.

Situated on a hill, the castle dominated the countryside, as much a part of the landscape as an outcropping of rock or an old tree.

At one time the hill must have been more abrupt than now, but debris from the castle itself had made the approach more gradual. On the north were three round towers, all partly in ruin, and on the south three towers, one of these square. This and the tower at the opposite end of the south wall were relatively intact.

The court or bailey was enclosed almost completely but the great hall was in ruins, its roof fallen in. My first action was to make a thorough search of the ruin. The curtains around the inner bailey provided a carefully contrived series of stairs and passages that communicated with every part of the castle so reinforcements might be rushed to any point from the keep.

The keep itself was of three stories, vaulted and pierced by arrow loops at each story. At each level, doorways offered access to all parts of the fortification.

From the keep there was an excellent view of the surrounding country, and all approaches could be observed from concealed positions. Yet what I sought was a way of escape. As Plautus has said, not even a mouse trusts himself to one hole only.

Such ancient castles always provided themselves with one or more secret exits as a means of sortie or escape, which also might be used to smuggle in supplies during a siege.

The square tower, which was the keep, was obviously the oldest part of the structure, and any passage that existed must have a concealed outer opening in a grove, a gorge, or at least a hollow. If I could find such an opening, I might more easily discover the inside entrance to the passage.

While Aziza slept I prowled the passageways, explored the donjons beneath, and studied the surrounding country from every window or breach. There might come a time when escape would be imperative, and it was necessary to know all the depressions, streambeds, and low ground, so one could keep from sight while fleeing. It was a lesson taught by caution: to stop nowhere without finding a way out, a means of escape.

Far in the distance lay Córdoba, but no villages lay near nor any habitation or road. Few traveled unless in strong parties well able to defend themselves, as there were bands of brigands and renegade soldiers wandering about.

The Castle of Othman was remote, alone, obviously unvisited. During my search I found no evidence that anyone had even sought shelter here in many years. It was far from roads, and from a distance appeared more to be a jutting crag than a castle.

For a time at least we would be safe, I hoped.

Returning to the bailey, I studied the interior court covered with grass and saw through the breach the ruins of the castle gardens. These were walled, and between the bailey and the gardens there was grazing for our horses for at least a week and perhaps longer. The food we brought with us would last as long, and might be supplemented by fruit from the garden, although there was little of it.

Sitting inside the keep, I gazed through an arrow loop at distant Córdoba and speculated on what the months had meant to me.

Aside from the lessons of the street and the chance to become more perfect in the use of Arabic, I had profited from conversations overheard, and intellectual discussions in which I had, at times, participated. I had read works by Aristotle, Avicenna, Rhazes, Alhazen, al-Biruni, and many others. I had delved into the sciences of astronomy, logic, medicine, the natural sciences, and necromancy. Each book, each author, each conversation seemed to open new avenues of possibility.

My skill with sword and dagger had improved, and with archery as well, yet I was not satisfied. I still possessed the gems brought from the sale of the ship and the ransoms, all except the sapphire, but I had no profession, no trade. I was a landless man, with all that implied. I belonged nowhere, had no protector, served no man. Which made me fair game for all.

It was a time of trouble, and the quickest way to success was war or piracy. Of navigation I knew more than most seafaring men, and I was steeped in the military tactics of Vegetius and others. The profession of arms was that for which I was best fitted, yet I inclined toward scholarship.

Scholars were welcome anywhere, with kings and cities vying for their attention. Yet I was a man alone, without family, without friends, without influence or teachers of reputation.

And what of my father? Was he truly dead?

"Mathurin?"

Aziza came to me along the passage, her face still soft from sleep, her hair awry, yet never more lovely than now.

"I thought you had gone."

"And left you?"

She came up beside me. "Will they find us here?"

"I doubt it. Can you endure this place for a while?"

"If you are here."

We sat together looking out over the plain of Andalusia. Far away, so far our eyes could scarcely make it out, there was movement on the high road that led from Córdoba to Seville. A few fleecy clouds drifted idly, casting shadows on the tawny plain.

We went below, ate from our small store, and drank water from the fountain. From under the trees I gathered sticks to keep inside in the event of rain, and Aziza, child of luxury though she was, gathered them beside me. We cleared a small room near the garden where we could sleep.

Looking about the ruin, I thought how quickly this could become irksome, less to me than to her who had never been without her comforts, never without a servant at call. For now the novelty and the strangeness appealed. There was also that other thing of which I thought, and which must surely come to her mind as well. If we were found together, we would both be killed, and for no other reason than that.

Questions haunted me. What had become of ibn-Tuwais? What was ibn-Haram thinking now, and where was he searching?

What worried me most was what would happen if some passing band of brigands chose to stop for the night. I had no illusions as to what would happen if they saw Aziza.

One I might kill, even two or four, but in the end they would kill me, and Aziza would be left in the hands of a rude soldiery, accustomed to rape or the casual women of the camp.

At sundown I killed a rabbit with an arrow, and we made a small meal of roasted rabbit and some grapes and apricots from the garden, conserving our meager food supply. After we had eaten we climbed up in the keep to watch the sunset.

Almost a half mile away there was a copse where a small cluster of trees grew, an unlikely spot for anyone to venture and less attractive than several other groves not far away. Shallow-seeming ravines led away from it in several directions. There, I surmised, would be a logical place for a tunnel exit.

Moreover, the inner entrance to such a tunnel must be in the keep itself, perhaps in the very room we inhabited. An hour's diligent search revealed nothing. It was Aziza who helped me.

"Near Palermo," she suggested, "there is a balanced stone in the wall of an alcove. They try to put the opening in some hidden place. Otherwise, there is risk of somebody appearing in the passage just as the secret door opens."

Of course! I was an idiot not to have thought of that, and there was an alcove out of sight of the door, a small place with an arrow loop, but the bottom of the loop was almost breast high. Beneath it was a solid slab of stone four feet high and three wide.

Crouching beside it, I shoved against the top. Nothing happened so I shoved against the bottom. Still nothing. It was not until I pushed against the left side a second time, bracing my back and pushing hard, that the slab moved. It too was stiff from years of disuse, but it did move.

It was balanced on an axis of polished stone that fitted into the rock above and below. It opened to allow barely twenty inches by four feet of opening, giving access to a steep, winding stair down the inside of a well-like space. The steps were but a foot wide and around them, utter blackness!

A misstep and a man would fall . . . how far?

Taking a small stone, I dropped it, listening. A long time after, it struck bottom.

Taking a candle from our small store, I lighted it. "If anyone comes, close the opening, but leave a small crack."

"I shall come with you." Aziza was pale and frightened. "I do not wish to be left alone."

"You must stay here. The stair may have fallen or the passage caved in. Let me be sure it is safe."

"Please let me come! If you die, I want to die with you!"

"I shall not die, but do keep watch for me. If anyone comes . . . hide."

So saying, I stepped through the opening and, clinging to the wall, prepared to descend.

Oh, yes! I was frightened. The ancient well had the odor of a place long closed, nor could I be sure there was an exit below, or that it had not been sealed by the action of water on stone over the years. Nor was there any guessing how old it might be, for this was the most ancient part of the fortress.

It was pitch dark, and the air was frightful. It would have been better to leave the passage open for a time and let the bad air, or some of it, escape. But we needed a way out, and that need might come at any moment.

Testing every step, I edged down and around the narrow well.

It was deathly still. Into this dark place there came no sound, nor did my candle shed more than a small circle of light.

Several times I paused to rest. I was sorry I had not begun counting the steps, for then I would know when I was beneath the surface of the earth. The well was within the wall of the keep, but as I descended it grew perceptibly wider.

At one place a step was half broken away; at another, rock crumbled beneath my foot, and the fragments cascaded into the depths below. The steps were slabs of rock set into the wall of the well like the rungs of a winding, one-sided ladder.

My candle flame stood erect, for there was no air movement. Had the flame shrunk? Was it true that where a flame would not burn a man could not live? Somewhere I had heard this.

Suddenly, I was upon a stone platform six feet square, and I paused to rest. Sweat drenched me, and the air was close and hot. My breath came hoarsely, but I could not be sure whether it was my exertions or the foulness of the air.

Starting downward again, I suddenly found a broken step! Cautiously, I reached with a toe, feeling for it. Putting my toe upon the broken step, I slowly let it take my weight. My foot settled . . . suddenly the step gave way. The stone crumbled, and my foot plunged down. Wildly, I grabbed at the wall. My fingers found a crack and clung. Precariously, afraid to even breathe, I clung against the face of the inner wall, trembling in every muscle. Then the true enormity of my disaster struck me.

My candle was gone!

When I grabbed at the wall, the candle had fallen, so I was marooned, clinging to a crack in the wall in abysmal darkness, unable to see or even move.

There was no light, nor could the eyes become accustomed to a darkness where there was a complete absence of light. I clung to the wall, trembling with fear, gasping hoarsely.

Slowly, my good sense returned. How long I clung there I have no idea, yet it seemed an eon of time before I dared move.

One toe rested in the tiniest crack; my fingers clung to another. Below me lay that black and awful pit, and my body became slippery with the sweat of fear. If I tried to lift one foot to another resting place, the other might slip off.

Another rock fell away under me, and fell and fell, and fell. Inside me was a vast emptiness in which fear had turned my guts to water. Always I had hated being locked up, hated barred and closed places. My muscles ached, my fingers were growing numb, only the weariness in my muscles gave me a sense of passing time. Perhaps it was no more than minutes, even seconds, yet it seemed forever.

Win or lose I must make an effort, for if I remained hanging there, I must surely fall, and there was no one to come to my rescue.

Somewhere below me was another step. Yet, suppose it, too, was gone? Suppose this was the purpose of the steps? To let some doomed prisoner believe in escape, to let him descend into darkness, only to plunge off into space and die miserably on the bottom?

Careful not to put too much strain on my fingerhold, I put out a tentative, exploring toe.

14

Beneath me there was nothing but space. Moving my toe carefully along the wall, I felt for a foothold. My fingers were aching, and the one leg that had a perch was trembling uncontrollably. How much longer I could cling like a fly to that sheer wall I had no idea.

Feeling along the wall with my free toe, I encountered an obstruction. It was further over and somewhat lower down. Carefully, I stretched still further, finally getting my foot upon solid rock.

An instant I held myself there, gathering strength and will, then with my right hand I reached out further, trying for a handhold. When I found it, it was the tiniest edge of a rock that had not been fitted properly. It offered only the barest fingertip hold.

Moving with extreme care, I shifted my other hand and foot and stood upon solid rock once more. But I remained in absolute darkness with nothing to strike a light.

Without a light I could not go back up the steps, and every move was made at the risk of my life, yet I had no choice but to continue. If I was gone too long, Aziza might try to find me, and the thought of her on those steps was frightening. So I must continue to the bottom, feeling my way down, hoping there would be no missing steps.

The air was close, and I found myself fighting to get enough into my lungs. There was no time to waste, for I had heard of men dying in old tunnels or long-closed spaces.

How long it took I had no idea. In the darkness there

was no way of estimating time. It seemed I had been clinging to that wall forever, inching my way down, streaming with perspiration. In this dark well I had no way of knowing whether it was taking minutes, hours, or days.

Suddenly, my foot was upon earth, but when I moved I felt something break under my feet. As I squatted down, my fingers touched the smooth surface of a skull and some broken bones.

Feeling about, my hand found the skull again, touched the eyeholes. I jerked my hand away . . . some poor wretch like myself who attempted a way out and was left here to die.

I felt oppressed, as if something were pushing against my chest. My hands groped for the wall. There had to be a way out.

Twice more my feet crunched on what had to be broken bones, but my searching fingers on the wall found no crack, only solid, unbroken stone.

Crouching, I began a second turning of the tower base, this time feeling lower down for any crack, any break in the wall that might mean an opening. I found nothing.

The very thought of climbing up, of enduring that nightmare again was . . . My eyelids drooped, my muscles seemed to give way, and I sat down. My brain warned me that the foul air was killing me. Soon it would rob me of consciousness, and I would fall to the floor to die as had the others.

And Aziza? She would be alone, waiting. Waiting up there in the golden sunlight for a man who could not return.

Earth, I thought, an earthen floor.

I could dig, but dig into what? In which direction? Back into the hill or away from it? And how deep into the earth did the foundations go?

Deliberately, like a drunken man, I forced my mind to view the problem. My will to live was fighting the foulness of the air. I forced myself to another circling of the wall. If worse came to worst, I could at least attempt

the climb. The air would be fresher the closer I got to that
open crack.

I could not, I would not, give up.

Suddenly, my fingers encountered a step. I found the
lowest one and sat down. Think . . . I must think. My
mind fumbled with the idea.

If there was a way out, my brain must find it. My
skull throbbed heavily, and I tried to force my thoughts to
deal with the problem. Leaning my elbows on my knees, I
held my aching head in my hands. My leg felt cold.

Cold . . . cold because I was soaking wet. Yet I was
hot. I was perspiring, so why should my leg be cold?

Air! It had to be air! Cold, fresh, wonderful air!

I dropped to my knees, my fingers tearing at the
earth against the wall, seeking the life-giving breath of air,
seeking the opening. My fingers found nothing, only cold
stone. No opening . . . *nothing!*

Yet there was air, a trickle of it. Something I had
done, some unwitting movement, some pressure of my
body when searching around the well, perhaps my weight
on the lower step. Flat on my face, I pressed my mouth
against the opening and inhaled deeply.

Again and again. Slowly the cool air revived me. Life
returned, energy returned, my brain cleared.

My skull still throbbed, but now I could think, the
dullness was gone. Eagerly, I dug my fingers into the
crack and tugged. Nothing happened. My weight on the
lower step seemed to make no difference. I pressed against
the wall, felt for each particular stone. Nothing happened.

Then—I scarcely believed it. I heard a sound, a whisper of movement hardly to be detected.

It was the first sound other than my own breathing
that I had heard in what must have been hours. Yet it
sounded as if something or someone were scratching at a
stone!

Pressing my mouth to the opening, I said, "Is someone there?"

A low cry answered. "Mathurin! You are alive!".

"I've no light. I lost my candle on the stair. Can you find the door?"

For a few moments there was silence, then I detected a faint stirring outside. She was doing something, what it was I could not guess. Suddenly, she spoke again. "It's a lever, just like the other one! But it's too high for me to reach!"

"Tap on the wall with a rock! Show me where it is!"

The tapping was frenzied. It was high, all right, too high even for me. Evidently, some step or platform had fallen or sunk into the earth. I could barely touch it standing on tiptoe.

Unable to see in the darkness, I had to judge its position; then I leaped upward in the darkness, grasping for something I could not see . . . and grasped it with both hands!

My weight came down on it, and slowly, a section of the wall moved. Cool air rushed in . . .

It was not open wide enough for me to escape, yet my hand reached through and grasped Aziza's, and for a time we simply clung to each other. Then sanity returned. "It's the bottom of the door," I suggested, "if you could dig the earth away?"

Dropping to her knees, she dug desperately, gasping for breath. Once again I heaved at the door, and this time it moved enough for me to emerge.

She caught at me, and for a moment we clung together as if drowning. After a long time I drew away and pushed the door shut with my shoulder.

The opening was a mere crack in the rock cleverly utilized and masked by brush and roots. The lever itself had folded back into the crack, and even now I had to look carefully to detect it. With gentle fingers I rearranged the vines, moss, and leaves we had disturbed.

"However did you find this place?" We were in the copse, the very place I had studied as a possibility.

"I'd seen you looking at this place, and I have lived in several castles, not only the one in Palermo. Such places as this were used. What you could not see from where we

were is that a part of the copse is right below the wall; you
were looking at a place further away. The trees disappear
for part of its length, then there's another patch of them.

"You were gone so long I was frightened. I started
down the steps after you. I called and called, but there
was no response, so I went back before I had gone far. I
was afraid you would come looking and find me gone.
Then on the second morning—"

"The *what*?"

"Oh, Mathurin! Didn't you know? You have been
down there two days and a night!"

Down there in the darkness, how could one know?
How long had I sat on the step in the darkness? Had I
slept? How long had I been on the steps, feeling my way
down, sometimes with long pauses while my feet or hands
explored for resting places?

My hunger now told me what she said was true, a
thing forgotten in my horror at dying there in the darkness
as had those others whose bones crunched beneath my
feet.

The Castle of Othman remained as we had left it. The
Barb greeted me with a whinny, extending his nose toward me. I rubbed his neck for a minute or so, talking
gently to him. Then I went to the fountain, and stripping
off my shirt, I bathed away the sweat and dust. Wrapped
in my robes once more, I rested while Aziza brought me
food, then I slept.

A long time later I awakened. It was not yet morning,
although the sky seemed lighter. I lay still, staring upward
and thinking about our situation. Our food was almost
gone, and we could remain here no longer.

The only solution seemed a return to Córdoba or to
travel on to some other town such as Seville or perhaps
Toledo. By now the men of ibn-Haram would have searched
the city and its environs. A return might be in order.

If careful, we might even return the way we had
come, thus escaping the guards at the gates of the city.
We might even continue to hide at the home of ibn-
Tuwais. Getting to my feet, I went to the window and

looked toward Córdoba. It was not yet light, but I could see for a good distance across country. Nothing moved.

Descending the stair, I went to the garden. What few grapes there had been we had eaten. The apricots, only few in number, were also gone.

We had no choice. We must ride away from the Castle of Othman.

15

When Aziza awakened I waited until she had left the fountain and returned inside. "We have food for no more than a day," I told her. "We will have to go."

"To Córdoba? We cannot."

"We will be safer there. If we start for somewhere else, we may fall in with brigands or soldiers."

"Yusuf is trying to make the roads safe."

"No doubt . . . in time. They are not safe yet."

She was silent for a moment, and I said, "It is safer for you. It is the last thing they will expect. I have some money."

Before noon I led the horses to the copse and picketed them where they were concealed by the trees around a small meadow. We must escape. If necessary, we could use the tower, and with candles and much care we could manage now that I had taken that route. With care we could last out another day and each day was a small victory for us.

Where else could we go? Her friends could not be trusted, for some were certainly now allied to Yusuf or ibn-Haram. Others were afraid of him. After the storm that must have been raised, any young man traveling with a beautiful girl would draw attention. In Córdoba I could lose myself among the students and find something to do. It was not in me to long remain idle. Even now I was chafing to be learning.

It was almost dusk when we saw the riders. There were at least a dozen, and they rode in a compact group heading for the Castle of Othman.

"Quick! We will hide in the passage!"

Swiftly, we gathered all we had brought and removed what signs there were of our presence. Much had already been done, as we planned to leave. As we closed the door behind us, we could hear the sound of hooves in the courtyard.

Crouching on the small landing in the darkness, we waited. We had left nothing, of that we were sure, yet there would be trampled grass and evidence that someone had been there. We hoped they would believe it had been brigands.

A subdued rustling sounded beyond the stone door, large sounds no doubt, but faintly heard from here. Moving back, I brushed against something I had not seen before. Another set of steps led upward. The stairwell was very small, but moving quietly we climbed upward to reach a small room not more than four feet wide but twelve long. There was a stone bench, a rusty halberd.

Then I saw a narrow crack where the stones should have fitted but which had been purposely left to allow a viewer to watch what transpired in the great hall, and due to the collapse of walls, it also offered a view of a part of the outer court. Snuffing our candle, we peered through.

A half-dozen men were in view, soldiers all. Outside in the court we could see others, searching all about.

As I watched, the officer in command turned and I saw his face clearly. It was Duban.

My mouth had opened to call out when Aziza clapped a hand over it, shaking her head violently.

"But it is Duban! He will help us!"

"They would kill you. You have been too long alone with me."

"But—!"

"No matter. They would kill you, anyway."

"Of course," I agreed, "I am a fool."

"Whatever you are, I love you."

Startled, I looked at her, and she returned my gaze with wide eyes. "I mean it," she said. "Not that it will matter. They will marry me to whom they wish if it will aid their cause."

When they had ridden away we descended the stair and went to the top of the keep. From there we could watch over the entire countryside, and the riders were far away now, riding swiftly toward a high road where dim movement could be seen.

We could no longer remain here. They had found nothing, but they might return. It was obvious someone had been moving about in the courtyard and the garden.

"You were right," I admitted, "I should have known what they would think."

"I am important to them," she said. "They want me because I am useful for bargaining. They hope to seal an alliance with me." She shrugged. "Women such as I know this is what is expected, and sometimes the match is a happy one."

"And if it is not?"

"We manage, somehow. We have known what was expected of us, and some become very clever at politics and intrigue. Some simply find a lover; some sink into whatever life they have with their children, and often they are enough."

At nightfall we left the Castle of Othman, walking hand in hand down the slope to the copse where the horses were tethered. The black well had left me uneasy, and I had a premonition I had not seen the last of it, yet now I knew its secrets, or some of them. A thing to be remembered: There among the bones lay the largest part of my fallen candle. Such things can be the price of life or death.

We rode, keeping to low ground and darkness, to the entrance to ibn-Tuwais's tunnel. Once inside we heard no sound. We rode to the hidden stable, left our horses with plenty of feed, and reentered the beautiful apartments where we had first hidden.

No sound came from beyond the wall. We detected no movement in the house. Had ibn-Tuwais been taken away to be tortured or killed?

There could have been no evidence of my presence left in the house, so the search must have been purely routine unless they had previous knowledge of my presence.

But how could that have been?

When for a long time we heard no sound, I pushed on the slab and it pivoted gently. There was a slight scrape of stone on stone but no other sound. With drawn sword I went through the door.

A rustle of garments, and a familiar voice. "Kerbouchard? Come in. You are safe."

The voice was that of Mahmoud.

Stepping into the room, we found him reclining upon a divan, one of the books of ibn-Tuwais in his hand. He arose and came to us, bowing low to Aziza.

"We feared you had been captured or killed. Ibn-Tuwais got word to us to wait for you here."

Why did I not trust him? There was no reason for mistrust, and we desperately needed a friend.

"When you could not be found they arrested ibn-Tuwais. He has told them nothing."

"But how could they know I had lived here?"

He shrugged. "Someone saw you, I suppose. Spies are everywhere, and as you should know, we Berbers trust no one."

He glanced at Aziza. "Ibn-Sharaz is said to be angry over his daughter's disappearance, and Prince Ahmed— you can imagine how he feels."

Mahmoud seated himself and clapped his hands for a slave. The man who came was strange to me, yet I recalled having seen him once. Was it in Mahmoud's home? The slave began to spread a low table for a meal, and after our poor fare of the past week, my mouth watered.

"You must remain here for the time," Mahmoud suggested, "and we will arrange to get you out of the city."

Mahmoud was my friend; there was no earthly reason for not trusting him, yet the situation left me uneasy.

Mahmoud was a Berber, yet I did not believe he had any connection with Yusuf or ibn-Haram. His friends had all belonged to the previous ruling group, the Almoravids.

I liked it not at all. In effect we were prisoners in the house, trusting to Mahmoud for food as well as information, and I had seen his eyes stray toward Aziza. Was it with envy or jealousy?

Mahmoud was ambitious, and Aziza was a pawn in a struggle for power, a struggle in which I was merely in the way. Reluctantly, I had to admit she would be better off with Prince Ahmed than with me. At least she would be assured of comfort, food to eat, and freedom from pursuit.

What had I to offer but love? I was a drifting adventurer, a man living by his wits and his blade. I had neither family, fortune, nor friends.

When Mahmoud had gone Aziza came at once to me. "Of what are you thinking?"

"I do not trust him."

"Neither do I."

"You would be safer with Prince Ahmed."

"But happier with you."

No doubt she believed what she said, yet I could only think of the city out there, teeming with potential enemies, devoid of friends.

"The slave is a spy," she warned. "Be careful of what you say."

"We still have the horses."

"Yes."

Was there reluctance in her tone? She had been brought up to a life of luxury and ease, living in the saddle or in occasional ruins could become old very soon. Our stay at the Castle of Othman had been idyllic only up to a point.

Restlessly, I paced, filled with uncertainty, always aware of the presence of the slave. He was busy, but close by.

My bow and arrows had been left on my saddle. My scimitar and dagger were with me. There was little food in the secret room, but I could get more. The question was, when to move?

The time was now.

All my instincts as well as my intelligence warned me there was no time to lose. The walls seemed suddenly oppressive, and I wished desperately to be free, to be outside, riding across the tawny plain.

Turning to Aziza, I said, "You must think, and you must be honest both with me and with yourself. If you escape with me now, you will be tying yourself and your fortunes to me, perhaps for always. You cannot go back."

"I do not want to go back, Mathurin. I wish to be with you."

"All right. We will go, now."

The slave had been gone from the room; now he returned suddenly. I went at once to the storeroom and began packing food.

"If you will but tell me what to do, Master, I will do it."

"Just stay where you are and be still. I will do it myself."

He turned to leave the room, and I stepped before him, my hand on my scimitar. "Sit down!" I commanded.

His lips tightened, and he grew suddenly wary.

"Try to leave," I promised, "and you shall choke on your own blood."

He backed away and seated himself on a cask. Swiftly, I finished my packing and went out of the door, locking it behind me.

Aziza was waiting. "Hurry, Mathurin! They—"

The outer door opened, and I heard footsteps and the clank of arms.

Wheeling in my tracks, I pushed to open the door into the secret room. The stone door swung inward.

Four men faced me with drawn swords.

16

When I opened my eyes my cell was unchanged, and I lay upon the filthy straw that for three months had been my bed.

For a long time I lay still, remembering the expression on the face of Mahmoud as he stood behind the four swordsmen.

"I am sorry, my friend," he said smugly. "You were in the way."

Aziza had cried when they took her from me, her lovely features contorted with weeping.

One other face that I was to remember, a tall, handsome man with a smartly trimmed beard. He looked at me coldly as if I were some sort of insect, then looked away.

Prince Ahmed!

"Throw him into prison," he said, "and when he has suffered enough, kill him."

He could not forgive the days at the Castle of Othman with Aziza. That I had even looked at the bride of Ahmed without her veil was an insult.

Three months in this vile place? When and how would they kill me? Or had I been forgotten?

My Berber guards were savage, bitter men, yet they were fighting men, and for this I admired them.

They left me my books. When taken from the house of ibn-Tuwais, I had been allowed to bring the books he had given me, and from time to time, mysteriously, I had received others.

Was Mahmoud to be thanked for this? Or had Aziza contrived some means of having them smuggled to me?

One thing I had done. Before being taken away, I cleared ibn-Tuwais of any complicity in my activities; aiding in this was proof that I had paid him for my quarters. As no Arab would accept money from a friend in such a case, they had believed my story, and he was freed.

During those three long months, I had studied the geography of al-Idrisi, far superior to anything of the kind available in Christian Europe.

Eratosthenes, a scholar of 194 B.C. in Alexandria, had devised a method for calculating the diameter of the earth, and al-Mamun in 829 had figured its diameter to be 7,850 miles. Also during these three months, I had read the translations of Hippocrates and Galen by Hunayn ibn-Ishaq.

There was only straw upon the floor of my cell and one small window to offer light. When the wind blew rain into the cell, I had to crowd under the window itself to keep dry, and it was always cold, damp, and unpleasant. One day a guard came to my door and handed me a package in which was wrapped the work on surgery by Albucasis.

There was little to do but read, although each day I exercised to keep my body fit. The food was bad, but it was no worse than aboard the galley.

My mind was forever occupied with thoughts of escape, yet I now knew the passage outside my cell to be impossible. There were four Berber guards in that passage, and at the end of it a guardroom in which a dozen more were wont to gather to talk and to gamble. My small window opened upon a sheer cliff that fell away for hundreds of feet.

Al-Idrisi I loved. The great Moslem geographer had much information about the far corners of the earth not obtainable elsewhere. The Arabs, because of the pilgrims who came to Mecca from all parts of the world, were in an excellent position to gather geographical knowledge.

My restlessness increased. Prince Ahmed would not permit me to live. His pride would not allow it. Sooner or later the order would come through.

When my guard was not around, I often grasped the lower sill of my window and chinned myself, pulling my-

self up until I could peer through the bars. All I could see
was blue sky and an occasional drifting cloud. Yet one by
one I tested the three bars.

They were set in the stone window frame closer to
the outer edge than the inner, and the castle was very old,
dating back to earliest Visigothic times. The wall itself was
exposed to driving rains, and over the years the stone on
the outer edge might have eroded away.

Testing them, I found one was very slightly loose in
its socket, so it became a part of my exercise, my daily
routine, to work at the bar. Twisting it, I found I could
occasionally loosen fragments, a fine sand that could itself
be used as an abrasive.

Occasionally, I would pour a few drops of my water
into the hole, and as I was a man of more than usual
strength, it seemed possible to push the bar free at the
bottom, breaking away the thin edge of stone that remained.

The other bars were seated solidly, yet the edge of
another hole was thin, and if I could work the first bar
loose and use it as a lever . . . ?

My guard on this day was a slender, knifelike man
with a lean face and high cheekbones. He was a warrior
and looked it.

Several times I made efforts to engage him in conversation, to no avail until I commented that I hoped my
horse was being cared for.

"The dappled Barb? Maybe after you are killed they
will give him to me."

"You are a man who would understand such a horse,"
I agreed.

There was a change in his manner. He seemed inclined to be friendly. Our talk was of horses, then it
switched to camels. The Berber was a desert man and
seemed pleased when I showed some interest in camels.
Of them I had learned a little from Hassan, the servant of
John of Seville.

At the end of an hour I had learned a few things. The
castle in which I was imprisoned was on a lonely crag
some distance from Córdoba, and the walls fell into a deep

gorge on all but one side. The idea did not frighten me, as from boyhood I had climbed about on the lofty cliffs of my native Brittany. Heights did not disturb me, and I had learned how to use every tiny finger grip, every crack, every opening in the rock.

My beard had grown; my clothing was unclean, and the straw on which I spent my nights was forever clinging to it. Yet that clothing was still sufficient to cover me, and sewn into the seams were the remaining gems I had kept from the galley.

That night when the cell was dark I labored long at the loosened bar and the second one also. By daylight when I lay down to sleep there was some movement in the second bar.

The guard awakened me by bringing food. On this morning he did not seem disposed to talk nor would his eyes meet mine.

"The order has come then?"

He shrugged irritably and closed the door behind him. Then he said quite distinctly. "You are to be strangled."

"When?"

"Tomorrow."

"You may have my horse."

When he spoke, there was something in his tone I could not fathom. "I already have him. He is in the stable at my house in the village, with your saddle and your weapons."

Was he boasting? Or trying to give me information?

"Wait. Is anyone near us?"

"No."

"I must escape. I have a diamond. Help me and it is yours."

"I would be killed. Prince Ahmed is furious." He chuckled. "It is said the beautiful one murmurs your name in her sleep."

He hesitated at the door. "You have friends who wish you free."

"Aziza?"

"It was not she who sent the books. But I cannot help you."

"You were asked?"

"Yes."

"By whom?"

"I cannot say, only that she is very powerful in some places. Yet even her influence cannot reach beyond ibn-Haram and Prince Ahmed."

She?

I knew no woman who might wish to help other than Aziza, nor any person. Perhaps John of Seville—but he would have no knowledge of my danger.

When he had gone I wasted no time. From my guard's manner I knew he would not mind if I escaped, but he would take no hand in it himself.

Besides, what could he or anyone do? The passage was filled with men, the outer court also. One could not buy them all, nor would they risk the reprisals of ibn-Haram.

Hoisting myself to the window, I grasped one bar with my left hand, the other with my right. With all my strength I pushed on the right-hand bar.

Nothing happened.

Bracing myself, I drew the right-hand bar back in its socket, only a tiny distance, then smashed it outward with all the power I could muster. For an hour I worked until drenched with sweat and my knees and arms became raw with chafing against the rock wall.

My guard returned with food, and if he noticed anything, he gave no indication. Only, as he was leaving, he commented, "Twice men have tried to climb down the wall; each was dashed to pieces on the rocks below. It is seven hundred feet to the bottom.

"My house," he added, "is not a pretty one, but it is painted pink. It is the only pink house outside the walls."

When he had gone there would be no one nearer than the guardroom. I ate what meager food there was, then scrambled to the sill.

Desperately, I went to work. Escape tonight or die

tomorrow; die upon the rocks below risking my life for freedom or be strangled like a sheep.

Grasping the loosest bar, I gave a tremendous shove and something gave. Rock grated, and I shoved again. The bar came loose at the bottom; the top slipped from its socket. I now held in my hand an iron bar three feet long, slightly beveled at one end. An hour later the second bar was free.

Thrusting my head from the window, I looked off into a vast, unbelievable space. The cell in which I was imprisoned was set upon the rock of the clifftop, but the precipice fell away in a sheer drop for two hundred feet and was then broken by several crevices that seemed to run down the face of the cliff.

Studying the wall below my window, I carefully noted the knobs and projections that might offer fingerholds. Returning to the floor of my cell, I drank what remained of the water, then lay down for a brief nap. Within the hour my body might lie broken and bloody on the rocks below, but I would never be strangled by the retainers of Prince Ahmed.

Awakening, I rinsed my mouth with the few drops I had missed of the water, then climbed to the windowsill and went through the window, feet first. Gripping with my fingers on the window ledge, I groped with my toes for the hairline of rock where the building rested, and found it.

Always agile, and adept at rock climbing, I knew the trial before me would be the worst I would ever meet. In my belt, tied there, were the two iron window bars. Clinging to the ledge with my fingertips with one hand only, I leaned down and thrust one of the bars deep into a crack in the wall.

Letting go the sill, I let myself fall, catching the bar with both hands. Had the bar slipped or the rock crumbled— but neither happened. A gust of wind caught my body; I heard distant thunder. My toe found a crack. Holding to the bar behind me with my left hand, I leaned down and wedged the second bar into place.

Farther along the cliff face was a vertical crack some three feet wide and but a few inches deep. Edging my way, handhold by handhold across the face of the rock, using the second iron bar, which I had recovered, for the first I had abandoned in place, I made my way to that crack.

Rain spattered on the rock face around me, and a gust of wind, harder than the first, tore at my clothing. Placing the sole of one foot against the edge behind me and my knee against the edge in front, using my hands with care, I began to work my way down the crack. After a few feet of descent the crack deepened so I could also oppose a shoulder against the edge behind me. In this way, using a technique often applied during my boyhood climbs along the rocky shores, I descended for at least sixty feet.

There, for the moment, I had a good foothold and rested as wind and rain lashed at my body. Below me the cliff was a smooth sheet offering absolutely nothing in handhold or foothold. At the bottom, however, glimpsed briefly in flashes of lightning, I perceived a ledge a few inches wide of another rock sheet that overlay that on which I waited.

Gingerly, I edged out on the smooth surface, flattening myself against the rock. Then I let go and began to slide. There was a moment of sheer panic at the thought of the vast depth below and what would happen if I overshot the ledge or failed to stop myself there.

Braking my slide with elbows, body, and toes, I slid, rapidly gaining speed. Grasping at the rock for anything to slow my speed, I felt a sharp sliver of pain as a fingernail tore loose, and then my toes thudded against the narrow ledge, and only my body weight against the rock kept me from being thrown clear.

Clinging to the rock face, I fought away the fear and took slow, deep breaths of the cool air. Gasping hoarsely, I waited, struggling to calm myself and prepare for the ordeal that lay before me.

How far down I had come I had no idea, but there

was no returning, no stopping now. Escape and freedom lay before me; around me, death.

The inches-wide ledge on which my feet had come to rest seemed to extend along the face of the rock and to slant downward, so clinging to the rock face, I edged along. Time ceased to exist. At times the narrow ledge became no more than an inch wide. Then it grew wider again, and suddenly I found myself in a shallow cave, hollowed by wind and rain. There was room to sit down, and I did, but first I looked up, waiting for a flash of lightning. It came, and I was no more than a hundred and fifty feet from my cell!

Only the sharp urgency of my position and the knowledge that I could not remain where I was started me moving again. It was not in me to wait for death nor to give up to despair. Somewhere my father, if still alive, was a prisoner, and I must free him. Sucking my torn finger, I studied the rock. Then handhold by precious handhold, I lowered myself. Twice I found narrow chimneys down which I could lower myself for short distances. Once a ledge of rock crumbled under my toes, and only the grip of my fingers saved me. Another time only my closed fist in a vertical crack held me suspended above a black gulf. I had only to open my hand to fall to my death.

It was some time after the rain had ceased that I became aware of it, so intense was my concentration on the task before me. Thunder rumbled in the gorges like a sulky bear in a cavern. The face of the rock became rougher. I moved more swiftly until suddenly I slipped and fell, and I was brought up with a jolt that smashed my skull against a rock.

Half stunned, I lay there for several minutes before I rolled over and climbed drunkenly to my feet. Distant lightning flashed, and I looked around me for a way down—and there was none. I was standing in the bed of a dry creek!

A rumble from upstream warned me a flash flood was coming, and I ran, stumbling, across the creek and up the far bank, only just in time.

Pale yellow edged the clouds in the east. Now for the pink house, and my horse!

I had been all night on the face of the cliff.

My forearms were raw, the skin torn and lacerated. My knees were in the same condition, and I walked in pain. There was a cut on my skull from which blood issued, but most painful of all was the lost fingernail.

My head throbbed with a dull, heavy ache, but I was down.

I was free!

17

Eastward I fled, eastward astride the fast-running Barb, and before the noon sun was in the sky I took to the hills, riding into rough, broken country. It was a land of naked mountains, serrated ridges, lofty towers, and natural fortresses, forever unused by man, impregnable beyond comprehension.

Sweat trickled into my raw wounds, and the blazing sun caused my head to throb with pain. Nowhere could I find water, and there was but little food in the saddlebags. Yet my only safety lay in losing myself in the empty mountains, reputed to be the hiding place of brigands.

It was nearly sundown when I heard the tinkle of a bell.

Riding along a rocky slope, I came upon the droppings of goats and tracks of their tiny hooves. Topping a ridge, I saw them before me. At least two hundred goats guarded by three men and two huge, savage dogs.

With them was a girl.

She walked several steps toward me and stood, feet apart, her flimsy skirt blowing in the wind. Her hair was wild and uncombed, but there was a fine insolence in her eyes and manner, and under the flimsy skirt her body had an outline that turned my mouth dry and made my pulses pound.

She held her ground as I allowed the Barb to pick his way through the scattered rocks. The men shouted at her, but when she continued to stand they left their goats and walked toward her, and me.

All were armed, and they were taking in my horse

131

and scimitar as if they already possessed them. I was doing the same with the girl.

"What do you want?" she demanded insolently.

"Food and wine," I said, letting my eyes say more than my words, "and perhaps a place to rest."

She looked at me boldly from under long lashes. "Food and drink you may have. As to rest, you will find little here!"

I took my foot from a stirrup. "Ride?" I suggested.

She looked at me, then tossed her head and, thrusting a bare foot into the stirrup, stepped up beside me. I put an arm about her waist.

"Which one is your man?" I asked.

"Of them?" Her tone was contemptuous. "None of them! Although each wishes to be. They are afraid of my father."

"They are fools."

"Wait." She gave me a cool glance. "You have not met my father."

The three shouted at her to get down, but she swore at them, swore wickedly and with eloquence. I surmised she was younger than she looked, but whatever her age, a wildcat, and worth the taming.

"Get down!" The shouter was a big young man who looked like the casual offspring of some Visigoth warrior. "Get down!" he shouted. "Or I shall take him from the saddle!"

"Try it," I invited, "and I shall ride you down."

He glared at me, but his courage was all in his mouth. My hand was on my scimitar, and my horse within two jumps of him, and the Barb was a horse who started with a bound. Had he started to lift his bow, I'd have cut him down like the swine he was, but he was a big-muscled swine, and I began to wonder what the girl's father must be like. I was to find out.

She pointed down a worn path, and we followed it, the Barb pricking his ears and quickening his step. A moment and we rounded a bend into a beautifully green valley, completely hidden by the barren hills. On the floor of the valley, crowning a small knoll, was a walled ruin, an ancient castle that had been repaired somewhat.

As we rode up to the gate, out walked the biggest man I had ever seen.

He was a head and a half taller than I, and half again as broad. His hands were huge, his eyes fierce. He wore a black beard, and his hair was to his shoulders, black as a raven's wing.

He gave me the merest glance, yet his eyes lingered on my scimitar and the Barb. "Get down from there!" he shouted at the girl, as if she were two fields away from him.

She started to obey, but deliberately, I held her back and kissed her lightly on the cheek.

"He will kill you!" she hissed, then dropped to the ground, sauntering away with that fine, impudent way she had.

He took a swift stride toward me, reaching for the bridle. Sidestepping the Barb, I drew my blade. "Keep your hands off, my big friend, or you will be lacking one of them."

He took a second look at me. He was big, tough, and mean, and he was used to men being frightened of him. Before he could speak, I spoke quietly. "I have not come for trouble. Your daughter was kind enough to invite me for food and drink. If you can provide them, I shall be on my way."

He waited while I could have counted a slow ten, then said, "Get down. Come in."

"I would care for my horse first."

"Alan will do it." He gestured toward a slim, dark young man with quick, intelligent eyes.

Swinging down, I said, "Take good care of him. He's a fine animal."

His eyes lighted up. "Of course," he said. Then under his breath he warned, "Be careful of my uncle. If you touch Sharasa, he will kill you. And," he added, "he may kill you, anyway."

"A man who wishes to kill," I said, "must also be ready to die."

Sharasa held the door for me as I entered. Her father was already at the rough board table, pouring wine from a flagon. There was bread on the table, cheese, and a haunch of mutton. Suddenly, I realized I was ravenously hungry.

A half hour earlier there had been nothing else on my mind, but Sharasa—such influences can be distracting.

He stared at me from the opposite end of the table. "I am Akim," he said. "This is my valley."

"And I am Kerbouchard, a soldier."

"Bah!" he sneered. "There are no soldiers now! In my young days—"

"In your young days," I said, "the soldiers were no better than now. I will share your food and wine, my friend, but do not think I am one of your goats, or one of those sheep you call men. I am as good a man as you are, or ever were."

He glared at me, furious. He liked me not one bit, and I liked him no more, nor was I to be put upon by boasting. I could match him, lie for lie, boast for boast. It was true I was no soldier, although trained in arms. My blade had been blooded as a good blade must be, yet at such a time the truth is only for those lacking imagination. If it was war he wanted, I would match him war for war, battle for battle, and lie the better as I was the better read.

Reaching across the table, I took the mug from in front of him and shoved mine at him. "You would poison me," I said, "before you would try me with a sword. I trust you not at all."

He tore meat from the slab of mutton before me, but taking out my dagger, I cut thin slices from mine, letting him appreciate its razor-edge.

He drank with me, eating some of the bread, but my eyes were busy. These were no simple shepherds, but thieves when opportunity offered. No doubt this place had seen the spilled blood of many an innocent traveler, but I would not be among them.

Akim had the look of a seasoned campaigner, and he would be a dangerous man in battle, but such as he would not be turned aside by soft words. Such as he would kill those who submit, respect only those dangerous to them.

My seat, purposely taken, allowed me to watch the door, and no one could come up behind me. Akim had noticed this, and there was surly respect in his eyes.

Sharasa brought more food, a bowl of fruit and some choicer slices of meat. She walked away from me swaying her hips, and Akim swore at her. She flipped a corner of her skirt at him, and he half started from his seat.

"She's a likely girl," I said. "Have you found a man for her?"

There was a glassy look to his eyes when she stared back at me. "I will kill the man who touches her."

I grinned at him, cheerful with filling my stomach. "Is that what the sheep are afraid of? Well, it does not frighten me. She would be worth it. And as for the killing, two can play that game."

"When you finish eating, get out of here."

"You mean you have decided against robbing me? Better think again. That's a fine horse out there." My dagger slid into my hand, and again I cut a paper-thin slice from the roast. "You might be able to get it, and then again, you might not."

Sharasa returned with a pitcher of cold goat's milk. I could see the sweat on the sides of the pitcher. She had taken this from a well or a cave.

Pouring some into my empty cup, I drank, and over the edge of the cup I closed one eye at her. She put her chin up and flounced away.

"I shall stay the night," I told Akim.

"All right," he said mildly, and I was wise enough to be afraid.

Akim was no coward, and he had a half-dozen men to help him, but he was accustomed to fear. In the old days he would have met my challenge at once, but he had been spoiled by the fear of those around him, and the idea of facing again a man who was unafraid took some getting used to.

For me the bold way was the only way. Had I come to the valley in fear, I would be dead by now.

As for Sharasa, I had no time for dalliance even should such be possible. Yet she was such a woman as could topple kingdoms and lay dukedoms in the dust. Given her presence and manner, with the proper clothing . . .

Akim got suddenly to his feet and strode from the room. I remained, finishing my goat's milk.

Sharasa came quickly. "You must go! He intends to kill you! I know him!"

"Even with your hair uncombed and in that rag of a dress," I told her, "you are more beautiful than any princess, and I have seen a few."

She flushed, and unconsciously, a hand pushed at her hair. "I haven't—I mean there's nobody—" She fled from the room.

A few days ago I had been in prison, expecting to be strangled, yet I had escaped. By now half of Spain was searching for me or aware of my disappearance.

Too often had death brushed me closely. I had faced it in the Castle of Othman and again on the sheer face of the cliff. Now each moment of life was a moment stolen from eternity. I wished to live, and tonight Akim planned for me to die.

Sharasa could be trouble, yet a woman worth having must be fought for, or stolen.

Akim returned to the room putting a fresh bottle on the table. "More wine?"

Cheerfully, I reached around the bottle to the flagon Sharasa had brought earlier. He liked it none at all, but said nothing.

The others came in then, and Sharasa returned. Despite their animosity they were hungry for news, so I told them of Córdoba and Yusuf's plans to rid the country of banditry.

The various governments of Moorish Spain had been

until this time unanimously tolerant, accepting Christians and Jews alike and allowing them to practice their religion. Visigoths who owned land were permitted to keep it, paying only a small tax.

The Almohads, mostly Berbers from North Africa, a strong white people long resident there, were a strict, fanatical lot, and Moorish Spain was changing under their control. Yet there continued to flower there a brilliant society alive with creativity.

Only in the Athens of Pericles, the Alexandria of a few centuries later, the Gupta period in India, or that great Tamil renaissance from 300 B.C. to A.D. 300 had there been such a period as now existed in Moorish Spain.

The Arab mind, deprived of any but casual contact with the world of art and intellect until after the time of Mohammed, was an infinitely curious and acquisitive mind, and the Arabs fell upon knowledge, the science and skills of the Persians and the Central Asiatics, as rapaciously as they had fallen on their enemies with the sword.

Under the caliphs of Islam, scholars were honored as never in the world's history except, possibly, for some periods in China. This was true in Baghdad and Damascus, in Tashkent and Timbuctoo, in Shiraz, Samarkand, and Córdoba.

Yet now, in this lonely valley in the hills of Spain, I came for the first time to really appreciate the power of the spoken word. So far the sword had been my weapon, and I had not learned that wit and wisdom are keys to open any door, win the heart of any woman.

There is power in the word whether written or spoken, for words can create images for those who have not themselves seen.

Carried away, for when was a Celt not eloquent?—I spoke of Cádiz, of Seville and Córdoba. I spoke of the crowded streets, the bazaars, the women, the clothing, the weapons. I spoke of sword dancers and jugglers, of the magic of color, lights, and beauty. The candles smoked and the hours drew on, but all sat spellbound.

And I? I was the captive of my audience, yet not

eager to escape, knowing that with every word I made myself more secure, and with every word doors opened wider.

Of the Court of Oranges I told them, of parks hung with bronze lanterns, and I wove with my words a tapestry that all could see. I told them of the Great Mosque with its twenty-one archways decorated with terra cotta mosaics in red and yellow, of doors covered with burnished brass, of the fourteen hundred columns that support the roof of the mosque. I spoke of lattices of alabaster, of marble walls, and how during the month of Ramadan the entire mosque was illuminated by twenty thousand lights.

Returning to the Court of Oranges, I spoke of the hot still days, the sound of falling water in the fountains, the shuffling feet of the worshipers, the scent of jasmine, rose, and orange blossoms. Of travelers from foreign lands, of pomegranate, apricot, of vines and palms . . . ah, what did I not tell them?

A listener who hung on my every word, his eyes glowing with excitement, was Alan. This one, I thought, is worth saving. He has the soul of a poet, imagination, and intelligence, for such as these is the world made.

"I am tired," I said at last. "I have ridden long this day." Turning to Sharasa, I said, "Will you show me where I am to sleep?"

Akim scowled. "Alan will show you." He paused. "No need for you to ride on. Stay a few days."

The big young man sneered. "You come with fine talk, but you come in rags."

I smiled at him. "Do not get into a sweat, my big-chested friend. When the time comes, you will get your whipping. Do not beg for it beforehand."

A moment I paused. "If you wish to know, I have but lately escaped from prison." I named the castle. "I have enemies, and they seek me now. My enemies are your enemies also, for I have told you of Yusuf and his seeking of all who lurk in the mountains."

Turning to Akim, I suggested, "Put out a guard and

choose a place in the hills to which you can escape. I warn
you. They intend to sweep the hills, and they will find
you. Hide what is of value and your flocks."

It was a concession from Akim that he suggested I
stay on, and I learned then that many a victory is easier
won with words than a sword—and the results are better.

"I shall stay, Akim, and you shall tell me stories of
your wars. I venture you will have stories worth the
telling."

"That I have." That he was pleased was obvious. "It
will be good to talk to another soldier."

Alan came with a candle, and I followed him. In
Moorish homes a room was rarely set aside for sleeping.
One slept wherever one might be, yet Alan showed me to
a room where there was privacy, and brought me water
with which to bathe. When I followed him from the main
room, I caught the expression in the eyes of the bastard of
the Visigoth, if such he was, and that expression was not
pleasant.

That was one victory that must be won with a sword.

Sharasa stood in the doorway as I passed, her head
tilted back against the doorjamb, looking at me from under lowered lashes.

And that was a victory that must be won with other
weapons.

18

After two days nothing had been resolved except some of the wrinkles in my belly. Sharasa was just as elusive and just as attractive, but surprisingly, Akim and I had become friends.

The stories he had to tell were of war and bloodshed, of risk and riot, of scaling walls and single combat. Akim, unwittingly, was teaching me much of war, and not knowing what might lie before me, I was eager to learn.

He had fought for and against both Goth and Moor, surviving many a bitter battle in the breaches of city walls, in house-to-house combat, and of fighting in the streets.

The bastard son of the Visigoth was called Aric, and I knew he intended to kill me. Aric had decided Sharasa was for him, and until I arrived on the scene, it had seemed to him inevitable. He glowered about, casting threatening looks in my direction.

Sharasa was often about, yet vain as I might be, I knew much of her interest was in what I had to say of clothes, cities, and the behavior of other women. This, Aric was too stupid to understand. Sharasa, I think, had long had her own dreams, none of which included Aric. My words fed those dreams.

Alan, too, was never far from me when I talked of Córdoba.

Turning to him one evening when we were briefly alone, I said, "Alan, you must go to Córdoba or Seville. You would be happier there.

"Go to Seville," I advised, "find John of Seville, and tell him Kerbouchard sent you."

Akim overheard and turned sharply around. He had heard no name for me but Mathurin, and at the time not too many Europeans had family names.

"Kerbouchard? Your name is *Kerbouchard*?"

"It is."

He slapped the table with the flat of his hand. "Why did I not see it? You resemble him, Kerbouchard the Corsair!"

What a ring he gave the name! What a sound!

"I am his son."

"I saw him once. It was in Almería, that city of pirates and rovers of the sea. He came with a dozen ships loaded to the gunwales with loot!

"Ah, how we stared! Our mouths watered to see it! Gold, silks, spices, jewels . . . he unloaded them all. Had he asked for volunteers, the city would have emptied to serve him.

"There was never another like him, not one! He had raided the isles of Greece, captured a rich prize off Tripoli, looted another within sight of Rhodes!

"There was a soldier with him, a man I knew from another time, another war. His name was Taillefeur, he—"

"*What?*" I caught Akim's wrist. "Taillefeur was with my *father*?"

"You know him? Then you know him for a rascal, though a first-class fighting man. Yes, Taillefeur was with him, and I wondered at it, for he was not a man to serve another unless he could betray him for a price, and there were many who offered prices for Kerbouchard.

"Taillefeur fought beside me at the defense of Caltrava in 1158. We fought in the breach together against the Moslems, but I never trusted the man."

Taillefeur had been with the Baron de Tournemine, my father's enemy. Was it he who brought news of my father's death? Might he not have betrayed my father, if betrayal was his way?

It was a thing to consider.

On the morning of the third day Alan came to me. "Be warned," he whispered, "Aric means to kill you."

It was time for me to ride on. I wished the big lout no harm, but my destiny lay outside this valley. Moreover, I feared the soldiers of Yusuf would find even this long-hidden valley.

On this morning I arose early and rode down the valley toward a deep pool where I had often gone to bathe. The sky was dull with clouds with a suggestion of coming rain, yet the swim would refresh me, and tomorrow I must be on my way to wherever I was going.

Which of us knows the direction of his life? Who knows what tomorrow may bring? Often, when pausing at a crossroad, I have wondered what might lie waiting on the road not taken?

Drawing up in the shelter of some willows, I tied my horse where he could feed but would nevertheless be hidden from a chance passerby. Disrobing, I walked to a rock and plunged into the pool.

For a few minutes I swam, then returned to the rock from which I had dived and began to dress. Yet scarcely had I begun when I heard an angry cry. It was Sharasa!

Swiftly, I plunged through the curtain of brush and found myself standing in a cave mouth with Sharasa not ten feet from me and Aric facing us both, holding my scimitar taken from my saddle.

"I will kill you now," he said. "I shall kill you and her, too!"

"He has done nothing. He did not know I was here."

"You expect me to believe *that*?"

Well I knew the razor edge of that scimitar, and I was half naked and unarmed. That blade would sever an arm like butter.

"Leave him alone. He has done nothing."

The shock of his sudden appearance was gone now. He had given me the moment I needed, and my mind grasped desperately for some escape. Nor was there a rock or a stick upon the cave floor. There was nothing. There was no weapon.

He had moved to block any escape, and there was no

way out. I must meet him, face to face. My life was at
stake here, but Sharasa's was also.

Warily, I advanced a step toward him, my hands
down. It surprised him, I believe, because he had expected me to shrink from death as he would have done.
Only death had become a constant companion, and I was
not prepared to die, not at the hands of such as he.

He held the scimitar awkwardly and not like one
accustomed to swordplay, yet he was an agile and powerful man. The fury in him might work to my advantage.

There was little room for maneuver, yet I advanced
another step, working a little to his left, studying his
position.

My father, a skilled fighting man, always told me to
notice the position of a man's feet, for if a man can be
taken off-balance he can be beaten. There is a limit to how
far a man can reach without shifting his feet.

Behind me now I could hear Sharasa's hoarse, frightened breathing, and I knew I was fighting for her life as
well as my own.

If I threw myself at his legs, I might throw him, yet
the edge of that blade could sever a finger or a hand, and
if he sprang back as I moved in, he could run me through.
Suddenly, he leaped, slashing wickedly. Only just in time
I sprang back, and the tip of the blade just missed me. I
made to dive at him as the blade swept past, but he was
quick and shifted ground.

He lunged then, the blade at arm's length. With the
palm of my hand I slapped the flat side of the blade as it
thrust at me, knocking the point out of line with my body.
Instantly, I stepped in, hooking my right leg behind his
leg and smashing him under the chin with the butt of my
palm.

He grunted with pain, and tripped by my right leg,
he fell backward. Thrown hard to the sand, he landed on
his back. Promptly, I kicked him under the chin and
wrenched the scimitar from his loosened grip.

He sprang up, staggered, and would have lunged at
me, but I slapped him alongside the skull with the flat of

the blade. He fell to the sand, and for an instant I was tempted to finish him off.

"No, Mathurin! *No!*"

I drew back, for I had no desire to kill him. "All right, he shall live, but we must go."

Returning to my horse, I finished dressing and strapped on my dagger and the scabbard of the scimitar. I took Sharasa up beside me, and we rode back to the farm.

We rode swiftly, and my usual awareness was dulled by the events of the afternoon and the dangers in facing Akim. Dropping Sharasa to the ground, I swung down and started through the door. I shouted for Alan and stepped through the door into a room filled with soldiers.

Akim was sprawled on the stone floor, bathed in blood. At least two of the attacking soldiers had been killed, and others nursed wounds. That much I glimpsed before a wicked blow struck me across the head, and I fell, striking the floor on my face.

In a moment of slipping consciousness I heard someone say, "Leave him to burn. Take the girl, but gently. She will make a fit present for Zagal."

With all my will I struggled to move, but could not. A wave of darkness engulfed me, and through the darkness I heard the crackle of flames.

19

Heat blasted my face; smoke rolled over me. My eyes opened to find crackling flames within inches of my head. Rolling over, I struggled to rise, only to fall headlong. Still too weak to rise, I crawled through the smoke to the door.

Twice I collapsed; twice I started again. My head was heavy as a cask; my mind would not work. Fighting toward the air like an animal, groaning with effort and only half conscious, I somehow reached the outside.

For days I lay around in a daze. The ruins finally stopped smoking, and I managed to bury the remains of Akim and those others who had been killed.

Alan was gone, so was Sharasa.

My horse had been taken, and even my poor jacket with the gems sewn into the seams had been taken or thrown away. My dagger had been inside my shirt and unseen. It was all that remained.

Fortunately, they had not found the cave near the well where the goat's milk and cheese were kept. There, also, was some wine.

My clothing was filthy. Some had been charred by the flames, and I had no outer robe. My turban had kept me from being killed by the blow but had suffered in consequence.

At the edge of the well I sat drinking cold goat's milk and munching cheese, reflecting on the misfortunes that attended me. Surely, the old gods must have cursed me to have each move end in disaster.

I was alone. The nearest city was miles away over

rough country infested by brigands, many of whom would kill for the sheer pleasure.

Aziza was lost to me, and now Sharasa.

My face had been horribly blistered by the flames, but owing to the treatment I had given, methods learned during my study of medicine, it would heal, I believed, without leaving a scar. But meanwhile, the skin was tender, and my beard had grown greatly. It would be long before I dared shave or even trim my beard.

No one in Córdoba would know me now. My elegance was gone. Shabby, half starved, ugly with beard and healing scars on my body, I looked more the beggar than a student or a gentleman. All I possessed, aside from what I wore, was an old blanket found in the stable.

Mahmoud? Ah—Mahmoud! He deserved my attention, and I was determined to see he received it in full measure.

Finding an old waterskin, I cleansed it as well as possible, then filled it with goat's milk. Wrapping up a cheese, I started upon my way.

It would be a long walk to Córdoba.

A week later I sat upon the old Roman bridge that crossed the Guadalquivir to Córdoba. It was an ancient bridge built in the days of Augustus, repaired only recently.

The day was hot and sultry. Along the high road passed an unending stream of people, camels, donkeys, and carts going to and from the city. Footsore and exhausted, I stumbled to my feet and joined the procession, walking toward the city that had given me so much, and had taken so much from me. Yet it was a city I could not yet leave.

Money, decent clothing, and weapons I must have. The burns, the blow on the skull, and privation had left me weak, and I tired quickly.

There was the beginning of a plan shaping in my brain. The crews of my father's ships had been men from many lands, and I had grown up speaking a variety of tongues, none of them well, but since then I had become proficient in Arabic and improved in both Latin and Greek. A sailor from my father's crew had come from Miletus, and there were several others from Greek islands. Often they had told me stories, and the smattering of their tongue I had acquired had been added to aboard the galley. There was in Córdoba a branch of the Caliph's Society of Translators and it was in my mind to try there for any task, no matter how small.

First, I must have clothing. No better hiding place could be found than among scholars, and it would provide a chance to learn, to have access to books.

My studies until now had taken no definite trend, nor was I planning that they should. Knowledge might be power, but it was also the key to survival. My knowledge of navigation led to my escape from the galley; my small knowledge of medicine helped to heal my burns.

Even in a comparatively small city, and Córdoba was a large one, a man can lose himself by choosing another way of life. Within cities there are islands of people who had no communication outside their own island. It has even been surmised that people cannot know more than a certain number of people with comfort, which some believe has led to the classes in a society as well as to the exclusiveness of groups. If I chose one of those islands remote from those I had known, I might live as isolated as in another country.

Before me the gate yawned. Several soldiers loitered nearby. My skin tightened, my heart began to throb. This was the moment of danger. Forcing myself, I walked on, keeping my eyes to the road. My flesh crawled as I drew abreast of them, but then as I stepped through the gate, I heard a familiar voice.

"The check must be thorough. Until the Caliph ceases to search the mountains, we must beware of brigands who might seek to hide within the city."

It was Haroun! It was the voice of Haroun!

Stealing a glance, I saw him in the uniform of an officer and sitting a fine black horse. So he, too, was among my pursuers! He had never been as close to me as

Mahmoud, although there had been a sort of quiet friendship between us. The moving line was carrying me past, but I glanced back again. It was a mistake.

Our eyes met; for an instant our gaze held. In his eyes there was first surprise, then puzzlement. He started toward me, but a cart drawn by four oxen pulled between us, and his path was blocked. When I looked back again he had turned away.

Hunger gnawed at my vitals. The only thing of value I possessed was my dagger, which was also the last tie with my father and my home.

Finally, I could walk no more, and I sank down with my back against a building. The sun was warm; the air, filled with fragrances. Oranges, melons, grapes were being sold about me, yet I starved. Voices were lifted in argument; whips cracked; wheels rumbled over the pavement, and there was the pleasant aroma of coffee from a stall nearby. Exhausted, my head tipped forward, and I slept.

Awakening, I was chilled to the bone. The sun was gone, and the bazaar, empty. My sleep seemed not to have rested me, and my bowels were a void where hunger growled.

My muscles had cramped and stiffened; my face was sore, and there was nowhere to turn. In despair, I looked about me.

Why was I such a fool? If I were a prisoner, they would at least feed me. Or would I be strangled at once?

Gloomily, I stared around the bazaar, scattered with fruit skins, drifted leaves fallen from the trees, and all the usual debris left by traders. Soon the sweepers would come, and after them, the lamplighters.

My dagger held release. I could die.

Die? But I was Kerbouchard, the son of Jean Kerbouchard the Corsair! Had I not started to find my father and seek my fortune? Was I a coward, to quit so soon? I, who had ridden out of Cádiz, my cloak sewn with gems?

There were smells about me, but the worst was the smell of my own unwashed body, of my stale clothing. I started to rise, glimpsing behind a booth an orange, fallen from a stand nearby. My eyes went to the orange and then to the booth's owner, who was preparing to leave.

Strolling over, I picked up the orange, but the man turned to me, glancing from the orange to me. "It is mine. Give it to me, or pay me."

"I am hungry," I said.

He shrugged. "So? Pay me. Then eat."

"I have no money."

The skin on his face tightened. He eyed me with open contempt. "Give me the orange, and be gone."

The dagger was in my waistband. If I drew the dagger, the orange might no longer be so dear to him, yet there were soldiers at the far end of the market area, and he had only to lift his voice.

"You accept not the word of Allah?" I asked gently. " 'To eat thereof, and feed the poor and the unfortunate'?"

"Allah has his troubles, I mine. Pay me. If Allah wills you to be fed, then you will be fed, but not by me."

Staring, I brought all the intensity of my gaze upon him. As I advanced a step, he involuntarily retreated. "There is no god but Allah," I said, "but there are devils."

He liked not my words and took a step back, glancing right and left as if for escape. "There are devils," I said, "and there are curses." Lifting my hand, I pointed a finger at him and began to mutter in my own Breton tongue a phrase or two of Druid ritual, but nothing to do with curses.

His features went stiff with horror. I had forgotten how lately these people had come from the desert where savage gods ruled and superstition was the order of the day.

"No!" he lifted his hands as if to shield himself. "Take the fruit and go!" Seizing a small clutch of bananas he thrust them at me. "Take these also, but go. I am a poor man. I have done no harm. I did not know. I thought . . ."

Jerking the bananas from his hand, I glared at him, then strode away, inwardly pleased at my good fortune. Truly, there was power in the word.

Walking along, I ate the bananas and the orange as
well. It was overripe and not to my taste, but it was food.
Then I rinsed my hands in a fountain and dried them on
my shirt. With food in my stomach my mood expanded. I
began to think of a place to sleep.

If curses were to be the answer, I could invent horren-
dous ones, but there must be simpler solutions. Why
should I lie in a cold and dusty street when I might rest
my head on the shoulder of some wealthy widow looking
for solace? Yet if such there were, they would not look
with favor upon me in my rags.

There is, after all, an atmosphere that hangs about
success that is favorable to the breathing of beautiful women.

No doubt this follows some law of physics, some
aspect of feminine instinct or of feminine laws of survival.
Despite my tattered clothing and bruised body, I still had
my wits. Somewhere, somehow, I would find a bed.

The last of the day was gone, the side streets were
shuttered and closed, becoming caverns of darkness, empty
of life.

There were lighted streets in Córdoba, but upon
these walked the young men of fashion, roistering soldiers,
men out upon the town. Many of these had I known, but
none could I count as friends. I could beg, a few coins,
perhaps?

No, not the son of Kerbouchard.

My feet strayed into a narrow alley between two high
walls of baked clay, beyond one of them I heard a feminine voice, softly singing. A haunting song of love sung by
a lonely voice. Beyond, the sound of falling water.

My eyes estimated the wall. It would not do to be
caught in the women's quarters of a Moslem house. Men
had been killed or castrated for less.

However—I leaped, catching the top of the wall,
swinging up to lie flat atop it. Had the music missed a
beat? The fingers throbbed the strings of the *qitara*, and
the plaintive voice lifted again. The words yearned with
memories of the desert, dunes, and palm trees, of the
black tents of the Bedouin.

The song's words hung inquiring into the night; the water fell in a fountain, and there was a heavy smell of jasmine, a sense of delightful coolness after the day's heat. Swinging my feet over, I dropped to the ground, and the music of the strings whispered away and faded, leaving only the memory of sound.

Feet shuffled by in the street I had quit only in time, and I looked about me, feet apart, hands on my hips.

"Who are you, and what do you want?"

There was a difference in the tone, not that of a frightened girl nor of a woman of the harem. There was unexpected assurance, a voice accustomed to command. My refuge lay in frankness.

"I am a man without money, a man with many enemies. My only food in days was a little fruit in a market, nor do I have a place to sleep.

"However, despite my garb, I am a man of honor, a warrior, and a son of warriors, a man who can sail a ship, compose a rhyme, discourse upon the laws of men and nations, fight a duel, or treat a wound."

"Leave this garden at once, by the way you came. If I am forced to call my slaves, they will kill you."

"There is no deliverance from a destiny decreed by Allah," I said with my tongue in my cheek, "but surely it cannot be my destiny to be sent to starve by one so lovely? If I am here, it was only because of you, of your voice, of the song you sang. Your song called to me. I had no will but to answer."

Taking a step nearer, I said, "You see in me a Celt, the son of Kerbouchard the Corsair, a wanderer, a man without home, family, or lands, but if you have use for a sword, I know the blade."

"You must go."

Did I detect a softening of resistance? A relenting? A suggestion of growing interest? Man's greatest advantage in the battle of the sexes is woman's curiosity. She was in the shadows, beyond the reach of my eyes, yet the voice was of a woman both young and well-bred.

"If you drive me from your garden, my enemies may take me, and if they do, I shall be strangled."

"These enemies of whom you speak? Who are they?"

Ah, the shrewdness of it! I was fairly trapped, but the risk was one I must accept. Perhaps I stood in the garden of an enemy, of one with allegiance to those who sought me.

No matter, I had trusted to honesty thus far. I would persist. I must stake all, and hope that emotion would rule rather than political favor.

"Prince Ahmed is my enemy, as is ibn-Haram."

She moved slightly, to see me better, I guessed, for she was still in darkness. "To have such enemies you must be more than a mere Celtic adventurer. I had not heard that Prince Ahmed was—ah?"

She paused as if remembering.

"Prince Ahmed? Are you the one then? The one who spent a week with Prince Ahmed's bride? If so, you are the toast of Córdoba."

She paused. "What is it you want?"

"Sanctuary until I am rested. A bath. Clothing, if it can be obtained. I can stand being hungry but not unclean."

"Step into the light."

I did so. "See?" I said mockingly. "I am dirty, I am ragged, but I am a man."

"The story of your escape is repeated at every gathering in Córdoba, Seville, and Cádiz."

She stepped into the light. She was small, deliciously shaped. She indicated a door. "Accept what I am giving. Demand more and I shall call the guards."

I bowed. "Thank you, Princess. I am most grateful."

"What has happened to your face?"

Briefly, I explained, but only the part about returning to the house, being struck down, and left for dead.

She asked but few questions, but each was to the point. Her manner puzzled me. This was no wartime widow, nor yet a wife. Her questions were those of one skilled in obtaining information.

When I dropped over the wall I'd have been pleased

to find only a corner where I could sleep in security, to be on my way in the morning, but there was mystery here. Her eyes held a calculating expression that had nothing to do with my physique.

Women in the Moslem worlds of Spain or the Middle East were not restricted and had attained eminence in the field of letters. Many had attended universities and had a liberty unbelievable to Christian Europe. With all the talk of chivalry among the Franks, women were considered mere chattels.

The house in which I found myself was not large, yet showed every evidence of affluence.

A robe was thrown over a marble bench when I emerged from the bath, and I donned it. A moment later she returned and without a glance at me, placed a bundle of clothing on the bench.

My face was still too tender to shave, but I trimmed my beard in the Moslem fashion and dressed myself. The clothing was the plain but substantial clothing of a man of means, of quality but unobtrusive. There might be five thousand in Córdoba who would dress in similar fashion.

She awaited me in a small room that adjoined her living area, and on the table there was tea, bread, fruit, and a few slices of cold meat and cheese.

Her name was Safia. While we ate she questioned me about my activities, and I told her of my escape from the galley, of my studies, my imprisonment, and my flight.

Safia was older than I, older than the girls I had known, and it was obvious her interest was not in any minor escapade. Quite simply she told me she had plans with which I might help, and that might be profitable to me.

She indicated a pile of rugs and pillows on the floor. "You may sleep there."

"Of course. Where else?"

Her eyes narrowed a little. This woman had a temper. "We will talk in the morning."

Again, from the sands of despair I had salvaged the water of well-being. The future remained in doubt, but I had eaten, drunk, bathed, and was freshly clad. Beneath me, when I finally lay down, was a bed not too soft.

Safia, my lady of the fountain, had the body of a siren, the face of a goddess, and the mind of an Armenian camel dealer. What ideas she had I could not surmise, but Córdoba was a place of intrigue, an art in which the Arab mind was uniquely gifted.

Was she an Arab? A Berber? A Jewess? I could not guess, nor had she given me the slightest hint or clue. Her few questions and comments when I related my story gave evidence that she was well aware of what was happening in Spain, and there was no doubt she was involved somehow, in some way.

No doubt I was to be involved also. No doubt I was a tool to be used, but a tool that would be careful of his own interest, and his own life.

My fingers felt for my dagger. At least, I had that. Tomorrow, with luck, a sword.

In the meantime there was sleep.

20

Córdoba was a universe, a universe in which revolved many planets, each isolated to a degree from all others. Now, following the night meeting in the garden, I inhabited one of those planets.

My world was made up of those who worked, as I now did, for the Society of Translators. Those and the few shopkeepers I met in the daily round of my new life. It needed but a word from Safia to take me to a hearing from the scholars.

My excellent handwriting satisfied them, but then it was requested that I read aloud and translate from works both Latin and Arabic. On the table was a volume of the *Canon* of Avicenna, known here by his proper name, ibn-Sina. As I had studied it previously, my translation was satisfactory.

They gave me the task of copying the *Index of Sciences* compiled by al-Nadim in 988.

Each daybreak I arose, dressed sedately, and walked through the streets to the library. There I was among older men, far more interested in the matter of the manuscripts before them than the personalities of their fellow workers.

In the evening I walked home through a park, occasionally sitting down to read under the trees. During all this time I saw few people, none whom I knew.

My work was painstaking yet fascinating. Two months passed in this quiet endeavor. My trained memory absorbed facts easily, skipping all that was unnecessary, but avid for that information that might be of use.

My command of Arabic improved, as did my knowledge of both Greek and Latin, and from Safia I was learning Persian. As the streets were dangerous for me, I avoided those where I might encounter someone whom I had known, but my hours were such that the chance was slight.

Despite my initial confidence, Safia had not found me irresistible. In fact, if she was aware of my maleness at all, it escaped me. This made our relationship simple yet quite pleasant.

That she possessed a mind quite out of the ordinary was immediately obvious, also that she was engaged in some occupation that required secrecy. It soon became apparent, although she told me nothing, that she was the center for many sources of information. Little happened in Córdoba of which she was not aware, nor in Seville, Toledo, Málaga, or Cádiz.

The fact that our relations remained as simple as they were was in part due to the daughter of an innkeeper near where I lived. We had passed each other on the street occasionally, never speaking, but mutually aware. She was a full-bosomed lass with dark Moorish eyes ringed with black lashes, and as I have said, we often passed each other. And then there was a day when we did not pass.

My childhood training in Druidic lore had given me memory and the habit of learning, and for me to copy a book was for me to know it. Among other things I found in the library was a veritable storehouse of maps, many ancient and long out of date, some very new. Some of these were the portolans used by merchant mariners in navigating, trading, living along the coasts. The best of these I copied on bits of parchment, and soon I had a packet of charts of my own.

Then one day John of Seville visited the library and spoke to the various translators. When he greeted me as an old friend, there was a subtle change in the atmosphere. In the cloistered stillness of the library, among rolls of parchment, my big shoulders must have seemed out of place. Despite my efforts at maintaining a subdued profile, it was obvious I was a man of the out-of-doors, of the sea, and the battlefield. John of Seville was a noted scholar, and to be his friend was to command respect.

"You have lived an eventful life, Mathurin," John suggested, his eyes twinkling.

"I was not aware it had attracted attention."

"You have made enemies, but you have also won friends."

"Friends? I have no friends."

"Am I not your friend?"

"I am honored, but I scarcely believed you would remember. But other friends? I know nothing of them. The one friend I thought I had was he who betrayed me to my enemies."

"But when you escaped, was there not a horse waiting for you?"

"You know of that? Then who am I to thank?"

"I am not at liberty to say. Let it suffice that somebody believed you were too good a man to die in such a way, at such a time.

"Someone," he added, smiling, "who believed in your somewhat unique abilities to believe that given a chance you could escape."

No more would he tell me. He asked about my work and was impressed when I repeated pages of an ancient manuscript.

"I envy your memory. It was training, you said?"

"For generations, on my mother's side of the family, there were Druids. They were the masters of our history, lore, and ritual, all committed to memory. I do not know if a good memory can be inherited, but we all had such memories, and then there was the training—"

"Yes?"

"I cannot speak of it. Only this I can say. It is a method of using the mind as one uses a burning glass. If one focuses the sun's rays through such a glass, the heat becomes intense and will start a fire. With us it was a matter of focusing the attention, so that what we saw once

was ours forever. Although I must say, repeated readings
are a help."

After the visit of John of Seville, I found myself
included in small gatherings of the translators when they
met away from the library, so in a small way I became a
part, a listening part, of that great city.

Often I heard of Valaba, the beautiful woman I had
seen in a coffeehouse with Averroës. Her home, it seemed,
was a gathering place for beauty and intellect.

In the library I read translations of Heraclitus, Socrates,
Plato, Empedocles, Pythagoras, and Galen. Hunayn ibn-
Ishaq, who translated Hippocrates and Galen, had also
translated Plato. I made several copies of each of these
works, for at first I was given more copying to do than
translation.

Then I was given a book to translate from the Persian,
The Qabus Nama, written by Kai Ka'us ibn-Iskander,
Prince of Gurgan, in 1082. It was a book of advice to his
son, considering all aspects of his life as a prince and as a
man.

In his chapter on enemies, I came upon this passage:
*Ever remain aware of your enemy's activities, secret or
otherwise; never feel secure against his treachery against
you, and consider constantly ways in which you may
outwit or defeat him.*

My eyes lifted from the page. How could I be sure
ibn-Haram or Prince Ahmed did not know of my presence?
How could I be sure I was hidden from them simply
because I stayed away from old acquaintances?

Thus far I had not followed the advice of Kai Ka'us.
My enemies had acted against me, not I against them.
Should I give thought to preventive warfare? And to secur-
ing my own position, for was I not vulnerable?

Thus far I had trusted to my blade, my strength, and
my luck. It was insufficient. I must build defenses, and
the only defense possible was that offered by influential
friends. I had none.

Could I not spy out his position? Discover his

intentions? Duban had told me ibn-Haram was a supporter of Yusuf but was himself ambitious for power.

So then, I needed friends; I needed information; and if not able to defeat my enemy, I could at least elude him.

My face had healed; my strength returned. New blood seemed to flow in my veins. The coffee shops were beyond my small income, but there were other shops to which I might go and drink sherbet and listen to the idle talk.

Desperately, I wanted a sword, but dressed as a scholar, I must proceed carefully not to excite curiosity.

On a warm day I found myself in a remote bazaar and was glancing at some sandals while actually studying the swords in an adjoining booth. They were fine weapons of Damascus and Toledo steel.

Suddenly, a man stopped almost beside me and chose a scimitar from among those exposed for sale. He tried the balance of the weapon, whipping it through the Persian manual with skill. I started to move away when suddenly he spoke. "Here, Scholar, try your hand. Would you not say this was a fine weapon?"

I knew that voice. It was Haroun.

Keeping my face averted, I said, "I know little of weapons, emir. I am a mere student."

He spoke in a lower tone. "Do not play with me, Kerbouchard. I know you."

Looking directly into his eyes, I said, "I have had little reason to trust my old friends."

"Because of Mahmoud? He was always jealous of you, and when Aziza showed interest in you rather than him—he is very vain, you know."

"And you?" I asked bitterly.

"I am still your friend," he replied calmly, "if you will have it so. Did I not let you pass at the gate?"

"You knew me?"

"Not at once. Only after you had passed. It was your walk. I dared not speak to you, for the soldiers would have been curious. After that I looked for you but could find you nowhere."

We went to a cubbyhole of a place to drink sherbet and talk.

He wore the uniform of one of Yusuf's crack cavalry regiments. He was a square-built man of great physical strength and was maturing rapidly under the harshness of the military training. Less agile in conversation than Mahmoud, he never spoke without thinking.

Haroun was one of those calm, relaxed men who are capable of tremendous outbursts of dynamic action. I knew the type well, for my father had been such a man.

"You have plans?" he asked.

"To learn, and to learn more. To find if my father lives, and then to see more of the world. I have thought of India."

"I, too, have thought of it, but who knows anything of India?"

"I know of it."

"You?"

"There are books. Arab ships sometimes sail there, and there is a route through the desert." Looking around at him, I said, "My destiny is there, Haroun. I feel it."

He arose. "Perhaps one day we will meet there, or we might go together." He gripped my shoulder. "It has been good to see you. Like the old days."

He stepped outside into the evening. "And Mahmoud? Do you see him?"

"Mahmoud is an important man now. He is close to Prince Ahmed."

"I think of him," I said, "but there are others who come first."

"Be careful," he warned, "you tread upon loose sand."

"One thing more. Do you know the name Zagal?"

"He commands many soldiers, and rules a *taifa*. Is he your enemy, too?"

I told him the story of Sharasa and of Akim. Until now I had believed the attackers had been men sent by Yusuf; now I discovered Zagal was a minor ruler of one of the smaller principalities into which Moorish Spain was divided.

"It is nothing," I said. "I would simply like to know if she fares well."

"From what you have said I imagine wherever she is, she will be doing well." He smiled. "If you attempt to protect all the girls you meet, I foresee an active life."

We parted, but I felt better. It was good to know Haroun was still my friend. However, I had not told him what I was doing, and I wandered about to make sure I was not followed before going home.

It was that night I told Safia of my father, and that despite reports of his death I believed he still lived. She asked me a number of questions about the galley, its crew, and where he had been bound. Then his age, description, and any scars or marks upon his body.

"You should have told me sooner, but no matter. It is possible I can learn something about him."

Before I could ask her how she could possibly get such information, she handed me a key. "Go to this place." She described it. "You will find four horses. Look at them and decide if they have speed and strength. Then I wish you to take one day each week for the next four weeks and buy supplies for a trip."

"You are going away?"

"*We* are going. I told you I might have need of you." She turned to look at me. "Mathurin, if I have need, it will be a desperate need. I want nothing spoken of this. Do not go near the horses by day, and when you go, be sure you are not followed."

"When?"

"When I will. You seemed to be a man of enterprise, and it was such I have needed. Is your friend Haroun to be trusted?"

"I am sure of it."

She smiled at my surprise, for I had not mentioned his name to her. "It is my business to know. It is yours to be ready to help me as I have helped you. One day— soon, I shall have to leave this city quickly."

"You have only to speak."

"Please do not misunderstand. I have done what was necessary, and you came offering your services."

"And I shall not withdraw them."

The scent of jasmine was heavy in the garden, and I thought of that night, months ago, when I came over that wall, hungry and in rags, in a city filled with enemies. Yes, I was in her debt.

Moorish Spain was a hotbed of intrigue, and plots were forever developing across the Strait of Gibraltar in North Africa, the homeland of the Berber. In Navarre, Castile, and León their rulers looked south toward the luxury of Andalusia with envy.

Realizing time was short, I intensified my study. Medicine and military tactics held first place, but navigation, history, philosophy, chemistry, and botany I studied also.

The key to success in Arab countries of the time lay in none of these. The Arab is by nature a poet. His language is filled with poetry and wonderful sounds, so much so that even state papers were written in poetic form, and the extemporaneous poet was the most sought after of all men.

The Qabus Nama had a chapter of advice on the writing of poetry. Whether the son of the Prince of Gurgan profited by his father's advice, I did not know, but I did. The prince had died a hundred years or more before my time, but his advice was still good.

One by one I checked escape routes from Córdoba, and I became familiar with the hours of closing the gates, and which guards were most strict or casual. From time to time I shared a bottle with those who would drink, for most Moslems would not.

Sometimes I frequented the low dives, making the acquaintance of mountebanks, jugglers, troubadours, and even thieves. I listened to the storytellers in the bazaars, thinking this might someday be of use. I practiced with the lute, and here or there I dropped a coin in a hand, or bought a meal.

It became known among them that I was the Kerbouchard who had sold the galley and who escaped from the castle where Prince Ahmed had me imprisoned. Bits of information came my way. Ibn-Haram had gone to North Africa. Prince Ahmed had still no son.

No longer was I employed at the great library, for Safia wished me ready to move at a moment's notice, yet the library was open to me, and the scholars welcomed me. Safia supplied me with money, and the fact that I was earning the money removed my reluctance at accepting it.

There were elaborate catalogues listing the books of the library, some of which were illustrated with great beauty, bound in aromatic woods and embossed leather inlaid with gems.

Among the books that came to the library were some written on the bark of trees, upon palm leaves, among bamboo or the wood of trees cut in thin slices. Others were written on animal skins, bones, thin plates of copper, bronze, antimony, clay, linen, and silk. Papyrus, leather, and parchment were common.

Some were in tongues none of us could translate, such as those from Crete or Thera or Etruscan ruins.

There were scholars at the library who read in Sanskrit, in Pali, Kharoshthi, and even the ancient Kashmir script, Sarada.

Day after day I buried myself in my work, and now that I no longer was engaged in copying or translation, my studies went further afield, for I delved into that great storehouse of manuscripts untouched and unread.

One night Safia came to the room where I slept. "I have news."

"News?"

"Your father may yet live."

"What?" My heart was pounding.

"His galley was sunk off Crete, but he or somebody who resembled him was taken from the sea and sold into slavery."

"Then I must go to Crete."

"He is no longer there. He was sold to a merchant in Constantinople."

My father was *alive*!

"I must go."

Safia shook her head. "It would be foolish. Those who discovered this are making further inquiries. When I have news, you shall have it."

Filled with impatience, I had yet to wait. Safia was right, of course. To dash off without further knowledge would be to set myself adrift once more. First, I must know what merchant bought him and if he was still the owner, or if he had sold him, to whom?

I had waited this long. I could wait longer. I would have to trust that Safia would not fail me just as I would not fail in my duty to her.

21

Where Safia procured the horses I did not know, but all
were of the *Al Khamsat al Rasul*, the five great breeds
superior to all other Arabian horses. Two were *Kuhaila*,
one a *Saglawi*, the last a *Hadbah*. Only the third horse
was a stallion, the first two and the last were mares,
preferred by the Arab.

They were handsome animals, and the groom who
cared for them was a desert Arab, a deaf mute.

Obviously, the horses were his life and could be in no
better hands, but I took time to caress them and become
acquainted, feeding each a few fragments of *naida*, a con-
fection made by soaking wheat for several days, allowing it
to dry, then pounding it into cakes.

After visiting the horses a second time, I left by a
roundabout route so that I might not be followed, and I
discovered myself in the corner of a bazaar where there
were several *karob* and wine shops. Hurrying past, I was
stopped by a cool but familiar voice.

"If you wish to know, ask Kerbouchard!"

The voice was that of Valaba.

Turning, I saw her standing in the entrance to a wine
shop, two young men beside her. She wore the Byzantine
costume affected by some of the fashionable women of
Córdoba, a tunic of pale blue that reached to her ankles
and a mantle of dark blue embroidered with small Moline
crosses of gold.

"Kerbouchard," she said, "knows the far regions of
the world. Ask him."

One of the young men, slender and pale, merely

glanced at me, taking in my rough student's clothing. The other, a big, loose-jointed young man with mildly amused eyes, was more interested.

"We were speaking of the earth. Is it true that some Christian theologians believe the world to be flat?"

"Theologians," I said, "should go to sea. The roundness of the world is proved every time a ship disappears over the horizon."

Valaba turned toward the interior of the shop. "Kerbouchard, it is good to see you again. Will you join us? I would have you tell us of the lands beyond Thule."

"Beyond Thule?" The tall young man put his hand on my shoulder. "Are there such lands?"

"They are a mystery only to scholars and writers of books. Fishing boats go there each season. I am a Celt, from Armorica, in Brittany. Fishing boats have sailed to those far lands from our isle of Brehat since before memory. Nor were they alone. Basque and Norman boats have been there also, and those from Iceland."

"Tell me of those lands."

"That I cannot. Our boat went for fish, and the land is remote, its people savage. When we caught our fish we came home."

The fair-skinned young man was bored. He was also haughty. His look was disdainful. "A fisherman? In a student's clothing?"

"We are all fishermen after a fashion," I said. "Some fish for one thing, some for another." I smiled at him. "Tell me? What are you fishing for?"

He stared at me, shocked at my reply. Before he could speak, Valaba said gently, her eyes showing her amusement, "You do not understand, Roderick. Mathurin Kerbouchard is *Count* Kerbouchard. In his country it is customary that all boys learn the way of the sea."

The title, of course, was nonsense, although it had been said there were such at some bygone time. The rest of what she had said was simply the truth. I wondered how she knew so much. Or had she merely surmised? Titles had never impressed me. They were given to the

servants of kings. I knew one who got his by helping the
king on with his trousers each morning, or whatever he
wore. We Kerbouchards were servants to no man. My
father often said that he knew of no king with a family
half as old as his own. Not that the age of the family was
important, many an old tree bears bad fruit.

Roderick did not like me, but the other young man
was interested. He ordered wine for us, coffee for himself.
"You are a scholar, yet you have been a man of the sea. It
is a rare combination."

"There is knowledge at sea to be found nowhere else.
Lately, I have been reading accounts of many voyages, but
so much is left out. The sea has an enduring knowledge
passed from father to son for generations.

"It is our custom in sailing from our land to the great
fishing grounds in the west to sail to Eire, the green island
beyond England. From there it is but five or six days with
a fair wind to IceLand, and but two days, perhaps three,
to the GreenLand. From there it is another five days or
less to the fishing grounds.

"Our fishermen and those of Eire learned of these
lands by watching the flight of birds, for when birds which
nest only upon land fly off over the ocean, there must be
land beyond. Where they flew, land must lie waiting, so
fishermen followed a flock as long as it could be seen, then
another flock until it was lost to sight, by then they could
see mountain peaks on the far land.

"Over the years our people have found many lands,
and the monks from Eire, seeking a hermitage, were often
there before us. Such men already lived in the Ice Land
before the first Vikings came. The Vikings speak of it in
their own sagas.

"Explorers and discoverers are often those who draw
attention to what simple people have been doing for years.
I doubt if any land has ever been found where some
hunter, fisherman, or trader had not been before."

"Such men would not have the courage for such
adventure!" Roderick said.

"Who speaks of courage? Or adventure? The men of

whom I speak have time for neither. They fish for fish to eat or sell."

The big young man agreed. "Mas'udi speaks of this in his geography. The seafarers go and return while the geographer sits in his study and tries to shape the earth and its lands according to a theory of his own."

Valaba was saying nothing, toying with her wine glass and listening. The big young man puzzled me. He had the hands and shoulders of a peasant and the face of a thinker—if such a face there is. It was the face, at least, of a thoughtful man.

His clothing was rich, and the one jewel he wore was a magnificent ruby, yet I could not place him. He was no scholar as such, nor did he have the appearance of a soldier.

We talked long, of the writings of al-Bakri, of Hind, and of Cathay. Over the wine glasses the conversation moved and sparkled over many topics and half the globe.

Valaba suggested, "You must come to my house tomorrow. We are having many guests, and ibn-Quzman will sing."

Ibn-Quzman, a wandering minstrel, had taken the *zajal*, a popular form used by troubadours, and given it real distinction. He had become the delight of Córdoba as well as Toledo, Seville, and Málaga. Naturally, I knew of him, yet I had never expected to hear him sing.

Even now I dared not. At such a gathering there would be spies who might report my presence to ibn-Haram or to Prince Ahmed.

"O Light of the World!" I said. "I would choose to spend my life within the sound of your voice, but if I came to your house at such a time, that life would be short, indeed."

The big young man smiled. "Come," he said, "I want very much to speak with you again, and you need not fear arrest. You have my word."

He arose, and Valaba and Roderick moved with him. "Do come," she said, "and have no fears."

They left, and excited by the afternoon, I walked

slowly back along the streets. Who was the friendly young man, scarcely older than myself, who accompanied Valaba?

Safia heard my story. "Mathurin, you are indeed fortunate. The young man with the big hands? He had a strong, rugged face? A wide smile?"

"He did."

"It is Ya'kub, the eldest son of Yusuf himself, and his favorite."

Abu-Yusuf Ya'kub was much talked of in Córdoba. Between himself and his father there was a rare understanding all too uncommon between Moslem rulers and their sons. Yusuf knew Ya'kub had no ambition to rule before his time, or at all, for that matter.

Extremely able, educated in the business of government, Ya'kub preferred to assist his father and remain free of the sharp focus of public attention.

Safia seated herself and poured coffee. "But Valaba!" she exclaimed. "First, the bride of Prince Ahmed, and now Valaba, the most beautiful woman in Córdoba! I should be surprised, but I am not. After all, you are extremely handsome."

"I scarcely know her."

"She knew you well enough to see that your horse awaited you in the guard's stable."

"What? You cannot know what you are saying! She could have had nothing to do with that!"

"Nevertheless, it was she. It was her gold with which your guard gambled at the end of the corridor so he might not hear or see what happened in your cell.

"She could do no more. Had you escaped in any other way the guards would have lost their heads. Not that I would mention it. Such things are better accepted and remembered than talked about. It could do her harm."

"She has power in Córdoba."

"Yes"—Safia was bitter—"and so had I, upon a time, but power is a breath on the wind and soon lost." She put her hand on mine. It was the first time she had ever touched me. "Mathurin, do not fail me. I have nowhere else to turn."

"I have no answer but to say I shall not fail you."
Pausing, I said, "You have never told me what it is you
do."

"Whatever it is will soon be at an end. Believe me, I
could not do less than I have done."

Fear was upon her, it flowed in her veins, shadowed
her eyes. That she was engaged in some intrigue was
obvious, and that she had sources of information was
obvious. More than that I did not know.

It was midnight when I left, for she feared to be
alone. I left by a small gate in the garden wall, for I now
had a place to live close by the horses. Holding to the
deepest shadows, I went along the small alleyway to the
street. I hesitated before emerging.

Nothing.

The air was tight with danger, nor did I like to know
there were enemies at whom I could not strike because
they were unknown to me. And still, I had no weapon but
my dagger. Drawing it from the scabbard, I glanced at the
blade.

A Berber soldier saw it and laughed. "It is a toy!" he
sneered. "Stained only with milk!"

"The milk left no stain," I said, smiling, "but come to
me, and we will see if a dog's blood will stain it."

The sneer left his face. "It was but a jest. Who would
die for a jest?"

"You could." I held the blade in my hand, waiting.

"You are crazy!" He walked away down the street,
glancing over his shoulder at me.

So I sheathed my blade in its scabbard rather than his
belly and walked homeward, smelling the jasmine and
thinking that no doubt he was right.

A man would be crazy to risk dying in a world where
there was jasmine.

To say nothing of Aziza, Sharasa, and Valaba.

22

The major consideration of the world of the twelfth century after Christ was Islam, and so it had been for more than five hundred years.

Never before had a single idea created, in terms of conquest and culture, an impact such as the religion given to the world by Mohammed, the camel driver of Mecca.

Christianity, the other great moving force of my time, had in a thousand years won to its teachings only a few lands in western Europe.

On the other hand, in the space of one hundred years following the death of Mohammed in 632, the Arabs had carried the sword of Islam from the Atlantic to the Indian Ocean, holding at one time most of Spain, part of southern France, the isle of Sicily, all of North Africa and Egypt, all of Arabia, the Holy Land, Armenia, Persia, Afghanistan, and almost a third of India. The empire of the Arabs was larger than that of Alexander the Great or of Rome.

They came with the sword, but they retained the best of what they discovered. Much that we know of Arab science was born from the minds of Jews, Persians, Greeks, various Central Asiatic peoples, and the Berbers, but it flowered under Arab protection, impelled by Arab enthusiasm.

A scholar was welcome everywhere and might travel thousands of miles, welcomed in each city by a sultan, a bey or emir, presented with gifts, honored, escorted, entertained, and, above all, listened to with attention.

Here and there were signs of change. Rulers came who were ignorant or cruel men whose interests lay elsewhere than with the propagation of knowledge. Indications of decay were evident under the flush of greatness, yet for more than five hundred years the Arabs carried the torch of civilization.

A fever of discovery lay upon the world; old libraries and bookstalls were ransacked for books; scholars from all countries were welcomed; men delved, experimented, tried new things. Nothing like it had ever happened within the memory of man. The Greeks of Athens had thought, speculated, and debated, but the people of the Arab world experimented, tested, explored, and reasoned as well. New ideas did not frighten them, and the stars were close to them in their deserts. Their ships, with those of China and India, had made the Indian Ocean as busy a place as the Mediterranean.

Among other books I had found and read *The Periplus to the Erythean Sea*, a guide and a pilot book to all the ports of the Indian Ocean and adjacent waters; the *Hudud al-'Alam*, a geography and guide first published in 982, as well as the work of Sharaf al-Zaman Tahir Marvazion, *China, The Turks and India*, written in 1120.

Until the beginning of the Conquest, the Arab had lived on the outer edge of civilization, subject to its influences but accepting little of its teaching. A practical people, they were not inclined to speculate or form theories. They introduced the objective experiment and the accurate observation of phenomena. Their lives as shepherds, desert travelers, or seamen had given them a working knowledge of the stars that developed into a study of astronomy.

Arab ships had sailed to China, to Malacca, Sumatra, Borneo, and Java. Their religion had been established in islands unheard of in Europe, and where their religion went, trade followed.

The pilgrims who made the hajj, the pilgrimage to Mecca, brought with them itineraries, and these helped to build the geographical knowledge of the Arabs.

At the library most of the books had leather covers on paper of good quality but handwritten by such as me. They were of a size easily handled or carried and convenient for use. Several lists had been prepared of available books, one of those *The Fihrist of al-Nadim*, to which I often referred.

Haroun and I had taken to meeting in a wine shop near the great mosque. We often drank a date wine flavored with cassia leaves or ate *Foūl Madumnas*, a dish of beans, hard-boiled eggs, and lemon, into which we dipped bread, eating as we talked.

We talked of alchemy, into which I was delving, of the writings of Jabir ibn-Hayyan, known to the Franks as Geber, who experimented in al-Kufah about 776, and of the writings of al-Rhazi, the greatest in chemical science. Jabir had described the two operations of reduction and calcination, and advanced almost all areas of chemical experiment.

It was the good talk of young men to whom ideas are important, to be alive was to think.

"Tonight," I told him, "I go to the house of Valaba!"

"You are fortunate," Haroun said ruefully, "you will go as a guest, I as a guard!"

It was night upon the banks of the Guadalquivir, and under the orange trees, under the palms and the chinar trees, there was music and laughter, the soft play of light from many lanterns, the stir and movement of people. Bronze lamps threw their light through colored glass from trees and balconies. It was a colorful, shifting, and kaleidoscopic scene.

From across the spacious court a haunting voice sang to the music of a lute and a *qitara*, a song filled with the sad loneliness of desert spaces.

Only an hour ago I had been staring in discouragement at my dull student's clothing, longing for just one of the gems lost with my ragged coat. True, I had bathed, and I had brushed my clothing with care, but it looked like nothing more than it was.

I would not go.

I would look like a skeleton of death at a place where

all was elegance and beauty. I would not shame myself nor the memory of my ancestors.

A slave appeared, and a genii could have come no more suddenly. "Oh, Master, I come from Abu-Yusuf Ya'kub! He begs to offer tribute to Your Eminence!"

With that he took from his shoulder a long bag. Opening it with a gesture, he drew out of it a magnificent suit of clothing, a mantle . . . everything.

Now I stood beneath the palms wearing breeches called *sirwal*, baggy breeches of black, of the thinnest wool, carrying a sheen like silk; a short jacket called a *damir* of the same material and trimmed with gold; a *zibun*, or shirt, of the finest silk; a crimson sash of silk, and a mantle of black wool of the same material as the suit, but brocaded with gold and crimson. My turban was of dull but rich red, and in my sash I wore a jeweled dagger sent me by Ya'kub, but alongside it my Damascus dagger that had been my companion through so many troubles.

Valaba would be somewhere about, and Ya'kub would be here. The gift from Ya'kub surprised me, although it was customary to make such presentations to traveling scholars—gifts of clothing, horses, purses of gold coins, sometimes slaves were given when a scholar shared his knowledge with a ruler.

Suddenly, my name was spoken. It was Averroës. The *qadi* smiled and put a hand on my shoulder. "So? Valaba has captured you at last! She has been looking forward to this, Kerbouchard! It is not often we have a distinguished geographer among us, and particularly one who has sailed the seas himself!"

Geographer? Who was I to argue the point? Call me what they would, I alone knew my ignorance. True, I had read more of geography and studied more maps, charts, and portolans than most, and I had sailed what to Moslems were unknown seas, yet I was woefully ignorant of so much I needed to know.

The term "unknown seas" distressed me. Man has gone down to the sea since the beginning of time, and often left accounts of his voyages, yet so much has not been told. The call of the horizon finds quick response in the heart of every wanderer.

We of the Veneti had legends of sailing to distant lands, faint, cloudy stories of brooding cliffs and crashing waves, of temples, gold, and strange cities. Julius Caesar wrote in his *Commentaries* about our great, oak-hulled ships with leathern sails, but he knew nothing of what ports they visited or with what strange cargoes they returned.

Perhaps records of their far-flung voyages had been kept in the great destroyed libraries of Tyre, Carthage, or Alexandria.

We strolled across the garden, Averroës and I, and many turned to look, for the *qadi* was a great man and a noted scholar. We talked of geography, medicine, and the stars, and I told him of remedies used among our people, and of healing herbs of which my father had spoken.

Ya'kub came toward us, walking with Valaba. There was a somewhat surprised look in her eyes to see me in my new finery, gratifying to me.

We walked among the trees, followed by all eyes. This stroll was sufficient to make my fortune in Spain, yet who they were meant less to me than what they were saying and that I, a mere wanderer, was accepted as an equal by Averroës himself.

Wherever my eyes turned there were beautiful women, fingertips stained with henna, the luster of their eyes heightened with antimony. Many wore a comb at the back of the head attached to a scarf of gauzy material, but all their costumes were striking and beautiful.

The Prophet forbade the wearing of silk, but he who was a good husband should have understood women better than that. These all wore silk, and many of the men did as well.

Silk had come to Spain with the Moors, and by the tenth century was the principal export, ornamental silks and tapestries being shipped to all the ports of the Near East. Until the birth of the silk industry in Spain the Coptic silks of Egypt and the Sassanid silks of Persia had been preferred. Now the Spanish silks superseded all others.

Almería was especially known for its turbans for women and damask for drapes. Lightweight, contrasting to the heavier satins, velvet and damasks were made in Catalonia and Valencia. Court robes and vestments for the clergy were ordered from Spain by most of the Christian nations.

For a moment Valaba and I were alone. "It was gracious of you to invite me here. I have done nothing"—I waved a hand—"to compare with these, although I have ambitions."

One eyebrow lifted slightly. "I suspect your ambitions, Kerbouchard, and if stories of the Castle of Othman are a criterion, I suspect you would find plenty of cooperation out there."

She studied the crowd. "Sixty or seventy of the people here might be ranked among the most brilliant in Córdoba, and perhaps twenty more who will be their equal in a year's time, but few of them will be better informed than you."

She looked directly into my eyes, and hers were very beautiful. "Be sure of this, Kerbouchard. You would not be here unless you belonged here.

"John of Seville has kept pace with your studies, and only last week Averroës was reading a book on alchemy translated by you from the Persian."

"Introduce me to your guest, Valaba." The tone was cool. "I do not believe we have met socially."

It was Prince Ahmed.

His eyes were utterly cold.

"Prince Ahmed," Valaba said, "my very good friend, Mathurin Kerbouchard!"

"And *my* very good friend!" Ya'kub appeared from under the trees where he had been talking with Averroës.

"Of course, Your Eminence." Prince Ahmed's eyes were bitter. "These are your domains." His pause was brief. "But I understand that Kerbouchard likes to travel."

"Believe me, Prince Ahmed," I said, smiling, "you

must forgive me if I avoid your city. You make a guest almost too welcome!"

"Without assistance you would still be my guest. Sometime I expect to learn who assisted you."

"Assisted me? I assure you, sir, I was alone on the face of that rock, very much alone. No one could have helped me in that situation. If you doubt me, try scaling that cliff yourself."

"I am not a performer."

"Each of us plays many roles. Some are heroes, some villains, and some merely"—I paused slightly—"mountebanks."

His face went white under the olive skin, and for an instant I thought he would strike me, but he turned abruptly away. His back was stiff as he walked away, and Ya'kub turned to me. "You make enemies, Kerbouchard."

"I did not choose him for my enemy, Your Eminence; he chose me. He owes me some months in a dungeon."

"He has been paid in laughter," Valaba said.

Then at a signal from Valaba, ibn-Quzman sang, a low, haunting melody, the love song of a desert rider, following it with a wild, fierce song of war and vengeance. Yet I could not lose myself to the music as I wished. There were enemies who might even dare the displeasure of Ya'kub for the pleasure of spilling my blood. Powerful friends could make armor of a word, and from their lips a phrase could be a shield. This had I witnessed tonight.

Yet I placed less faith in the words of men than in my own hands and the steel behind my sash. That man who is no longer on guard is one who invites death.

Ibn-Quzman crossed to Valaba as she stood beside me, and I said, "I envy you. You sing more beautifully than any other."

"You are Kerbouchard? We must talk one day of the Celtic bards and their songs."

"And you could explain the writings of al-Mausili. I know too little of music to understand all he has written."

"You know of him? His uncle, Zalzal, they say, played the lute better than anyone."

We talked idly for a time, and when he had gone on, Valaba put her hand upon my arm. "Ya'kub wishes to make a place for you."

Ya'kub overheard the remark and came over to us. "Loyal men are not easily found, Kerbouchard, and there are dangerous days before me. I could make a place for you that would allow leisure for study."

"I am sorry."

He was not pleased, and I hastened to explain. "There is no prince I had rather serve, but I have a mission and but lately have received a clue."

Briefly, I explained. "If my father lives," I added, "I must find him; if he is indeed dead, I must know. Nothing else would keep me from serving you."

"I had thought of you as commander of my personal bodyguard." He smiled slightly. "Rumor has said you are skilled with a sword."

"May I suggest a man?"

"I trust few men, Kerbouchard."

"This one can be trusted. I would stake my life upon it, and he is here tonight, in command of the guards around these walls. He proved loyal to me in time of trouble."

"His name?"

"Haroun el-Zegri."

"I know the man." He listened to the music, then said, "Come! Let us dine."

On the table where food awaited us I saw sugar for the first time, white, gleaming crystals. It was something of which we in Christian lands had heard but never seen. We had for sweetening only honey or sweet grasses.

There were heaps of food in infinite variety. Plates of *carra bige*, a pastry sausage of chopped almonds and walnuts mixed with sugar and over which melted butter had been poured. This mixture was rolled into a thin pastry and baked for fifteen minutes or so. It was served with a spoonful of *natif*, a fluffy mix of sugar, egg white, and orange flower water.

There was rice with sour lemon sauce, pilaf Egyptian,

shebach, an Egyptian fritter, green and black olives, brains fried in batter, artichoke hearts also fried in batter and served very hot, and *kebaeba*, a mixture of red meat, pine nuts, and crushed wheat. There was *louzine saparzel*, a Syrian dessert of quince, ground almonds, and cardamom seeds served in small squares. There was rose jam, made of rose petals, sugar, and lemon.

There were skewers of beef, lamb, and veal, smoking hot and ready to be served in a number of sauces and styles. There was wine from Portugal, Italy, and Greece as well as coffee, sweetened with sugar.

The moon arose, holding its light beyond the minaret of the great mosque, and Valaba said, "Then you will be leaving soon?"

"At any moment."

"We have hoped you would remain. Ya'kub is a good man, and the time is near when he will need good men about him."

"It is well to think of Ya'kub. He is a rarely fine man."

She turned toward me. "I think of you, too, Kerbouchard. The way you take is filled with risk."

"Are there other ways?"

"For some, even for you, perhaps. You are a strange man, Kerbouchard. You are an adventurer yet a scholar."

"There have been many such, even Alexander, and Julius Caesar. I but dabble in scholarship. Learning to me is a way of life. I do not learn to obtain position or reputation. I want only to know."

"Is not yours the best way? To learn because one loves learning?"

"There are places I have not seen, Valaba. I would feel their suns upon my face, the brine of their seas upon my lips. There are too many horizons, and too many dreams of what may lie beyond those horizons."

"What are you seeking, Kerbouchard?"

"Must one seek something? I seek to be seeking, as I learn to be learning. Each book is an adventure as is each day's horizon."

"What of love, Kerbouchard? Did you love Aziza?"

"Who is to say? What is love? Perhaps for a time I loved her; perhaps in a way I love her still. Perhaps when a man has held a woman in his arms, there is a little of her with him forever. Who is to say?

"A ruined castle, an ancient garden, a moon rising over a fountain . . . love comes easily at such a time. Perhaps we loved each other then; perhaps we do not love each other now, but we each have a memory.

"Love is a moment of stillness that sometimes a word can shatter to fragments, or love can be a thing that endures, a rich deep current that flows unending down the years.

"I do not think one should demand that love be forever. Perhaps it is better that it not be forever. How can one answer for more than the moment? Who knows what strange tides may sweep us away? What depths there may be or twists and turns and shallows? Each life sails a separate course, although sometimes, and this is the best of times, two lives may move along together until the end of time?

"Listen to the music out there. Is the song less beautiful because it has an end? I believe each of us wishes to find the song that does not end, but for me that time is not now.

"You see?" I spread wide my hands. "I have nothing. I have no home, no land, no position. I am an empty gourd that must fill itself.

"I would owe no debts to destiny, Valaba, nor could I exist on the bounty of another. I am not a lapdog to be kept by a woman. I do not know what awaits me out there beyond the rim of things, but destiny calls, and I must go. For you and me, today is all we have; tomorrow is a mirage that may never become reality."

"You speak well, Kerbouchard. Did you learn that on those bleak northern moors?"

We were walking slowly through the shadows, away from the crowd, away from the music. There was a dim, unlighted court ahead of us, and through the open gate to that court I could see the lights of the house.

Two chinar trees leaned their great trunks close above the path, and there were rose bushes beside them. Valaba started to go ahead of me when I heard a sound, *a faint chink of metal as a blade brushes against twigs*!

Catching Valaba's arm, I whirled her to one side, and my dagger came from its sheath as men closed around me.

My life was saved because I did not hesitate or step back as expected. It was ever my way to go toward an enemy, and I went now.

He stepped from behind a bush and held a sword in his hand.

23

He held his point low. When he saw me moving toward him, his blade came up, but he moved too slowly, and I was already past the point. Before he could step back, I had put my dagger into his belly.

Turning sharply around, I faced three men with drawn swords.

Valaba screamed, and one of them turned toward her, another swore at him. Outside the garden there were running feet, and the three men moved to kill me.

These were hired assassins, and neither honor nor glory lay in a victory over them, nor could I defeat them in any way except by surviving.

Valaba was at the gate, but they would not dare harm such as she. She was safe enough.

Feinting a lunge that brought them up short, blades up, I spun around quickly, put my blade between my teeth, jumped, and grasped the top of the wall. With a quick motion I swung my legs over the wall and dropped on the far side. Behind me I heard Haroun and his guards surrounding the garden, but there was nothing further to be gained here. I left the garden and, by a roundabout route, hastened to my quarters.

On the bed lay a message with but a single word in Persian.

Come

Safia was waiting, but if she noticed my handsome clothing, she gave no indication. Gesturing to some clothing on a bench, she said, "Change into that. You must disappear."

"Disappear?"

"You must not return to your quarters. Whatever you have there will be packaged and sent to the library." She indicated a small pile of gold coins. "Take that. You must go to a place I will designate, and remain there until I call you."

"The time is near?"

"You were attacked tonight, were you not?"

"You knew?"

"They were not enemies of yours, but of mine."

When I dressed I resembled one of the many foot-loose mercenary soldiers ready to sell their services to any cause.

Beside the armor was a sword. As I picked it up, my blood surged with excitement. What a *blade*! The balance was beautiful, the feel of it—I ached for combat.

The room was small with one door and a window that opened upon a wall that ran for some distance between a double row of trees, shaded and crossed by their branches, creating a leafy tunnel, concealed from both sides. The wall ended at an aqueduct near a street.

Safia's planning astonished me. The section where I now waited was shabby, inhabited by mercenary soldiers, camp followers. The street near the aqueduct was where our horses were stabled and waiting. Not far from it was a small postern gate.

Days passed, but there was an ample supply of food; an olla suspended from a ceiling beam contained water. There were books, also.

I made but one friend. Khatib was a sly man with quick hands and a quicker brain. No longer young, there was little he did not know of the ways of the beggar or the trickster. Squatting on his heels by the doorstep, he regaled me with news from the streets, as well as about our neighbors.

He had a face of old leather, and an odd way of
peering from the corners of his eyes as if to gauge the
effect of his comments. He seemed to like me, and I liked
him, but I dared trust no one.

My identity was that of a Frankish soldier and former
pirate, something I was qualified to carry off, for aside
from my brief experience, I had countless tales from my
father and his crew.

From Khatib I learned tricks of the hand and juggling,
for he had once traveled with a company of tumblers and
jugglers, some of whom were thieves.

My reading was done only at night and behind closed
doors. To be able to read marked a man, and there is
always gossip.

It was at this time that I read *The Ring of the Dove*,
by a young Spaniard of Moorish extraction who devoted
his time to an exploration of amorous play and its accompa-
nying phenomena. It struck me as an intriguing area for
study.

Khatib was another sort of book, one I never tired of
reading. Within that cunning, fertile, amoral mind lay all
the devious tricks and devices men have learned over
thousands of years, or so it seemed. He also possessed
qualities of dignity and loyalty that would have been a
lesson to any Christian or Moslem.

With Khatib I often went to a room in an ancient ruin
where tumblers and jugglers gathered to practice their
arts or to acquire new tricks. Ever athletic and handling
my body with ease, I took part in their training, to learn
their somersaults, flips, and cartwheels. Some of these I
had learned as a boy from others of my age, but now I
became an adept.

Nearby was the Street of the Booksellers where over
one hundred dealers gathered along one street. They had
been established there since the time of the Abbasids.
Al-Ya'qubi states that in his time, about 891 in the Christian calendar, these shops were already here. Many of the
keepers of the shops were letter writers for pay, authors of
books, and literati of various sorts. The shops not only

were where books were sold but were centers of intellectual discussion.

Several times I bought copies of ancient manuscripts, smuggling them to my room under my robes. One of these was from the private collection of the great Egyptian physician Imhotep, and it concerned treatments for diseases of the eyes, the skin, and the extremities.

Around the bookshops I never tired of loitering, listening to discussions, examining Egyptian papyruses, Chinese paper, scrolls, or parchment. Córdoba manufactured its own paper and had its own printers.

Chinese prisoners had, in 751, introduced into the far-off city of Samarkand, the art of making paper from rags or linen, flax or hemp. A paper mill was established in Baghdad in 794, and paper replaced parchment in all government offices. By the tenth century paper was readily available in the Moslem world, and with the advent of paper, books became plentiful.

Idling along the streets of the bazaar, I talked with the weavers and their masters, fascinated by their skills. By their feeding, the peculiar worms who spin the silk a variety of shades had been created. White cocoons came from white mulberry leaves, but if the worms were fed the dwarf mulberry, the cocoons were of yellow, and fawn cocoons came when the worms were fed from the castor bean plant. These secrets were known to few outside the trade, and not to all who worked with silk. The Arabs, who were master weavers, experimented with many kinds of leaves, and it was whispered to me that one had devised a silk that would poison the wearer because the leaves fed to the worms were poisonous to humans but not to them.

This silk was extremely rare, and robes or drawers were sold only to a few secret customers. Robes were rarely made of this material, as it was most effective when in contact with the skin. Often the buyers were women of the harem who wished to do away with some rival, or the sons of kings, eager for power.

Drawers, shirts, or turbans were the garments most often made of this material where the poison was made more effective by the body's heat. The wearer would die, often in a fit of madness, but with no indication of poisoning.

One Arab was reported to be feeding his worms a special formula made from leaves of the Indian trumpet vine so the worms would produce a scarlet silk. This was, however, only a rumor.

Fine dyes were available, the best red coming from an insect associated with oak trees, an insect called *kermes* by the Arabs.

Restlessness sat heavily upon me, yet I could not be long absent from my quarters, for when Safia needed me, it would be suddenly and desperately. She had provided food, shelter, and clothing when needed, and more than that, if anyone could discover where my father now was, it would be she. That she was in mortal danger, I knew.

Sometimes I suspected her of dealing in magic, yet none of the signs were there, and reared as I had been in the old knowledge that is never written, the signs would be obvious enough. Had not each of my grandparents been buried with the oak and the mistletoe?

Our family memories went back to the time when a Druid temple topped the isle of Mont-Saint-Michel, long before any Christians came to build there. Had my ancestors not studied in the secret temples of the lost city of Tolente, destroyed by the Normans in 875?

Had I not myself been consecrated times over? The first at *Men Marz*, a tall gray stone near Brignogan on the coast where I was born?

The Druids were gone, it was said, or had never been, but customs and traditions die hard on our rugged Armorican coast, and there were those who still go to the old places in the wilds of the Arré and Huelgoat.

Among those wooded hills, beside the foaming torrents, among the boulders there are places we of the old knowledge have not forgotten, nor shall we forget. It was there I had been taught the history of my people, a history that reaches back beyond the first Celts who came to Brittany. Some of them migrated to England and to Eire, fleeing before the Romans, only to return many years later to add to the Celtic population of Brittany.

Again I thought of Valaba. Did she ever come to the Street of the Booksellers? Would I see her there?

Safia had not come, and might not come for days.

I would go to the Street of the Booksellers.

24

Stripping, I bathed in the small tub in a corner of the room. This was an old Visigothic house, and the bath had been added after the Moors arrived.

Constant exercise with the tumblers, swordplay, and wrestling had developed my back, shoulders, arms, and legs. I had grown no taller, for I achieved my height early, but I had filled out and was much broader and deeper in the chest. My waist was trim, my hips narrow, my legs strong but slim.

When I landed in Spain I had no beard to speak of; now I wore one trimmed in the latest style, and a mustache. After bathing, I trimmed my hair and beard. My hair was black with a tinge of red when seen in the light, a heritage from Celtic ancestors.

On the inspiration of the moment I donned my coat of chain mail. It was new, finely made of small links, bearing the mark of a great armorer from Toledo. It was remarkably light in weight. Then I slung my sword from my shoulder, which was the style of the Moor.

The street was empty but for a disconsolate donkey, and further along the street two camels lay where they had been saddled for a trip. Odd, for camels to be leaving at night.

The Street of the Booksellers was brightly lit. Here and there groups of students gathered, and strolling among them, I watched for Valaba but saw her not. A feeling of depression lay heavy upon me, nor could I shake it off. Several of the booksellers spoke, obviously willing to engage in discourse, but on this night I was not interested.

After a while, despairing of finding Valaba, I started back. Nothing had been gained by my walk. Valaba was busy elsewhere.

A beggar came from his corner to seek alms but when close he whispered, "O Mighty One! Return not. Fly! If your enemies are not there, they soon will be."

Beggars were friendly with street players and singers, and by now I was considered one of them. Yet I dared not accept the warning, for Safia would be coming. All was dark and still when I neared my room, yet I detected a stirring in the shadows not far away.

Entering my room, blade in hand, I searched until sure I was alone, then I went to the corner where I could sit on my bed and not be seen, where I could read. My small light was hidden, and the door was left open a crack to detect any movement outside.

The book I chose was a rare volume from the library of the great mosque. The book had come to my hands in a strange way. I was searching a stack of uncatalogued manuscripts with a view to bringing them to some kind of order, when the stack toppled toward me, revealing a narrow door fitted into the wall. As nothing was kept there but old manuscripts, books collected but unlisted from the time of al-Hakem, it was possible the existence of the door was unknown to anyone in the library.

The door was locked, but my curiosity aroused, I picked the lock with a skill I had acquired from street people. Facing me was a small room, comfortably fitted but thick with undisturbed dust. It was a private study, perhaps that of al-Hakem himself. No doubt it was here that the caliph, one of the great scholars of the Arab world, had done his own research into ancient manuscripts.

Among the fifty or so books there were some with which I had long been familiar, but lying on the table in a sort of leather envelope was a book written in Arabic but translated from the Chinese of Tseng Kung-liang. The original title had been *Wu Ching Tsung Yao*, written in 1044. Translated the words meant *A Compendium of Military Art*.

Opening it, I had found a careful study of the military art of the Chinese and the Mongols as well. What most intrigued my interest was the description given of an explosive powder used by the Chinese in warfare. Included among notes at the back of the book was a formula for making this powder.

Nothing like this had been used by the Moors, and it was unknown in Christian Europe, but here in my hands lay the method of manufacture, information on its use, and something of its reactions when contained in bamboo, wood, or metal.

From notes written in a careful hand this book must have come into the hands of al-Hakem shortly before his death. Those caliphs who followed lacked his interest in books, and this room had been forgotten.

Pocketing the book, I had locked the door and piled the manuscripts into their original position. Many of the manuscripts were duplicates of others already translated, and it might be years before they were again disturbed.

Military art had been a major interest of mine, and the book I now held was a treasure. Such a book might easily win a man a kingdom. It might also blow high the walls of the castle of the Baron de Tournemine.

I had safely hidden it in another section of the library and had earlier in the week dared sneak into the great mosque to remove it for further study. Now I read this book once more, for it was my intention to commit the entire book to memory. The formula, which was the core and essence of the book, I had memorized within ten minutes of opening it for the first time, but there were other items of importance.

Yet I could not concentrate. My ears tuned to the slightest sound from the dark street outside, and I finally tucked the book inside my shirt and put out my candle.

For some time I sat in the dark with a naked sword upon my knees, then suddenly I was sharply alert, listening.

Something or someone had fallen in the street outside. I heard hoarse panting and a sound of something dragging. A faint moaning, as of someone in dire pain, came to me, and I opened the door wider, the oiled hinges making no sound.

"Kerbouchard! *Help me!*"

It was Safia. Staggering to her feet she half fell across the threshold. Catching her with my free hand, I eased her to the floor. Sheathing my sword, I knelt beside her.

"*Go!*" she whispered. "They are coming! They made me talk, and they will kill you, they—!"

Despite the risk I lit the candle. Her robe was soaked with blood, and she had been beaten until the flesh was cut to the bone in places, and her feet were a pulp from a terrible beating upon the soles.

"They believe me dead. I could not let you—but go! I release you from your promise. I had no right—"

Slinging the sack which contained maps and some precious books over my shoulder, I wrapped her in a fresh robe and picked her up.

Moving might kill her, but if found here, she would certainly be slain. Crawling through the window, I drew her to the wall beside me, then closed the window. Risking a fall, I carried her along the wall in utter darkness, leaves brushing my face and my clothing.

At the stable the horses were undisturbed. Saddling two and putting halters on the others, I tied Safia into her saddle and led the horses outside, closing the door behind me.

The night was cool, almost cold. The great arches of the aqueduct threw shadows upon the pavement. Tonight I would leave Córdoba. Would I ever return? It was a city I loved, and although it had taken much from me, it had given more.

The ride would be brutal. It might kill Safia, but we had no choice. Riding in the shadows, I went to the postern gate. As I had hoped, there was no guard. Ignoring her moaning as she became conscious, I rode for the hills, stopping for nothing. What Safia had done to warrant the torture I neither knew nor cared. Whatever it was had ended disastrously.

Before daylight I found a hollow beside a small stream. Taking Safia from her horse, I went to work. Not for nothing had I read the *Canon* of Avicenna and other great teachers of medicine. I bathed her wounds, using what medicines I had in my own small kit. Treating her lacerated back, I bound up her wounds.

She had lost blood and was unconscious while I treated her. The sight of her feet horrified me. It had taken more courage than a person had a right to possess for her to come to warn me on such feet. The sun was high in the sky before I ceased to work, nor was there any way of judging how successful I had been. Now all rested in the lap of Allah.

Safia was drawn and pale, and when her eyes opened, it was only to stare wildly about and plead for water. There was grass for the horses, and water, but we could not long remain here. Toward nightfall she became conscious, so I could feed her some soup.

Once more I tied her in the saddle. I was taking her by a roundabout route to the cave where long ago I had fought the Visigoth.

It was a lonely place, but the cave was hidden, and there was water. We could hide there until Safia was well or until she died.

At daylight, after concealing the horses on some grass among the willows, and while Safia slept, I took my sword and bow to prowl about. In a small copse I found a few of Akim's sheep banded together with one big old ram for protection. I put an arrow into a lamb that strayed from the flock and, butchering it, carried the meat back to the cave.

Later, following the stream, I found another cave, larger, roomier, still better hidden, so I moved us there.

Treating Safia was the first test of my medical knowledge and a severe test for a more experienced man than I. However, Safia began, slowly, to recover. First, hers was a struggle for life, then for health, and mine was a struggle for our very existence. The food kept with the horses was soon gone, but the sheep seemed glad to have me about. If they noticed the inroads upon their number, it was no more than they expected.

Some of Akim's crops had seeded themselves, and I found a little barley, some fruit the birds had not eaten, and once I killed a wild boar.

Several parties of riders appeared, and one rode to the ruins of Akim's place, but I had erased all evidence, and they found nothing.

When Safia could sit up and fend for herself, it became easier, for I could go further afield to forage for food and the herbs needed to treat her.

Trouble came without warning. Three mercenary soldiers rode up to the cave just as I was mounted to ride away. I saw them the instant before they saw me and drew my sword, keeping the left side of my horse toward them, my sword resting on my knee, point forward.

No doubt they thought me some peasant, easily frightened, for when they rode up one said, "Get off that horse, or you will have a split skull."

The third man who held back somewhat said, "Rig, see what's in the cave. I think we've found ourselves a woman."

Unmoving, I sat my horse, and the first speaker started for me just as Rig started to swing down. Touching a spur to my Arab, I leaped the horse at him, knocking him to the ground. At the same time my sword came from behind the barrel of my horse.

My sudden lunge at the dismounting soldier had brought me up on the left of the first man. He threw up his arm, and he had no shield, and the edge of my blade cut deep into his arm and shoulder.

Our horses were pressed together, and commanding my horse with my knees, I thrust my sword into his side.

The third man was fleeing, but sheathing my sword, I leaped my Arab after him, bringing up my bow with an arrow ready. His heavier, slower horse was no match for mine, and I overtook him swiftly, unleashing an arrow that shot him through. Catching up his horse, I despoiled him of armor and weapons and returned to the cave.

The man whom I had knocked down was no longer in sight, but I had no doubt where he was. Dismounting, sword in hand, I entered the cave.

Safia was against the wall, her dagger in her hand.

"You are a fool," she was saying. "He will kill you!"

"Maybe, but I shall have you first."

He leaped at her, but instead of using the dagger as he expected, she struck him across the face with a brand from the fire. His attention had been concentrated on the knife, and he had not seen the glowing stick she held down beside her. The swing through the air ignited flame, and he sprang back. It was not my fault that he fell against the point of my sword, although maybe I did push, just a little. If a man is determined to die, who am I to fly in the face of destiny?

"We were lucky," I said.

"Yes," she admitted, "but you have skill, also."

Our venture of the morning had been rewarding. We now had three more horses, three helmets, two coats of mail and a breastplate, daggers, swords, and some other gear. There were only four dinars between them, but we had money of our own. Yet it was time to move.

During the long days in the cave Safia had taught me more Persian than the little I had learned, and also some Hindi. Born in Basra, daughter of an emir by a slave girl, she had been given a fine education and betrothed to a Bengali prince. His death left her alone, but in Baghdad she married one of the old Abbasid dynasty and engaged in intrigue to seize the caliphate of Córdoba for him. Failing in that, she had become a spy, selling information to all who could pay.

It was now four months since our flight from Córdoba, and although her body was wasted from the long illness, she was now fit to ride. The soles of her feet remained so tender she could walk only a few steps.

Often when bathing in the pool or prowling the ruins of Akim's farm I wondered how Sharasa fared. Had she done well? Where was she now?

Resuming the battered armor of a mercenary, but armed better than before, I led back to the road, but this time we traveled away from Córdoba.

"There is a man in Constantinople," Safia said, "who might know of your father. It is he you must find."

We sold our captured horses as well as the armor and weapons. The four horses Safia had acquired originally we kept. We were not apt to find their equal.

Safia had given me her jewels to store safely back in Córdoba, and I had remembered to bring them, but we hoped not to touch them. Riding in the fresh, clean air was raising color in her cheeks, and the dead, lackluster expression of her eyes was gone. Outside Toledo we met a group of travelers and joined our force to theirs. Now that we would be traveling beyond the areas controlled by the Moslems, we would be in even greater danger. Banditry existed in Moslem territories now, too, since the breakup into many small *taifas*.

It was in Zaragoza that we met Rupert von Gilderstern, a mountain of a man, at least two inches taller than I and many pounds heavier. His huge face both long and wide, possessed a beak of a nose and two chins. Although he looked fat, he gave no impression of softness, and despite his massive size he moved with ease and grace. He spoke with the voice of an oracle and the commanding presence of a god.

Arriving at a wayside inn, we found the courtyard filled with packhorses and mules. Standing wide-legged at one side of the court was a man the like of whom I had never seen. "We will have the packs off. Check your beasts for scratches, wounds, or abrasions. We will have no animals unfit to bear burdens here."

He ignored our arrival and looked at no one. He spoke strongly and clearly. "Look to their hocks, check their hooves for stones. Brush down the hair upon their backs, a lump of twisted hair can cause chafing. No man will see to himself until his beasts are cared for."

Obviously, we had encountered a merchant caravan, and this huge man was the *Hansgraf* or captain of the train. Such caravans took merchandise up and down and across Europe, traveling by age-old trade routes dating from ancient times, long before the Romans. Some followed the old Amber road that led from the Baltic to the Mediterranean over which amber had been taken to the pharaohs of Egypt, to Solomon himself, and to Hiram of Tyre.

These parties of merchants, bound together by an oath of fidelity, were well-armed, prepared to resist attack by brigands, or *Raubritter*. There were barons who charged down from their castles hoping to plunder a caravan. Many a castle was lookout for such as these.

The *Hansgraf*'s caravan of the White Company of traders was a rich one, and immediately I realized this could be our salvation. Our route led eastward through mountain passes where danger lurked, yet with such a caravan we might travel safely.

Choosing an empty corner of the yard, I unsaddled and tended my horses, and no horse in the yard could compare to ours.

Several times I saw the eyes of the *Hansgraf* upon me, or glancing from me to Safia, who stood nearby. When my animals were cared for, I gathered my weapons and went inside.

A dozen men were seated about the table, eating and drinking, several of them already drunk. They stared at Safia as she entered, and one spoke aloud in the Frankish tongue, an insulting phrase that Safia did not understand.

Reaching across the table, I took him by the beard, the worst of insults in a Moslem country, and dragged him across the table. Jerking down on his beard, I shoved a handful of grease and suet into his opened mouth.

"Keep your filthy mouth shut," I said, "or next time I'll force a sheep down your throat."

Wiping the grease from my hand on his shirtfront, I released him and shoved hard, toppling him back over the bench choking and gagging.

Two of the others, flushed with drink, half started to rise. "The lady," I told them, "will be treated as such. If you wish to take issue with me, I shall split your skulls like melons."

We chose a table at the far side of the room, and I saw the loud-mouthed one stagger to the door, gagging. It would be a while before he wagged his tongue over another woman.

Glancing up, I saw the *Hansgraf* looking across the room at me.

We ordered up a bottle of wine and a chunk of roast beef and settled down to eat. Safia had recovered except for her too tender feet, and the cool air had given her a fine appetite.

A shadow loomed beside our table. It was the *Hansgraf*. "Nobly done! That swine was well served. Do you travel far?"

Gesturing to the bottle, I said, "A noble wine, *Hansgraf*, will you join us?"

"A moment, at least."

He seated himself, and again I was amazed at the size of him. He must have weighed half again my own weight. He was clad in black: black hose and black tall boots, a black cloak over all.

"You are a soldier?"

"Of fortune," I said, "a fighting man, if necessary, but something of a scholar as well. I travel eastward," I added, "and the lady Safia travels to her home in Shiraz."

"It is a far place." He measured me again with appraising eyes. "Do you have capital to invest? Ours is a merchant company, our goods bought and sold in common, profits shared. If you would like to join us, we can use strong men."

"Would I share with the company?"

"You would be one of us. Your sword must be ours, also. We will have need of swords, I believe."

"And your route?"

"By way of Pamplona to Pau and Avignon. We go eastward but by way of the fairs."

So it was that I, who had been a scholar, a geographer, and perhaps a physician, became a merchant.

A merchant with a sword.

25

The tawny hills lay like sleeping lions along the narrow track. Far ahead, leading the convoy, was the *schildrake*, or standard-bearer. Behind him rode six armed men, selected for their skill with weapons, and then the *Hansgraf* himself.

The caravan was made up of nearly five hundred pack animals, mostly horses and mules but cattle also. These last would be eaten when their packs were sold or shifted to mules. They walked in pairs because the track was narrow, with armed guards along the flanks of the column.

Four women accompanied them, and there were sixty-two men, hardened by constant travel and intermittent warfare. All were shareholders in the venture, and in von Gilderstern they had a very superior commander who maintained sharp discipline. If any failed to live up to standard, he was dropped at once. His goods were purchased, and he was left wherever they happened to be.

That morning Gilderstern had stood with his feet planted upon the earth and stared at me, hands on hips. The stance was typical, I was to learn. "You are a Celt?"

"From Armorica, in Brittany, near the sands of Brignogan."

"I know the place. And the woman? She is not your wife?"

"She is a lady to whom I am indebted. And she *is* a lady."

"I assumed as much. Tell me, and no offense intended. Is she well-behaved?"

"As man to man, yes. We are friends. Good friends,

but no more than friends. Also," I added, "she may be of
much value. She is a lady who deals in information. She
was at the center of things in Córdoba until enemies
caught up with her. I helped her escape as she had once
helped me."

The *Hansgraf* nodded. "We go north to Montauban,
then to the fairs of Flanders, back to those of the
Champagne. It could be a year before we reach the sea."
He glanced at me sharply. "You were ready to fight. Are
you a quarrelsome man?"

"I am not."

"For your information, we are like a family here, in
loyalty, in cooperation. All quarrels or disagreements are
settled by me. At any time you are not satisfied or prove
less than you need to be, we will buy you out, and you go
your way.

"The company protects all its members, and all trading companies stand ready to aid each other."

Under gray skies we moved forward. The great fairs
of Flanders and the Champagne attracted merchants from
all the countries of Europe. The honor of being the oldest
fair was believed to belong to St. Denis, but there were
fairs at Ypres, Lille, and Bruges almost as old as St. Denis.
The greatest of the Flanders fairs was at Ghent.

By the earliest years of the twelfth century the fairs at
Bar and Troyes as well as those at Lagny and Provins were
long established, and those in Champagne had become
the money marts of Europe, clearinghouses for debts contracted in all Christian and many Moslem lands.

Fairs lasted from three to six weeks, and it was customary for merchant caravans to travel from one fair to the
next. Large fairs operated at Cambrai, Château-â Thierry,
and Châlons-sur-Marne.

The laws of the lands had given many unique privi-
leges to the fairs and the merchants who attended them,
all with a view toward attracting trade. Merchants doing
business at the fairs operated under a special *conduit*,
under protection of the ruler of the land through which
they traveled. A special group of armed men, the "guards

of the fairs," maintained order, and a letter bearing their seal assured safety to all who bore them.

No merchant traveling to or from a fair could be held for any debt contracted outside the fair, and all were free from fear of arrest for any crime dating from an earlier period.

The right to play cards or roll dice on saints' days was also permitted to the people of the caravans.

The greatest route was that which we were about to follow, from Provence to the coast of Flanders, to Champagne, to Cologne, Frankfort, Leipzig and Lubeck in Germany, and then perhaps on to Kiev or Novgorod, ending our trade in Constantinople.

The company, the word taken from *com-panis*, meaning bread-sharer, had come into being to share perils of travel at a time when the roads were beset with brigands, robber barons, and armies of warlike monks who left their monasteries to attack and pillage caravans.

The first merchants had apparently been landless men, the drifters and adventurers that arise from any population in ferment. Often they were younger sons, outcasts who acquired money through local trade or were financed by officials of the church with secret loans. Some began as peddlers or hawkers in the towns, and acquiring a stock of goods, they took to the highways with others of their kind.

One of the merchants who rode ahead of me dropped back to talk. He was a thin, hawk-faced man from Lombardy named Lucca. "You have done well," he said. "Von Gilderstern is the best *Hansgraf* on the road. In Swabia last year he began his own fair at a river crossing, for he can smell a market as other men smell a flagon of mead. Our wealth is rarely idle, or our hands, either."

Lucca glanced at me. "The word is that you are a scholar? What manner of scholar?"

A fair question. What kind of scholar was I? Or was I a scholar at all? My ignorance was enormous. Beside it my knowledge was nothing. My hunger for learning, not so much to improve my lot as to understand my world, had led me to study and to thought. Reading without thinking is as nothing, for a book is less important for what it says than for what it makes you think.

"A good question," I replied, "but I am merely a seeker after knowledge, taking the world for my province, for it seems all knowledge is interrelated, and each science is dependent to some extent on the others. We study the stars that we may know more about our earth, and herbs that we may know medicine better."

"You are a physician?"

"A little of one. So far I have had more experience in the giving of wounds than the healing of them."

"If it is experience you wish, you will have your fill of both. We often deal with robbers who barter with a sword."

"Then we will give them fair trade." A thought came to me. "Is there not a fair in Brittany, then?"

"A small one, perhaps. Sometimes we go to St. Malo, but there is a robber baron there who ranges far afield."

"Tournemine? Would that be the name, by chance?"

"By chance it is. You know the man?"

"Does he carry a scar upon his face? So?"

"He does, and I wish it were his throat."

Placing my hand upon my dagger, I said, "This point put it there. He killed my mother, all our people. If we go that way, I may pay him a visit."

"Alone?"

"How else? These past years I have remembered him."

"We must talk to the *Hansgraf* of this."

A spatter of rain began to fall as I rode back along the column. We topped the rise and looked upon a fair valley, masked now with rain, at the far end the gray tower of a castle. It was a lonely and forbidding sight, with the Pyrenees beyond, their crests lost in clouds.

A slashing rain began to fall, but we pushed on as there was an inn ahead with a large stable where many of us could sleep.

Safia was hunched in her saddle but looked up when I came alongside. "I like the rain," she said. "It is good to feel it on my face."

"Enjoy it then, for we shall soon be inside."

We were tired and looked forward to the inn with pleasure. A pot of mulled wine, a loaf, and a bit of cheese—I was learning how easily one could be content. Yet I sorely missed my books, for there had been no time to turn a page since leaving Zaragoza. Ahead was the mountain pass of Roncevalles famous for the *Song of Roland*.

"The castle yonder?" Safia said. "Do you know whose it is?"

"It is an ugly place. I like it not."

"It belongs to Prince Ahmed. You are in his lands now."

What was it he had said at the party of Valaba? *These are your domains, but I understand that Kerbouchard likes to travel.*

My eyes strayed to the castle. I was a fool to put myself in my enemy's hands. "He must not learn that I am here," I said, "I must tell the *Hansgraf*."

Leaving Safia, I galloped swiftly to the head of the train and explained the situation.

Von Gilderstern sat his horse like a monument, looking down the valley toward the inn. "You have done well to tell me of this at once. What have you in mind?"

"To ride for the mountains. I see no reason to implicate you in my affairs."

"A noble thought, but a foolish one. In those mountains lurk brigands who await travelers. Remain with us. You are one of us now, and your troubles have become our troubles."

He changed the subject. "Lucca informs me you know the Baron de Tournemine. Do you know his castle?"

"I know it. I rode there with my father when he told the baron the limits of his power. The baron did not like it."

"An evil man, but a strong one. Under the pretense of keeping order he rides far afield to demand tribute, and he makes war upon merchants."

"I shall seek him out."

"We will talk of this again, in the meantime be assured that our company stands with you."

The gray towers loomed ominously through the rain. I had no doubt that we were watched, for such a body of men would be immediately reported.

Beyond the village, which was a cluster of houses, was a huge old inn. There was a court with a strong wall and wooden gates that could be closed against attack. Our burdens would be taken inside the court while the animals would, for a time, graze upon the meadows. On such a night as this all would stand guard in groups of twenty men each.

Prince Ahmed, Lucca told us, was rarely here, and he had protected the caravans that passed through his domains, occasionally trading with them.

The *Hansgraf* drew up by the gate and sat on his powerful horse. He rarely made gestures, but each was a command. I have never known a man who better understood his role. He accepted rights due him without comment or apology, and he made the responsibilities of command seem a privilege.

The pack animals were stripped of their packs and led at once to the meadow, but the horses of the guards were kept inside and grain fed, ready for instant use.

The *Hansgraf*, erect upon his horse, directed all arrangements with movements as skilled as those of an artist at his canvas. "You," he said as I passed, "the four hours after midnight."

They were the only words he spoke during the whole process of arrival.

This was a nightly affair for these men, and few directions were necessary. Many had visited this inn before, and the business of arrival, unloading, storing, and disposition of the animals was simple indeed.

By now I knew most of the company, but aside from the easygoing Lucca the one I knew best was a lantern-jawed man named Johannes, from Bruges. His history as a merchant was typical. A landless man, born in Bruges and left an orphan by the plague, he had begged, struggled, and fought his way to manhood. On a voyage at sea he helped in the capture of a prize and came ashore with a little money in hand.

Inland there was famine; at the port there was grain, so he bought both mules and grain and carried them inland and sold his grain for a good price. Everything was raised on a local scale, and there was no transportation away from the rivers, so famine might exist only a few days' travel from an area of plenty.

A new class of citizen had come into being in what had been an exclusively agricultural society. The old ways when a few strong chieftains held all the land about them, and serfs worked for them, were changing. A new kind of wealth and a new means of creating wealth were being evolved. Merchants thrived on discontent. They brought to people things they needed but also created new desires by displaying cosmetics, fabrics, silks, jewels, and many simpler items.

Guido was a peasant from the Piedmont. His family had been wiped out by war. A young boy at the time, he had drifted with the refugees before an invading army and had come at last to Florence. For the first time he saw a ship, saw men coming ashore with modest wealth, so he shipped out.

His voyage ended in the Greek isles, his ship sunk, a few castaways reaching shore. They had stolen a boat, raided a village, and gone off to sea again. His second voyage ended in failure, but the third was a success. He gambled, lost all but a few pennies, but with that small sum he bought candles to sell to pilgrims and went from that to furnishing others with goods to sell. A few years later he joined a merchant caravan.

The first companies of merchants I had been told had been little better than brigands. Made up of ne'er-do-wells, vagabonds, and thieves, they robbed and pillaged as they traded. Order entered the enterprise; the fairs were organized, and companies of merchants became a recognized institution.

The inn was large, but when we crowded into it, forty

strong plus our five women, the room was no longer
spacious. One third of our men were with the animals in
the meadow or on guard about the walls. Other travelers
were present. A friar on a pilgrimage, the prioress of a
convent with a small escort and two nuns, a pair of soldiers returning from the wars, and a cattle drover who had
just sold his stock.

It was hot and stuffy inside. The wet clothing of our
men steamed. The room itself was none too clean, but the
food was, and there was plenty of it.

I approached Safia as she sat resting. "To bring you to
this? I am sorry."

"I have known this before, Kerbouchard. Not here,
but in Persia, in my own land. Do not worry, all will be
well."

The door opened suddenly and we all looked up.
Quickly, I looked down again. Several soldiers had come
into the room, and the officer commanding the soldiers
was Duban. I glanced about for a way to escape. There
was none.

In a moment he would see me.

He turned his eyes and stared directly into mine.

And in his look there was recognition.

26

He crossed the room, and I arose to face him. As I stood, Johannes placed his sword upon the table before him, as did Guido. Duban did not fail to see them.

"You have friends," he commented. His eyes were not unfriendly.

"Good friends," I replied. "And you, Duban?"

"I am a captain. I serve and am served. It were a better thing if you did not stop here this night. There is a small inn at the entrance to the pass. I would advise it."

"Duban, I am now a merchant, and a merchant travels with his *hanse*. Your prince threatened me. He imprisoned me, but I am a patient man."

"You do not search for Aziza?"

"No."

His eyes searched my face for the truth, and it was there if he was the man to see it.

"Your prince has chosen to be my enemy. So far I am not his. But tell him this, if you will: that if I become his enemy, I shall not rest until he is dead, but he must await his turn. I have an older enemy."

"You are a bold man, Kerbouchard, a fit son for the father."

I bowed. "I have far to go to equal Jean Kerbouchard, and far to go to find him. Meanwhile I am *your* friend."

Duban held out his hand. "Farewell, then. May fortune favor your sword."

As he walked away from me there was a sound of sheathed blades; then for a moment I thought them

sheathed too soon, for the door of the inn opened and
Aziza entered.

She was not alone. With her were several women and
a half-dozen eunuchs. She was beautiful, a little rounder,
and possibly even lovelier than I remembered, but her
face had a stillness I did not remember.

Duban had no opportunity to warn her, and her eyes
met mine across the room. Met mine, hesitated briefly,
then passed on. Aziza had made her peace with her new
life and had forgotten the Castle of Othman.

And I? Well, not exactly. I remembered the Castle of
Othman. This tribute have I always paid to women. I have
not forgotten.

What greater tribute than to remember a woman at
her loveliest? And in her moments of enthusiasm?

When I seated myself beside Safia, her eyes twinkled
slyly. "She was, well, restrained."

"Why not? I am a vagabond in dusty armor, and she
the wife of a prince." Pausing a bit, I added, "I hope all
the women I know do as well.

"Safia, I think no man should ask more than the
moments. He should accept what the gods offer and make
no demands upon the future."

"I think a day will come when you will make demands,
Kerbouchard."

On that I had no comment, for the future is the
future, and I place no trust in the reading of the stars. And
do we not all look for the time when there is *one* girl, or
for women, one man, who does not pass on?

Safia? She alone was unreadable, beautiful again, and
a mystery forever. She was soft and lovely as a *houri* out of
paradise, yet quiet, with much of the queen in her presence.
There was steel in her, a command of herself and those
about her such as I had seen in no other woman. For the
first time since the death of her Bengali prince, she was
now cared for, protected, and I believe she liked it.

On the next morning as we rode away, I turned in my
saddle and glanced back at the sullen gray walls of the

castle. On the west side of the tower I could see some blue domes and near them a flat-roofed dwelling.

Farewell, Aziza, farewell . . . what was it my acquaintance in the Cádiz tavern had said so long ago? *Yol bolsun!* May there be a road!

How passed the days? How the weeks? Northward we moved, ever northward, occasionally pausing at fairs, occasionally trading at castle or town. Twice were we attacked by brigands, and once there was a swift raid when a *Raubritter* swept down upon us.

We lost a man that day, but we had seen them coming and had twenty bowmen waiting in a ditch and behind a hedge. Seven attackers left their saddles at the first flight of arrows, and then we closed with them.

The *Raubritter*, a huge man in black armor, charged my part of the line, and I rode to meet him. He dealt me a mighty blow on the helm that swept me from the saddle, the first time I had been unhorsed. Shocked and raging, my head ringing from the blow, I sprang at him. He missed a hasty stroke, which left him off-balance, and I jerked him from the saddle. On the ground, blade to blade, we fought on the wet sward, rain falling upon us.

He was a strong swordsman and sure of victory. My Frankish upbringing had taught me much, but the Moors were adept at single combat, and soon I was pressing him hard. He thrust at me in a feint, then flicked his sword up at my eyes and nicked my cheekbone, showering me with blood.

Our blades engaged, then disengaged, and I thrust at his throat. My blade laid open his face, and with a quick twist, not bringing the blade back to guard position, I cut across his throat, but only a scratch.

My head was throbbing from the blow I had taken, and my legs, strong as they were, were tiring. He missed a strong blow at me, and I cut back with my Damascus blade, which was steel that was truly steel, and the edge bit through his helmet. He staggered back as a final thrust finished him.

Turning, I saw we were surrounded by our men, and they gave me a round cheer.

My legs were trembling, and Safia came to stanch the blood from my cheek, where ever after I would carry the scar. The blood worried me less than the realization that had he dealt me such a blow with a sword like mine, I would now be lying dead upon the wet grass. I had been careless, dangerously careless.

With the *Raubritter* dead we attacked the castle, rushing upon it before the drawbridge could be lifted. It was my first opportunity to see how my companions functioned as a fighting unit, for compared to this our other fighting had been mere skirmishes. Sweeping through the castle halls, they put to the sword all who resisted. We found several village women who had been captives there and freed them. We left the pigs and fowls for their enrichment but thoroughly looted what else there was of value. The *Raubritter* had long terrorized the country around, and the villages greeted us as saviors.

Day after day we moved north. The fair at Montauban lay behind us, and the next was far away. We would cross the Seine, von Gilderstern told us, at Mantes.

It was a place I knew, for William the Conqueror had been killed there when his horse tripped on a burning brand. William had massacred the male population of the town, which he then claimed for his own.

We camped on the Vilaine not far from Rennes on a pleasant night with scattered stars. Looking about me I thought, *This is my land; these are my people*.

A peasant squatted by our fire and his face had a vaguely familiar look. Finally, it came to me. He was from the holdings of Tournemine. There was a shifty look in his eyes, his hair matted and dirty.

As he had not noticed me, I walked quickly to where the *Hansgraf* sat over a glass of mulled wine.

"Unless I mistake him, he is a spy. I suggest we have half a dozen of our men appear sick and appear careless. If so, we may draw an attack by Tournemine."

The *Hansgraf* considered while he drank, then agreed.

Within minutes twenty of us were rolled in our beds, and we watched the peasant as he nosed about, then saw him slip silently away. Later, we heard a horse galloping into the night, a horse he must have left waiting for him.

My admiration for the *Hansgraf* was never greater than now, for he moved with swiftness. How far off the enemy awaited we did not know. We laid our bundles of goods out to appear as sleeping men, and the fires were supplied with wood to keep them burning.

Men were sent out to warn of Tournemine's approach while several of us guarded the women, our goods, and men wounded in the fight with the *Raubritter*.

They came with a rush.

We heard the thunder of their hooves, coming with a suddenness intended to overwhelm at one stroke. All must have appeared serene and simple to them, for they charged pell-mell, thrusting swords or spears into what they thought were sleeping men. In that moment when all was confusion our men let fly a flight of arrows.

Tournemine, veteran fighter that he was, saw the trap at once, and even as the arrows were loosed he shouted for a withdrawal.

The arrows struck home, and we charged from a copse where we had been hiding. A huge man in armor loomed over me, swinging a battle-ax. His blow, enough to have cut me through side to side, missed. My swift Arab horse darted past him, and I swung a wicked backhand blow with my sword.

It caught him where intended, on the side of the neck where there was no armor. The ax dropped from his dead hand, and his horse galloped away, the man's head dangling. The shouts of men and the clang of weapon upon weapon were loud in the night.

How long? A minute? Two minutes? In all this time I caught no glimpse of Tournemine.

We gathered together as planned, thirty strong, and pursued, overtaking two stragglers whom we cut down, then fearing another attack, we circled back to our camp.

We lost no men and had but four with minor wounds. The attackers lost four men at camp and two out on the plain. We captured three wounded prisoners, and five horses were taken.

The *Hansgraf* strode among them. He was a monumental figure of a man, and now he stared at the prisoners, glaring first at one and then another. "Now, thieves," he said, "I have it in mind to hang you for the ravens. There are strong branches here, and we came provided with rope. It is hanging long delayed.

"Or shall it be fire? What think you, Lucca? Shall it be fire?" He pointed a finger. "The fat one yonder would make a merry blaze. Can you not see him frying in his own grease?"

"You might run a lance through him," Johannes said seriously, "and turn him over the fire as on a spit. I saw it done in the Holy Land, and you have no idea how long it takes them to die."

"Perchance they have something to tell," Guido suggested. "No use to burn them if they talk."

"Bah!" Lucca said. "They know nothing? Burn them!"

The fat man stared from one to the other, his features twisted by fear and horror. The second kept shifting his eyes, glancing from side to side, licking his dry lips. The third was a sullen rascal who glared his contempt. We would have nothing from him.

"What could they tell? Tournemine's castle is impregnable."

"Hang them, or burn them and be done with it," I said, "Tournemine's castle is too far from here to be worth the riding. Open their bellies and leave them. They will die slow enough then."

Our talk was having the effect we wished. Two of them were thoroughly frightened. The fat man kept swallowing as if he felt the noose tightening.

"There would be nothing at the castle worth the riding," Lucca said, "and we haven't time for a siege."

"There's loot!" the fat man said suddenly. "There's the goods of two caravans taken last week and of a household raided. I tell you there is plenty!"

"Shut up, you fool!" The sullen one spoke in a fury. "I'll smash your skull for this!"

"You will smash no skulls," the *Hansgraf* said. "If you live out the hour, it will be because of my whim, and I am not given to whims." He thrust a finger at the fat man. "Hang him!" he ordered.

"*Please!*" The fat man screamed, wetting himself in his terror. "I told you! And there's the postern—"

The sullen one sprang at him, but the *Hansgraf*, with amazing speed, grasped him by the hair and flung him back into place. "If you move or speak, I shall run you through myself." He drew his sword. "Now then"—he spoke to the fat man—"you mentioned the postern gate?"

There was a postern gate needing repair. It could not be closed properly, and it was on a dark side of the castle near the woods.

The fat man talked freely, as did the other. When they were through we had a clear picture of what lay before us.

"How many are in the castle," I said, "who plundered the manor of Kerbouchard?"

There was instant stillness, the eyes of all three were upon me. If frightened before, they were doubly so now.

"Kerbouchard is dead," the fat man said.

"He lives," I replied, "and soon he returns. Now an answer to my question."

"It was long ago. Several years ago. It was before my time."

The surly one was staring at me, his eyes alive with alarm for the first time.

The second prisoner pointed at him. "He was there. Ask him."

"You were not?"

"I was left behind at the castle."

The sullen one was staring at the ground now, but sweat stood out on his neck and brow. "Kerbouchard is dead," he muttered.

"He lives," I said, "and I am his son."

"Hah! The cub! The old wolf's cub!"

"He was there when they murdered your mother," the *Hansgraf* said. "Lucca, Guido, hang him!"

We left twenty men with the goods and the women. The rest of us, strong men all, mounted to ride. We rode swiftly through the night, striking a route I well knew that would take us through the dark forest of Huelgoat, a much faster way than that taken by Tournemine.

Forty men, we rode through the night, pausing for a quick meal and a nap in the dawn light. Our mounts, toughened by long marches, carried us swiftly. Each had brought an extra horse, and we changed mounts repeatedly.

Our two prisoners rode with us.

Johannes had been riding behind, and on the third morning he caught up to us. "We are followed," he warned. "Perhaps thirty riders."

"Tournemine?"

"I think not. It looks like Peter."

We turned off the road to wait, weapons ready. Suddenly, the *Hansgraf* uttered a sharp exclamation and rode out of the trees.

The short, square man riding at the head of the column thrust out his hand. "Rupert! By all that is holy!"

They clasped hands, and Peter said, "We met one of your men, and he guided us to the caravan. We left half our force there and have ridden to overtake you. If my brother wishes to take a castle, then I wish to take a castle."

I was amazed. "They are brothers?" I asked Johannes.

"Rupert would make three of him, would he not? But Peter is a first-class fighting man and a good trader. He learned from Rupert."

We rode on, nearly seventy strong, and as evening

came, we halted on the crest of a hill, looking across a brown-green valley at the Castle of Tournemine.

The site was a pleasant one, a low knoll in the midst of a valley protected from the sea winds and the chill of the high plains. It was an ancient site, rebuilt and occupied by the Tournemines.

Dismounting at the edge of the wood, we waited for the sun to go down. Around the castle there was no movement nor any sign that we had been discovered.

"If that postern gate can be opened," Johannes said, "we shall be soon inside."

"No matter," I said, "I know the way. I can take us into the fortress tonight."

27

The Castle of Tournemine was little more than a camp walled in stone. More often such places were built on natural or artificial hills surrounded by a deep ditch and were usually built of heavy timber.

The site in this case was of an old Roman station, and some initial stonework had been done. Tournemine had come to the spot with a following of landless adventurers, built the wall into an ovoid shell some thirty feet high, and inside the shell erected a round tower approximately one hundred feet in height.

Only once had I been inside that castle wall, and once inside the keep. I had gone with my father to issue a warning to the baron, accompanied by only a dozen horsemen. No more were necessary. The name of Jean Kerbouchard was a known one, and six of his galleys with upwards of five hundred fighting men lay alongshore.

Tournemine, but lately arrived, had been raiding about the country, and we came to issue a warning.

Tournemine was a black-browed man and his features darkened with a fury he dared not express as we strode into the keep. All about were the men of Tournemine, yet he knew if one arrow were loosed, the men of Kerbouchard would see his fortress razed to the ground.

My father was not one for diplomacy. He walked to the table where Tournemine sat and drew a rough outline of Brittany with a piece of charcoal from the fireplace. He marked upon it the position of Tournemine's camp. It was near the village of Plancoet, not far from the sea at St. Malo.

Taking the charcoal, he drew a line north to south across Brittany and through the camp of Tournemine. "If you dare to raid west of that line I shall come back here and hang you from your own battlements."

Tournemine's face was rigid with mingled anger and fear, but my father was a man to make men tremble.

My father picked up the table, and with his own hands he broke off the legs and tossed them aside. Picking up the table with its rude sketch, he placed it on the mantle above the fireplace.

"Leave it there," my father said. "If I ever hear it has been taken down, I shall come back to see you. Do you understand?"

Tournemine, his jaw stiff, struggled for the words. "I understand," he muttered.

From that day forward, each time he returned from a voyage my father inquired about the table, and each time it was reported to be in position. Tournemine, day after day, had to face that table and stare at that which remained a mute indication of his limits, his smallness. Only when my father was reported lost at sea had he taken it down; only then dared he raid to the westward.

"If we cannot enter through the postern," I said to the *Hansgraf*, "there is another way. I have seen Johannes throw a spear. If he could throw one over the wall with a line attached to the middle of the spear, one of the lighter men could go up the wall carrying a heavier line."

"Exactly," Peter agreed. "If the falling spear did not alarm them and if it caught across an embrasure."

"It is worth a try," von Gilderstern agreed.

Slowly, shadows gathered. Darkness surrounded the trees under which we stood, and pressed in against the walls of the fortress. Fog drifted in from the sea, covering the lower valley.

How many men would be inside? Not many, for Tournemine had little to fear in this corner of Brittany. It was doubtful if he had even been threatened since my father went off to sea.

Ours was an old, old land and had known many

changes, its people evading trouble when possible, prepared to fight when it was not. The Celts had come six
hundred years before Christ, it was said, to mingle with
people already present.

The great stone monuments, the megaliths, and dolmens were already in place and had been so for centuries.
There were tombs here that were more than a thousand
years old before the first pyramid was built in Egypt.
When the Romans invaded they defeated the native peoples one by one, the Namnetti, the Redones, and the
Veneti. Finally, in 407 B.C. the Romans left, and raiding
by pirates began. In 460, the Celts, who centuries before
had gone to England, returned to give the land its name of
Brittany. They had returned from Great Britain to Little
Britain where many of the King Arthur legends took place.

Through all changes the people tilled their fields,
fished the wider fields of the sea, and fought when the
need arose. It was a harsh land and bred the kind of men
to whom the wastes of the sea were an invitation rather
than a threat.

When fear chained the mariners of Florence and Genoa
to their narrow seas, the Veneti and their kindred had
long sailed the dark waters of the Atlantic. The Irish
monks whom the Norsemen found waiting for them on
IceLand were only a few of those who ventured upon the
far waters. Many of the Bretons had become corsairs, as it
was a richer living than tilling thin soil or fishing.

Rain began to fall and I donned my helmet. Peter was
standing beside his horse, and Johannes came to take the
bridle of his.

The *Hansgraf* said, "Bring the prisoners to me."

When they stood before him, features faintly visible
in the darkness, he addressed them. "You have said the
postern is easily entered? Your lives may depend on what
happens in the next few minutes."

"I am sure of it!" the fat man protested. "If I could
speak to the guard—but there is not always a guard."

"Lucca, take ten men. Scratch on the postern, and if

there is a reply, let this man identify himself. If he does more, kill him.

"Peter, take Johannes and ten men who are agile and go over the wall. Whoever is first inside, swing wide the gates."

We moved into the darkness, muffling the sound of our going. It was a somber, frightening time as seventy armed men moved down a grassy slope and across the valley, our armor glistening from the rain. The fortress walls loomed dark and ominous. We saw no lights, hidden by the walls. How many awaited us? Ten? Thirty? A hundred?

My face felt the rain upon it. For the last time? I breathed deep of the damp, cool air, felt the firmness of my seat in the saddle, the good feeling of the sword hilt in my hand. There were no stars, only the glint of rain-wet metal.

How still the night! Where now was Aziza? Where Sharasa? And Valaba?

Did my mother lie warm in the earth? Did she know I rode to avenge her? Did she realize how often in the still hours of the night I thought of her? How I wished I might have been there to defend her, saved her perhaps, or died beside her?

Did she know I loved her still? If the dead live only in the memories of those they leave behind, then she would never die while I lived. I had not seen her die and for that I was grateful. To me she yet lived, only apart.

We rode to war. What matter if only a small war. Is the blade less sharp? The arrow less deadly? My blade this night would avenge not only my mother but my Arab teacher and all the others Tournemine had slain.

I am not a noble man. I am not really a brave man. I fight because the blade is my business and I have no other. Perhaps I fight because of the fury that comes over me when I am attacked. My motives are often less than they should be. I fear I am sometimes a trickster and a conniver, but, I told myself, tonight my blade would draw blood in a good cause.

What other choice was mine? I was a landless man,

and there was nothing lower, nothing less vulnerable. One was attached to a castle, serving some great lord, or one was nothing. We merchant venturers, we were the first of a new kind of man, creating a new kind of wealth.

We drew up, shivering a little, for the night was damp and chill, and stared up at the walls, which were very high. Guido, who had gone to the main gate, returned.

"Tournemine is here. They came back before us."

"So be it. The attack goes forward."

We moved down, side by side, no whisper between us. I glanced at Johannes with his spear. What had seemed a simple feat suddenly grew large and dangerous, for the wall was high, the outline of the battlements difficult to make out.

Johannes stepped down, and we cleared his line for him. He held the javelin, sighting at the wall, then he took several quick, running steps and threw it hard and high into the night.

We waited, holding our breaths, but there was no sound. Johannes took up the line and pulled on it until it was taut. The spear had fallen inside and was now caught across the embrasure, a lucky stroke, as it might have come through the embrasure point first.

Peter tied the heavier line to his waist; then taking the line in his hands, he began to walk up the wall. There was still no sound from within. Were they waiting for us with drawn blades?

Peter disappeared into the darkness above, and suddenly his line slackened and the heavier line shook with his signal. Instantly, I grasped the line and went up, hand over hand. My acrobatic training proved its value, and I climbed swiftly.

Almost at the embrasure I heard a gasp, then a body fell past me.

Swinging through the embrasure, I glimpsed Peter down on his face, whether dead or wounded I could not guess, and then a half-dozen men ran along the wall walk toward me.

There was no use being quiet now. I let out a savage yell: "A Kerbouchard!" And sprang at them.

My shout startled them, that unexpected but feared cry stopped them where they stood. The shock of that cry saved my life. I was closer behind Peter than expected, and that cry, so unexpected after all this time, brought Tournemine's men a shock. My blade leaped at them, and a sword came to meet it. I was in a desperate fight with the three closest men, but the walk was narrow, and all could not reach me at once.

Behind them and from the postern, which opened on the castle yard, there was a shout and a clash of blades. Again the men facing me faltered, and my thrust went by the blade of the nearest man, taking him in the throat, above his breastplate.

He went to his knees, interfering with those behind him. Again I shouted, "A Kerbouchard!" The old war cry of my father's men. It seemed to strike fear into those opposing me. I pushed forward, thrusting and slashing, and then Johannes was beside me.

He swung a great loop over the men before me and jerked it tight. One fell, another, his arm pinioned, could not lift a blade to stop mine.

Now our men were swarming over the wall, and from the yard I heard the great gates creak open. A fire sprang up, and someone tossed brush on the flames. Beyond them, firelight dancing on his scarred face, was my enemy.

Tournemine stood in the doorway of the keep, staring at the fight in the castle yard as if he could not believe what was happening. A glass was in one hand, a bottle in the other.

"A Kerbouchard!"

Down a ladder I went, and Tournemine sprang back and tried to close the door, but my shoulder struck it, and he fell back. I followed him through and faced him, at last.

"You are not he," he said; "you are not Kerbouchard."

"I am Kerbouchard, and you carry my mark on your face."

His fingers went to the scar, then dropped to his sword. "So I shall kill you at last!"

"No, Tournemine, I shall kill you. You have taken down the table."

He went white to the lips. How that insult must have rankled! How many nights he must have stared in hatred at the table he dared not move, that evidence of his submission, of his weakness.

Yet now he was confident. I was only the boy he had seen escape across the moors. He came at me, a smile of contempt on his lips, and I began with care, for he had the reputation of being a swordsman.

He turned my blade and lunged, but I parried his blow, and for an instant he was out of position. I could have killed him then, but his quick death would not satisfy me. So I struck him on the side of the face with the flat of my blade, a ringing blow that staggered him.

My taunt was deliberate, and in a burst of fury he came at me, and I was fighting for my life. Desperately, at times almost wildly, I fought off his rush. He nicked my wrist, narrowly missed my throat, and moved in steadily. Suddenly, I shifted my feet, feinting as I had been taught in Córdoba. He reacted instantly, according to pattern, and my point touched him over the eye. I felt the point touch bone, and blood showered over him. He drew back and I moved in, trying for his throat.

There was bleeding from my wrist, and I was afraid the blood would make my grasp of the hilt slippery. Outside, there were sounds of fighting, and we might yet be defeated, for the men of Tournemine must now outnumber our own small force.

How long did we fight? Who had the better blade? Up and down the room we fought, but then my constant training began to tell, the hours of training, the tumbling and acrobatics as well as my time at the oar. Also I saw that my Moorish tricks bothered Tournemine, for he knew them not.

To simply kill him was not enough. He must taste defeat, savor it like bitter ashes in his mouth. I wanted it there in his teeth. I wanted him to know, this man who murdered my mother, killed our family servants, and destroyed our home. I wanted him to taste defeat.

So I pressed Tournemine harder, relying upon the Moorish style of swordplay. My point touched his throat, drawing blood; then slashing down swiftly, I nicked his thigh. His steel mail prevented me from running him through the body, narrowing my target.

Coolly, deliberately, I began to teach him what he did not know. Sweat beaded his brow, mingling with the blood that trickled into one eye and down his cheek.

"You should keep to killing women, as you murdered my mother. You will die soon, Tournemine, and when you do I shall sink your body in the *Youdig* quagmire of the *Yeun Elez*."

He had lived in Brittany and knew the *Youdig* was believed to be the entrance to Purgatory and that the bodies of traitors and evil beings were cast into its bottomless sinks.

His face paled, but his eyes flashed with hatred. He lunged at me, but I turned his blade and laid open his cheek.

The doors opened, and Johannes entered with Guido. Their blades were sheathed. So, we had won.

Have done then I decided. I feinted, but Tournemine's wrist had tired, and his point came up too slow to parry. I ran him through the throat and let my mother's murderer slide off my blade to the floor.

The *Hansgraf* entered. "Was that the man?"

"Yes, that was the man."

Remembering, I asked, "Peter? How is Peter?"

"Sore wounded and like to die. That is why I have come for you. If there is help that will save him, do what you can."

"Johannes? I want the body of Tournemine. I want nothing else from this place. Only that body."

So I turned from the dealing of death to the saving of life, anguished at the little I knew of healing.

Tournemine was dead; Peter must live.

28

My way led westward and south to complete my vow, so I drew off from the column and watched them pass, the body of Tournemine across the saddle of my spare horse.

Peter von Gilderstern lay in a litter between two horses, his wounds bandaged. He had lost blood, but I had given him salt water to drink, which was good for shock, we believed, and helped to replace lost blood.

They would return to their caravans and then proceed to the fairs. When I disposed of the body of Tournemine, I would hope to join them.

"Allow me to ride with you," Johannes suggested. "I would share your trouble."

"No, this task is my own. I ride alone."

So I watched them go, driving the cattle, the sheep, and horses packed with the loot from the baron's fortress. When they were but a thread of darkness on the road, I took my way.

It was long since I had seen those rugged Arré and the Huelgoat forest, but with the light rain falling it was a fit time for such a ride to such a place.

In summer the moor was overgrown with purple heather, but now the heather was dark with rain, the earth soft beneath my horses' hooves.

Days later, under somber skies, I rode into the barren solitudes of the Arré. It was a brooding land, a dark land, an ancient land of haunted hills, mysterious fens, of dark morass. Here the Druids held their weird rites under the oak trees, of which a few remained mingled with beech, fir, and pine. Here they had cut the sacred mistletoe from the limbs with a golden sickle, catching it in a white robe as it fell.

The Elez stream flowed from the dreaded bog called *Yeun Elez*, trickling away to become, in a farther land, a merry, friendly stream that gave no hint of its origin at the very mouth of the nether regions. Here was the *Youdig*, a seething, sucking hole where anything dropped therein is sucked down. Many believed it the mouth of Purgatory or something worse, where we Bretons had cast witches and other malefactors. A treacherous quagmire supposed by legend to be unfathomable.

Here one might see the dreaded *Ankou*, the death spirit, female and a skeleton, that we Druids knew to be the survival of the Death-Goddess of the dolmen builders.

Where the Elez flows from the quagmire it was a dark and sullen stream, its banks haunted by black dogs with eyes of fire who rushed upon travelers who chanced upon the region unawares. Here were the haunts of werewolves and vampires, all manner of unclean things.

No tracks saw I, either of man or beast except a lone raven who dipped a black wing at me with a hoarse cry of warning as it flew by.

A gloomy, cloud-shrouded land where the soil was thin over rocks, and clumps of dark woodland gleamed with the eyes of *teursts*, those black and fearsome things, or of *gorics*, evil creatures only a foot high who guard treasures in secret caves or ruined castles.

At each stream crossing I rode wary of *night-washers* who wash the clothes of the dead in streams at night, and who drag unwary travelers into the water to help them wash. If the traveler refuses, or attempts to escape, they break his arms and leave him to drown. Evil things they are, with hollow eyes that stare from black and empty sockets into one's very soul.

As a child I had been brought to this place by my mother's uncle, himself a Druid, a priest, diviner, and magician, said to be possessed of all human as well as supernatural wisdom. It was said he could bring storms or

illness, and I, who had been bred in the tradition, was
taught some of what he knew.

Darkness came, lightning flashed weirdly in the sky,
and I came at last to the *Youdig*. Getting down from my
horse, I unleashed the body of Tournemine and carried
my grisly burden to the stone only we Druids knew, the
stone that marked the only path to the *Youdig*.

Thunder rolled among the sullen hills, and rain whispered among the dark pines and over the empty moor.
Step by step I carried his body along the narrow way, each
step taken by number, each with care until directly before
me lay the pit.

It was flat and ugly water, occasionally bubbling, rank
with corruption. This was the heavy lip of the nether
world. Holding Tournemine's body high above my head, I
held it so until lightning flashed, then with all my strength
I heaved it outward, and it fell, landing with a splash on
the dark, ugly water.

The arms flailed loosely as it fell; the black body
struck the surface lit green by lightning. It lay there, the
rain falling upon the wide-open eyes, and slowly the body
sank, the face upturned and last to submerge, dark water
flowing into the open mouth and eyes.

As it disappeared, one pale hand remained above the
mud and water, seeming to clutch one last time at the life
it left behind and to all things of this earth.

"There, Tournemine, destroyer of homes, murderer
of women, evilest of evil creatures, there by my promise
you sink into the *Youdig*, swallowed by the morass of
evil."

After a long moment alone, I stood, a dark figure
amid the darkness, then I turned and picked my way
back. My horses, frightened by this place, welcomed me
eagerly. Mounting, I rode away down the faint track to the
north.

Not until long after did I know that a son and a
nephew of Tournemine had fled the castle during the
fight, going east to the forest of La Hunaudaye, where

deep in a trackless wood, haunted by wild boar and deer, they built another castle that may be seen there yet.

Westward lay my homesite, and that night rain fell on its roofless floors, its fallen stones. The house where I had grown up. Before our time it had been a Roman villa, and who knew what else before that. In Brittany all things are timeless, and whatever lies before is only a page in what lies before that and before that. I, trained in the ancient lore, knew history before history, where no beginning is, and no end will be.

We know there are shadows for the shadows of things, as a reflection seen in a mirror of a mirror. We know there are circles within circles and dimensions beyond dimension. Reality is itself a shadow, only an appearance accepted by those whose eyes shun what might lie beyond. We of the Druids know the lore we have withheld and kept for ourselves alone, passed down father to son, from times beyond memory. We few hold this knowledge in trust for those who can grasp the awfulness and incompleteness of time.

Along the high trail, among the barren hills, along the lonely moors I rode with my two horses. Lightning flashed, then ceased, and thunder died rolling away to mutter among the far-off hills. The rain ceased to fall, and I drew up and removed my helmet to let the last few drops fall upon my head.

I was empty now; Tournemine was dead. He who knows his enemy is dead feels a loss as much as he who buries a friend, and the thought of Tournemine had long haunted my memory.

Nothing lay behind me now but the shell of a ruined house and the grave of my mother. The moors where I had run and played and hunted as a boy, they lay behind me.

My way was eastward. My father might yet live, and if so he must be found, whatever the circumstances, whatever the cost.

Now I could go as a warrior goes, with a debt paid, the blood of my mother avenged.

Eastward.

First, the caravan, the fulfillment of my duty to Safia.

And so I rode from the vile sink of the *Youdig*, nor did I look back.

29

There is a saying that one should "Trumpet among the elephants, crow among the cocks, bleat among the goats." For a man traveling in a strange land it is good advice.

Far to the north was the caravan with my goods, and with Safia. It was many days distant, and days add to miles. The people were strange to me, and I to them, and in many languages the words for stranger and enemy are identical.

My armor was battered, my clothes nondescript, but my horses were of the finest, although disguised somewhat by their winter coats. My sword was of the best, and in my pocket there was gold.

Yet a man is often betrayed by his heart, and lout that I am, I am often taken in by those who plead, by those who suffer. It is a wise man who tends to his own affairs, but who is wise always? One is betrayed by his own memories of hardship.

There was a night when I arrived at an inn. Stabling my horses, I went inside.

A fire blazed on the hearth, the bare board tables were wiped clean, and a few men sat about, not talking, looking downcast and beaten.

When I entered they glanced up, then shifted their eyes quickly, for such as these had no good to expect from a roving soldier. The poor devils had been robbed often enough.

The host brought, at my order, a loaf, a hand of cheese, and a haunch of mutton, good fare for the time.

"Wine," I said, "a flagon of wine." My eyes went past

the innkeeper and it seemed the sitting men were lean in rib and flank, hollow in the cheek. They stared hungrily, then averted their eyes. "Join me," I said, "there will be a glass for each."

They came, willingly enough, accepting the wine and glancing hungrily at my mutton, so I cut a slice for each.

"It is little enough we find to eat or drink," one fellow said, "a gruel of millet and a carrot or two. They take our sheep and cattle, and today they took our honey which we planned to take to the fair."

"We are tenants," another said, "but you would not believe it to see how we are treated. The *maire*, the agent who presides over the estates, he takes all, and the lord never comes to see how we fare."

"The honey," the first man said, "was from bees we hived of an evening, and the bees gathered nectar from the heather. The *maire* had no claim upon it, but it was taken, and you may be sure the lord will never see it."

After they had gone and I still sat, enjoying the fire, the host came over, and I invited him to join me, which he did.

My host was a proper man with a proper gift of tongue, and he talked freely when drinking another man's wine, although never a drink did he offer to buy himself.

"Poor fellows! It is little enough they have and few who come this way offer to share, as you have. You noticed Jacques, did you not? He put his slice of meat in his pocket, and bread, too, all the while making believe to chew so you would think him eating? He will take the bread and meat to his wife and children and swear to them he ate his while here.

"Jacques it was, and Paul. They hived the bees and hid them, planning the yearlong to sell the honey at the fair to buy clothing for their youngsters, and then the *maire* took it from them. He's a skinflint, that one, you will never see such a hunger for money as his."

The fire was warm, and the wine had a fine body. Our glasses were filled once more, and my mind began to work, thinking thoughts of which I should be ashamed, and I should be ashamed that I was not ashamed.

The thought of the honey, the *maire*, and the poor defrauded peasants aroused my ire, but thoughts of honey brought thoughts of bees. Now bees were something we had upon the moors at home, and I understood them well.

"The *maire* is a skinflint you say? A lover of money?"

"Aye, he would cheat his own mother, and willingly, if he could have a coin by doing it."

"He must have a store-place at the *cour*. Does he keep what he has in the house with him, or a separate place?"

"You think to steal it? You'd have no chance. The storehouse is in his own home, his bed hard by, and the table where he eats sits at the storehouse door. He has ears like a cat. You'd have no chance. You may be sure Jacques has thought of it, he's that desperate."

"The *cour* now? Is it the large building by the stream?"

It was, indeed. Mine is a conniving sort of mind, and the men who shared my meal had been honest, hardworking folk. By Allah, I thought—and then realized I must stop thinking of Allah, as this was the wrong land for it—I would lend them a hand.

"Tell Jacques," I said, "to move his hives into the willows across the stream, and move them tonight, under cover of darkness. If what I plan can be made to work, he shall have his honey back."

Leaving the host to ponder on the sense of that, I returned to my horses and rode along the road to the *cour*.

At the door I pounded angrily. Suddenly it opened, revealing the *maire*, furious. Much of what he had stolen from the serfs he had been putting behind his belt, which thrust out before him.

"Here, here! What is this? Go away from here!"

"What? You would send away a traveler with a gold coin? I want but a meal and lodging, and I could not stomach that vile inn." I took a bright new gold coin from my pocket. "Put me up, good sir, and this gold coin shall be yours."

He looked from my rough clothing to my fine horses and took the coin from my fingers. He trusted me not at all, but the gold insured his hospitality. "Come in, then," he said.

Lucky it was that I had appetite, for I ate a second meal and drank a better wine.

"My tongue has a taste for sweet," I said. "Do you have sweet grass? Or honey?"

"I have honey, but it is hard to come by."

"But the gold coin? When did you have such a coin for a night's lodging?"

He opened the door behind him, and there was the storehouse, a fine long room with louvered windows. He went to one of five large jars, at least a hundred pounds of honey, and dipped a taste for me.

"You are free with your coins," he said, staring at me from his mean, pig eyes.

Refilling my glass from his bottle, I shrugged. "It is nothing. If others knew what I know, all would have gold. Look you—" From my shirt I took a leathern wallet and shook several coins upon the table, all bright, new, and shining. "This I have, but it is time for more. Gold is nothing for we who know, and blessed be the Good Lord we are so few!"

He stared at me as I swept the gold into my purse and returned it to my shirt. I gulped another glass of wine and stared wisely into the glass. "I have been serving in the wars in Andalusia, fighting the Moor. Ah, those Moors! They are the ones who understand gold!"

My glass was empty, and I filled it again. "Bright, is it not? Bright, bright new gold!" I winked at him. "If I had a place, a place to work for a few days, you and I might share a pretty thing."

"Of what are you speaking?"

"Why, the Moors, and what one taught me to keep my knife from his throat.

"He was there among those bottles and tables, working at God knows what, when I surprised him. As I would with any other Moor I intended to have his heart out. Then he showed me a piece of gold, bright, new gold."

"Gold?"

"Gold. What is now needed is a quiet place in which to work. This"—I touched the wallet in my shirt—"is all I have, and I shall need more when I come to Paris. I need a place"—I gestured—"a quiet place such as this, and we would share, fifty-fifty."

Oh, he took the bait! He gulped it down so quickly I had to think rapidly to keep ahead of him. There was a room where I could work. He would get the necessary equipment. "One thing, there are plants I need which must be gathered in the dark of the moon. If I make haste—"

It was quite dark, yet I remembered the plants needed were growing beside the road. When one has such training as mine, one cultivates habits of attention. When riding I was ever aware of what herbs grew along the way, and many grow along the ditches of Europe that are important medicinally.

The one in which I was now interested was sometimes called the corn rose. The season was late, but the seeds would be there, and I had seen a few wilted blossoms. When spring is late the flowering will be late, but wild poppy grows along the roads where it is convenient.

When I returned, two glasses of wine had been poured, and the bottle remained on the table. Had there been time I would have made a syrup, but there was none. I moved toward the table, then I paused. Why bother? The *maire* was out and the storehouse near.

Swiftly, I opened the door, and although the room was dark, I knew where the honey jars were. Quickly, I uncovered each of them and opened the louvered windows a bit. Returning to the main room, I gathered my sword and gear.

The *maire* hustled back into the room, and from the expression on his features I knew he had been up to no good. "Where have you been?" I demanded. "Up to some deviltry, no doubt."

"No, no!" he protested. "Household business, nothing more."

He stared at me and the bundle I had brought back from the ditches. "You found what you wanted? May I see?"

"You may not. I no longer trust you."

We argued, and I became angrier; finally I said, "I do not trust you or this house! Come with me to the inn. If after two days all goes well, we will begin to make gold; otherwise, I shall have nothing to do with you."

He protested, argued, and I remained adamant. Finally, still protesting, he went to the inn with me. As we entered, I glanced at the host, and he nodded, ever so slightly.

I would be delaying my trip, but not for long. I must keep the old man from his house for two days, perhaps a bit less or a bit more.

"You locked your house?"

"Naturally! There are thieves about." He gestured at the shabby men tolerated by the innkeeper. "Such as these."

"If they are here, they cannot be stealing."

"Give them a chance, and they will steal."

"The honey tasted very good," I said. "Do you keep bees?"

"They do, and what is theirs is mine. It is part of what they owe."

"And you send it on to the lord of the estate?"

He shot me a suspicious glance. "I do."

"You have taken their honey, but if they now get more, will you take that, too?"

He chuckled. "It is impossible! If they can get more honey this season, they can keep it, and sell it at the fair if they wish."

The next day was dull, for the *maire* was a narrow, bigoted, unhealthy man who thought of little but squeezing the peasants and no doubt robbing his lord. Despite his restlessness I kept him at the inn or in the fields, always with the peasants in sight.

"We must watch them," I insisted. "They might steal something you could not steal in turn."

"What was that?" His sharp little eyes stared.

"I said they might steal as much as they feel they earn," I replied.

They did not steal, for we observed them carefully, and I, who am a curious man, did some other watching. Things, I decided, were going well.

At a table in the inn I said, "Today the peasants stole nothing. Do you agree? They did not leave the fields?"

"They did not!" The *maire*'s face was smug with satisfaction.

"Bear witness," I said to my host, "the *maire* states the peasants stole nothing, that they did not leave the field."

The innkeeper was puzzled, but the *maire* was staring suspiciously. I, being a sometimes evil and conniving man, enjoyed it all very much.

"The gold? When do we begin with the gold?"

"Soon," I said, "I had to be sure the peasants were busy and not watching us. What we do must be done in secret."

It was dark before the *maire* returned to his home on the second day, and I was well pleased with myself and the inimitable ways of nature.

Jacques came wearily to the inn, accompanied by Paul. "Wine! A flagon for my friends, the sellers of honey!"

"You jest. What honey have we to sell?"

"Tomorrow," I said, "look to your hives. You will find them filled with honey."

They did not call me a liar, for the wine was on the table, and I ordered another leg of mutton. This time I cut a slice for each, and a thick slice for each of those at home. "Now fall to. When you look to your hives tomorrow you must be skeptics indeed if you think you have no honey."

Suddenly, there was a tremendous clamor outside, and the *maire* burst into the room, accompanied by two of the watch. "Seize them!" He pointed at Jacques and Paul. "They are thieves! They have stolen my honey!"

"Hold!" I lifted a hand and, rising to my feet, stood taller than either of the watch. "Your honey is gone?"

"All of it! Every bit!"

"But we have watched the peasants for two full days. Did you not say this day that they had stolen nothing? Did they ever leave the fields? I, too, watched closely, and not until nightfall did they go to their homes or leave their work."

"He said they had stolen nothing," my host said, "that they had not left the fields."

The men of the watch looked to the *maire* who did not know what to say.

Leaning across the table and putting on my sternest expression, I said, "This is a plot to defraud the lord. By claiming the honey stolen you could keep it all yourself, depriving your master of his just share." Turning to the men of the watch, I said, "See to it the *maire* delivers three large jars of honey to his lord, even if he must buy them himself."

Gathering my cloak about me, and picking up my gear, I said, "I shall go now, but I shall speak of this matter. It demands investigation. It seems all matters here need investigation."

"No!" the *maire* protested. "I will deliver the honey to my lord."

"See that you do, and see that you steal no more from those who work for him." I leaned across the table. "Think you, my fat friend. You know they did not steal the honey, then is not the hand of God in this? Or a spirit, perhaps? Be wary, my friend. The good man Jacques and good man Paul are men to treat with care."

Stepping outside, I drew the door shut after me and started for my horses.

The *maire* rushed after me. "But the gold?" he protested.

Drawing my cloak about me, I said, "A man who will

cheat poor peasants and attempt to defraud his master is no man to have for a partner.

"Moreover"—I almost accidentally held out my hand—"I shall ride to your lord to report this . . . unless it pays me to take another route."

His fat jowls quivered with agitation. "There would be trouble! Much trouble!" He leaned toward me, putting a purse in my hand. "Take another route! Oh, please, take another way!"

A short distance down the road I drew up before a peasant's hut. Leaning from the saddle, I rapped loudly. A frightened woman opened the door, and I gave her the purse.

"This is for Jacques to share with the others," I said. "Tell him it is from Kerbouchard, the man who commands bees!"

With that I rode into the night, reflecting on the habits of bees. Busy creatures they are, avid in their search for sweets, flying into every bush, every crevice . . . every window.

Busy creatures, indeed, but no fools. They gather nectar from flowers to make honey, but even a bee will not gather nectar if there is ready-made honey at hand.

30

The France to which I returned was vastly different from Islamic Spain, and I learned to take no part in discussions, yet it went sore against me. We Bretons are inclined to silence, but, nonetheless, Celts have a love for argument. It was hard to be silent, but usually I was.

The universal lack of cleanliness, as well as the overbearing pride and ignorance of both nobles and churchmen, astonished me.

For all their effect on the Western world, the Greek thinkers, except for Aristotle, might never have lived. Of Muslim and Jewish thinkers and scientists nothing at all was known, and the practice of medicine was frightening.

During time past I had become accustomed to the easy give-and-take discussion in Córdoba, to the hot, lazy baths, and lighted, paved streets. Everywhere in Córdoba, Toledo, Seville, and Málaga there was wit, poetry, excited discussion of ideas.

Yet even in France I found a growing curiosity, a willingness to listen and a desire for learning among the young.

Here and there in the monasteries scholars such as Peter Abelard were thinking, writing, talking. They were few, and often in trouble, but their number was growing.

At long last, a month after our leave-taking in Brittany, I rejoined the caravan.

They were at Cambrai. Difficulties had arisen at Bruges and Lille, and those fairs had been avoided. Business had been good, and I returned to find our silk sold but for a few bolts and our money invested in the cloth of Flanders.

We turned southeast to Châlons-sur-Marne, and six weeks later went on to St. Denis, near Paris.

It was at St. Denis that Safia said, suddenly, "Mathurin, I shall leave you here."

She had been quiet since my return, and I knew she had problems she did not confide in me, nor did I question her. As long ago as Montauban she had received a message from her old associates, and now she would resume where she had left off.

"I shall miss you."

Her eyes held mine. "Do you still wish to find your father?"

"More than anything."

Her eyelids seemed to flutter a little, and I knew she knew more than she cared to tell me. "It would be better if you did not think of him again."

"He is dead?"

"No, but he is beyond your reach. I fear for your life if you persist."

"I have no choice."

She was silent. We were in a small grove on the banks of the Seine. Tomorrow we would ride into Paris and say our good-byes there. We had been good friends, with mutual admiration and respect. She was a shrewd, intelligent woman, one of a network extending through the Islamic world, and there were several such, working for different ideals, different causes, and there was war between them, a war unseen, untalked of, but a vicious, deadly war nonetheless.

Finally, she asked, "Have you ever heard of the Old Man of the Mountain?"

"Of the Assassins? Yes, I know of them."

"He has a fortress high in the mountains, beyond the Caspian Sea. There are several castles, as a matter of fact, but only one concerns you. It is the fortress of Alamut."

"My father is there?"

"He is a slave there, and, Mathurin, nobody—and I mean *nobody*—enters that castle unless he is one of the Assassins."

"You are sure he is there?"

"Our spies are everywhere. This word has now come to me. All I know is that as of three months ago, he was still well and strong."

"But a slave?"

For such a man to become a slave seemed impossible. His fierce strength, his sharp intellect, his indomitable way—I could think of no man less suited to slavery than he.

Of the Assassins I knew only what was generally believed. They were a Persian sect, a branch of the Ismaili, who in turn were a branch of the Shi'a, one of the great divisions among the followers of Mohammed.

A young Persian Shi'ite, Hasan ibn-al-Sabbah, joined the sect in 1071 and became the first Grand Master of the Assassins, the first "Old Man of the Mountain." He turned murder into a political weapon, making himself feared throughout the Islamic world and even in Christian Europe.

From the stronghold of Alamut, Assassins were sent out, doped with hashish to kill enemies of the Old Man of the Mountains or to attack caravans and bring their goods to him. From his fortress he sent orders to kings and sultans, and more than one, under threat of assassination, complied with the wishes of the Old Man.

There was a legend to the effect that Hasan-ibn-al-Sabbah, Omar Khayyam, and Nizam-al-Mulk, as young students, had entered into a pact. All studied with the same master; all were talented, and it seemed certain that at least one of the three would rise to power. It was agreed among them that whoever won success would share equally with the other two.

Nizam-al-Mulk became vizier of the mighty Seljuk empire, and Omar, the scholar, mathematician, and poet, chose a pension that would provide support while he pursued his studies. Hasan, on the other hand, insisted upon a position at court where he soon became rival to Nizam-al-Mulk himself.

Finally, outwitted and disgraced, he fled from the

empire and established himself at Alamut, from which point he directed the assassination of Nizam-al-Mulk.

A story was told of the Garden of Alamut, a secret valley in the mountains nearby where all manner of delicious fruits, gorgeous flowers, and shading trees were grown. There were fountains that flowed with wine or milk, and all about were beautiful, sensuous women.

Youths from desert tribes were invited to Alamut, drugged and transported into this interior valley. For a few days they lived as they had never lived upon the harsh and infertile desert.

Until this experience these desert youths had known nothing but dates, camel's milk, and goat's flesh. Suddenly they were surrounded by all manner of luxuries and permitted to enjoy the company of women of such beauty as only appear in dreams.

They were doped again, taken back to the outside, and told that the Old Man had transported them to Paradise and could do so again, at will. Furthermore, if they died in his service they would be returned to Paradise.

Then these young men were sent to slay the enemies of the Old Man, and because they were given hashish to make them fearless, they became known as *hashishans*, or assassins.

Stories were told of the Old Man and those he had slain. Every death of a possible enemy was attributed to him, no matter how it came about.

And now my father was a prisoner in Alamut. Somehow I must go there, enter the fortress, and get him out. I said as much.

"I knew you would want to go there, but there is nothing I can do to help you, nothing at all."

"I expect no help. The task is my own. I now know he is alive, know he is in health, and the rest is up to me."

"I need not warn you, Mathurin, but the Old Man has spies everywhere. If you speak of your intentions, he will know. Even here he may have spies, so tell no one of your plans."

We listened to the rustle of the river, and the stirring

of the leaves. "Safia? You are sure you will be all right now?"

"I have friends, Mathurin, but I will need money. If you agree, I will take what cash we have, and you keep the goods, and the horses."

"It is unfair. The value of the goods and the horses far exceeds what we have in gold."

Behind us the camp was stirring. Guido was singing, and we could hear the laughter of Johannes. "I shall miss them, as I shall miss you. We were fortunate to find them when we did."

"And I was fortunate to find you when I did," I said. "Do you remember that night, Safia? I had no place to turn and enemies everywhere."

"You have been a good friend to me." She looked up at me. "Mathurin, I wish .. ."

What she wished I was never to know, for at that moment there was a call from camp.

The *Hansgraf* and Peter awaited me, with them were Lucca and Johannes. "We need your advice. Safia informs us that you have much knowledge of the science of lands, and even maps?"

"I have such knowledge."

"East of here? Do you know the lands of the Magyars and Petchenegs?"

"I have read Marvazi, and others. They offer little."

"Do you know Kiev?"

"It is a large market town, the largest in northern Europe, but the way there is dangerous, and the Petchenegs are a savage people."

"No matter. Our two caravans, Peter's and mine, will muster more than one hundred and fifty fighting men."

Having heard much of the fierce steppe tribesmen, I was worried about the idea. The *Hansgraf* listened gravely to my objections. "We have missed the fairs at Bruges and Lille while the fair here at St. Denis is a small one. There will be trading at Lagny and Provins, but if we go eastward, there are fairs at Cologne and Leipzig. It seems to me if we take the cloth of Flanders to Kiev and sell it there and buy furs to take to Constantinople, we will make good trade."

There had been rumors of restlessness among the steppe tribes, and I was disturbed. Safia was awaiting me, and I told her of what was planned and what I feared.

The deep sea can be fathomed, but who knows the heart of a woman? We had known each other for many months, and she was always disturbing to me, yet there is a moment in the acquaintance of a man and woman and once that moment is passed it may never be recaptured. Not at least with the same essence.

We had met as equals, rarely a good thing in such matters, for the woman who wishes to be the equal of a man usually turns out to be less than a man and less than a woman. A woman is herself, which is something altogether different than a man.

"I shall escort you into the city. It is not well that you should ride alone."

"All right."

Silence fell between us, and I searched my heart for a key to the silence and found no words.

Paris was no such city as those to which I had become accustomed, but a shabby little place with muddy streets and a people suspicious of strangers.

My father told me how fishermen had settled an island in the Seine and started a town called Lutetia, raided many times by the Vikings. Finally, the Count Eudes and Bishop Gozlin fortified the island and organized the townspeople to fight off the Vikings, who then went downstream to settle in the land named for them, Normandy. The Northmen came to be known in the Frankish lands as Normans.

The city of Paris, if such it could be called, was actually three cities. On the island where Lutetia had been and where Notre Dame now was were the seat of government and the palace. The bishop lived on the island. On the right bank, separately administered, was the Town, the shops, markets, and the six great guilds. There were the money changers, goldsmiths, and bankers. This area was ruled by the Provost of Paris. On the left bank, only beginning, were the "schools" with their own laws, administrations, and customs. The Bishop of Paris was himself a feudal lord, a great landed proprietor with as much power as the king himself.

The ancient site of Lutetia was called the "Isle of the City," but the king and the bishop who lived there had less to do with what was called government than members of the guilds or even the argumentative and often ribald students of the university. The Romans, I noticed, had not kept themselves to the island, for there were the remains of an amphitheatre and a few arches of an aqueduct on the left bank.

Safia and I parted at the bridge, for I had no desire to cross into the realm of officialdom. The further one can remain from the powers that be the longer and happier life is apt to be. Moreover, prolonged leave-takings made me uneasy.

"You will be all right?" I asked.

"Only this can I tell you. I shall be here for some time. Some friends, it does not matter who, plan to introduce silk manufacture to Paris."

"It is a good idea, Safia. Times are changing. Only a few years ago towns lacked importance. They have ceased to be merely places of refuge and have become markets. You have seen it. Traveling merchants are ceasing to wander and settling in the towns. You are wise. Where there are women there will be a market for silk."

We said no more, but parted with one last, lingering glance. I rode away, unhappy as was she.

The old Roman road to Lyon led me toward the edge of town, but I turned aside, seeing a gathering of young men. Walking my horse closer, I paused to listen. A group of young men sat about on bundles of straw listening to a lecture. This was the place of the Fouarres, and one of the first schools in Paris.

Some glanced askance at me, sitting my fine Arabian horse but wearing battered armor, sword at my side, bow

and arrows slung on my saddle. No doubt they wondered at such a man being interested in their discussion.

The lecturer, a thin man with a sour face, was expounding upon Bernard's condemnation of Abelard for his application of reason to theology, and praising Bernard for his sentence against Abelard, whom he called a heretic.

"Nonsense!" I said irritably. "Bernard was an old fool!"

Every head turned, and the teacher stared, aghast. "How dare you say such a thing?" he demanded.

"I dare say anything," I replied more cheerfully, "because I have a fast horse."

Several of the students laughed, and one shouted, "Well spoken, soldier!"

"Have you no reverence?" the teacher demanded.

"I have reverence for all who ask questions and seek honest answers."

"A philosopher!" laughed a student.

"A wanderer in search of answers," I said, then to the teacher, "You asked if I have reverence? I have reverence for truth, but I do not know what truth is. I suspect there are many truths, and therefore, I suspect all who claim to have *the* truth."

Walking my horse a few steps closer, I added, "I have reverence for the inquirer, for the seeker. I have no reverence for those who accept any idea, mine included, without question."

"You are a heretic!" he threatened.

"I am a pagan, and a pagan cannot be a heretic."

"You ride an infidel horse."

"My horse has never committed herself, but judging by her attitude on a frosty morning, she is an unbeliever."

There were subdued chuckles, and the teacher's eyes narrowed. "You ridicule the Church," he threatened.

"Who mentioned the Church? On the contrary, I have great respect for religion. My objection is to those who are against so many things and for so little."

"What are you for?" a student called out. "Tell us, soldier."

"What am I for? Being a man, it is obvious. I am for women."

This drew a burst of laughter.

"My only trouble is, I am unacquainted in town."

"Stay the night, soldier! We will introduce you to Fat Claire!"

"It is a theory of mine," I countered, "that as a seeker for truth I should find my own answers, and my own women."

"Tell us, soldier, in your travels have you discovered if the world is round or flat?"

"It is round," I said, "a fact known to the Greeks and to the Arabs as well. For that matter, it is known to the people of Hind, which is far away."

"Do you know this of yourself, soldier, or is it by the word of others that you speak?"

"That the world is round I know of my own experience, for I have sailed far out upon the ocean-sea, and I know it is known to the Arabs from converse with their teachers. As for the Greeks and those of Hind, I have read their books."

"You read Greek?" The teacher was astonished now.

"Greek, Latin, Arabic, some Persian, and some Sanskrit," I said, "and much of what lies in a woman's heart."

"I think you lie," the teacher said.

"It is the eater of chillies," I said, "whose mouth is hot." Then I added, "Teacher, when you say I lie, say it with a sword in your hand."

Several of the students arose. "Soldier, the hour grows late. If you will not accept our recommendation of Fat Claire, then by all means come with us to see what else Paris has to offer. Also, we would test the wine of the country with you to see if your palate does justice to your intellect."

"By all means, gentlemen! Lead on, lead on! A true philosopher will never refuse a lass, a glass, or an hour of conversation!"

Turning to the teacher, I said, "I meant no disrespect to you or what you teach, only ask questions of yourself."

"The bishop will ask the questions," he said darkly, "and he will ask them of you!"

"Put him on a fast horse then," I said, "or he will ask them of the wind."

31

The Church of St.-Julien-e-Pauvre had been built upon the site of an ancient fortified priory, a part of which remained.

It had been the custom for travelers arriving late at the gates of Paris to spend the night at the priory, but when the site was taken by the Church, several inns came into being.

These inns eked out a precarious existence until schools began to appear on the Left Bank. Most of the teachers had been given their license by the chancellor of Notre Dame, but due to crowding, the desire for greater liberty of expression, or other reasons, they had moved across the river, leaving the Isle of the City.

In later times licenses would be granted by the abbot of the monastery of St. Genevieve.

No shelters being available for these schools, they were held in the open air, the students seated on their bundles of straw. Later some took shelter in the Church of St.-Julien-e-Pauvre until it became famous for fierce debates and student brawls.

With schools on the Left Bank, students flocked to the inns, and although many of them managed only the most precarious existence, their very numbers kept the inns alive. However, among the students, adopting their attitudes, garments, and the protecting arm of the Church, were a number of renegades, thieves, panderers, and cutthroats. These were tolerated by the students, and some became students or catered to them.

This area on the Left Bank came to be called the

university, meaning in this case simply a group of persons. Originally the students had met under the cloisters of Notre Dame, and teaching still continued there. Those who migrated to the university were the most ribald, disrespectful, and freethinking, and more often than not, the best intellects.

Hungry for learning, young men came to Paris to learn, many of them walking for days to reach the city. Only a few had sufficient money to maintain themselves. Books were scarce, paper expensive, teachers diverse in attitude. After three years a student might be received *bachelier-des-arts*, but two years more were required to get his master's degree or license. To become a doctor of medicine required eight years of study, and to earn a degree of doctor of theology the student had to present and defend four theses. The last of these was a challenge only the exceptional dared attempt, for the candidate was examined from six in the morning until six at night, nor was he allowed to leave his place to eat, drink, or for any other purpose. Twenty examiners, relieving each other every half hour, did their best to find flaws in the preparation of the student.

The language of the students was Latin, and for this reason a part of the area became known as the Latin Quarter.

The common room of the inn was a dingy place, low-raftered and dark. Several board tables stood about, each surrounded by benches. A huge roast was turning on a spit as we entered, filling the room with a fine, warm smell. One of my student companions, Julot, dropped to a bench, and I seated myself opposite. His was a hard, reckless but intelligent face, with a ready smile, and he had a pair of strong hands.

"Did you mean it when you said you had read books? A lot of them?"

"Of course. They are sold along the streets in Córdoba."

"They sell books in shops?" His disbelief was obvious. "Religious books?"

"Everything. Philosophy, medicine, law, astronomy, astrology, poetry, drama, what you will."

Julot grabbed his companion's arm. "Did you hear that? They sell books along the street as if they were onions or fish! What I would give to see a sight like that!"

"There are dozens of public libraries in Córdoba, and you can read what you like."

"Let God have his temples and cathedrals," Julot said passionately, "if they will give us libraries!"

The one called The Cat brought three bottles of red wine to the table, and when I placed a gold coin in his hand he stared at it. "A scholar with money! What have you done, robbed a priest?"

They brought slabs of roast beef to the table. Plates were almost unknown in Europe, and the meat was served on slices of bread.

We drank wine, ate roast beef, and gestured with the meat bones as we talked. We argued, protested, debated. Their eyes were alive with excitement, and they vied with one another to have their questions answered, arguing furiously over the answers or probable answers.

Had I read Hippocrates? What of Lucretius? What did I think of *On the Nature of Things*?

"What of Avicenna? Who was he? Where did he come from? We have heard his name, nothing more."

"One of the greatest minds of this or any age," I said, "he has taken the whole field of knowledge for his province."

Their excitement was a tonic. They knew of John of Seville, of Averroës, and of al-Biruni, yet only by name, and even those were whispered about. As I talked, I kept an eye out for spies, for there were those who wanted no teaching that might weaken their power, and they were hard on any deemed as heretics. Being a pagan, I was theoretically free from persecution, for by Church law a pagan could not be prosecuted for heresy. At least, not at the time. However, I was skeptical about the interpretation of such a law, and strangers were forever vulnerable.

Students crowded about the table, for despite their often rowdy ways, there was a genuine hunger to know what the world outside was thinking. They wished to know what had been thought in ancient Greece, in Rome, and Persia. There is no curtain knowledge cannot penetrate, although the process can be slowed.

Even as we talked, there were those in the monasteries who were moving cautiously into areas of knowledge hitherto forbidden. There were abbots and bishops who were overlooking the fact, but observing with interest.

It is a poor sort of man who is content to be spoon-fed knowledge that has been filtered through the canon of religious or political belief, and it is a poor sort of man who will permit others to dictate what he may or may not learn.

Those about me had tasted the wine of learning and liked the bite of it on the tongue. Their appetites had grown with tasting, and they were no longer content merely to wonder and question, they wanted answers. Civilization was born of curiosity, and can be kept alive in no other way.

Of Moslem poetry they knew nothing, so I recited for them from Firdausi, Hafiz, and el-Yezdi. As to Avicenna, I told them what I could: that he was born in Bokhara in 979 and died in 1037. By the time he was ten he knew the Koran from memory, had studied the Arab classics, and by the age of sixteen he had mastered the existing knowledge of mathematics, medicine, astronomy, philosophy, and had lectured on logic. Before his death he had written more than a hundred works, including the *Canon on Medicine* of more than a million words.

Suddenly, the door burst open, and in the door stood the hugest woman I had seen, but large as she was, there was still a shape to her. She was no taller than the average man present, but in girth she would have outdone any two of them, possibly any three.

Her plump cheeks were wide with smile, her large blue eyes truly beautiful. Around her, like pigeons fluttering around a barn, were half-a-dozen girls.

"Where is this paragon of a man? Where is he?"

The group about the table parted, and standing, I

bowed low. "No paragon, Claire, but who would be a paragon in company where you stand? How can the Good Lord have given you so much beauty when it meant depriving so many others?"

"A gallant speech!" She came down the room to our table. "Now there's a man, girls!"

She took up our bottle and filled a glass. "They tell me you've a tongue for blasphemy. Is it true?"

"Blasphemy? Not unless it is blasphemy to seek the truth. No, I am no blasphemer, but something worse, I am an asker of questions."

"And you are not a rascal?"

"In this company?" I glanced around in mock horror. "How could anyone as innocent as I be considered a rascal in such company as this? No, the teacher was talking nonsense, and I stated a contrary opinion, that is all."

She seated herself, and the wenches gathered around, a comely lot and fit to start a man's blood boiling had they been cleaner.

"They tell me," I said, straight-faced, "that you, too, are a professor."

"A professor? I? I have been called a lot of pretty things but never that. Perhaps a philosopher. Men come to me with their problems."

"And who could solve them better?"

"I am Fat Claire, and I deny neither the name nor the title. Young man, Fat Claire is a name that is given respect!"

"How could I believe otherwise? I had scarcely met these gentlemen before they were assuring me of the high quality of your accomplishments."

I called to the waiter. "Another bottle of wine. When I am out of funds, I shall leave."

"Stay, we need your kind in Paris."

"If you open a school," Julot said, "I shall be the first to sit at your feet." He turned to Fat Claire. "He is not all banter and wit. He has studied in Córdoba where they have more books than priests!"

"And studied more than books, I should say," she replied wryly.

The girls gathered about with the students. "Stay with us, soldier, and we shall give you such entertainment as you will not find in Córdoba."

"I have heard of your entertainment. My father was here long ago. He fought Vikings on the river below Paris."

"Your father? And who might he have been?"

"Kerbouchard. It is an old name upon the sea."

"The son of Kerbouchard." Fat Claire's look was appraising. "Yes, it could be, though no two men looked more and yet less alike. We know your father here, and bless him. He fought the Vikings well enough, fought them in the streets of Paris as well as on the river.

"I was a girl then, and the Vikings came up the river, and our town was empty of soldiers. They came with no warning, and had it not been for your father and his men, much good French blood would have run in the gutters that night. He followed them up the river and arrived behind them when they had begun their rampage. We were ready to flee to the island and burn our bridges as we used to do when he and his men took them at sword's point."

She put down her glass. "So you are the son of Kerbouchard? He was a strong man, and narrow in the hips."

Julot leaned toward her. "Claire, I have a thought the teacher was ill-inclined to our soldier. He might start an inquiry. If so, we might have to flee quickly."

She glanced at me. "Are you alone? Have you friends?"

"None here. I go to meet them now. I have my horses, and some gear."

She did not ask where my friends were, for she had learned discretion in her own school. If the time came when I must escape, I preferred it to be by my own route. That man is a fool who would descend into a well on another man's rope.

For one day I had done enough, and I was uneasy, for

that teacher had seemed a narrow, vengeful man who would not have enjoyed my comments. It was a night's ride to the fair, and if I did not start soon, they might be gone.

Peter Lombard, the student of Abelard, was no longer Bishop of Paris, and I had small hope such a straight-thinking man would succeed him. Had Peter Lombard still been bishop, I would have trusted my case to his hands, but I had no desire to lie in prison while they made up their minds about me or subjected me to torture. It had been my experience that the political or ecclesiastical mind is laggard in making decisions.

Whatever plans one has were best kept to oneself, for those with whom you share them might themselves share them with someone else, and he is a wise man who mentally keeps a hand on the door latch.

To die for what one believes is all very well for those so inclined, but it has always seemed to me the most vain of solutions. There is no cause worth dying for that is not better served by living.

The air in the inn was close and hot, but the talk that ebbed and flowed in the room was at least the good talk of men of ideas. Yet a restlessness sat upon me, not alone because of what might come of my comments on Bernard of Clairvaux, but because of my realization that by coming here I had stepped back in time from Córdoba.

The ideas that excited these young men with their good minds were ideas of the dead past. The ideas of Plato are also of the past, but they are fresh with each new generation. Many of the ideas here were ideas already passed by in Córdoba and elsewhere. They were going up the blind alleys of man's thinking, bickering about ideas from the dusty corners of philosophy where old debris had been swept to be forgotten. It was depressing to see such eager young men, restless for change, obsessed with ideas, many of which had never possessed validity and would never have occured to Plato, Avicenna, Aristotle, or Rhazes. What this generation needed was another Abelard, or a dozen such.

In Moorish Spain, in Baghdad, Damascus, Hind, and Cathay, even in Sicily, the thinking was two hundred years in advance of this.

The merchants of the caravans, while they kept their thoughts to themselves for safety's sake, were generations ahead of these students, for they had traveled and they had listened. Yet the spirit of inquiry was alive here, and where it has a free existence, ignorance cannot last. There was fresh air entering the dark halls of ignorance and superstition.

Such men as Robert of Chester, Adelard of Bath, and Walcher of Malvern were making astronomical observations, or translating Arabic books into Latin. This was the beginning of something, yet I had ventured back into a world from which I had come and found it an alien world of which I was no longer a part.

In a sense I had always been alien. My Druidic training had taken me deep into a past that held more than the present, and along with it had been my father's accounts, returning home after voyages, of a world beyond our shores. I had mingled with the men of his crews, almost half of which had come from other lands, other cultures, until I had become a stranger in my own land.

"Fill up, soldier!" Julot clapped my shoulder. "Fill up and tell us more!"

How much could I tell them? How much dared I tell them? What was the point at which acceptance would begin to yield to doubt? For the mind must be prepared for knowledge as one prepares a field for planting, and a discovery made too soon is no better than a discovery not made at all.

Had I been a Christian, I would undoubtedly have been considered a heretic, for what the world has always needed is more heretics and less authority. There can be no order or progress without discipline, but authority can be quite different. Authority, in this world in which I moved, implied belief in and acceptance of a dogma, and dogma is invariably wrong, as knowledge is always in a state of transition. The radical ideas of today are often the conservative policies of tomorrow, and dogma is left protesting by the wayside.

Each generation has a group that wishes to impose a static pattern on events, a static pattern that would hold society forever immobile in a position favorable to the group in question.

Much of the conflict in the minds and arguments of those about me was due to a basic conflict between religious doctrines based primarily upon faith, and Greek philosophy, which was an attempt to interpret experience by reason. Or so it seemed to me, a man with much to learn.

The coins in my pocket were few, the hour late. "It is time to go, Julot. I shall leave you to Fat Claire and The Cat and your friends."

"But you have just come!" Julot showed his dismay. "Soldier, we would learn. You have knowledge we need."

"You are your own best teacher. My advice is to question all things. Seek for answers, and when you find what seems to be an answer, question that, too."

"It is very hard," The Cat said.

"Listen to him," Fat Claire said, "what he says makes sense."

"Ask her," I suggested, "the value of experimental science."

"Soldier," one of the girls interrupted, "you told us of the poetry spoken in Spain, poetry often made upon the moment. Make us a poem for Fat Claire!"

She was an elegant wench, this one who spoke, a buxom lass whose best features were quite outstanding. She was a bold hussy with a swish to her hips, red gold hair, and lips . . . !

"A rhyme, soldier! Give us a rhyme? Give us a song!"

"It was their ability, not mine. I would make a sorry poet."

"Your father was not so hesitant," Fat Claire said, "but the poetry he made was of a different kind." Her eyes sparkled with humor. "Of course, I was many pounds younger then!"

"My father was a seagoing man," I admitted, "and no doubt he laid the keel of many a pretty craft. It is the way of seafaring men and has no doubt contributed much to the spread of knowledge. It is possible that the Greek approach to Trojan women inspired an appreciation for their philosophy."

It was in my mind to give them a poem, however, and I stood in my place, putting a foot on a bench, and was about to speak when the door opened.

There stood the teacher, pointing a finger at me. Behind him were a dozen soldiers.

"Take him!" he said. "That is the man!"

32

"**Q**uick!" Julot caught my arm. "Out!" We sprang through a sudden opening in the crowd as a brawl exploded near the door, blocking the path of the soldiers. A glance over my shoulder let me see The Cat struggling along with two other of my attentive listeners.

Ducking around the chimney, we escaped through an almost hidden door in the chimney corner and out through the kitchen.

The stable showed darkly under the trees, yet even as we approached it, two soldiers with pikes intervened. One held his pike leveled at my stomach while the other stepped forward to disarm me.

As the pikeman reached for my sword, I grabbed him by the upper arm and spun him into the man holding the pike, throwing both off-balance. Julot was already moving to the stable. Whipping out my blade, I parried a thrust of the pikeman, and stepping past the pike, I put the point of my blade through his thigh.

As the second man started toward me I said, "My friend, if you wish to see another sun, step back. I have no quarrel with you and want none, but if you step closer, I shall spit you like a duck."

"Why, I have no quarrel with you, either, so away with you. I shall see to my friend."

"Thanks," I said, "and Godspeed."

Julot appeared with the horses, and I sprang to the saddle, breaking away down the lane between rows of poplars. There was a shading of lemon light in the sky where the sun would be an hour from now.

"Julot," I said, "this is no quarrel of yours, so be off for Paris and lose yourself there. I've a fast horse and can play hare to their hounds as long as it amuses me."

"You ask me to leave a friend?"

"I do so ask," I said, "for I have a place to go."

"Fat Claire would skin me alive. She had a feeling for you, and you have no idea what you missed."

"There are other women, but I have but one neck. Be off with you now."

"You take this too lightly, my friend. Talk such as yours is not tolerated. There has been too much free-thinking, and even we of the schools must bridle our tongues. If you are found, you will burn as a heretic."

"But I am a pagan!"

"Who is to say? They'll burn you, soldier, for there are those about who have a liking for the odor of burning flesh—and no taste at all for the teaching of Peter Abelard."

The fields were white with frost, and we kept our horses to a brisk trot, saving them for swifter flight if need be. An immediate return to the caravan might involve my friends, for which I had no desire. Yet escape I must, and once with them, they would hide me. It had been done before, with others.

"There's a small village this side of Melun. Fat Claire told me of it. If we are separated, go there and ask for a man named Persigny."

"Is it far from the road to Provins?"

"The direction is right."

If I could meet the caravan at Provins, at a fair to be held there, it was unlikely I would be found. Search in such an unlikely place was almost out of the question, for I had not the look of a merchant.

During an hour we made many turns and twists among farms and lanes. Once when a party of horsemen appeared, going toward the city, we took hasty shelter in a stable where Julot relieved the hens of several eggs.

Day came to a land brown with autumn and a gray sky with lowering clouds, a sky that promised rain.

Julot shivered in his rag, nor was I clad for the

weather. From time to time I thrust my fingers into my shirt to warm them.

"There is a castle nearby, a place called Blandy. The lord of the castle is a brigand with a penchant for attacking merchant caravans, which we must avoid. But there is a chapel at Champeaux, built in the time of Clovis, and the monks are friendly. Abelard was a teacher there, and most are of his persuasion. The man Persigny is their friend also."

A fine rain began to fall, turning the atmosphere to a steel mesh, but we huddled our shoulders against the rain and the cold and hurried on. There was need for shelter and warm food, for Julot's hands were turning blue, and his cheeks were drawn, his eyes hollow. He looked half starved, and no doubt he was, for many students barely existed while carrying on their studies.

Monks had scattered gardens and vineyards through the Brie forest, and here and there were old farmhouses, lying in ruins from past conflicts. The woods were dismal, a web of black branches interlaced overhead, a track marked by pools of rain that lay like sheets of steel across the way. Riding past such a ruin, we came in behind it to leave no tracks where we entered. We rode through weeds and brush and walked our horses through a breach in the wall, entering an ancient hall where a few disconsolate bats hung from the ceiling.

Gathering sticks for a fire, we built it carefully wanting no visible light nor smoke to warn a passerby. When flames sprang up we stretched our cold hands toward their heat, two dark and crouching figures, rain-soaked and cold, seeking as man has ever sought, the consolation of fire.

"It is good, the fire," Julot said.

"The companion of vagabonds. Few men are so poor they cannot have fire."

"You knew your father?"

"Aye."

"My mother was a peasant girl; my father, a soldier in some army or other. She never knew which army or where he was from. He was a gentle man, with a handsome beard, so much and no more could she tell me."

"Men without fathers often place more emphasis on them than others would. A mill does not turn on water that is past."

"Perhaps, but without family a man is nothing."

"You are mistaken. Your church has given opportunity to many men without family, the army, also."

"One must conform, and I conform badly."

"Be a philosopher. A man can compromise to gain a point. It has become apparent that a man can, within limits, follow his inclinations within the arms of the Church if he does so discreetly." I smiled at him. "Remember this, Julot, even a rebel grows old, and sometimes wiser. He finds the things he rebelled against are now the things he must defend against newer rebels. Aging bones creak in the cold. Seek warmth, my friend; be discreet, but follow your own mind. When you have obtained position you will have influence. Otherwise you will tear at the bars until your strength is gone, and you will have accomplished nothing but to rant and rave."

"Compromise is an evil word."

"Think a little, Julot. All our lives we compromise, and without it there would be no progress, nor could men live together. You may think a man a fool, but if he is an agreeable fool you say nothing. Is that no compromise?

"Victory is not won in miles but in inches. Win a little now, hold your ground, and later win a little more.

"A man should not compromise his principles, but he need not flaunt them, as a banner. There is a time to talk and a time to be still. If a wrong is being done, then is the time to speak out.

"Study, Julot, gain prestige, and people will ask you solemnly for advice about things of which you know nothing."

"I like not the sound of it," Julot grumbled. "I am a fighter. I fight for what I believe."

"There are many ways of fighting. Many a man or woman has waged a good war for truth, honor, and freedom,

who did not shed blood in the process. Beware of those
who would use violence, too often it is the violence they
want and neither truth nor freedom.

"The important thing is to know where you stand and
what you believe, then be true to yourself in all things.
Moreover, it is foolish to waste time in arguing questions
with those who have no power to change.

"There! My sermon for the day is finished. No doubt
I will make at least some of the mistakes I have advised
you against."

"You preach well," Julot grumbled. "Now see if you
can preach us up a meal."

"You have eggs; there is water and a fire. If we can
find a kettle, we can boil our eggs, or a piece of metal on
which they can be fried."

"The idea is yours," Julot said, "do you find the
kettle. After all, who robbed the hen?"

Rising, I hitched up my sword belt. "Do you sit warm
and snug. I shall venture out into the cold and storm."

"Go ahead. Make something of it, but come back with
a kettle."

To tell the truth, I was confident. This ruin was such
a place as would attract vagabonds, and where a kettle
might be hidden for some future time. Stepping out into
the rain, I began scouting every corner of the ruins.

My search brought me nothing but a greater soaking
from the rain and the realization that the ruin was more
extensive than imagined. And then I saw the path.

It is my weakness that I can never resist a path or a
bend in the road, although usually the bend in the road
when rounded only reveals another bend, as topping a hill
only shows another hill before you. Yet I could not resist.
I followed this one into the forest, my hand upon my
sword hilt, my eyes questing at once for danger and a pot,
a kettle, or something edible. From a tree I saw a great
streamer of bark ripped away, which brought to mind a
way in which we had often made baskets or boxes as a
child.

Our problem was solved. Searching for the bark

needed, I found some chestnuts the squirrels had over-looked. Studying the earth for more, I found something else.

A footprint.

A tiny, pointed toe. A track made by a slipper never intended for the forest, nor for a lady to wear walking in the wilderness. It was a slipper for dancing, for the halls of a castle.

Squatting on my heels, I studied the footprint. A damp leaf was pressed into the earth. Lifting it, I saw the earth was damp underneath. As it had begun to rain only a short time before, a brief rain already turning to sleet, there was a good chance that track had been made since the rain began. How long ago? A half hour? An hour?

What was such a woman doing in the forest at such a time? Unless she had been all night in the forest, she must have left some castle before daybreak.

If such was the case, somebody must come looking for her, which meant our ruin would be searched as an obvious place of hiding. Hence we must leave at once.

But where was *she*?

Rising to my feet, I looked carefully around. The track had come from the direction in which I was going, and had she come further than this, would I not have seen her tracks? I had been searching the ground for whatever might be useful and could scarcely have missed them.

No doubt she had seen me and had hidden herself nearby.

"If you can hear me"—I spoke loudly—"please accept me as a friend. I know not who you may be, but those who come seeking you will find me, and I would be far from here before they arrive. It may be I can help you."

Rain fell softly on leaves, freezing there. It was growing colder. "There is little time if you are to escape. I have a friend and horses nearby."

A long, slow minute passed, and I began to walk away. Then there was a sudden movement, and a voice called out, "*Please!* I am in great trouble!"

She stood beside some brush where she had hidden

herself on my approach. She was slender, wore a cloak reaching almost to the ground, and carried in her hand a small bundle.

"Mademoiselle!" I bowed. "If I can be of help . . . ?"

"Oh, you can! You can! I must not be taken!"

"Come then." I took her hand and helped her through the grass, something she was perfectly capable of doing without me, but I have observed the easiest way to reassure a woman is simply to be courteous, as with anyone else.

Julot glanced up from the fire as we appeared in the opening. He stared as if he could not believe his eyes. "Ah, Kerbouchard! There is no one like him!" he said ironically. "He goes into a dark forest at daybreak and returns with a beautiful woman! It is easy to see you are a sailor's son!"

"We must go," I said, and explained.

My horse rolled her eyes at the lady but did not object when I put her into the saddle. She had an understanding rare among beasts.

33

It was dark when we reached the village. On the skyline beyond the cluster of houses and the trees loomed the towering keep of Castle Blandy.

The hour was past sundown, and the houses were shuttered and dark. Travelers by night were rare and not welcomed in the small villages. God-fearing folk were in their homes or inns before darkness, and only thieves, vagabonds, and evil things roamed the night.

The streets were muddy from recent rains, and our horses' hooves made no sound. The cottage of the man we sought lay at the edge of town, bordering on the lands of the chapel. Julot rapped upon the door.

There was a cautious movement within, and Julot spoke softly. "Fat Claire is our friend."

"What do you seek?"

"Sanctuary and freedom."

The gate opened then, and we rode in. Persigny stared hard at the woman, but seemed reassured when he looked at Julot.

"Who are you?"

"I am Julot, a student of Paris, and a friend of Fat Claire's."

"And the lady? One of Claire's?"

"No!" My tone was sharp. "Truly a *lady*, but one who must be far from here before another day is gone."

"Inside!" He gestured toward the door, then took our horses to the stable for water and grain.

The floor was stone-paved, unusual in the houses of peasants—if he was one. Obviously, it was very ancient, and the walls were thick. The shutters seemed formed from solid boards and fit snugly, allowing no light.

A woman brought a steaming dish of stew with large chunks of meat and many vegetables. She also brought an earthenware jar containing wine.

As we ate, Julot explained our plight, and Persigny listened without comment. It was my feeling he had assisted in many such ventures and was not surprised. He was a tall man with a tuft of gray curly hair atop his head, a sparse beard on a thin, ascetic face.

"They have no patience with freethinkers," he commented, "and we have already been alerted to watch for you." He glanced at Julot. "You have not been identified, so when you leave him, you are safe."

His attention went to the girl. "You, madame, are in serious trouble."

He turned to me. "This lady is the Comtesse de Malcrais, bride of Count Robert, possessor of vast estates in the Holy Land."

"This man was not involved in my transgressions—if such they are to be called. I fled into the forest, and he helped me."

"Nonetheless, he has been seen with you this day. From what I hear of the Count he will not believe your meeting was accident nor your traveling together innocent."

"Before I return to him," the Comtesse said quietly, "I will kill myself. It was not by my choice that I became his wife, nor am I his wife except in name. After we were married he spent the night drinking and fell asleep at the table. I heard his friends laughing because he was drunk on his wedding night, so I fled into the woods."

"What of your family?"

"My father was master of Saône, one of the greatest Crusader castles in the Holy Land. By marrying me Count Robert becomes its master. He abducted me and brought me here against my will."

"If you do not protect her," Julot said, "I shall. I know of this Count Robert. An evil man. He is no husband for a lady such as this."

Food was prepared for us to take with us. It was doubtful if any had seen us close to the village, but there are always prying eyes, and we could not be certain.

"Where can you go to escape him?" Persigny said. "He is a man of great influence, with the Church as well as the King."

"I go to Provins. Once there I shall be with friends."

"To Provins? Ah! Perhaps that makes the problem less difficult. To Provins, indeed."

"If word has come this far, it will have been carried further. The high roads will be watched."

"There are back roads, and our horses are swift," I said.

"Eat," Persigny said, "and get some sleep. Perhaps I have a way."

We continued to eat, and for the first time I saw the Comtesse de Malcrais with her hood thrown back. Her hair and eyes were dark, her skin like cream, her lips soft and beautifully shaped. She might have been nineteen, perhaps less, in any event a ripe age for marriage when most were wed at twelve and thirteen.

Her figure was lovely, and she had beautiful, expressive hands. She caught my eyes upon her and smiled, a warm, friendly smile . . . I would it had been otherwise.

"What has been said is true, and I must warn you. Count Robert will not rest until he has me again."

"How does it come you were in possession of the Castle of Saône?"

"From my father, but from my first husband, also. A woman cannot hold a castle, and when my first husband was killed, it was necessary for me to marry. It is the custom in the Holy Land for a widow in possession of a castle to marry again, at once, so the castle will have a strong man to defend it. The widow has no choice, for if such castles are to be held against the infidel, it must be as I have said.

"Count Robert envied my husband the possession of Saône and its lands, which pay tribute. I believe it was he who murdered my husband."

"Murdered?"

"Supposedly by a band of infidels. I think, and Colin thinks, it was Count Robert and his men."

"Colin?"

"The captain of those who defend the castle, and a good man. It was he who helped me escape, but I was taken again and married in the Church so there could be no question as to the validity of the marriage. Count Robert has enemies in the Holy Land."

"I dislike to hurry you"—Persigny arose—"but what is to be done must be done by night, and in silence." We arose, and I gave my hand to Julot who would remain here for a few days, then become a pilgrim wending his way to Paris.

From my saddlebags I took a small, hand-bound book in leather containing my own translations of Lucretius and Suleiman the Merchant.

The first was one of the great philosophical poems of all time, the second the account of a traveler in China, written in 851, containing information about commercial dealings between China and the Moslem world. Suleiman also refers to a strange custom of the Chinese, who used fingerprints as signatures, maintaining no two fingerprints were alike and could not be forged. It was a practice already hundreds of years old in that land.

"Take this," I said. "I wish it were more."

"Ah, a book! I have never owned a book. You mean it is mine?"

We parted there, and I followed Persigny into the night, the Comtesse walking beside me, the horses following. We went down a lane between stone barns and hayricks, then crossed a pasture and paused at the edge of a dark wood.

After a moment of listening we followed a narrow path into the wood to the edge of a pool. Beyond it was a grotto. In the distance a large building, no doubt a château, loomed against the sky.

The pool was divided by a stone wall as were some artificial lakes to facilitate cleaning. On one side of the wall was water, the other side an empty hollow. Walking out upon the wall, Persigny lifted a sluice gate and the water began falling into the empty side of the pool. When the water had emptied, he went down into the hole where the water had been, brushed aside some sodden leaves, and catching hold of an iron ring, a ring that fitted neatly into a crack between the floor stones, he opened a stone door.

Obviously, there were counterweights, for the door swung back easily, revealing a ramp. Motioning for us to follow, he went down the ramp, and he closed the opening behind us. Above, we could hear the water once more falling into the pool.

Meanwhile he lighted a candle, and we glimpsed stalls for twenty or more horses, all empty now, and storage bins with grain and hay, long unused. He pointed down a long passage opening before us.

"Follow it, and you will arrive in Provins. Make no sound, not even a whisper, for the first half mile. At a point not far distant this passage passes close to a secret passage from the Castle Blandy. The lord of that castle has never been aware of this one, but we did hear someone moving in their passage once."

Looking off into the darkness, I had doubts. "What of air? What of light?"

"Take a supply of candles or torches. You will find others at intervals. Air circulates in the tunnel by some means we have not discovered, but if more is needed, you will find occasional rings in the wall. Pull on a ring, and a small opening will appear. Stand by the openings to breathe, but when you pass on, be sure the openings are closed."

"And at Provins?"

"There are catacombs of a sort beneath that city. There is a maze of subterranean passages, some of them dating to a time before the Romans, but be careful where you emerge. Listen, first."

Still, I hesitated. I had my fill of such places before this. "To Provins? It must be thirty miles!"

"The distance is not important. The passage was built over several hundred years and a long time ago. Monks carrying grain or wine from one monastery to another were often robbed by such barons as he who inhabits Blandy, so this tunnel was built to enable them to come and go as they wished.

"There were many monks; few knew or cared what they did, and this passage is known to none outside the Church and only a few inside. It has not been used for many years, but the account of it is hidden in the archives."

"I would not deceive you. I am escaping because of words spoken of which some teachers did not approve."

He shrugged. "There are shades of opinion, my friend. We here are followers of Abelard, and pleased to be so."

"And Fat Claire?"

He looked me in the eye. "She is my sister."

Holding my torch high, I looked down the passage as Persigny walked away. "Are you afraid, Comtesse?"

"Yes, but I have often been afraid and, no doubt, shall be afraid many more times. No one, in our world, I think, lives without fear." She turned to me. "I do not even know your name."

"Mathurin Kerbouchard, but I am not, as I appear, a soldier. I have been many things, a man of the sea, a translator of books, a vagabond, a merchant, and occasionally, a physician."

"You are a landless man?"

What happened at my home, I told her, and of what took place later, with Tournemine.

"A man who handles a sword need not long be landless. The followers of William of Normandy did very well for themselves, and Roger of Sicily, too."

"You could become a knight," she agreed, "or win a patent of nobility."

"It interests me less than you would believe. The difference between a brigand or wandering soldier and a noble is scarcely a generation."

"It is a bit more than that, I think."

"Or less. It might take several generations to achieve a Count Robert. It seems to me that blue blood only becomes important when red blood begins to run thin."

Being of the nobility, she did not wish to agree with me, but no doubt, she knew her own family history. I did not know hers, but could guess. The Crusaders may have had noble motives, but loot was at least a secondary object, and their desire to free the Holy Sepulcher did not stop them from capturing and looting a Christian city or two.

We rode for some time in silence, and when the air became close and hot, we stopped near one of the rings in the wall and, tugging on it, found that it opened stiffly to let in cool night air. A moon had arisen, and we could see woods and fields. The opening was in some kind of a wall, a castle, perhaps. We breathed deeply, waited a few minutes in silence, then closed the opening and went on.

"Where do you go?" she asked.

"To Provins, where I have friends. If they are not present, I shall await them, then on to Kiev."

Startled, she turned to stare at me. *"Kiev?"*

"Yes."

"But it is far!"

"From there I shall go to Constantinople, to Trebizond, and even further."

"It is my way, too. I must return to Saône."

"Come with us. My friends are many, and there are women among them. We travel well."

She did not reply, and for a long time there was no sound but our horses' hooves on the stones beneath. A trickle of water ran along the center of the floor, water scarcely a half-inch deep.

"The book you gave your friend? What was it?"

Briefly, I explained, adding, a little smugly I am afraid, that it was my own translation.

"You read Latin then? And Arabic?" She paused. "I have known few people who could read."

"The nobility rarely read. It might make them think."

"You are not complimentary."

"How many have you known who knew much but war, hunting, or drinking?"

"I believe you do not like us."

"I like *you*. You are a very beautiful woman."

We opened another notch to breathe the air. It was almost day, and we could see rolling hills and a flock of sheep.

"I have never been alone with a man before, one to whom I was not married."

"You have no need to be afraid. I shall warn you beforehand."

"Warn me? Of what?"

"It is far to Provins. Perhaps I shall wait until then. Perhaps even longer."

"I thought you were gallant."

"A word of more than one meaning, as you may know. Yes, I believe I am gallant. If I made love to you, would I be less gallant?"

"Without my permission, yes."

"Oh, I should have your permission! I wouldn't think of it otherwise."

She turned on me, her eyes sparkling with anger. "Do you believe, for one minute, that I would allow you, a vagabond, a landless man, to make love to *me*?"

"Of course."

"Never . . . unless you take me by force."

"Don't keep harping on that idea. It sounds too much like an invitation. No, no matter how much you expect me to, I shall not. I shall wait. The kisses of a woman who has been humbled are the sweeter for it."

"You are the most egotistical man I ever met." Her tone became cool. "We will discuss the subject no longer."

"If I discuss it, you will leave me?"

"I cannot escape you, you know that."

"A satisfying thought, is it not?"

We rode on in silence until finally I said, "A true gentleman is at a disadvantage in dealing with women. Women are realists, and their tactics are realistic, so no man should be a gentleman where women are concerned unless the women are very, very old or very, very young. Women admire gentlemen, and sleep with cads."

How far we had come I had no idea, but we had ridden most of the day. During our occasional stops, we gave the horses a chance for fresh air also, and I took time to study the construction of the tunnel. It seemed to have been built at intervals over an extended period. Judging by the masonry, I believed the tunnel must have been built for some distance, and then work ceased for many years and then was begun anew. From place to place the styles of the masonry were different, and even the materials.

No doubt it had taken several hundred years to complete it, but there need have been no shortage of manpower during that time. Yet wars and political confusions within the Church may have caused stoppages.

We came upon old entrances walled up and several places for escape from the tunnel; yet where they emerged, I had no idea nor time to investigate.

At one of the places where we stopped for fresh air, we shared our bread and meat, but she remained cool.

"What is your given name?" I asked.

"I am the Comtesse de Malcrais."

I smiled. "You can call me what you wish."

"I have several ideas about that!"

"Good! You have imagination, at least. Share them with me? What would you call me?"

"An unmannered peasant, a boor, an impossible, ungallant person—oh, I could think of many things!"

"Well, not bad, but they are rather the usual names, are they not?"

"I expect you are accustomed to them."

"I have some names for you, too." She stiffened, her nostrils flaring a little, her lips tightening. "You are beautiful; you have a very provocative mouth, one that was meant for kisses. Your shoulders are lovely. As for your legs . . . I haven't seen enough of them to express an opinion, but probably they are ugly."

"They are not!"

"I am sure they are. However, you have a warm color, especially right now, and very, very beautiful eyes."

"You make jokes."

"No, you *are* beautiful. Your lips would be very soft to kiss, very warm, and I think—"

She got to her feet. "It is late. I think we should be moving on."

"Of course." Helping her into the saddle, I felt her arm stiffen. I mounted, and we rode on in silence. When next we stopped for air it was dark and the air was colder.

"We are close now, Comtesse."

"My name is Suzanne!"

"Yes. We are close now, Comtesse."

She lifted her chin at me; then we rode on until we came to the end of the long tunnel, and there was a stable there, too. Like the first it had been long unused.

"I do not know what lies outside. We must be prepared for anything."

I drew my sword.

"All right," she said, "I am ready."

Reaching up, I took hold of the ring. For a moment, I hesitated, then I pulled on the ring.

As the door grated and swung slowly open, I stood with my left hand holding the bridle, my right hand gripping my sword.

34

The door swung on its counterbalance, and we stood in a vaulted, deserted room. All was dust, a few ancient boards piled against a wall, and cobwebs. The room seemed not to have been entered for years.

There were arrow ports, and as we walked our horses across the room, I peered out. It was dark and still. The air from the arrow ports was cold.

The view was that of a narrow street, a crooked street where we could see but a few yards in either direction. Unbarring the door, we went outside, closing the door behind us.

The door had been so rigged that when it opened, the bar lifted automatically, and when it closed, the bar fell into place once more. Mounting, the Comtesse and I walked our horses along the street into the town.

All was dark and quiet. We needed shelter and a place where we could remain out of sight until the von Gildersterns' caravan arrived if it was not already here. And we needed food.

We found an inn on the outskirts of town, one that gave indication of being well-appointed. The common room was crowded, and the host came to us at once. His glance was hard and suspicious.

"Is this the inn patronized by the *Hansgraf* von Gilderstern?"

His manner changed. "Hah? You are a friend of the *Hansgraf*? This is not the inn to which he comes, but I know him well. He came often to the inn of my father, beyond the walls. He will be here for the fair?"

"I am a merchant of his caravan. I left him at Montauban to meet my sister. We are to join him here."

"Ah? You were not at St. Denis? We heard he was there." He turned. "Pierre! To the yard! See to the merchant's horses!"

He took up a massive ring and keys. "I have a fine room. I was saving it for the *Hansgraf*, hoping to get his business. I hope you will recommend us."

"See that we are not disturbed, and notify us at once when the caravan comes to town."

He led the way to a comfortable room with two beds and a large fireplace. He knelt and lighted the fire upon the hearth.

He brought a pitcher and a bowl. "I would have known she was your sister," he said. "You favor one another."

"*Merci*. There could be no greater compliment," I answered, smothering a smile at the shocked expression on the face of the Comtesse. "My sister is the loveliest of women."

When he had gone she turned on me. "How dare he say such a thing! It is nonsense!"

"A good sign, I thought. People often fall in love with those who resemble them because they can imagine no beauty greater than their own. That may be why you are falling in love with me, because we resemble each other."

"I am not falling in love with you." Her tone was icy. "We are to sleep in the same room?"

"There is no other way. Had we asked for separate rooms, they would not have understood. It is not the custom for husband and wife, brother and sister, or whatever, to remain apart in strange inns. A woman by herself is in danger."

"And am I not in danger here, with you?"

"That would depend, madame, on your definition of danger. Some people are afraid of one thing, some of another."

"If you come to my bed, I shall scream for help."

"Madame, if I come to your bed, I shall not need help."

She removed her cloak with an angry gesture, and I took it from her and hung it on the wall.

"You were quick to tell them who you were, but why Montauban?"

"If one would remain hidden, Comtesse, one must be obvious, not mysterious. Had I not told them who I was and who you were, they would have been curious, which leads to imaginings. I identified myself as a merchant here to meet a known caravan. My identity is established, and we are no longer of interest.

"Moreover, I did not want us associated with the road from Paris. If soldiers come searching for us, the innkeeper might have mentioned that we had come by that road, and they might have come to ask whom we had seen on that road."

"You are good at this. It inclines me to believe you have often been a fugitive."

"Beautiful women are the wives or daughters of powerful men. Naturally, I have been a fugitive."

"Do you make a practice of this? Of running off with strange women?"

"All women are strange until they become familiar, but I have forgotten other women. How could even a memory be left after having seen you?"

"You are lying."

"Perhaps, but even a lie may carry truth. It is a paradox, but is not all life a paradox?" I paused. "Now shall we lie down together and discuss paradoxes, life, and strange meetings by the wayside?"

Before she could reply, our meal was at the door, and we ate in silence, as we were both tired and hungry. As the warmth of the fire and wine crept into our tired muscles, I thought of her home. "Tell me about Saône," I said.

"It was built long ago on the foundations of an earlier, Byzantine castle. It was to guard the southern approaches to Antioch. They built upon a promontory jutting out to the westward, with a gorge on either side. Two deep ditches were dug across the neck of the promontory, one of these to defend the approach to the gate, another to divide the castle into two sections in the event the first was taken.

"You know about such things, but the castles were built to defend land the Crusaders had won, and many of the Crusaders did not return to their homelands, but stayed to rule their vast estates in Lebanon.

"There are subterranean storage chambers for supplies; there are mills to grind grain, as well as wells and cisterns for water. The castles were sited so they could communicate with each other by signal fires, but if the distance was too great, they used carrier pigeons."

"It must cost a fair amount to keep it all going."

"We have income from a dozen villages and much land, but a few years before my father was killed he had to be ransomed from the Arabs, which cost many thousands in gold."

"What will you do if you return to Saône? Will they not want you to marry?"

"I must, to hold the castle and the land, but there are others than Count Robert. He knows that, too, and will not want me to return to Saône except as his wife." She glanced at me. "He will kill you if he finds us together."

"What better place to die? In your arms, I mean."

She was exasperated. "Are you never serious? You are in danger, far more than you believe."

We slept in separate beds, but I was sure she had a knife and was prepared to defend herself, and I am quite sure she remained awake most of the night. I, on the other hand, slept deeply and well.

Knowing little about women's thoughts, I have no idea how the Comtesse felt about me. She was, I suspect, ready to use the knife during the first hour and perhaps during the second. By the third hour I suspect she was wishing I would make some attempt so she could settle the matter and get some sleep. Her state of mind after that I would not attempt to assess.

When the sun came up, I went down to the common room and ate my breakfast, taking hers to her.

"Did you sleep well?" I asked, all innocence.

"I slept *very* well!"

"Good. The caravan should arrive today, and you must be rested for travel."

During the afternoon, dressed in a cloth coat and cap, I risked a visit to the town. My clothes were such as a prosperous merchant would wear, so with the influx of people for the fair I was not likely to attract attention. However, I did a little advance work for the caravan and discovered the *Hansgraf* was well known here.

It was evening before I returned. The Comtesse was awaiting me. "How much longer must I be cooped up here?" she protested. "It is maddening!"

"Go now, if you wish. Count Robert may not be in the town, but I am sure he has spies here."

"You might at least stay with me!"

"I have matters to arrange, but I thought you might prefer to be alone. It must be difficult for you to be in a room with a mere merchant."

She did not reply to that. Today, she looked even more beautiful and had wrapped her braids about her head in a perfectly enchanting way, and she was wearing pearls. Knowing a bit about such things, I thought it was obvious they were worth more money than I had ever seen.

The Comtesse wore a clinging white gown, a close-fitting garment with tight sleeves above the elbow, falling wide and open below the elbow. With her dark hair and eyes she was astonishingly beautiful. How she managed with the small amount of clothing she brought with her, I had no idea. Yet the result was certainly worth the effort.

I told her about the town, a pleasant, walled town where our arrival had been accepted without curiosity, yet I was wary. Not for a moment did I underestimate the jealousy of Count Robert, who wanted not only the castle but the girl as well. The former meant the power equal to that of a crowned king, and the loveliness of the Comtesse was answer to the second consideration.

While in town I purchased a fur-lined tunic that came to my knees, and new leather boots that pulled on over plain hose. The boots came to just above the calf and were beautifully made. Walking in the town, I carried no sword, but I had two daggers beneath the tunic that could be reached through a slit in the front just above the belt.

There was knocking at the door. It was the innkeeper. He was visibly nervous.

"There have been queries about a lady. Knowing you for a friend of the *Hansgraf*, I said nothing about—about your sister."

"Who made the inquiries?"

"Soldiers of a Count Robert. He rode into town this morning with about thirty men, and I am sure they will be back."

"Do you wish us to leave?"

"Would you? But stay until the night. The *Hansgraf* should be here by then."

Taking up my sword, I placed it conveniently on the table. Glancing again at the innkeeper, I decided to trust to his discretion.

"What I have said is true. I am a merchant of the caravan led by *Hansgraf* Rupert von Gilderstern. As you have guessed, the lady is not my sister. She was to be forced into marriage with Count Robert. A castle is at stake as well as the happiness of the Comtesse."

He dismissed the explanation with a gesture. "It is nothing. Count Robert comes, he goes. In a lifetime I shall not see him again, but each year the *Hansgraf* comes to Provins, spends much money here, brings much business. He is a good man much respected. Do not worry."

When he had gone the Comtesse turned quickly to me. "You must go! If you are found with me, he will kill you!"

It irritated my masculine pride that she thought me so easily killed. "Madame, we Kerbouchards do not kill so easily. This blade"—I gestured to the sword—"has taken the life of one baron not long since. No doubt it can take the life of another."

"You killed a *baron*?"

"After we had taken his fortress by storm. Barons, my Comtesse, bleed as easily as merchants or peasants. This one bled like the thief he was. The Baron de Tournemine—"

"Tournemine?"

"Not a relative, I hope?"

"No, but a captain at the Castle of Saône once served him, a man named Taillefeur."

"Trust him not. I believe he betrayed my father, and he tried to rob me. He is a mercenary without their virtue of loyalty. If he is not in the pay of Count Robert, I would be surprised."

"I trust him."

"Others have, to their cost. Once I nearly cracked his skull, and only wish I had struck harder."

She was frightened. "If I cannot trust my own captains, then whom can I trust?"

I bowed. "You may trust me with your castle, your wealth, your life, but not too many nights in the same room with you."

Her eyes were amused. "You have spoken so much of that, merchant, that I wonder if you are not just a talker."

Stung, I started to reply, but she laughed, and turned her back on me. That white dress did admirable things to her hips, which were shapely, very—

A sudden uproar in the street took me to the window. Six men-at-arms clustered there, and with them was a tall, powerfully made man with a swarthy face and thick black brows. Nobody needed to tell me this was Count Robert.

Turning swiftly, I said, "Do you remain here, and make no sound. I shall go below." Belting on my sword, I turned to the door.

She caught my arm. "No! *Please!* He will kill you!"

Bending my head, I kissed her lightly on the lips and regretted that I must leave.

"Wait for me. If I die, I take the memory of your lips

with me." Adding, for my own information, that I did not intend to die. Too much remained to be done.

Count Robert was approaching the steps when I appeared on them. "Stand aside," he ordered, "I wish to mount the stairs."

"At the head of the stairs," I replied, "is one room. It is my room. You have no business there."

"Stand aside, I said!" His black eyes were cold. "Or I shall spill your innards and walk over them to the room."

"If you come up these stairs," I said, "we shall see whose innards lie upon them." I drew my sword. "Come, if you wish. You can bite on this steel."

Coolly, he stepped back and motioned to the men behind him. "I do not fight with commoners. These do it for me."

"An excuse for cowardice," I replied.

Count Robert gestured at the men-at-arms. "Kill him," he said.

"If they advance one step," a voice called out in a haughty tone that once heard could not be forgotten, "I shall hang the lot of them, and you higher than the rest.

"I am the *Hansgraf* Rupert von Gilderstern, of the White Company of traders. This man is a merchant of our company."

"I have thirty men!" Count Robert declared.

"And I have five times that number." The *Hansgraf* stood on the landing inside the door, feet apart, hands clasped behind him. "They are veterans of more than three hundred battles, Count Robert. Any five of my men would take your thirty and spit them like frogs."

The *Hansgraf* put a hand on his hip. "If you have had no experience of war with a merchant caravan, Count Robert, this will be a lesson to you, a lesson you would not live to appreciate."

The *Hansgraf* stepped down into the room, and a dozen of his men followed after. Months of hard riding in all kinds of weather had darkened and toughened their faces. Their armor bore dents from many conflicts. They were lean, muscular men ready for whatever must be done.

Count Robert's men lowered their weapons, and giving them an ugly glance, Count Robert strode from the room, followed by his men.

The *Hansgraf* held out his hand. "You disappear, then appear again! It is good to see you, Kerbouchard!"

Then he added, "I would suggest you disguise the lady, and we will go to the market where we are known."

The Comtesse appeared at the head of the steps. "I am ready, *Hansgraf*, and you have my thanks."

She came down the steps wearing the old cloak worn when we first met in the forest, the hood covering her hair.

Turning to me, she said, "From the actions of the Count I can see it is not only the rascals who have rascality." She looked up at me. "And not only the nobles, Kerbouchard, who have nobility!"

35

The fair at Provins was one of the largest in France during the twelfth century. There was a fair in May, but the most important was that in September. Now the unseasonably cold, wet weather had disappeared, and the days were warm and sunny.

Long sheds without walls covered the display of goods. Silks, woolens, armor, weapons, leather goods, hides, pottery, furs, and every conceivable object or style of goods could be found there.

Around the outer edge of the market where the great merchants had their displays were the peasants, each with some small thing for sale. Grain, hides, vegetables, fruit, goats, pigs, and chickens, as well as handicrafts of various kinds.

Always there was entertainment, for the fairs attracted magicians, troupes of acrobats, fire-eaters, sword-swallowers, jugglers, and mountebanks of every kind and description.

The merchants usually bought and sold by the gross; hence, they were called *grossers*, a word that eventually came to be spelled *grocer*. Dealing in smaller amounts allowed too little chance for profit, and too great a quantity risked being left with odds and ends of merchandise. The White Company had come from Spain with silk and added woolens from Flanders. Our preferred trade was for lace, easy to transport and valued wherever we might go.

Merchants were looked upon with disdain by the nobles, but they were jealous of the increasing wealth and power of such men as the *Hansgraf*, Lucca, Johannes, or a dozen others among us.

The wealth of nobles came from loot or ransoms gained in war or the sale of produce from land worked by serfs, and there were times when this amounted to very little. The merchants, however, nearly always found a market for their goods.

At the Provins fair there were all manner of men and costumes: Franks, Goths, Saxons, Englanders, Normans, Lombards, Moors, Armenians, Jews, and Greeks. Although this trade was less than a century old, changes were coming into being. Some merchants were finding it profitable to settle down in a desirable location and import their goods from the nearest seaport or buy from the caravans.

Artisans had for some time been moving away from the castles and settling in towns to sell their goods to whoever passed. Cobblers, weavers, coppers, potters, and armorers had begun to set up shops rather than doing piecework on order. The merchant-adventurers were merely distributors of such goods.

The finest cloth was made in England and Flanders, woven from wool clipped from sheep grazing on the damp grounds near the sea where they grew the finest wool. Cloaks made from this wool were in great demand, and the greater the distance from the point of origin the better the price.

This was the reason the *Hansgraf* and his company had decided upon the venture to Kiev.

Such cloth was worth fifty times its cost in Kiev, and furs purchased there would bring a fine profit in Byzantium or Italy. Such an extended journey, if successful, could make the fortune of every man present.

The Church looked upon the merchants with disfavor, for trade was considered a form of usury, and every form of speculation considered a sin. Moreover, they were suspicious of the far-traveling merchants as purveyors of freethinking.

Change was in the air, but to the merchant to whom change was usual, any kind of permanence seemed unlikely. The doubts and superstitions of the peasants and nobles seemed childish to these men who had wandered far and

seen much, exposed to many ideas and ways of living. Yet
often the merchant who found a good market kept the
information for his own use, bewailing his experience and
telling of the dangers en route, anything to keep others
from finding his market or his sources of cheap raw material.

Regardless of what the Church as an institution felt,
the convents, monasteries, and churches were among the
merchants' best customers. Vestments worn by Church
prelates were usually the product of Moorish weavers. I
found them, with few exceptions, eager for books or news
and to listen to the experiences of the merchants. Despite
attempts to impose a pattern from above, the priests and
monks in villages and towns were a part of the change that
was altering the face of Europe and tempering its opinions.

One such came to my stall in the market to buy a bit
of brocade for a vestment. We talked of the material, of
Córdoba, of books, and finally of medicine.

"The Arabs," I said, "believe in absolute cleanliness
of the hands and instruments before beginning an operation."

"I have heard"—he looked at me with worried eyes—
"that Maimonides has ventured to criticize Galen himself."

"And rightly so."

He was shocked. "Is there nothing on which we can
place a finger and say, 'This is so, this is correct'?"

"Perhaps, but the one law of the universe seems to be
change. Everything is in a state of flux, and it is better
so."

He shook his head in disagreement, yet not in total
disagreement, I was sure. "Speak softly," he said, "such
remarks are better unheard."

A thought seemed to occur to him. "You are not he
who—?"

He knew I was the one.

Nor could I well deny it, for he might question others
to verify if I was the man who disputed the teacher at the
university.

"I trust your friendship. What I say is as one scholar

to another. At the end of the fair I leave Europe, probably never to return."

"What was it you said?"

"That Bernard of Clairvaux was a fool in taking issue with Abelard. I believe Abelard was a fine scholar, and we need more like him."

"I agree with much of what he taught." He looked at me. "You are fortunate to travel. Possibly a pilgrimage is what I need."

We talked of changes in the laws of the Franks brought about by the presence of the merchants, by their dealings with each other and with the towns. Charlemagne had begun it by promoting travel within his empire, but the merchants caused basic changes in the law by introducing elements foreign to earlier thinking.

In a civilization based primarily upon agriculture, with all law based upon the use of land, we merchants brought new considerations. Authority stemmed from the king, the Church, and the great barons, and all property was rooted in the land. Merchants were subject to few of the existing laws, so they had evolved codes of their own for use among themselves. Local courts began to have recourse to these laws in settling disputes in which merchants were involved.

These laws made the merchant a privileged person, free of the laws that bound the citizens. The barons, enjoying taxes paid by the merchants as well as the trade they introduced, offered special treatment to merchant caravans.

The tall young monk whose special interest was the law was intrigued by this. It fitted his mind for the acceptance of change.

The Comtesse, who had never witnessed a fair, was very excited. Donning a costume from Arabia that one of the wives in the caravan offered her, she emerged to enjoy it.

People had come from miles away to sell their goods or simply to enjoy the performances and the excitement. Aside from our own caravan, now merged with that of

Peter, five others were present. One was Italian, another was from Armenia; Germans from the shores of the Baltic, Venetians, and Netherlanders were all attending the fair.

We merchants had our own *argot*, and our signals to warn of impending trouble. Within a few minutes after the fair opened all the merchants knew about Count Robert and who it was he sought. Among us we numbered more than a thousand tough, seasoned fighting men. The jugglers, magicians, and acrobats were our allies also, and the various companies knew each other from many previous meetings. No matter what differences they might have with each other, and they were few, all stood together against trouble.

Suddenly, at my elbow, there was a word. Turning, I saw the wrinkled, wily old Khatib! Khatib, from Córdoba! My friend the beggar, the thief, the purveyor of information!

"Ah, but it warms my heart to see you!" He gestured. "I am with the jugglers."

Opening a hollow in the handle of his dagger, he took out a rolled up bit of writing.

> *I have not forgotten.*
> V.

The Comtesse saw it, glancing quickly from it to me. "From a woman?"

Khatib grinned at me, bowing elaborately to her. "What leopard does not recognize the tracks of another leopard?"

He spoke in Arabic, but she replied quickly, "You liken me to a leopard?"

We were astonished, for neither had guessed that she spoke Arabic, yet why not? She had grown up in a castle in an Arab land.

"All women are huntresses; all are deadly."

"I am not surprised that this man is your friend," she said to me. "You think alike."

Without comment I showed her the note. She lifted an eyebrow, then handed it back. "I wonder what you could have done that would make anyone remember you past the second day?"

"I do not expect to be remembered," I said, "only enjoyed."

Suddenly there was a burst of cheers, and we turned to see a man doing a handstand with one hand atop a tall pole held by another man. Then the jugglers, a sword-swallower, and others were crowding about.

"It must be wonderful, to live like that!" the Comtesse said.

"It is a matter of viewpoint," I said, "the man on the pole has a crippled child whom he lives for. The sword-swallower is an orphan who knew neither father nor mother. They have many troubles, Comtesse."

"You *know* them?"

"They are my friends," I said, "and I can even do some of their acts."

"You amaze me."

"All things fascinate me, and I love skills. Then, who knows? Some day I may need to disappear. Who remembers the face of an acrobat?"

Days passed, and trade was good, but I was uneasy. Count Robert was not a man to yield when so much was at stake. Moreover, he was a good hater. I had seen it in his eyes. The fair had been one of our most successful, and now we prepared to leave. But we were not leaving alone, for after many conferences the other caravans planned to join the *Hansgraf*, as he was widely known for his business acumen.

No cloth of Flanders had been marketed in Kiev, although occasional cloaks of the material had been seen there, some sold by their owners for outrageous prices. An Armenian among us who had traded there said the market for silk and lace would be very good.

The night before we were to leave, a message arrived. It was pressed suddenly into my hand at the market.

If you would know the whereabouts of your father, come to the east postern.

Mounting Ayesha, one of the mares, I rode into town. Only Safia knew of my father, Safia and the Comtesse.

Leaving the mare in the shadow of the wall, I watched the postern.

Time passed and no one approached. Was this a trap? If Safia was here, where was she? For an hour I waited, but there was no sound, no movement.

And then I noticed something I had not seen before.

The gate stood ajar.

36

Beyond the gate . . . what?

For several minutes I studied the situation. Had the gate been open when I first saw it? I did not believe so, but how could I be sure?

Suppose Safia waited there? Or someone else? Perhaps an enemy?

No matter, if there was news of my father, it was news I must have.

So be it. If this was a trap, let them spring it. As I edged along the wall to the gate, my attention was riveted upon it. Stepping out from the wall, I started toward it.

Around me were two dozen armed men, all with drawn swords.

The open gate had been a trap. It had been the bait that distracted my attention, that demanded I focus upon it, a focus that distracted me from the buildings around and what might be there. The gate was pushed wider, and Count Robert came through.

"How did you know of my father?"

Count Robert's smile revealed his even white teeth. He was pleased with himself. "My men listened around the market. There is always gossip . . . a word here, a word there."

There seemed no escape. Could I reach him, kill him, before they killed me? Could I throw my blade, javelinlike, into his throat?

"Are you going to fight me then? Or avoid it?"

"Fight you? Why should I fight you? I shall simply

have you whipped for your insolence, and when I am tired
of watching you whipped, you will be hung."

They formed a wide circle about me, but I had my
sword in my hand and knew I would never be taken alive
to be whipped like a slave.

A wild, weird cry sounded. My every sense became
alert.

"Sheathe your sword!"

Those surrounding me stared about, wildly. The voices
seemed to come from nowhere. "Pay no attention!" Count
Robert believed the shout had been for his men. "*Take
him!*"

An instant I had hesitated, then slammed my blade
home into its sheath. A rope dropped beside me, and
grasping it high as I could reach, I went up, hand over
hand! The rope had dropped from a balcony in the gate
tower, and up there was Khatib with Lolyngton, one of
the acrobats with whom I had rehearsed in Córdoba.

Luckily, not one of the soldiers of Count Robert was
an archer, or my body would have bristled with arrows. As
it was, they charged the gate tower, but as they did so,
several of our men appeared with arrows in place and
bows bent.

As I swung myself over the balcony rail, the *Hansgraf*
appeared, stepping out upon the balcony. As usual he was
clad in black, his only ornament a gold chain slung about
his waist in two loops.

"Count Robert!" He spoke pompously, but with enormous effect. "Enough of this nonsense! We will not be
distracted by you! My messenger has gone to His Majesty,
who, as you may well surmise, is delighted by the heavy
duties we pay from our combined companies!

"Now, sir, you and your men will drop your swords
where you stand. I allow no time for discussion. Upon my
ceasing to speak if one man still grips a sword, he will be
killed by my archers.

"Then you will depart from Provins, being out of the
city before the sun is in the sky, or my men will hunt you
down and hang you like the dogs you are!

"We are busy men! We have no time to play at war with you! *Drop your blades!*"

Swords rattled on the pavement. Count Robert's face was swollen with anger, for he stood in the light of the moon, clearly seen.

"Now," the *Hansgraf* said, "*March!*"

And they marched.

When I came to our house beside the wall, the Comtesse ran to me. "Oh, you are safe! You are safe!"

"Thanks to the *Hansgraf*."

"It is Khatib you must thank. He suspected something and went to the *Hansgraf*. I never saw men assemble so quickly."

"Out upon the high road, Comtesse, there is no time. One is prepared, or one dies in the next breath. Attacks are without warning."

We were silent, realizing with almost the same breath that we were standing in each other's arms. She started to draw back, but I drew her gently to me, and she came closer, almost with relief. We stood that way for several minutes before I took her chin in my hand and kissed her gently on the lips.

"I have been a fool," she said then.

"Who is not a fool? Often when one is in love one can only win by losing."

She nestled her head on my shoulder. "There is probably something profound in what you have said, and I shall think about it, some other time."

"Like many things, it only sounds profound, so waste no time upon it. There are other things to think of, and to do."

She drew back quickly. "It is broad daylight, and—"

"We must pack. It will soon be time to move."

She wrinkled her nose at me, but we packed our few things. This time, however, we had taken advantage of the fair to supply ourselves with clothing and whatever might be necessary.

Because of the long trek across Europe, it was decided that we should remain together with our *Hansgraf* as leader. The associated companies would comprise more than a thousand men and, with their pack animals, would make a formidable assembly, but one that required much food, extensive grazing en route, and considerable advance planning. From the companies we had men who knew eve·y bit of the route we must follow and the problems to be faced. Also, we must send forward scouts who would locate grazing for our animals, camping sites, and estimate the possible difficulties to be encountered.

Never shall I forget the morning when the five companies of the first contingent led off on the long march to Kiev.

In the Frankish lands we would keep to two groups, but upon entering the wilder country, where towns were farther apart and castles even fewer, we would travel together but with an advance guard of fifty picked horsemen. Two companies would follow, and a short distance behind, the main body. Finally, there would be a rear guard of twenty horsemen.

We often sang as we marched, and there was always the sound of the marching drum, a sound I shall hear all my life, so deeply is it imbedded in the fibers of my being.

The walking drum . . . a heavy, methodical beat marking the step of each of us. That drum rode on a cart at the rear of our column, and the pace of the march could be made faster or slower by that beat. We lived with that sound, all of us, it beat like a great pulse for the whole company and for those others, too, who had their own drums to keep their pace.

Our armor was not uniform, nor our helmets. Our weapons were of all kinds, although the number of our archers was greater in proportion than any army of the period. We also had a company of slingers whose skill with that weapon was beyond belief. Our horses and draft animals were of the best.

Hardship and storm were daily companions, keeping our bodies conditioned and our minds prepared. We lived with expectation of trouble, a small world that moved under its own power, that could defend itself, and had.

On this trek we had several carts other than that carrying the drum. Some carts carried supplies; some were homes for the women while on the march. These were two-wheeled carts, and ours was driven by Khatib.

Eastward we marched with the turning leaves, the greens changing to brilliant reds and yellows. The green fields turned to brown, and the crops that covered many of them had been reaped, leaving only stubble. Here and there we stopped, holding small fairs of our own, buying or trading for additional supplies and picking up what information we could of the road ahead.

We were attacked the first time near the Meuse, and the second time on the Rhine. Both times we came off well, and the second time we pursued the attackers, overtook them, and captured their horses, stripping the men of armor and weapons but permitting the survivors to go free.

Nightly camps were each a fortress, our columns like an army on the march. We awakened to a trumpet call, marched upon a second, and all our waking days were accompanied by the rhythmic throb of the walking drum.

We heard its muted thunder roll against the distant hills, through sunlight and storm. That drum was our god, our lord and master, and a warning to potential enemies.

The *Hansgraf*, on one of his several great horses, led off each day. He consulted often with the *doyens* who commanded their companies and with merchants whose judgment he respected.

Lolyngton, chief of the acrobats and performers, had become my close friend, and occasionally with him, I departed from the convoy to hunt. He was a master archer, and together we killed several boars, stags, and a number of hares to augment our food supplies.

Upon one of these forays we stumbled upon an ambush. We had seen no travelers, no sheep, nor any riders for some time when Lolyngton and I came suddenly upon a wide band of muddy tracks.

Riding away from that track, we rode cautiously up the slope of a long hill and dismounted. Creeping forward, heads low, we peered over the crest. A half mile away to the north lay the track along which our company would come, and hidden in a copse near the road were several hundred armed men, well mounted.

As many of our men were needed to drive cattle or to handle pack animals, we could muster less than half the force that lay waiting. Had such a force struck without warning, they could have done untold damage, perhaps even destroyed us. No way of avoiding them existed, and a sharp conflict would mean casualties and death.

"If we could strike them now," Lolyngton suggested, "surprise would be on our side."

The fact that we would not now be surprised was an advantage, but how to make the most of it?

When we came in sight, what would they do? Lolyngton said, "Were it me, I would wait until a part of our column passed before attacking."

This was my own conclusion, and probably theirs. Our column would be divided and in confusion, but suppose there was no confusion?

Riding swiftly back to the column, we reported to the *Hansgraf*. He listened attentively, first calling around him the *doyens* as well as Lucca and Johannes. Sarzeau, *doyen* of the largest company other than our own, was a good man, as was Flandrin.

My idea was explained to them. My suggestion was that, as the attack could not be avoided, the column continue along, but when the attack began, that portion which had gone ahead and those who were still behind would each swing around and take the enemy on the flanks.

Quietly, we rode along while all members were alerted. Sarzeau had several carts covered with bull's hide, impervious to arrows. In each of these would be three archers.

Forty horsemen were detached to fall back and to circle and take the enemy from the rear, using the route Lolyngton and I had found. Plans were made, and the disposition of the defenders took place while the column continued to march. Command of the forty horsemen was given to me. "You scouted the route, you know the way."

Lolyngton volunteered to come with me, our party then fell back, substituting for the rear guard.

From the crest of the hill we saw them come storming out of the woods. Our convoy broke, swinging around with military precision, and the attackers were met by a flight of arrows. Military archers were as yet few in any army, and among mercenaries turned outlaw, it was the same. Arrows took several men from the saddle, and then with a shout, we charged down the slope.

The attackers had been caught fairly between the two lines of our convoy and were meeting fierce resistance when we charged into their rear.

We struck them hard, sweeping several of their horses off their feet. A gigantic rider swung at me with a sword, but an arrow took him in the throat before he could complete the blow, and I charged by, slashing another rider across the biceps and seeing his arm fall loose, hanging by a thread.

Lolyngton, drawing off to one side, used his bow and arrows with precision and skill, wasting no time, utterly cool, yet bringing down rider after rider.

A sudden blow swept me from the saddle, and I fell, foot caught in the stirrup, but Ayesha stopped abruptly. Kicking my foot loose, I came up just in time to see a lance point coming at my chest.

Deflecting the lance with my blade, I thrust deep into the attacker's side, blood pouring down my blade and over my hand. Suddenly, the sounds of fighting ceased, and the attack was over.

Victory was ours, but at what cost! The smith, a burly man who was our best ironworker, was dead. A Lombard, one of our best archers, a man whom I had never really known, had also been killed.

Sheathing my bloody sword, I gave myself over to treating the wounded.

Johannes had a spear thrust in the side. It had missed the heart, but he was losing blood. Binding it tightly, I got him stretched out on a blanket, and while Suzanne tended

him I extracted an arrow from the corner of a man's eye.
The eye itself was uninjured, and fortunately, for I knew
little of eyes. The arrow had struck the bridge of the nose
and the eye socket, wedging there, and the man was more
shocked than hurt. A fraction of an inch and he would
have lost the eye, and perhaps worse.

From one to the other I went, taking what emergency
measures I knew, then back to continue the treatment.

The *Hansgraf* watched while I worked. "There are
fourteen dead, and how many wounded?"

"Thirty-seven, and some with scratches of no importance."

It was very good, considering the numbers involved,
but a long trek stretched before us, and we could not wait
beyond the night. There might be further attacks.

Our attackers had lost three times our number of
dead largely due to the precision of our archers. There
were also some of their wounded left on the field.

We collected armor, weapons, and horses from the
field. The *Hansgraf* was worried.

Johannes, his strong right hand, always cool of head,
and cautious in advice, was sorely wounded. It might be
weeks before he recovered—if he did. Flandrin, one of
the *doyens*, had been injured, and we had scarcely room
to carry them in the carts. Suzanne was the first to volun-
teer hers.

It was a forbidding sundown with red flame in the sky
and brown grass taking the color of fire. From our camp
came the moans of the wounded.

Then, as darkness came, from out on the hillside I
heard a low cry, the desperate, wailing cry of a wounded
man. Listening, I heard the cry again.

And I who was considered a physician could not
ignore the sound.

37

Kiev we found a muddy, disagreeable town, but the weather was excellent. We camped in a forest not far from the Dnieper. The weeks of trekking the vast plains, rivers, and mountains had dealt harshly with us.

There had been a short, fierce engagement at the crossing of the Danube, where we lost two men, and eleven were wounded. In Buda one of our men had been killed in a brawl, others injured. By the time we arrived at Kiev we had forty-seven men who must be carried in carts.

A large part of each day was devoted to checking their wounds or prescribing for illnesses. For such a large body the number was not excessive, but as every man had a job, their work fell upon the shoulders of the others.

Our trade in Kiev was all we had hoped for. Woolen cloaks from Flanders commanded prices many times greater than we paid, and within two weeks our merchandise was gone, and our carts and packhorses were heaped high with furs, ermine, marten, fox and wolf skins, elk hides, and much else.

In the ninth century a few bands of Norsemen had swept over this land, defeating the Slavs and establishing themselves in a series of fortified enclosures called *gorods* for protection against the people they ruled. Novgorod was one such, Kiev another. Kiev was the largest trade center, and its prince was superior to all others.

To the east lay the Moslem world of Baghdad, Damascus, Aleppo, and Samarkand. To the south lay Constantinople and the Byzantine Empire, formerly the Eastern Roman Empire, called so but rarely now.

Arab, Jew, and Byzantine traders filtered into Kiev and were quick to establish a working relationship with the rulers from the north. The slave trade, providing slaves for the harems, shops, and large homes of Byzantium, was remunerative. The *Hansgraf* disapproved of serfdom (he was, I believe, born a serf) and would have none of it. He was on good terms with the Scandinavian traders who had settled among the Slavs and were called Russians by the native peoples.

In Córdoba I had read the writings of Constantine Porphyrogenetus who traveled here in the ninth century, and his works were the source of much of the information I had given the *Hansgraf*.

Each year there gathered at Kiev a great fleet of boats, and after the melting of the ice, this flotilla descended the Dnieper to the Black Sea, sailing to Constantinople with slaves, furs, and products of the northern lands. Boats also went upriver, and from there the caravans traveled across country to the Baltic, following a part of the Amber Road.

By the time we arrived in Kiev much of this trade had ceased to exist. Far to the east there was restlessness among the wild tribes of the steppes. The Petchenegs, sometimes called Cumans, had swept across the trade route to Baghdad, and they had almost cut Kiev off from Constantinople by driving their hordes into the lands north of the Black Sea.

Kiev was, in many ways, a more enlightened city than Paris, for Paris lay under the domination of an autocratic Church that was only beginning to broaden its intellectual base, and Kiev, utterly pagan, but drawing upon both Christian and Moslem cultures, was a town where all ideas were of interest.

There was little agriculture about the city. Nomadic herdsmen, dark-eyed and savage fellows with Mongolian features, stalked the streets in tight, well-armed groups, talking to no one. There were tall, blond Vikings from the north, a fierce, piratical people, many of whom had become excellent traders.

"Sometime," I told Suzanne, "I shall write about the relationship between piracy and trade. The one always seems to precede the other, and the most successful pirates have become traders, perhaps on the idea that it is easier to defraud a man than kill him.

"Trade is much superior to piracy. You can rob and kill a man but once, but you can cheat him again and again."

"You are cynical," Suzanne said. "They only sell them what they want."

"If people were sold only what they wanted, there would be little trade, my lady. The soul of business is to inspire people to buy that which they neither want nor need.

"Take our Lucca, for example. Fur makes his neck break out in a rash; yet at each fair in Flanders he wore fur-trimmed robes with such style, such elegance, that many were prevailed upon by their wives to buy cloaks in which they looked neither stylish nor elegant, and which their own woolens far outclassed in many respects."

"Mathurin, has the *Hansgraf* said when we would go south?"

"Soon. He is negotiating with the boatmen to travel with them, but I fear it will come to nothing. They have their own cargo to carry, and we have too many people."

"But if we go overland we must pass through the country of the Petchenegs!"

"The boatmen probably hope we will be attacked. Our goods will be in competition to theirs, for they will be carrying furs also, and gold."

Rising, I belted on my sword and donned a cloak, one of our woolens, purchased in Flanders. "The decision will be made today."

Trade was no longer of interest to me. What I wished for now was Constantinople, a meeting with Safia's friend, and then to do what could be done to free my father—if he still lived.

We had met many travelers, and each I prodded with
questions about Alamut and the Old Man of the Mountains as well as his Valley of the Assassins. Little it was
they could tell beyond what I already knew. They all
agreed that escape from the Valley was impossible, to
enter it equally impossible.

We gathered about our fire in the woods outside
Kiev, an oddly assorted group. Sarzeau was there, his
wounds mended now, but oddly surly. The *Hansgraf* was
flanked by Lucca and Johannes, the latter pale and thin
after his long illness. Flandrin, Grossefeldt, and the others, all
were present. The *Hansgraf* had failed to negotiate a ride
downstream, and the disappointment was great. Following
the long trek across Europe with its fighting and hardship,
they longed for the lazy drift down the river and the sail
across the Black Sea.

Sarzeau was grumbling. A good man and a fighter,
since his wound he had changed. Lucca, commenting on
it, said, "He thinks his luck has run out."

It was obvious he intended to bicker with the *Hansgraf.*
Grossefeldt, a stubborn, hard-headed man but a good
leader, was seated beside him.

Yury Olgevichi was present. He was a leader of a new
faction in Kiev, and I suspected him of some association
with the tribes to the south. There was little on which to
base my suspicion, but I believed he had done much to
see we were denied passage on the boats. Khatib spied
upon the meetings and assured me this was true. One of
his wives was a Magyar woman.

What the *Hansgraf* had in mind, I did not know, but
as we entered the meeting, I whispered to him the news
Khatib brought.

Yury I had seen before and did not like, nor did I like
the way he looked upon Suzanne. It was not only her
beauty that interested him but the importance of Saône.
To possess such a castle would give him immeasurable
prestige, and I suspected Yury of ambitions toward Constantinople itself. Not many years past a prince of Kiev

had led an attack on the Byzantine Empire, driving deep into their territory.

With a strong castle to the south, a fleet on the Black Sea, and a strong land force made up in part of the tribesmen who had moved in south of Kiev, Yury might pose a serious threat to Constantinople.

He was a tall, powerful man with a reputation as a fighter and a statesman as well. If he possessed the Castle Saône, he could prevent supplies or men reaching Constantinople by that route as well as draw upon the manpower available there. He was a somewhat larger man than I, extremely strong, a dangerous antagonist.

The *Hansgraf* opened with a statement. "We have been refused transportation down the river to the sea. I propose we travel overland, following the Dnieper for easier travel."

My head came up, and I stared at him, but he ignored me. Follow the Dnieper? It was insane. The river flowed far to the east before taking a great bend to flow back toward the Black Sea. If he went overland, marching south, it was somewhat less than half the distance. To be sure, there was some protection along the river, but not much. To strike due south was the thing, but I did not interrupt.

Maps were almost nonexistent, and the few who knew the country chose to remain silent and await the *Hansgraf*'s plan.

"We could buy boats," Sarzeau argued. "It is foolish to go overland. We have looked forward to the river and a rest."

"We attempted to buy boats"—Lucca wished to avoid discussion if possible—"and none could be found. They can make more by carrying goods than men."

"We could build our own boats."

"We might build enough by spring," Johannes said, "or we can wait a month until the river freezes and use sleds."

Sarzeau started an angry reply, but Lucca spoke first.

"Whatever we do, the decision must be made here, now. The season is already late."

"What is the distance?" Grossefeldt asked.

"Perhaps six hundred miles. It is safer following the river."

Sarzeau was determined to object. "We can find boats. We have not looked up the river."

"You are free to look," the *Hansgraf* said, "but the rest of us should leave tomorrow."

"Tomorrow?" Grossefeldt exploded. "Impossible! It is too soon!"

"Already there is snow just fifty miles to the north. It can snow here. However, I shall hold none of you to our agreement of unity unless you wish to reaffirm it. We—our company—will leave tomorrow with all who wish to accompany us."

"I shall go," Flandrin said quietly.

Sarzeau and Grossefeldt hesitated, but I was not watching them, or listening. I was watching Yury Olgevichi. His face was blank and innocent, yet I believed I detected in his eyes a spark of satisfaction.

The *Hansgraf* rose. "At daylight, then."

Suzanne stood near me, and Yury crossed over to her, bowing. "Madame, if you would prefer the river, I can offer you my boat."

"With Kerbouchard and our company?"

"The offer was made to you, madame. After all, for a woman of your position the boat is more comfortable."

"I shall remain with the company. We have been quite comfortable, thank you." She half turned away, then glanced over her shoulder at him. "Have you visited Constantinople, Prince Yury? Have you walked its walls? It might be advisable. It might save much trouble and disappointment."

Startled and angry, he started a reply, but we walked away.

"So you have the same idea I have?"

"He has had little successes, and he mistakes them for great victories. He has connived and intrigued in

Novgorod and Kiev, and he believes he is prepared for Constantinople. Believe me, Mathurin, no people are so adept at intrigue as the Byzantines."

"And if it comes to war?"

"He will be defeated before he comes within sight of the walls. While he is planning to make a dinner of them, they will make a breakfast of him."

We stood together watching the sun sink, although the hour was early. There was a chill in the wind. Yes, I was ready to go, more than ready.

Leaves fell from beech trees at the camp's edge; clouds caught the reflection of far-off sun-flame, blushing at the sight.

I did not like Prince Yury.

38

The *Hansgraf* Rupert von Gilderstern led, mounted on his powerful charger. He sat erect in his saddle as always, holding his bridle reins breast high in his left hand. He was truly a monumental figure.

Some distance away was the bank of the Dnieper, on our right the fields of the few who ventured to farm in the neighborhood of Kiev.

Behind the *Hansgraf* marched his company and that of his brother Peter; a little further back came that of Flandrin. The others followed in their respective places, with Sarzeau and Grossefeldt bringing up the rear.

Of retainers I had but one, the thief, beggar, and philosopher, Khatib. Before leaving Kiev, I called the jugglers and acrobats around me, a motley group most of whom I had known from Córdoba.

"I have no claim upon you, but I fear that Prince Yury will attempt to seize the Comtesse, and I cannot always be with her. If you would help to watch over her, it would be the greatest of favors."

"Worry not," Lolyngton said. "Where the Comtesse is, we will not be far away."

We camped at the edge of a forest of beech and maple, our circle tight, our stock held under guard in a nearby meadow.

At sundown the *Hansgraf* called me to his tent. Peter, Flandrin, Sarzeau, Grossefeldt, and the others were present.

"Kerbouchard, you are our master of geography. How far to the sea if we travel directly south?"

"Half the distance of following the river, which bends far to the east."

"That is it, then. We strike directly south."

There was no argument. Even Sarzeau seemed pleased. If we could reach Constantinople before the boats, our market would be much better.

The *Hansgraf* arose. "Prepare to move within the hour."

We had started out of the tent; now all stopped. "What?" Flandrin protested. "*Tonight?*"

"Our enemies will have satisfied themselves we are following the river. Now we shall make forced marches. In ten days we shall reach the sea. If we are fortunate"—he paused, his eyes going from one to the other—"we shall do it in eight days, perhaps even in seven."

Outside, Sarzeau muttered, "He is a good man. Sometimes I think not, but I am wrong. What do you think of this move, hey?"

"There will be fewer river crossings, and the rivers will be narrower than where they enter the Dnieper."

"Yes, yes! Of course! I had not thought of that." He put a hand on my shoulder. "You are a good man, too, Kerbouchard. You should give up whatever plans you have and remain a merchant."

At first we used marketing roads traveled by farmers, then we cut across country, for there was no road the way we had chosen.

It was open country, for the forest line was falling behind us, although there were patches of forest and, of course, thick growth along the streams. By daybreak we had fifteen miles behind us.

On the third day we entered the valley of the Bug River. Far away on our right was the Volyno-Podolak upland, but aside from dips into streambeds, the country was flat or gently rolling, presenting few obstacles. Usually, I rode out in front, discovering the way, removing obstructions, alert for danger.

The Bug River was now our guide, and we followed the western bank. Oak, which had been plentiful, had

given way to beech; maple mixed with ash and occasional
elm. Game was plentiful, grazing excellent. The grasses
were blue or wheat grass, where we saw and sometimes
killed *saiga* antelope, red deer, roebuck, and wild boar.
From time to time we saw small bands of *tarpan,* or wild
horses. They were mouse-colored with a dark stripe down
the back.

Each company had hunters who ranged far afield to
supplement our supplies and to scout the land as I was
doing. By nightfall of that third day we had a hundred
miles behind us, approximately a third of the distance.
For the boats descending the river, progress would be
slow except for a short stretch through the rapids of the
Dnieper. Kiev was of no great elevation, and the rate of
descent, including the rapids, was not more than eighty
feet to the mile.

Long since we had crossed the Bug, which flowed
into the river we had been following from the northwest,
and now we approached the Chicheklaya.

Lolyngton, Johannes, and I had ridden far in quest of
game. We had seen several bear and one moose, although
no more than a glimpse, when Lolyngton suddenly drew
rein, lifting a hand. "I smell smoke," he said.

We were traversing a small meadow bordered by a
fine stand of ash, and we held our mounts, trying the
wind.

"A campfire," I said, "it can be no more than that."

We had seen no one in days, now we entered the
woods, picking our way. Johannes, who was not feeling his
best, remained with the horses. We wore chain mail with
tunics over it and conical helmets brought from Spain.

Threading our way, we came to a blowdown where a
number of trees had been felled by a great blast of wind.
We stopped well back under the trees, for an observer
who knows his business remains back under the trees
where he is concealed but can see just as well.

Clustered around a fire not over a hundred yards
away were a dozen strangely clad men. They wore conical
helmets, somewhat different from our own, and tunics of

hide that fell to the knee but were split up the sides for easy riding. Their boots seemed to be of soft leather, and they carried quivers of arrows and shorter, thicker bows than I had seen. They were swarthy men with broad, flat faces, narrow eyes, and square jaws. They looked a rugged and dangerous lot.

Eyes appear as dots at one hundred yards; mouth and eyes can usually be plainly seen at fifty yards, so we were actually somewhere between the two distances, not nearly enough if they gave chase.

These were the Petchenegs of whom we heard, hard-riding men from the steppes of Asia. Such as these had long ago attacked and destroyed Roman armies.

As we watched, one of the soldiers lifted his saddle and brought out a slab of meat. I recalled hearing such was their method of tenderizing meat, carrying it between the horse and the saddle and riding on it all day. The idea did not appeal to me, but the smell of broiling meat aroused our hunger. We drew back deeper into the woods, then returned to Johannes. "This must be reported to the *Hansgraf* at once," he said.

"Do you return. I shall circle about to find where they come from and if there are more."

"What of you? We shall move on, you know."

"Drive hard for the sea. If they are some distance from their main body, we will gain distance."

When they had gone I mounted and rode until I came upon the Petchenegs' tracks. At a swift canter I rode their back trail, and coming to a rise, I turned in my saddle. In the distance was the flat plain over which we had crossed with the caravan.

Riding a short distance along the rise, I found where a large body of horsemen had stopped for some time, facing the river.

They had seen us then, but how far away was their main body?

The day was warm; a slight breeze stirred the few leaves remaining and rattled skeleton fingers among the bare trees. A heron flew up from a sphagnum bog, and I followed the back trail of the Petchenegs. Topping a rise, I saw their camp lay before me, and my heart lay heavy within me, for the black tents spread wide upon the plain.

How many tents? How many horses?

Five thousand men? Ten thousand? I looked at the horse herd, and even allowing for three or four horses per man as was often the case with the Petchenegs, it was a great number. If they came against us, we would be swept up like leaves in the wind. We would be destroyed, trampled into bloody dust.

Flight, swift, driving flight, was our only recourse. The *Hansgraf* would suspect, when Johannes reached him, that the party we had seen were not alone.

By now our company would be moving, flying toward the sea, but their scouting party would be riding in, and their army would mount.

Could I stop them? Slow them, even a little?

Far off, a party of horsemen were riding toward the Petcheneg camp, and the man riding that magnificent gray horse, surely two such horses did not exist, that man I knew, even at the distance.

It was Prince Yury.

They were some distance away, and the idea came as naturally as such an idea can come.

The attack on the convoy must be delayed, and the Petchenegs kept in their camp, and there was nothing, or so I had heard, they liked better than to witness a good fight.

Prince Yury's presence could mean but one thing: that he had come to enlist their services against us if he had not done so already. Therefore, Prince Yury was my enemy.

Deliberately, I rode my horse into the bright sunlight, removing my tunic so the sun could strike my bright-polished armor. I wanted them to see me; they must see me.

"All right, Ayesha, let us hope you do not have a fool for a master and that his blade cuts sharply this day!"

Touching her lightly with a heel, I rode my mare

down the gentle slope toward the camp of my enemies. I sat very straight in the saddle. I rode at an easy canter.

Perhaps I rode to my death, but at whatever the cost there must be delay for the caravan and my friends. Without it they would have no chance.

Nor would Suzanne.

39

The people of the camp saw me coming from a distance, but I came as a visitor comes, and they had respect for visitors.

My route brought me into their camp at the opposite end from that of Prince Yury, as I intended. Immediately, I asked for the Khan.

They understood that word and no doubt believed I came as an ambassador or expected guest. They recognized my Arab armor, and there was murmuring among them as they looked at Ayesha.

Four horsemen fell in around me, and we came to a larger tent. There was Prince Yury, staring at me in blank astonishment, swiftly giving way to triumph.

"Seize that man! He is from the caravan!"

Knowing nothing of their tongue, I trusted to Arabic, which many of them would understand. "I have come to your camp of my own will. I have been told of the hospitality of the people of the Black Tents."

Their Khan was a square, powerful old man with bowed legs and a grim expression. "Why come you here?" he demanded.

"In Kiev it was said you were followers of Prince Yury," I lied cheerfully, to put my enemy on the defense, "but I do not believe the Khan of the Black Tents follows any man."

Ayesha stepped about a bit, and when she quieted, I said, "I have come here, trusting to your hospitality as well as your nobility, to challenge Prince Yury to combat.

"You are noted men of the sword and respect those

who fight. I do not ask your friendship, although to be your friend would make me proud; I ask only fair treatment, which I know you will give. The blood upon your swords has never been the blood of cowardice."

"You come here, in the camp of his friends, to challenge Prince Yury?" The old Khan's eyes glinted, and I felt I had won his respect where nothing else would have done so. These were men who loved daring. "Why do you seek him?"

"Because he tries to get other men to fight his battles, and because he is a knave, a coward, and a mongrel, fit only to be fed the meat of dogs!"

Prince Yury drew his sword. "By the gods! For this I shall have your blood!"

"Why fill thy belly on the east wind and give utterance to vain and foolish words?" I said contemptuously. "Will you meet me on foot or horseback?"

By now hundreds of the Khan's followers had gathered about, eager for the fight. Yet all that I could think of now were ways to make the fight last. The scouting party I had seen had not yet come in. Could I hold them when they did come? Every minute gained would bring my people closer to the sea, and the boats that should be waiting.

Suddenly, there were shouts and a band of horsemen charged into camp. Men rushed to them for their report.

It was the scouting party. I was too late.

Amid the confusion, Prince Yury stared at me with hatred. He pointed at me. "Kill him! His coming was a ruse to distract your attention."

"There speaks a coward," I sneered, "who would have his killing done by others."

"He has challenged you, Prince Yury," a voice said. "His challenge deserves respect. Do you fear him, that you shrink from battle?"

That voice! *Where had I heard it before?*

"He is our enemy," Yury replied coldly. "His coming is but to gain time."

"How much time do we of the Black Tents require?"

The speaker was behind me. "He has come to our camp as a guest, of his own will, and he shall leave it when he wishes."

"Who says?" Yury demanded, his voice hard with anger.

"I say!" He walked forward and stood beside me. "I, Abaka Khan!"

A moment I stared, then remembrance. "Abaka Khan! The man for whom I bought a drink in Cádiz, so long ago!"

Prince Yury hesitated, and I could gauge Abaka Khan's importance by that hesitation. Yury was suddenly uncertain of his ground.

"Do you speak for this enemy?" Yury demanded.

"Whose enemy? They have not attacked us. *You* say they are enemies."

"There is loot among them."

"And a woman," I said, "whom he hopes to take." Deliberately, I thickened my tone with contempt. "This dog cannot seize her for himself. He must have the Black Tents to win his woman!"

"Is this so?" The old Khan turned to Prince Yury. "You spoke of a woman when you told us of the caravan."

"The woman is important. It is a matter of politics."

Aside to those nearest me, I said, "What manner of mouse is this? That he claims politics as an excuse for taking a woman? Is he a man or a eunuch?"

Prince Yury heard my remark and took a step toward me, and the crowd opened to let him come, eager for the fight.

"A proper duel? Or do I spank you with my blade upon your bare bottom?"

"A duel it is," Abaka Khan said sternly, "and we will see it properly done. Come, Prince Yury? Will it be foot or horse?"

"Horseback," Yury said angrily, "and no quarter. A fight to the death!"

"Agreed." I spoke carelessly, and drawing my blade,

I rode Ayesha fifty yards down the course, walking her slowly, for we needed time, then turning to face Yury.

How long since Lolyngton and Johannes reached the caravan? How much time had I won? Was it twenty minutes? A half hour? An hour could mean five miles for the caravan, perhaps six at top speed. It was not much, but the sea was not far away. The *Hansgraf* would know how to use the time.

What I feared most was that the caravan might be caught crossing the Chicheklaya. Once across the river there would be nothing between them and the sea, less than fifty miles away.

"Steady girl." I spoke softly and caressed her neck, knowing she understood. Ayesha had been ridden in many a tilting and many a duel. She pranced eagerly, nostrils dilated, her delicate head bobbing as she tasted the bit.

The word was given, and we started forward. Despite my talk, which had been for the purpose of forcing a fight, I knew I was in trouble. Prince Yury towered several inches above me in height, and his long arms gave him a reach advantage. He was a powerful man with every appearance of the fighter.

His sword was ready. Suddenly his horse gathered speed, and of her own volition, Ayesha did as well. Charging, we swept at each other, but when we neared I simply parried his blow and slipped past.

An angry shout went up at my evasion, but wheeling Ayesha, I lunged at Prince Yury. Yury had turned, but despite the fact she had been ridden all morning, Ayesha was the quicker. My blade swung and was only partly parried, and Yury was off-balance in the saddle. There was a moment when I could have killed him, and it was seen by everyone.

For an instant there was stark fear in Yury's eyes, for he was powerless to prevent a thrust, and I was in position. However, the fight would have been over, and it was time I was battling for. Contemptuously, I lowered my blade. "You shall not die so easily," I said to him, and circled my horse.

There was a cheer from the crowd, who misunderstood my gesture, and then he was upon me again. We fought desperately, thrusting, parrying, circling. Once, Ayesha almost fell, his heavier horse pushed against her, and I reined her swiftly away. Seeing his advantage, Yury charged me, and only Ayesha's swift turn prevented our being run down.

Our blades clashed, and disengaging, I thrust suddenly. I felt my point tear cloth, and then his blade struck me on the skull, and my helmet rang with the force of the blow. Rushing his horse into me, he struck viciously. Off-balance I fell from my horse.

As my body struck the dust, a tremendous shout went up, and he wheeled his horse to ride me down. However, rolling free, I sprang to my feet, and as he leaned to strike me, I threw myself against the side of the charging horse and under his sword arm.

It was such a feat as I had practiced many times with the acrobats and bareback riders who would mount and dismount from running horses. Catching the pommel and Yury himself, I swung to his horse's back behind him. With one arm across his throat, I brought my sword up, but his horse wheeled suddenly, and we were both thrown to the ground.

Thanks to my acrobatic training I was instantly up, but badly shaken, and there was blood on my face from somewhere. Yury got up, but he had several steps to recover his sword, and the wild Petchenegs yelled angrily for me to kill him. This time I did not delay because of gallantry or an attempt to prolong the battle, I simply lacked the strength to go after him and needed to catch my wind.

He caught up his sword and came for me, all the fire and fury gone now. He was cold and deadly, meaning to kill me now with no further nonsense.

How long had the fight lasted? Only seconds, perhaps, certainly no more than a few minutes, but I no longer dared think of simply delaying. To survive at all, I must fight only to win.

He came at me, feinted and lunged. Springing away, I moved in again quickly and went for his face, narrowly missing. We circled, our blades touching, almost caressing, then mine leaped past his thrust hard. The point took him in the chest but at the end of my lunge. I felt his chain mail give before that lovely Toledo steel, and recovering, I saw a spot of blood on his chest only inches to the right of his heart.

We circled, and then he drove at me fiercely, demanding all my skill to ward off his attack. My blade lowered, and he drew his blade back for one tremendous swing, and there flashed into my mind how my father had once saved his life in a battle aboard ship. Dropping to one knee, as his weight came forward over his right leg and his blade started down, I thrust upward into his throat.

At the last it was more his doing than mine, for his descending blade and the force of his swing were enough to send my blade through his throat and into his skull.

He gave a choking scream, and his sword fell, banging on my helm. His body twisted as he fell, pulling the blade from my grip, but springing up, and with a tremendous jerk, I wrenched it free.

The old Khan rode out to me as I stood gasping for breath, holding my bloody sword.

"It was well fought."

"I owe him an apology," I said. "He was a brave fighter and a strong man. I but spoke to gain time."

"You are honest."

"You gave me opportunity; I give you truth."

Abaka Khan had ridden up beside the old warrior. "This is my son," the Khan said. "He was long from my side."

"A strong son makes a father proud."

There was a wineskin on the saddle of Abaka Khan. I indicated it.

"Abaka Khan, I once gave you a drink. I would have one now."

He took the wineskin from his saddle, and I held it

high, before drinking. "*Yol bolsun!*" I shouted. "May there be a road!"

"*Yol bolsun!*" The shout went up from a thousand throats, and holding the wineskin high, I squirted the wine into my throat, parched from battle.

Handing the skin back to him, I said, "It was a good drink. Remind me that I owe you one."

The old Khan pointed. "There is your horse. Ride to your company and tell them we come with the rising sun, and what they have we will take."

Stepping into the saddle, I faced them, the short, powerful old man and his tall, slender son.

"I shall tell them, and we shall meet you, but many of your men will die."

"Where there is gold"—he shrugged his heavy shoulders—"there is blood."

Turning my horse, I lifted my blade in salute, for they were good men and strong, but before this hour came again many would lie with their throats choked on the dryness of death.

"*Yol bolsun!*" I shouted, and the hills rang with their reply.

"*Yol bolsun!*"

40

The low shore that is the north shore of the Black Sea between the mouths of the Dnieper and the Dniester is cut far inland by a number of drowned valleys that form inlets in the flood plains of the coast. There are no forests there, only clumps of willow, black poplar, and European alder with some mixture of filbert, maple, pear, and apple. Wild grape vines climb into the highest branches of the trees.

The drowned valleys form long narrow bays or estuaries into which the rivers empty. Into one of these emptied the Bug, the river that had been our companion on our trek to the sea.

Between two of these estuaries we prepared to meet the attack of the Petchenegs, forerunners of the great Mongol tribes that even now were stirring restlessly on the far-off steppes of Asia.

Behind us were the waters of the Black Sea, on either side of us a fork of an estuary. The *Hansgraf* directed preparations for defense, and each of us knew it would be a fight to the death. There could be no retreat, and no escape unless the boats arrived. The forces arrayed against us outnumbered us by ten to one, at least.

On our right, beginning close along the shore of the inlet was a dense thicket of brush, its millions of branches tightly interwoven and overgrown by grape vines. This barrier, which the *Hansgraf* immediately elected to use, was several hundred yards in width and extended almost a quarter of a mile across the neck of land we had chosen to defend.

For horsemen this was an impenetrable barrier and a trap for all who might attempt it. There was a narrow stretch of sandy beach between the thicket and the water, and there we piled driftwood to make a barrier. Beyond this we sowed some hundreds of caltrops. These were made of metal or hardened wood so devised that one of their four points always stood up, a deadly defense against cavalry charges.

The remaining area we must defend was protected in part by a thick wood, a tangle of willow, poplar, and grape vines, along with some thorny brush whose name I did not know. Branches were cut from trees and wedged between other trees to make a continuous fence. Inside of this and outside as well were set up sharp-pointed sticks of all sizes, their ends thrust into the ground on an angle that faced a charge.

In the opening that existed somewhat east of center across the neck of land we built a hasty wall, and before this we scattered more caltrops.

Upon receipt of warning from Lolyngton and Johannes, the *Hansgraf* acted swiftly. Disembarking his people from the carts and loading all upon pack animals, he sent the carts on along the river while he scattered his riders and pack animals in fifty directions to meet at a definite point.

What he hoped, and what did in fact happen as planned, was for the Petchenegs to follow after the empty carts only to find them empty and abandoned except for rocks placed in them for added weight. By the time the Petchenegs discovered their mistake and scouted the many trails the company had reassembled, chosen its position, and was well along with fortification.

The men and women unable to work otherwise because of wounds or other disabilities were put to making more caltrops, a supply of which was always carried in the wagons, as the attacks most feared by the merchants were those from horsemen.

Many caltrops were carried out some distance into the grass to break the force of any charge against the defenses. When that position seemed relatively secure, the *Hansgraf* drew back a hundred yards or so and proceeded to build several islands of defense, small forts behind earthworks and brush that could break the force of any mass attack, divide the enemy, and subject them to cross fire. Into one of these secondary forts the women were taken, and such of the wounded that required care. Food supplies were divided among the forts. Within the one where the women and wounded would be, there was a spring.

The labor to prepare this defense was done with incredible swiftness. This was due to a well-thought-out plan by the *Hansgraf*, who had long since worked out a series of defenses covering almost every situation a caravan might encounter.

In the main our defense was against horsemen, and this was true wherever we might be attacked. Our bowmen were of the best, but we also had many who were adept with the sling, and a part of the shore near us was a pebbled beach, providing the best of ammunition.

By the time I reached the point of rendezvous these preparations were far advanced.

The *Hansgraf* knew it was the custom of steppe horsemen to charge a wall or hedge, and leap their horses over it, but the sharp stakes driven into the ground and pointed in the direction from which any charge must come, as well as the caltrops, rendered such a charge impossible. Many of the caltrops were invisible in the knee-high grass.

Sometime since, he had sent a messenger to Constantinople to hasten the boats that were to meet us and transport our cargo, but it was doubtful if they would arrive in time.

By daylight on the third day after my return, they found us. It had taken them that time to catch up as well as to work out the maze of trails we left.

Several thousand of the Petchenegs started for our fort at a fast trot only to pull up or turn sharply away when they saw the plain before our wall. Knowing the skill of their horsemen, I knew that some of them, weaving between the clusters of sticks and caltrops, would get through.

From a distance I could recognize the Khan sitting his horse and occasionally standing in his stirrups to study our defenses. How long would it be before he realized we were vulnerable to attack from the sea or the estuaries? A fact in our favor was that the Petchenegs, a steppe people, rarely knew how to swim and feared the water.

Suzanne awaited me at the outer wall of one of the islands of defense. Her face was pale. "Mathurin? How will it be?"

What reply could I make to such a question? Our defenses could be no better, considering the time we had and the situation, yet I was sorely afraid. Nor need she ask, for her experience was no doubt as great as mine in such cases. Her Castle of Saône had often been attacked when she was younger.

Yet it was I who had looked into the Khan's grim old eyes, only I who had seen his men up close, those savage, ill-smelling tigers of the steppe. They lived for war, knew little else.

Nor was I one to shield a woman from truth. Women are neither weaklings nor fools, and they, too, must plan for what is to come. He who does not prepare his woman for disaster is a fool.

"We may win, Suzanne, and we may not. If you are taken, demand to see Abaka Khan. He is a prince, a son of the Khan, and we know each other. Ask to see him; tell him your story. But if you can, escape. I shall try to prepare a way for you."

"And you?"

"Do not think of me. There lies the sea, beyond it is Constantinople where you have friends. Go there, by all means."

"Do you believe they will defeat us?"

"Suzanne, a wise man fights to win, but he is twice a fool who has no plan for possible defeat."

She put her hand on my arm. "Mathurin, I do not want to lose you."

"Nor I, you."

We stood together enjoying the morning sun and looking toward the dark line of Petcheneg horsemen, a cloud on our horizon.

A dark and terrible line, they stretched from one side of the neck of land to the other, looking across the plain from the ancient dunes where they waited.

With the immediate rush of work on the defenses past, we rested, gathered our strength, ate, talked, and awaited the attack.

Remembering what I had seen, those dark-faced men with their cold jaws and narrow eyes, I shuddered for those about me. The steppe riders hated all places that did not grow grass, cities were an abomination to them. They lived on mare's milk, curds, and blood from the veins of living horses, eating barley and meat when it could be had. Killing was for them a way of life.

"Even if we win," I said, "it will be an end of this, and it is a pity that every beginning should also be an end. I shall miss the walking drum, Suzanne, miss it indeed.

"That drum has been our pulse, and often have I wondered what it is that starts the drum of a man's life to beating? For each of us walks to the beat of our own drum, an unheard rhythm to all our movements and thought.

"Was it my father's disappearance that started me? Or did it begin in some Druid forest long ago when the mistletoe was cut from an oak tree with a golden sickle? Or perhaps it began when the blood of my mother and father joined?"

The *Hansgraf* came over to us. "A small boat has been found, and it will carry a half-dozen people. There are oars, and there is a sail, and it will not be long before the boats from Constantinople come." He turned his eyes to Suzanne. "The women of our company will go in that boat, and there must be one man." He looked at me. "You are not one of us. You will go."

"I shall remain. Khatib will go."

He did not protest, and I knew he wanted me with him. "Across the estuary is a forest of reeds. Khatib can take you to the boat. You should push off at once. No doubt you will meet the boats upon the sea."

He glanced at Suzanne. "Do you have friends there?"

"And in Antioch."

"Very well, then."

He walked away from us, a commanding presence; he moved with ease and grace despite his great size, yet for the first time I detected a shadow of something that frightened me. He who had seemed invulnerable was no longer sure.

How could he be? How could anybody be?

"Mat . . . ?"

They had started . . . a long dark line of riders coming at a fast walk.

Quickly, I kissed her. "Inside," I said, "until you leave with Khatib. Remember, he is an old reprobate, but you can trust him. If I live, I shall come to you at Saône."

How easily, at such a time, are promises made! And how vain the promises when destiny hangs in the balance!

My blade came easily from the scabbard, and I strode forward. My hand touched the shoulder of Khatib. "Go to Madame, thou evil-smelling one! Thou pirate! Thou thief! Go to her, and guard her well for me. See her into the boat that is waiting, then to Constantinople and Saône! See to her, Khatib, for she holds my heart in her hand!"

"A boat, O Mighty One! There is a boat, and you hold a sword? What madness! What folly! A beautiful woman, a wide sea, and a boat? And you choose a sword?"

"I have my honor, O Father of Lice! I have my honor, and I am a warrior!"

His evil old eyes twinkled. "Praise be to Allah that I am but a thief and a philosopher! I choose the boat!"

He paused, his eyes suddenly grave as he looked at me over his scrawny shoulder. "Do not forget this, Mighty One. He is a wise man who can choose the moment. It is not necessary to die to prove you are brave.

"Think well of the enemy, and of your brothers in arms, but when your moment comes, remember your horse! Remember Ayesha, that slim-legged beauty with her flower of a nose! When it is futile to blood thy sword more, mount and ride!"

Lolyngton walked to join me. His smile held grave amusement. "I am afraid, my friend, that in this play my part will not carry over to the last act. What a role for a mountebank!"

"And a soldier."

"Think you so? I have been called many things, but . . . a soldier? It has a sound to it, Kerbouchard."

They were coming now, trotting their horses, sitting high in their saddles, a black line of death riding. Then they charged!

They reached the caltrops; a horse reared and screamed in pain, another swung away, and our archers unleashed a flight of arrows. Horses reared and plunged; men fell, and arrows dropped among us, too.

We waited; our time was not yet.

"What are you glad for, Kerbouchard?" Lolyngton asked. "You have lived . . . what have you loved?"

"What is it that has made me happy? A deck beneath my feet, a horse between my knees, a sword in my hand, or a girl in my arms! These I have loved, and the horizon yonder, beyond which there is the unknown.

"What else have I loved? The mist of morning, the rose of evening, a wet breeze upon my cheek, and my father's hand upon my shoulder.

"And as for women? I have loved, in their own time, Aziza, Sharasa, Valaba, and Suzanne. For the moment I loved them, and for the moment, no doubt, they loved me, and who can say how long such moments can last? I drink the wine and put aside the glass, but the taste lingers, Lolyngton, the taste lingers!

"Who can forget a horse ridden, a boat sailed, a far coast seen in the morning's first light, a battle fought, or a woman loved? He who can forget any one of them is no man at all.

"Come, Lolyngton, they near the outer wall. Let us see what the future holds."

We walked together to the outer wall, and shoulder

to shoulder we waited. We could see their faces now, waiting in line again, just out of bowshot, and they were going to charge, weaving through the sharpened sticks, weaving in their fine arabesques among the teeth of death. Oh, it was a fine sight! The sunlight on their sharpened blades!

"What are you proud of?"

"There is so little, Lolyngton, so very little. There has not been time, that remorseless word. What have I done? Nothing! Oh, I have dreamed great dreams; I have moved across the land; I have learned so very little, but yes, I am proud that I hold a blade well; I am proud that I have read, and yes, that I am the son of Kerbouchard!"

They came then, a pageant of martial beauty in the stillness of morning; they came mincing their horses through the dagger-sticks, weaving and changing as though to some strange drill or unheard music, and we let them come.

One hundred archers crouched below the barricade; one hundred men with slings crouched among them, and back by the secondary defenses one hundred horsemen waited in reserve. Along the wall were pikemen and swordsmen and some with battle-axes. There was no fear, I think, but only waiting, and then the explosion of the charge, the horses suddenly gathering speed, the men hurling themselves at our wall!

"*Now!*" shouted the *Hansgraf,* and his raised arm came down, and the archers arose as one man and shot their arrows into the teeming mass. They shot at riders, for no man willingly would kill a horse.

"*Now!*" Again the command, and the slingers arose and hurled their stones, and then there were no more commands for each knew what to do. Around us were downed men and charging horses, arrows and stones flying, a crash and clash of weapons upon the wall. A horse screamed, and a man went flying and was impaled like a bug on a pin, arms and legs flailing against the death that came too soon.

A dark rider leaped his horse at the wall and came down beside me, and I swung at his face with my blade and felt the edge bite through his nose-bridge, and the man fell toward me, dagger in hand. Stepping back, I ran him through. An arrow tore through my clothes, and then all incident was lost, and there were only the terrible screams of battle, cries of agony, shouts, the clash of blade on blade, the whiplike sound of arrows.

They came and they came again, and there was no surcease. We fought and fought. My blade crossed steel with a dozen blades. Arrows whipped close; one stabbed my side, but ripping it loose, I fought on, all unaware.

They charged, retreated, then charged again. Some got into our circle, and died there. Many fell by the wall. We drove them back and pursued them with arrows, we hurled stones and threw Greek fire among them, but still they came. They fought like snarling dogs and died with teeth bared and blades still moving in the awful reflexes of muscles commanded by a mind now gone.

A man lunged at me with a sword who had cheered me a few days ago, and I thrust at his throat, and he yelled, recognizing me, *"Yol bolsun!"*

"This is your road!" I shouted, and ran a yard of steel through his chest, and his eyes flared, close to mine. He tried to stab me with a shortened sword, but I pushed him off. Knocked to my knees by a horse that leaped the barrier, I glimpsed an acrobat take a flying leap and land astride the rider's shoulders and go careening off across the field, the rider atop the horse, the acrobat atop the rider, cutting and slashing.

Johannes died beside me, and I killed the man who slew him. Guido fell, choking on his own blood. Lucca, grim and terrible, fell back and fought beside me, and together we drove a dozen riders back from the barricades.

And then the attack broke, and it was over . . . for the time.

41

Some sat down where we stood, and some went for water, others to have wounds bandaged. I myself treated the worst of these.

We had a dozen killed, twice that many wounded, and some horses were dead.

When there was breathing space I leaned on the barricade and rested my head on my arms. We had killed them well, but they died hard, and we knew what had happened was a mere skirmish that hurt them little, although they had lost four times our losses.

Suzanne brought a wineskin. The Petchenegs had come so quickly the women could not get away in the boat. "You are bleeding," she said as I drank.

Remembrance came to me, and I put my hand to my side, but the blood had already dried. There was a place where my hauberk was slit so I could ride, and when it was hiked up an arrow had hit me, but not hard. A glancing blow, no doubt. Later my side might stiffen, but there was no time to do more now, for they would be coming once more.

"It is bad, isn't it, Mathurin?" She had taken to calling me that, a name my mother had used for me.

"It is very bad," I agreed.

Several men were throwing caltrops out on the grass, but nobody was talking except in commonplaces, for there was nothing to talk about.

The acrobat, a dwarf, who had been carried away on the shoulders of an enemy, had returned. He had a nasty cut on his foot, which I treated, but he had killed his man.

The sun was high; a light breeze ruffled the water; a fish splashed, and a Calandra lark sang in the meadow where death lay, oblivious of the corpses.

"Mathurin . . . look."

Suzanne pointed upward, and my eye followed her finger to a great circling column that must have reached thousands of feet into the air, a column of pelicans flying, their white wings catching the sunlight. It was a lovely, peaceful sight.

"It is better than war," I said.

We stood together, holding hands, and I felt the sweat drying on my body and wondered if I would outlive the day. It was very good to live, to feel her hand in mine.

A steppe eagle circled nervously overhead. Perhaps its nest was out there in the thicket.

The *Hansgraf* said, "Be ready, my people. They come!"

This time they came with their ropes, of which we had heard, and with hooks on long poles, and they pulled up some of our sharpened sticks beyond the reach of our arrows.

Their short, strong bows that needed two men to string sent arrows among us, but we kept low, and waited.

Suddenly, they charged on the oblique, hitting our wall where it joined the forest. They thought to find a weakness there, and several tried charging into the forest itself, but they were thrown back by hidden barricades or were trapped and killed by our men.

We lost another man, pierced by an arrow.

The afternoon drew slowly on, and we dozed by the barricade, enjoying the sun. Careful to avoid attention, I went to examine the boat. It was wide of beam but a good sea boat. There was a cask of water and a sack of bread and meat.

It came to me then that we were not going to get out of this, and the *Hansgraf* knew it. He had known it all the time.

He stopped me as I came to where he stood, but he said nothing, and we simply stood together. "If you get out of this," he said after a bit, "I hope you find your father."

Our food had been divided and placed in the forts that were our secondary defenses.

They were oval in shape, one set slightly ahead of the others, and all were earthworks with sharpened poles pointing outward from them and walls of woven brush with earth packed inside. They would be hard to take, for an assault on one exposed the attackers to fire from the other.

There was another attack before sundown, and we lost two more men, and a dozen were wounded. It was long after dark before I could come to the fire and be seated. Suzanne had hot wine for me, and it tasted good. For a little while then, I slept.

Darkness came and in the night we heard the cries of birds, occasionally something stirring in the thickets. Nobody felt inclined to talk. We wished only to rest, for tomorrow would come the hardest attacks, and we were bone weary and exhausted now.

Sooner or later they would find how shallow the water was and ride around us, and we had too few men to protect ourselves and no time to build defenses there.

That would mean retiring inside our secondary defenses and a long, bitter fight.

The archers went about gathering what arrows had fallen inside our barricade. Nobody suggested surrender or bargaining with the enemy, had that been possible. The Petchenegs did not bargain, they killed. In fact, we had nothing to offer them, for they wanted nothing they could not carry on a horse. There was but one way, win or die.

So we slept, took turns on watch, talked in a desultory fashion or nibbled at food. Suzanne rubbed oil on my tired muscles.

"When we retreat to the forts," I warned, "go to the boat and waste no time getting away. Somebody must be in command there; let it be you, but trust to Khatib, for he has wisdom in all matters."

"You believe it will be necessary?"

"Yes, Suzanne, it will be necessary."

"I shall not see you again until Constantinople? Or Saône?"

"One or the other. Expect me, but protect yourself. Count Robert may be there, or another such as Yury."

"You killed him for me."

"I do not know if it was for you. Maybe it was because we wished to test our strength. Mostly it was for time. The *Hansgraf* needed time."

The fires burned low, only a few lingering flames that coveted the fuel.

"If some of the others cross your path," I said, "help them. Lolyngton and his people. They are only actors, you know, and much put upon. They are but shadows of the roles they play, and often there is only the shadow."

"Not Lolyngton."

"No, not Lolyngton."

"The best actor of them all is not an actor," Suzanne commented. "I mean Khatib. He performs on the stage of the world. I think he might have been a king or a vizier . . . in another life he may have been. He is a man of many faces and but one soul."

We were conscious of a presence, the *Hansgraf* looming over us. We arose and stood beside him.

"Do you know?" He spoke suddenly. "I was born but a few miles from here."

Somehow I had believed him Flemish, or a Bavarian.

"I am nobody."

"You are the *Hansgraf*."

He paused, then slowly nodded. "Yes . . . there is that."

He stood silent, watching our shadows on the earth where in a few minutes no shadows would be. "It is day, I think. It is morning."

"They will come soon," I said.

"Go!" He spoke angrily. "Do not be a fool! What is bravery? It is a sham!"

"Why do you not go?"

"I am the *Hansgraf*."

"And I am the son of Kerbouchard."

"You are both fools," Suzanne said, "but I love you for it."

They came with the first light, not the mad charge that had swept so many enemies from the field, but carefully because of our defenses, and we met them at the wall, knowing it might be for the last time.

This time I, too, used a bow, taking up one dropped by a fallen archer. My first arrow took a man in the throat at seventy yards. Two more hits and a clean miss before they reached the wall.

Swords in hand, we met them at the barricades, and the fighting was desperate. A shout arose from behind us, and glancing around, I saw the Petchenegs were swimming their horses around to take us from the rear. For some, there was even wading water.

We fell back then, fighting every inch of the way. Men fell, horses reared and plunged, cries of pain, shouts of fury . . . it was madness. Behind us the walking drum was calling us back.

A man came at me, swinging a falchion, one of those broad-bladed swords that will slice through bone as if it were cheese. I parried his blow, thrust, and parried again. He lunged at me, and only the fact that my foot rolled on a stone saved my life. I fell, and the thrust that killed Prince Yury saved me again. Rising, I joined the flight into our islands of defense.

Suzanne! Had she gotten away? Was she safe?

The enemy charged, circling our forts and shouting, but the earth and brush walls were strong, and we drove them off.

Again I seized a bow and, manning the walls, took aim at the attacking riders. Twice we drove them off. Their dead littered the ground. How many were slain? How many died in those fierce attacks?

An arrow struck me on the helm, and it rang with the force of the blow. Stunned, I momentarily fell back.

However, Toledo steel was no makeshift stuff, but the best, made by the finest craftsmen, and again it saved my life. The wound in my side opened again and was bleeding. A stone grazed the bridge of my nose, and my eyes were swelling shut because of it.

We fought on the walls, driving them back, holding them. Our horses fled back and forth, mingling with those of fallen Petchenegs, and the scene was one of bloody confusion.

The *Hansgraf* was here, there, everywhere, never showing fear, never weakness, always in cool command.

The attack broke, and they retreated, tearing down more of our wall as they left. Now they would prepare for the attack that would finish us off.

Many of ours had fallen. Many were wounded. I could treat only those in our island.

A cry went up. "The boats! The boats!"

And they were there, the boats that were to pick up our goods and ourselves.

They were out there, not three hundred yards off, and upon them was escape, on them was safety, on them lay our future, if we could make it.

We would be men on foot, fighting against horsemen, but we had no choice.

Within our fort there were perhaps two hundred men, few of them without wounds. There must be nearly as many in the others. To remain meant death, eventually; yet to go out and face those fiendish horsemen, magnificent fighters, those devil riders from the steppes . . .

"How many pikes are there?" the *Hansgraf* demanded. He glanced about, counting them. There were no more than forty. Against horsemen, pikes were the best defense. He lifted a pike to signal the others. In reply the men of Sarzeau lifted a forest of pikes . . . perhaps sixty. But there were no more than twenty among Flandrin's men.

Rescue lay off the shore. Rescue, safety, Suzanne.

"We will try. Here all will die, out there some may live."

The Petchenegs had drawn off, regrouping and preparing another attack. Because of dunes along the shore back where they were, they had not seen the boats.

Suddenly, the walking drum began to beat, and we poured from the forts, surrounded by a wall of pikes. The drum began the beat double-quick, and we started on a trot for the beach, holding our tight formation.

How much distance did we gain? Forty yards? Fifty? They came like the wind.

Low in their saddles, they threw themselves into our pikes, dying while they drove our men in upon themselves. Men went down and were trampled into earth. An acrobat whom I had known went down, his face obliterated a moment later by the hoof of a charging horse; yet he came up and threw his sword like a spear into the back of the rider.

We fought inch by inch. Men fell; we helped them up, and now the months of working together told, for men fought to save each other as only brothers fight. And we reached the shore.

Dense reeds and brush crowded our right flank, and eagerly we used that flank to aid us.

A shout went up, and we saw more Petchenegs riding in the water, coming to cut us off.

In the wild abandon of that fight I forgot who I was, where I was; thoughts of escape were laid aside. Grasping a heavy pike from the hands of a fallen man, I hurled it into the breast of a charging horseman. My sword cut a swath around me. A hand grasped my leg as an enemy tried to pull me down, and I kicked him viciously. He fell back, his neck broken.

We fought. A body fell from a horse and knocked me flat. Struggling to rise, I glimpsed the *Hansgraf* surrounded and cut off, laying about him with a falchion, handling the heavy blade with the ease of a dagger.

An arrow took him in the breast, and he wrenched it free and fought on. Lucca went down. Lolyngton I could not see anywhere.

Blood was running into my eyes, and a horseman charged at me, lance at rest. My blade turned his lance and thrust into his side, but the rush of his horse slammed me back and into the water. A horse fell near me, his hooves threshing in agony.

Struggling to rise, I gulped bloody salt water. Somebody struck at me with an ax, but my swinging sword slashed through his ear and deep into the side of his head. He fell into the water, and I put my foot on his chest to pull my sword free.

The drum was still beating, a heavy throb, pounding in my skull. Something struck me, and I fell back into the water. A horse leaped over me, his hooves missing me by inches.

Plunging riders were all about me, as our men fought deeper into the water. Some were already swimming for the boats.

Sarzeau, Flandrin, and others were bunched together; some were archers, some pikemen. One of the Petchenegs snaked out a loop, catching Sarzeau and jerking him from the crowd. Sarzeau's knife slashed the rope, and then he threw the knife with such force that it drove to the hilt between his attacker's eyes. The man and his horse plunged by me, his eyes blazing with fury still, the knife sunk to the hilt above his nose.

A wave of riders swung around and past me, a blow on the helm sent me again into the water. Consciousness ebbed, but I fought like an animal to live. A stirrup struck water near me, and I grasped the stirrup and leg and was pulled up. Dragging the man from the saddle, in the grip of a terrible fury, I charged the nearest horseman, knocking him from his saddle with the power of my momentum. I grasped his sword as it flew from the rider's hand. A rider was coming at me, and I struck his head from his body with one sweep of my sword.

A cold flash of reason swept over me, and turning, using the thicket for a flank, I rushed back into the water.

If I could just get to the boats! Men were swimming wildly for them; others were being hauled in. I thought I saw Suzanne in one of them. I clapped spurs to my horse, and then suddenly he seemed to trip. I went over his head into the water, and it closed over me as I sank. Coming up, I glimpsed a hole in the wall of the thicket, such a hole as is made by wolves or other game. Desperately, I clawed my way into it and lay gasping.

Such a hole as this had saved me long ago in Armorica, saved me from Taillefeur.

Would I ever see him again?

Suddenly, there was a voice speaking, the voice of Abaka Khan. "Another drink you owe me!" And a wine-skin struck the opening of the hole and lay there. Reaching out, I drew it to me.

With the last of my fading consciousness, I crawled deeper into the thicket. A strange hot darkness swept over me, a hot darkness that a long time later was cold . . . cold . . . so very, very cold.

42

A cold, heavy mist hung over the lowland plain, and there was no sound in my thicket but the lap of the sea against my shelving coast.

Over a tiny fire I huddled and shivered, a sick, hurt, almost helpless thing: my clothing in rags, my face overgrown with beard, my hair untrimmed.

Shivering, I stretched my thin hands toward the tiny blaze, for it was cold . . . cold.

My skull throbbed with an endless ache; my skin was blue where it showed through the rags. I had been ill for a long time, and my wounds had been frightful, far worse than I dreamed during the heat of battle.

How long ago had that been? Wrinkling my brow against the dull ache, I tried to estimate the time.

A month? Two months?

Through long, bitter, pain-wracked nights I had fought for life, struggling to hold the thin line against my wounds, against the cold, against hunger, thirst, and depression.

There had been a gash on my skull, cut to the bone after I lost my helmet, a blow that left me with a severe concussion that undoubtedly contributed to my recurring headaches. There had been two arrow wounds in my side from which I lost much blood and from which poison had gotten into my system. There had been a bad gash on my thigh, and a foot had been stepped on by a horse and almost crushed.

Somehow, between moments of delirium, I contrived to squeeze the moisture from some sphagnum moss and pack it into my wounds. It was a good dressing, and one of

337

the earliest I had learned. My father had told me of it
when describing the use of it at the Battle of Clontarf in
1014.

This saved my life, for it stopped the flow of blood.
That and the wineskin dropped by Abaka Khan, who in
the fury of battle had seen me crawl into my hole to
escape death.

The wine quenched my thirst and enabled me to
survive during those first bitter days when I dared not
move for fear of being discovered and killed. All around
the Petchenegs were looting what remained of our camp,
taking the furs we had traded for, taking armor from the
dead, and what valuables they possessed. Those found still
living were slain.

When at last they rode away, the field was left to wild
boars and vultures as well as a multitude of small creatures
and insects. For days, scarcely daring to move, wracked
with pain and shaking with fever, I could hear the boars
rooting and tearing at the bodies that lay on the field, and
the shrill cries of the vultures clashing over the flesh of my
old companions.

My sword was gone. Only my Damascus dagger
remained, and my old belt brought from home, which I
never relinquished. Once a wolf prowled into the tunnel
where I crouched, and I grasped my knife and awaited
him, answering his growls with my own. Finally he backed
off, still growling.

All this occurred during intervals of delirium, and
when at last I became fully conscious, I could not walk,
could scarcely move. My foot was horribly swollen, and I
had no way to tell if bones had been crushed or broken.

My throat rasped with dryness, now that the last of
the wine was gone, and my bones ached from lying on the
cold, damp ground. It was then I managed my first fire,
hitching myself to an elbow, reaching out with my one
useful arm to break twigs and draw nearer the dead brush
scattered about.

Flint I always carried, and my knife provided steel. I
made a spark that fell into dry leaves and grass, carefully

pulled together, then added small sticks. Breaking the sticks enlarged my sleeping quarters, and in scraping together grass for a better bed, I uncovered some small nuts, filberts, that grew on some of the brush. The small effort required to gather and crack the nuts exhausted me. Slowly, I ate the few I had found, then scratched for more.

The fire warmed me, something that felt like life began creeping into my veins, and with it came a raging thirst. My wounds must be bathed, my foot soaked. Also, I must find food.

What a scene of desolation awaited me! Broken pikes, some scattered fragments of armor, a broken sword, the torn and ravaged skeletons of several hundred men, and over all the smell of death, the stench of decay.

Prowling about, I found a dented helmet that would hold water. Near it I put the stub of a sword. The spring inside the fort had been trampled in, but with the point of a pike I dug it out again, and working with my one good hand, pausing frequently to rest, I scraped sand and mud from the hole. Water began to seep in.

Lying close by, I waited for water to gather, occasionally scooping a handful to my lips. Finally, taking a helmet filled with water I crawled back to my den, inching along, fearful of being discovered by wolves or, worse still, a wild boar.

Back in the thicket I heated water, then bathed my swollen foot and ankle. Finally, after finding a few more nuts and eating them, I fell asleep.

During the night I was awakened by the horrible sound of bones crunching in powerful jaws, and the snarling of beasts fighting over the ribs of my old friends . . . or enemies. Now they were one, nor could any man tell the bones of one from the other.

Those skulls out there, once so hot with anger, with love, with hate or desire or loneliness, they were empty now, playthings of beasts. The passions and dreams were gone now.

Where was all we had worked and bargained for?

What profit now from our long trek across Europe? How many had survived? Would even I survive? Was I merely prolonging an inevitable end?

Building my fire higher, yet careful not to allow it to escape its nest and burn my thicket, I sat close to its warmth, feeding small sticks to the flames, pondering upon the strangeness of destiny, thinking back to Córdoba and Valaba, remembering Suzanne . . . where was she now?

When morning came I bathed my wounds again and made a poultice of agrimony mixed with leaves of dittany, daisy, and wild delphinium, a plant I had seen growing in fields all across Europe. These plants had been used in treating battlefield wounds for many years, and I had read of dittany in the works of Virgil, Theophrastus, and Dioscorides.

When I had rested from searching for herbs, I rigged a snare, using several old bowstrings gleaned from the battlefield. The following morning I found I'd caught a marmot, which I skinned, cleaned, and roasted.

The weather grew increasingly cold, but I still could not walk, so to get around I crawled in the dirt like an animal. Hardest of all was to keep clean, although each day I managed to bathe in the sea.

Two weeks went by slowly, and my wounds showed signs of healing, although I had lost weight until I became a veritable bag of bones. My skin looked old, and I was always chilled. Twice in the early mornings I found the tracks of tarpan, a wild horse native to the country, and once the tracks of a huge bear.

One morning I found a bowstring that had not been cut or broken and kept it with me. Later, finding other pieces, I tied them together into a line all of ten feet long. Splicing another line to it about three feet from the end, I tied each of these ends to a rock, making a crude bola for hunting.

Several times I had seen flocks of bustard, and I kept from sight not to frighten them. When finally some came close, I threw my bola and caught one. Hauling the squawking bird to me, I watched the rest fly off. That night I made a royal meal.

It was the same day I began working on a crutch. Using part of an old pike pole, I took another section for a crosspiece and lashed it in place with a bit of bowstring. After three weeks of crawling, I was able to get to my feet at last.

And now I would start for Constantinople!

Ragged, dirty, emaciated, I was a far different creature from the man who only a few weeks before had been the lover of the Comtesse de Malcrais.

To Constantinople it was several hundred miles, I believed, but less than that by sea. But I did not have a boat, or even food, or anything in which to carry water.

Turning west I began to walk. Each step I counted, and when I had traveled one hundred steps, I paused to rest. With me I carried my stub of broken sword and the helmet.

At the day's end I huddled under some black poplars and looked back at the dark blotch beside the sea that was the thicket where so long I had huddled. Throughout the long day I had struggled, falling twice, but each time moving on. I had counted only three hundred steps.

Constantinople was going to be a long way off.

When day came I saw the tracks of horses. They were the clumsy, untrimmed hooves of the tarpan, but among them were the small, dainty hooves of Ayesha.

Should I whistle? She had been trained to come to my whistle, but who else might hear? Were the Petchenegs all gone? Nonetheless, I whistled shrilly, whistled, then whistled again.

A long time I waited . . . nothing.

It might be some other horse. Some of the horses in the pack train had small hooves, and some of the Petcheneg horses had, also.

Slowly, painfully, I started on.

This time I must have covered at least a mile before I stopped, and again I whistled.

For several minutes I sat waiting, and then started to

rise. Only I did not rise. I sat very still looking across the small clearing at a man opposite me.

He had emerged from the woods, a thin, scrawny man with a queer face. Indescribably filthy, he carried a sack over his shoulder, and in his hand, a stout staff. On his other shoulder were a quiver of arrows and a bow.

For several minutes he watched me, and at last I called out to him in Arabic. There was no response, and I began to grow worried. There was that about him that filled me with unease. He was little enough of a man, but crippled as I was, I was less of one.

With the wound in my side I could lift but one arm, and that with difficulty. My left leg and foot were still in very bad shape, and I could hobble only using the crutch. With my right hand out of action from the wounds and my left occupied with the crutch, I was virtually defenseless.

Calling out in the Frankish tongue, I struggled to my feet. Painfully balancing there, I waited while he crossed toward me, pausing about ten feet away. There was an evil amusement in his glance that filled me with horror. Suddenly, he took a step forward, and before I could guess his intention, he put the end of his staff against my chest and pushed.

The push thrust me off-balance, and I fell, striking my injured foot, which made me cry out in agony.

He came to stand over me then, and as if it amused him, he kicked me in the face. Not hard—I had been struck harder many times—but it filled me with fear. What sort of monster was this?

He sat down where I had been seated and stared at me, and then he said, in a kind of bastard Arabic, "You will be my slave."

Taking up his stick, he deliberately poked me in the mouth with the end of it, and he laughed when I made a feeble attempt to grasp the stick.

For upwards of an hour he sat there, poking me with the stick, occasionally striking me with it. At last he got up.

"Why did you whistle?"

This man was an evil creature, scarcely human. What he intended for me I did not know, and I lacked the strength to overcome even his weakness. Did I also lack the wit?

"A djinn," I said, "I whistled for a djinn."

The smile vanished, but a sort of crafty humor remained. "A djinn? *You?* Get up! You are my slave. Get up and carry my sack, or I shall set you afire. Yes, that is what I shall do! I shall set you afire!"

Carefully, I struggled to get my crutch in position, and he watched my every move, perhaps the better to cope with me.

After several minutes of struggling, I got to my feet. "The sack"—he pointed—"bring it."

"Take me to Constantinople," I said, "and you will be paid."

He gave me a scornful look. "You think me a fool, but I shall show you. You are my slave. If you do not obey, I shall hit you. I shall beat you or burn you."

Once on my feet I tried to get the sack to my shoulder but could not. He approached, and careful to avoid my one good hand, he placed the sack on my shoulder. Weak as I was, I almost fell under its weight, but finally I managed to take a step. He started on, only occasionally glancing back.

I could move but slowly, and finally he returned. "You are no good!" He spat in my face. "You are no good!"

Suddenly, he leaped at me and began striking and pounding me with his stick. Desperately, I lunged at him, but he sprang back and began dancing about me, striking and thrusting. Finally, I fell, and then he really attacked, beating me unmercifully with his stick, trying to throw dirt in my eyes. He was a madman. Yet if I could only get him close enough I had my knife.

At last he tired of beating me and built a small fire and began to prepare a meal. Once he came at me with a burning brand, poking it at my eyes. He burned my chin, and one ear was singed, but when I swung my crutch and tripped him, he fell into the fire. He screamed and rolled away from the fire, but while he cursed me, he stayed out of reach.

Something moved in the shadows beyond the fire. Firelight flickered on a silken flank.

"*Ayesha!*" The name burst involuntarily from my lips, and I saw her head go up, her ears prick at the familiar name.

My tormentor at the fire turned as if stung, and then he saw the mare. He leaped to his feet, staring at her and panting audibly.

"It is your horse?" His beady eyes shined with malice. "Call it. Call it over, and you shall have this!" He held up a filthy bone I would not have given to a dog.

To think of my mare in the hands of this fiend was frightening, but Ayesha, spirited though she was, could be caught when I was around. Unless something was done, he would have not only me to torture but the mare also.

"I can bring her to me, but she is frightened of strangers." Slowly, carefully, I shifted my sitting position. My fingers felt for the bola with its twin rocks, and the bowstrings. "I can catch her," I said, "but there is but one way."

Seated on the ground my hand was free. How far away was he? Six feet? "Come, Ayesha," I said, "come to me!"

She was not sure. She lifted her dainty nostrils to sniff in my direction and stamped the earth, not liking the smell. Little could I blame her, for between my captor and me the odor must have been frightful.

"Ayesha," I pleaded. "Come!"

She came a step nearer, then another. "Now, Ayesha! Come!"

He had taken a step forward, hardly able to restrain his eagerness, his attention upon her.

My hand shot out in a swift, darting motion shooting the rocks past his neck. The weight of the rocks did as they were designed to do and wrapped around his scrawny neck. With a jerk, I snapped him toward me.

He fell, and heedless of my injuries, I threw myself

atop him, holding tight to the line with my bad hand and grasping my dagger with the other.

He fought like the madman he was, scratching and clawing, fighting to be free of the strangling noose. He kicked viciously at my injured foot, and the agony was like a bolt of lightning. The pain left me gasping and weak. My dagger came up and drove at him, and he took a good inch of the blade before it struck bone.

He screamed and exploded into violent action. Tearing loose from my bad hand, he sprang erect, but all thought of hurt or danger was gone from me. I must kill! *Kill!*

He must die or I must, and I dared not fail and leave Ayesha to him. Throwing myself at him, I stepped for an instant on my injured foot and pain shot through me. He tried to spring back but fell on his back in the fire, and before he could move or rise I fell atop him stabbing and thrusting.

He screamed and screamed again, and then his struggles ceased, and his teeth were bared to the sky, his eyes wide. I fell away from him, nauseated, and crawled away from the fire.

A long time later, when I opened my eyes, Ayesha stood over me.

43

Evil comes often to a man with money; tyranny comes surely to him without it.

I say this, who am Mathurin Kerbouchard, a homeless wanderer upon the earth's far roads. I speak as one who has known hunger and feast, poverty and riches, the glory of the sword and the humility of the defenseless.

It was without money that I arrived in Constantinople.

Hunger inspires no talent, and carried too far, it deadens the faculties and destroys initiative, and I was hungry, although not yet starving.

Women have treated me well, bless their souls, and it has occurred to me that a man need know but two sentences to survive. The first to ask for food, the second to tell a woman he loves her. If he must dispense with one or the other, by all means let it be the first. For surely, if you tell a woman you love her, she will feed you.

At least, such has been my limited experience.

Yet such a solution was beyond me, for my rags lacked gallantry, and rags without firm, exciting flesh beneath them excite little compassion and no passion. A woman who will gather a stray dog into her arms will call the watch if approached by a stray man, unless he is very handsome, but not often even then, for there remains an occasional feminine mind of such a caliber that she might suspect him of more interest in her money than more intimate possibilities.

Now I was footloose in Constantinople, a ragged, penniless vagabond amid the glories of the Byzantine Empire. Around me were wealth, luxury, and decadence.

346

The two former I did not share, but decadence is the one attribute of the very rich to which the poor have equal access.

Decadence is available to all; only with the rich it is better fed, better clothed, better bedded.

Cities were built for conquest, and I, a vagabond, must conquer this one with what weapons experience had provided.

To a man without money, for I could not call myself a poor man, the obvious way to riches was theft. Thievery, however, is a crime only for the very ignorant, in which only the most stupid would indulge. There is a crass vulgarity in theft, an indication that one lacks wit, and the penalties far outweigh the possible gain.

To a man in rags all doors are closed. In my present circumstances only the humbler occupations would be open. I, son of Kerbouchard the Corsair, a seafaring man, a swordsman, a merchant, a scholar, a linguist, a physician, and even an alchemist of sorts, had the possibilities of being an acrobat or a magician, but what trade is beyond a man with wit?

Of what use are abilities if they are unknown? To make them known, and myself, was now my problem.

My health and physique were now too poor to be an acrobat. As a magician I must fall far below the average in such a city. As a mercenary soldier the way to wealth was too long, and I had a father to find and, once found, to rescue.

Lacking the necessary clothing, I could not be a physician, for a ragged, ill-dressed physician inspires no confidence.

A storyteller, perhaps? A weaver of tales? Thus far my flights of fancy had been reserved for the ears of women, for long since I had observed that masculine beauty as an enticer of the female is much overrated. Women are led to the boudoir by the ears. For one who talks well, with a little but not too much wit, it is no problem.

Where women are concerned it is the sound of the voice, the words that are spoken, and the skill with which

they are said, especially when combined with a little, but
not too much, humility.

A few coins, just a few paltry dirhems, these I needed;
so I would become a weaver of tales, since most who
practiced that skill dressed in rags, anyway. By such means
I would inform my listeners, if such there were to be,
what manner of man I was.

Ayesha, drawn by some internal magic of her own,
had brought me to the edge of a bazaar, and in the shadow
of a great old building there was shade, and in the shade,
a stone.

A stone polished, no doubt, by the posteriors of the
idle poor. With the stone came inspiration. Tying Ayesha
in the shade where she might poach a few leaves, I seated
myself on the stone and looked about at the passersby and
the loiterers.

Before I could open my mouth to speak there came a
frantic roar, and a great, bearded booby of a man came
rushing upon me, shouting and expostulating.

"Away! Be gone, vagabond! Do you not know that
you have taken the seat of Abdullah, the storyteller?"

He loomed over me, his beard quivering with rage,
his eyes bulging, his vast stomach agitated.

"I do not doubt," I replied coolly, "that others have
taken your seat, but I am not one of them. If it is this
stone to which you refer, I found it unoccupied. Now,
Father of Vermin, Son of Iniquity, begone! I am about to
regale these gentlemen"—my gesture included the growing crowd of amused bystanders—"with the harrowing tale
of a thief and the daughter of a sultan, a thief who crept
into her bedchamber."

"What?" He fairly screamed. "Nay! None shall tell
stories upon this spot but Abdullah! Away, or I shall have
out my sword!"

"Insect! You are too clumsy to hold a sword and too
fat in the belly to see its point!"

The fat graybeard grasped his sword hilt threateningly.
"Away! Or I shall have out thy heart! Draw your sword!"

"My mind is my sword," I replied, "and if you linger you shall feel its edge."

A crowd had gathered, eager as always to enjoy any argument or scuffle, and from their expressions they were pleased to see the pompous old storyteller getting the worst of it.

My eyes swept the crowd. Beggars and loiterers, but a few shopkeepers and artisans, also.

"What stories can you tell?" I scoffed. "You, who have done nothing but polish this stone with your fat behind? And I? What sea has not known my ship? What road has not left its dust upon my feet?"

He blustered and ranted and grasped his sword again, glaring wildly.

"Draw the sword," I invited, "and I shall spank you with your own blade, or pluck your beard, hair by hair!

"Look upon him!" I gestured toward the huge stomach. "Is this bloated thing a teller of tales, or a concealer of wealth? It has been said that Abdullah the storyteller is really Abdullah the Tale-Bearer, receiving rewards for information."

Leaning toward the crowd, with a wink to show I was not serious, I said, "Do you think that monstrous swelling is a *stomach*? If you do, you are fools. It is a huge sack in which he carries his wealth!"

Pointing at the huge stomach, I said, "I wonder how much wealth he conceals in that huge sack? Shall we open it and see?"

"No!" Abdullah shouted. "This man is a—!"

Drawing my dagger, I tested its edge with my thumb. "Come! Let us open this bag to see if I am mistaken or not. If I am wrong"—I threw my palms wide—"I will admit my mistake and apologize.

"Perhaps," I said deprecatingly, "it is only wind! But let us see. Come, Abdullah! A fair test! Let us open the bag!" I glanced around at the crowd. "I will wager this bag is filled with coins! Who will take my wager?"

The crowd joined in, amused at Abdullah's angry

astonishment, an astonishment rapidly changing to protest and the beginnings of fear.

A huge-shouldered man with an exposed, hairy chest pushed through the crowd. "I wager it is nothing but wind! There are no coins there! I accept your challenge! Open it up!"

"Come, Abdullah, you are a sportsman! Help us to settle our wager!" I reached for his sash with my left hand, the dagger in my right.

He sprang back with amazing agility for such a huge man, but in so doing, he stumbled and fell into a pile of camel dung. "Come!" I protested. "Do not hide down there! I shall have your sack open in an instant!"

So saying, I grasped him by the beard, a deadly insult in any Moslem country, and held the point of my dagger at his fat belly.

Turning my hand, I struck him lightly in the belly with the fist that held the knife. "Here?" I asked the crowd. "Or shall we open it here?" And I struck him lightly in the side.

"Try it there!" The big-shouldered man pointed with a toe at a spot just below the wide sash.

"Perfect!" Releasing my grip upon his beard, I lifted the dagger. "Now—!"

He shot from under my dagger like an eel from a greased hand, lunged to his feet, half fell against the building, and then fled, followed by the laughter of the crowd.

Some of the people began to drift off, but many remained. "There!" A Greek pointed to the rock. "You have dethroned the king, do you take his place and tell us a story!"

This Greek was a slender, graceful man in a rich semicircular cloak of maroon, decorated at the collar and lower hem with a richly jeweled band of embroidery. The jewels were pearls and garnets. Under it was a tunic that came almost to the knees. His legs were cross-gartered.

He gestured to Ayesha. "Your mare is of the blood. Such a mare would be the pride of a king."

"There are kings and kings," I said, "and the mare is mine."

From his sash he took a coin and tossed it to me with a careless gesture. It winked gold in the sunlight as I took it deftly from the air. "Come, Teller of Tales, let us hear what you can do."

Bowing low, I spoke mockingly. "O Mighty One! What is your desire? Would you have a tale of the Caliph of Baghdad? Or from the siege of Troy? A reading from Aristophanes? From Firdausi? Or would you hear of far seas and lands unknown to the Byzantines?"

"Can there be such?" He lifted a supercilious eyebrow. "Byzantium is the center of the world!"

"Ah . . . ?"

"You doubt it, vagabond?"

"I was remembering Rome, Carthage, Babylon, Nineveh . . . each in its time the center of the world, all ruins now."

He was amused. "Do you imagine this city will be as those? You jest."

"Had I asked in any of those cities, would anyone have believed they someday would lie in ruins? Each age is an age that is passing, and cities, my friend, are transitory things. Each is born from the dust; each matures, grows older, then it fades and dies. A passing traveler looks at a mound of sand and broken stones and asks 'What was here?' and his answer is only an echo or a wind drifting sand."

Bowing again I said gently, "Perhaps your city will draw new life from the steppes, new blood." I looked into his eyes and said, "Perhaps the blood here is thinning now, and perfume appreciated more than sweat."

"You spoke of Troy? What know you of Troy?"

"Perhaps no more than Virgil knew, or Homer. Yet perhaps something more, for I myself have pulled an oar in a galley."

"A slave? I suspected it."

"Are we not all slaves, occasionally? To custom? To a situation? To an idea? Who among us is truly free,

Byzantine? Yes, I have been a slave, but other things also, and a sailor upon Homer's wine dark seas, as well as those unknown to Byzantines."

"That again. What seas?"

"Have you read Pytheas? Or Scylax? Eudoxus? I have sailed seas Pytheas sailed. Shall I speak of them?"

"We would be diverted." The Byzantine did not like me. "Tell us, vagabond, and if the tale be good you shall have another coin."

"Know then"—I crossed my legs upon the polished stone—"that far to the west a cold finger of land thrusts into the dark waters of the sea called Atlantic. Strange and rockbound is that coast, and along its shores live a hardy folk who from ancient times have taken their living from the sea. From a time beyond memory they have quested far a-sea in search of fish.

"Know then, Byzantine, that long ago these men built great, oak-hulled ships that towered above the galleys of Rome; great ships they were with leathern sails and no oars. Within these ships men sailed to far lands, breasting the cold green seas to follow the trail of the great gray geese, which each year fly westward over colder and colder waters.

"They sailed to IceLand, GreenLand, even to the shores beyond."

"Beyond?"

"There are always the shores beyond, for this have the gods given to men: that we shall always have those farther shores, always a dream to follow, always a sea for questing. For in this only is man great, that he must seek what lies beyond the horizons, and there is an infinity of horizons that lie ever waiting. Only in seeking is man important, seeking for answers, and in the shadow he leaves upon the land."

"Shadow?"

"Man in himself is small, but his Parthenons, his pyramids, his St. Sophias, in these he conceives greatly and leaves the shadow of his passing upon the land."

He did not like me, for I offended his ingrown sense

of superiority. He was becoming aware of things he had not known, and the thought irritated him. Yet he studied me thoughtfully. "You appear to have some knowledge. From whence do you come?"

"From afar." I did not like him, either.

"Do you wish to sell the mare?"

"No."

"I might simply take her." He measured me with cool attention, and I guessed him capable of trying.

"I would not," I said, "for we understand each other, and I shall have her until one of us dies."

"That might be arranged."

That brought a smile, and the smile surprised him. "Then plan it well, Byzantine, for death is a visitor who can call upon any man."

"You dare to threaten *me*?"

"Threaten?" My surprise was as genuine as I could make it. "I but made a philosophical comment."

He tried to stare me down, to make my eyes yield. "I have thought"—he spoke coldly—"education to be a dangerous thing."

"How would you know?" I asked.

He went white to the lips and stepped as if to strike me, but I did not move. "I would not," I said, "unless you are prepared to accept the consequences."

For a moment we were eye to eye, then he swept his cloak about him and walked away.

Nearby, a young man had stood listening. "You make enemies easily. The fat storyteller is nothing, but this man is dangerous."

He seemed friendly, and I needed friends. "I am Kerbouchard, a wanderer."

"And I am Phillip."

"Of Macedon?" I smiled.

"Strangely enough . . . yes."

My audience, if such they could be called, were drifting away.

"You are dusty from travel," Phillip suggested, "why don't you come with me?"

There was little I wanted more than a bath and a change of clothing, and the gold coins would help me to some simple dress at least.

We walked away, leading Ayesha, who had been very happy near the bazaar. Phillip spoke of the young aristocrat with whom I'd had words. "He is named Bardas, a close friend of Andronicus Comnenus, the cousin of the Emperor, Manuel I."

A brilliant, erratic man, Andronicus was handsome, witty, and elegant, an athlete and warrior, beloved by the people who knew little of his true nature. He had been called the "Alcibiades of the Byzantine Age" and was adored by women, yet he was a perjurer, a hypocrite, and an intriguer.

He had gathered about him what was considered by many to be the intellectual and artistic elite . . . actually a group of bored men and libertines who were glib-tongued, talking much of art, literature, and music but without any deep-seated convictions upon any subject aside from their own prejudices. Mainly concerned with their own posturing, they were creatures of fad and whim, seizing upon this writer or that composer and exalting him to the skies until he bored them, then shifting to some other. Occasionally, the artists upon whom they lavished attention were of genuine ability, but more often they possessed some obscurity that gave the dilettantes an illusion of depth and quality. In the majority of cases what was fancied to be profound was simply bad writing, bad painting, or deliberately affected obscurity.

Suspected by Manuel of plotting against him, Andronicus had spent most of his life in exile. Now, at sixty, he had returned to the capital.

"Do not misunderstand," Phillip warned. "Bardas not only has power but he is vindictive, and he is close to Andronicus, who can be fiendishly cruel."

"It is unlikely I shall see him again," I said. "I must find a way to earn money, and I shall rarely be in parts of the city where I am likely to meet him."

"He prowls the markets," my friend explained, "and

might be anywhere. He dislikes women of his class and seeks out ugly, often dirty women from the slums. Except when with Andronicus, he avoids those who might be considered equals.

"He prefers women he despises and to whom he can be cruel without fear of retaliation. There has been talk of him in all quarters of the city.

"He maintains a group of ruffians who protect him. They are perjurers as well."

Phillip's house was a comfortable one, but ancient. The bath was a relic of Roman times, huge and luxurious. While I bathed he went to the market and bought clothes for me with the gold coins given by Bardas.

My problems were such as to discourage any man. My father was enslaved, suffering I knew not what indignities and torture. I was powerless against a castle that had defied the strongest kings, and the Old Man of the Mountain had spies everywhere. Even now they might know of me.

First, I must have a means to income. Behind lay the wreck of all I had done. Had our goods been sold, I should have been a wealthy man, free to move as I chose, even to hiring a group of mercenaries to assist me.

The *Hansgraf* was dead, all the members of the company I presumed dead, and if Suzanne lived, how could I go to her again with empty hands?

44

My two pieces of gold provided me with adequate clothing, and for that I owe thanks to Bardas, whatever else I thought of him or he of me.

After giving myself over to pure enjoyment of the hot, scented water, I began to consider my problem. My Druidic training taught me the basic principles of reasoning: to first define the problem, for a problem clearly defined is already half solved, to gather evidence pro and con, to discard the irrelevant, to formulate a tentative solution, and finally to put the solution to the test.

My problems were several. To recover my strength and health, for I would need them to bring about my father's escape; to obtain money to pay my way; to rescue my father from the Valley of the Assassins.

First, I must consider my route from Constantinople to the Elburz Mountains and the fortress of Alamut. Also, there was the question of the identity I must assume to conceal my purpose. Furthermore, I must explore all the methods of entering the fortress itself.

The man who was Safia's source of information must be reached.

A slave brought food and wine, and wrapped in a thick robe, I seated myself on a marble bench and began to eat. Phillip joined me, bringing two books, the *Chronographia* and the *Alexiad*. The former I had read, the latter I had not.

The first was by Michael Psellus, a young man whose life was devoted to scholarship and court affairs in the great years of the Byzantine Empire. Born in 1018, he spent his life at the imperial court, often in positions of importance.

The *Alexiad* was an account of Emperor Alexius I from 1069 to 1118, written by his daughter, Anna Comnena, one of the most brilliant women of her time.

Phillip broke bread and gestured to the books. "Books are rare in Byzantium now, but it was not always so. Once we had great schools, and books were plentiful, but the schools were abolished for religious reasons."

"And now?"

"We have schools again, but not such as they used to be."

He was a tall young man of slender, athletic build, with a narrow head and a long face. It was an austere face, but when he broke into a sudden smile it lighted up with humor.

His was an ancient family, although his father had been a mercenary soldier from Macedon. The house in which he lived had once belonged to Belisarius, Justinian's great general.

Phillip was an attractive sort but of a type I could not understand, for he did nothing. To one of my energy, this was beyond belief. Moderately wealthy, he had family position and a possibility of office, yet he preferred to while away his time. There were things he thought of doing. Travel to the Nile, to the Phoenician ports, to write . . . he did none of them.

When I told him of my experiences beyond the Black Sea, he said, "You were fortunate to get into the city. Every effort is being made to keep those away who have no definite purpose for coming or money to pay their way.

"You will be unable to find anything to do, Kerbouchard. Business is closely regulated by guilds and the government."

Manuel I, the present emperor, ruled well, but the city was past its era of greatness. I found much grandeur in the city, but sections were in ruins, inhabited only by thieves and beggars.

The most elegant shopping district lay away from the

Golden Horn and the Bosphorus. The great central avenue with arcades on either side extended for two miles
through the forums and past the shops. Clothiers, goldsmiths (who were also moneylenders), silversmiths, jewelers,
potters, leatherworkers, all had shops in the arcades. The
House of Lights, where the silk market was carried on,
was a noted place and lighted all night long. Silk had been
an imperial monopoly for many years, but weavers not
under imperial control had moved into the field.

Long before the time of Troy, which lay not far away,
this had been a trade crossing and market for products of
Hind, China, Persia, Central Asia, Russia, and Europe. As
early as 556 B.C., ships from China had come to the
Persian Gulf to trade with Ur of the Chaldees.

The city of Constantinople, also known as Byzantium,
was a rough triangle lying in Europe with its point toward
Asia. Protected on the landward side by a wall of eleven
gates, the peninsula lay between the Sea of Marmora and
the Golden Horn, separated by the Bosphorus from Asia.
Like Rome, Constantinople was built upon seven hills. On
the sides facing the Bosphorus and the Golden Horn these
hills were relatively steep, but they sloped more gently
toward the Sea of Marmora.

Strabo, the geographer of ancient times, said the Bay
of Byzantium resembled the horn of a stag, and when
flooded by the rays of the setting sun, the water shone like
a sheet of burnished gold, decorated by the tiny, gemlike
ships crossing and recrossing the waters of the Horn.

"If you have not heard the story," Phillip said, "of
how the Bosphorus was named, it will amuse you. It is
said that Io, the mistress of Zeus, was pursued by the wife
of Zeus and driven from land to land until finally she came
to the shores of the Bosphorus. Transformed into a cow,
she plunged into the water and swam safely across, therefore the strait was given the name Bosphorus which means
the Crossing of the Cow."

The Golden Horn I found to be four miles long and
about a quarter of a mile wide. Walls ran along the seaward sides of the city, but outside the walls and along the

shores of the Golden Horn were the quays and warehouses where merchant vessels tied up or anchored. Beyond
were the houses and resorts for seafaring men built upon
pilings over the water. Farther back, where the city wall
came down to the water, lay the imperial palace.

There were magnificent buildings—the Cathedral of
St. Sophia, the new Basilica of Basil I, and the Church of
the Holy Apostles. Near the area where Phillip had his
home was the Royal Portico and the Royal Library. There
were no public libraries in Constantinople.

Nor did I discover that easy intellectual freedom to
which I had become accustomed in Córdoba. Life was less
casual, restricted by law and custom.

We went one night to a wine shop, done in the
extravagant style of the Byzantines, a place near the Royal
Portico. A dozen men were seated about, drinking, and
talking in subdued voices. We seated ourselves, and Phillip ordered a bottle of wine and listened to the talk. Some
spoke of troubles to the north, some of trade, of their
mistresses or the amount of wine they had drunk the night
before. They spoke of gaming and the circus. Many seemed
to be partisans of Andronicus, the cousin of the emperor
who they hoped would replace Manuel I.

After the intellectual ferment of Córdoba the conversation seemed stilted and dull, and I soon became restless
and ready to escape the city, yet I desperately needed
money and tried to think of some way toward an income.
As I listened, an idea came to me suddenly. If books were
in short supply, why not copy some from memory?

How many did I remember? Their authors were hundreds of years dead and could only be pleased to have
their ideas in circulation once more. If I could copy several of these books, I might present them to those in a
position to aid my cause.

Monks and lay scribes were copying books, many for
export, but these were of a religious nature. Books of
other kinds were almost impossible to discover.

The door opened suddenly, and two men entered.
Beyond the door I saw others, perhaps a bodyguard. The

first was a handsomely built man with a beautifully shaped head and magnificent eyes. He possessed a regal quality that foretold his name. This was Andronicus Comnenus. Bardas was his companion.

They came to our table. Phillip arose hastily, but I, perhaps because Bardas was there, did not rise. It was my way to conform to the customs wherever I might be, but this time I remained seated.

"Rise!" Bardas ordered angrily. "You are in the presence of Andronicus Comnenus!"

"Respect him I do, but in my country it is not the custom for people of my order to rise in the presence of kings. Nor do kings interrupt when we are speaking."

Phillip paled, and Bardas was shocked. It was to his credit that Andronicus was merely curious. "From what land do you come? This is a custom with which I am unfamiliar."

"From Armorica, far west of the Frankish lands. Mine was a Druid family; in generations past we were priests and the counselors of kings."

His eyes sharpened with interest, and he seated himself. "Yes, yes, of course! I should have remembered! I supposed all Druids to be dead long since."

"Mine is a country where customs linger, but only a few pass on the old ritual and the old knowledge."

"Learned by rote, is it not? The father reciting to and instructing the son?"

"From uncle to nephew in my case. The Druids were from my mother's side."

He was as intrigued as I would have been in a similar case. "You interest me. I should like to talk of this. It has been written the Druids possessed secret knowledge, no longer known, and had great powers of the intellect."

Never had I attempted to use the knowledge in which I was trained as a child beyond the use of the memory itself. In Córdoba, to translate or copy a book was to make it mine, whether I willed it or no. As for the secret knowledge, I was among the few alive who had been trained in its use. Now might be the time.

Miracles were a matter of everyday acceptance here, and all manner of mysteries were believed in, some with reason, most. without. There were in the city and its vicinity temples where ancient rites of Greece were still practiced. This I had learned while with the convoy from Greeks who were merchants.

Andronicus was steeped in intrigue, accustomed to the buying and selling of information. "I have only arrived in your city," I said, "my wealth was lost when the Petchenegs attacked our caravan. I must find a means to recoup my losses or leave the city."

"Oh? You were one of the merchants with the *Hansgraf* von Gilderstern?"

Surprised I was at his knowledge, but he merely smiled. "We are informed of such things. It must be so, for we have many enemies, and the steppes of Russia are the homeland of many. Also, there were those who looked forward to trade with the *Hansgraf*. Well, I am sorry."

Phillip chose the moment to fill a glass for him, and one for Bardas.

Bardas also chose the moment. "There is reason to believe this man entered the city without passing the inspectors."

Andronicus ignored him. "Caesar wrote of the Druids." He glanced at me. "You have this knowledge?"

"My people were of the ancient blood. Such knowledge is passed generation after generation under a blood oath."

He glanced at me thoughtfully, a measuring, probing glance. "I would give much for such knowledge." He turned to Bardas. "Your purse," he said.

Bardas' features stiffened, but reluctantly he took out his purse. Andronicus hefted it in his palm an instant, then placed it before me. "Please accept this. We must talk soon."

He arose. "Come, Bardas." He lingered. "This ancient lore? I have heard of methods for developing the intellect, even for seeing the future. Is this true?"

"I do not know what you have heard." I spoke carefully.
"We have many secrets."

They departed then, but the glance Bardas threw my
way was pure hatred.

Phillip was silent, then he said, very quietly, "You
are a man of many sides, Kerbouchard. I know not what to
think of you."

"Think this of me. I am a man who must survive, and
along the roads I have learned a little, as a man will."

"You lost much in the attack of the Cumans. I do not
think you lost all."

"The goods of this world, Phillip, are soon lost. Fire,
storm, thieves, and war are ever with us, but what is
stored in the mind is ours forever.

"I have lost even my sword. All that remains is what I
have learned and some discretion in how it is to be used."

"It would be dangerous to deceive Andronicus."

"I shall not deceive him. Perhaps he will receive a
little more than he expects, and a little less."

We sat silent, and I said, "The man is brilliant, but a
dilettante. He would have my knowledge in capsule form
to be swallowed with one gulp. He wants the magic,
Phillip, but not enough, not enough."

"You do not know him. Whatever there is, he wants,
and when he gets it he hungers for more."

"When he discovers this knowledge of mine will take
ten years to learn if he is an apt pupil, and fifteen if he is
less than apt, his interest will wane.

"Such knowledge is born from pain, hunger, and
discipline of mind and body. The pain and hunger he
might stand, but the discipline? Never!"

"Can you see the future, Kerbouchard?"

"Who would wish to? Our lives hold a veil between
anticipation and horror. Anticipation is the carrot suspended before the jackass to keep him moving forward.
Horror is what he would see if he took his eyes off the
carrot."

"You are gloomy."

Of course, but it was not my way. Was it some feeling brought by Andronicus? Or Bardas?

"He is loved by the people. They wish him to be emperor."

"The mob always wishes to make its hero the emperor, but no sooner is he emperor than they have another hero they wish in his place.

"If ever you become a hero to the mob, Phillip, remember this: Every man who cheers you carries in his belt the knife of an assassin."

45

Alone in the room Phillip provided, I sat over a bundle of paper to begin earning my living. The purse Andronicus had given was ample, but I put no trust in gifts.

The favors of great men or women are like blushes on the cheeks of a courtesan—rare, nice to see, but not to be relied upon.

My possession of esoteric knowledge placed me in a position that, if handled with discretion, might move me into a position of importance. Andronicus might someday become emperor, and even now his power was second only to that of Manuel.

At this time I chose to make a copy of *The Qabus Nama*, a very excellent book by the Prince of Gurgan.

No other book taught so much about the practical business of living, and during the long trek across Europe I had read and reread its pages. Yet when I began, I chose one of the later chapters in which the Prince discusses the service of kings.

Scarcely had I begun when I remembered a thought I immediately wrote down. No doubt my present situation brought it to mind. *If at any time your Prince should pretend your position with him is sure, begin from that moment to feel unsure.*

There was a further thought that he who argues with a king dies before his destined time. These were thoughts to remember, and while I knew not the character of Manuel, beyond that he was a man who loved war and the chase, I placed no trust in Andronicus, nor Bardas.

Throughout the night I copied from memory the pages

of the book so often read, but as I had been trained from infancy in total recall, this presented no obstacle. I had only to write a line or a thought from a book, and its contents returned to mind.

When I had written until my lids were heavy, I went to the window and, throwing it open, looked out upon the night and the city. Over the glistening domes, beyond the dark and reflecting waters of the Golden Horn, I looked toward Asia.

Hidden in darkness beyond the mouth of the Horn, lay the Bosphorus and my destiny. Not only my father awaited me there, but something more.

Was it intuition? Was it ancient Druidic awareness? Or some atavistic memory calling me back?

We Celts had come, long ago, from Central Asia, or so it was told in the old songs. Was there within me some urge to return along the track of migrating peoples? Was something lost back there? Was I returning even as some fish return to the streams of their birth to spawn?

And my father? How would he be, that father of mine, the hero of my childhood? Old? Gray? Stooped? Would his fine strength be wasted away? Crippled? Blinded?

Might Andronicus open the gates of Alamut for me? Or Manuel? From all I heard no man could do this, but what was one slave? Perhaps . . .

At last I slept.

Cold dawn awakened me. Birds sang, water bubbled in the interior fountains, and I returned to my table once more.

This was the hour when the mind was fresh, the hour of first and greatest clarity. My thoughts flowed easily as water from a spring, and I wrote, wrote, wrote.

Phillip came, followed by a slave bringing food. "I heard you moving about." He picked up some pages. "May I?"

He read, nodding a bit. "This is fine stuff," he said then. "Will you ask Andronicus to sponsor it?"

"Not Andronicus," I said, "Manuel."

"The *Emperor*? But how will you see him?"

"I shall simply ask. Many things are not done simply because they are not attempted."

"How will Andronicus look upon this?"

"With doubt. But I am no retainer of his, nor of Manuel's. Andronicus will trust me no less, for he does not trust me now, and he may value me the more."

"You play with risk."

"I say what I have said before. I have a fast horse." Smiling, I put my papers together and stacked them under a marble paperweight at one corner of the table. "Come, let us look upon the town."

It was time to discover two things: the location of Safia's informant and, if possible, what had happened to Suzanne.

"It is a danger, Phillip, to live always in one city, for undue emphasis is placed upon the importance of those who live there. Often when compared to others, their shadows grow less.

"I have observed," I added, "that the steps of a man sound heavier when he is alone in the hall."

The street to which we found our way was a narrow avenue off the great central street, the Mese. It was a street of shops not far from the Baths of Zeuxippus.

The shop I entered was small, displaying goods from many nations, and the man who came to meet us was a Persian.

"Something?" His eyes lingered on me, for Phillip was so obviously what he was.

"Do you sell the goods of Córdoba? There is a leather of a certain quality. It has been used at the Great Mosque for binding books. The leather was suggested by a lady."

The leather he displayed was excellent, and Phillip was looking at some cloaks across the room. "A valley"—I spoke softly—"in the Elburz Mountains, and a slave in the Fortress of Alamut."

"The slave's name?"

"Kerbouchard . . . as mine is."

He glanced at Phillip, who was out of hearing. "Forget the slave. He tried to escape and by now may be dead."

"I shall go to the valley."

"It is your life." The Persian shrugged, then he said, "It has been reported that you are a physician."

"I am."

"You are spoken of as a bold and daring man."

"I have been fortunate."

"Such men are valuable. Come again when you are alone."

We turned toward the Baths, and glancing back, I saw a man emerge from the shop and hurry away. Safia I trusted, but what did I know of this Persian?

Day after day in the quiet of my room or beside the fountain in the garden, I worked at my writing, preparing first a copy of *The Qabus Nama*, and following it *The Art of War*, by Sun Tzu.

Each day we went to an armorer who maintained a room for exercising with weapons, and there I worked myself into condition again, rehearsing the tumbling to recover my old agility and working with weights to make the sword light in my hand. Several of the Emperor's Varangian Guard came there for the same purpose. These were Vikings, hired for the purpose of protecting the Emperor; all were noted for their loyalty and incorruptibility.

One of these, Odric by name, often practiced with me with swords. He was a stalwart, powerful man, skilled with all manner of weapons, and at first he bested me. But as my strength returned and my old skills came back, I often bested him—yet not as often as I might have done as I needed his help.

One day, while resting after a hard bout I explained what I was doing, copying the ancient book on the art of war and the lessons it taught. He had many questions, and what I hoped for happened. He mentioned me to Manuel.

The Emperor was a fine soldier, extraordinarily strong and active, intrigued by all that concerned war and fighting. He suggested Odric bring me to him.

We entered by the postern gate, passing into a secluded garden where trees offered shade, where jasmine, rose, and lilies grew. The Emperor was seated on a bench overlooking the harbor.

His hair was gray, but he was a handsome man, his features blunt and less classically handsome than those of Andronicus.

He arose quickly and turned to greet me. The laugh lines in his seamed brown face deepened.

"It is proper," he said, "that I rise in the presence of one who does not kneel to kings, and whom kings do not interrupt."

"Your Majesty is well informed."

"It is the necessity of emperors. Tell me, what did you think of Andronicus?"

"A brilliant, interesting man, even a fascinating one, but utterly unscrupulous and dangerous to the empire as well as to you."

"Know you not that he is my cousin?"

"Your Majesty, my ancestors were, as you know, advisers and confidants of kings. One rule we had: We told our kings the truth or what we believed to be true."

"It is a rare quality," he said quietly. "It is no wonder you were not interrupted by kings, nor that you sat at the head of the table."

"We had only our wisdom to offer, Your Majesty, and only our truth."

"So then, what would you have me do with Andronicus? You believe he would like to be emperor, do you not?"

"Yes, he would like to be emperor. There is nothing he would not do to be emperor. What should you do with him? As you are doing. Keep him, by all means. He will be the focal point for all your enemies, and while he lives, there is not likely to be another.

"Keep him, value him, and by watching him you will know by his associates who your enemies are. They will come to him as flies to honey, and to no other so long as he lives."

Manuel turned to his bodyguard. "You were right, Odric, this is a valuable man."

He turned back to me. "You have said he was both

brilliant and dangerous. Should I not fear that his plotting will destroy me?"

"No, Your Majesty. You know your enemy well, better than he knows you. Andronicus believes he is much more clever than you, and this will never permit him to guess the truth, that you are using him for a purpose. Also, I suspect Andronicus plots better than he acts."

Manuel stood with his hands clasped behind his back. "And you have been in Constantinople for only a matter of weeks? I fear how much you would learn if you were here for months!"

"Perhaps less; before too many factors are involved the vision is often clearer. There was once a man who preferred to visit a city before he learned the language. He believed he could better estimate its quality before hearing the comments of its citizens. He depended on what he could see, hear, and sense."

He asked about our defeat by the Petchenegs, or Cumans, as he called them. In detail I described their numbers, leadership, and attack. I described our retreat, our defense. Knowing him for a soldier, I gave a clear outline of the strategy and tactics of our defeat.

"Your *Hansgraf* was too good a man to lose. Had he come to Byzantium, I should have given him command of an army."

For more than an hour we talked, of wars and men, of tactics and the means to victory.

"There," he said suddenly, "lies the weakness of our city." He pointed across the Golden Horn toward the narrow harbor beyond. "If ships could get inside our great chain, the city might fall."

He glanced sharply at me. "When next you see Andronicus will you speak of this visit?"

"He will know of it, I am sure. Andronicus is one who would have many spies."

"And what will you say?"

"That I had a book to give you, in return for which I hoped a favor."

"The book is in Greek?"

"It is now." I handed it to him. "It came from a Persian source."

He opened the pages, glanced at them, became enthralled. The sun lowered; the garden grew cool. Glancing up, he said, "Please seat yourselves. I shall be long." He read on, occasionally turning back a page or two.

"You wished a favor? What favor?"

"I wish to get a slave from the fortress of Alamut, and if I cannot get the slave, I intend to enter the fortress."

He stared at me as if he believed me bereft of sense, then shook his head.

"The slave?"

"My father."

"It is impossible. The fortress is impregnable. It cannot be taken by assault, nor is any slave allowed to leave it alive. For years I have sought such a slave or someone who might tell me of the fortress and its defenses. There is no one. Nor is anyone allowed to enter who is not of their cult."

He stood up. "I should be glad to help, but what you ask is impossible. A dozen kings have tried it or planned it. None have succeeded."

He handed me the book, but I refused it. "The book was written for you, Your Majesty. Please keep it."

"I am in your debt. The book is a valuable one." He paused. "There is a place for you in my service."

"I am grateful, but I go to Alamut."

"You will need money. You will need horses."

"One horse I have; my others were taken by the Petchenegs, although"—the thought came to me—"if I could get word to Prince Abaka Khan, I might buy them back."

"Abaka Khan has been to my court."

The sun was gone, a cool breeze came over the water. "I have affairs to which I must attend. I am grateful, Odric, for bringing this man to me."

He extended his hand. "Think of another service I can do you. It will be my pleasure."

When he was gone we left by the postern gate, which

closed after us. Lights thrust into the darkness of the waters like golden daggers. A coolness arose from the harbor.

"You have a friend," Odric said.

"I like him."

"He is a soldier, as strong as any three of my men even today, and he has been emperor more years than I have lived."

At the end of the street Odric paused. "I return, but be careful. Our streets are unsafe for a man alone."

"I am not alone," I told him; "I have my sword."

46

It has seemed to me that each year one should pause to take stock of himself, to ask: Where am I going? What am I becoming? What do I wish to do and become?

Most people whom I encountered were without purpose, people who had given themselves no goal. The first goal need not be the final one, for a sailing ship sails first by one wind, then another. The point is that it is always going somewhere, proceeding toward a final destination.

Until now my task had been to find if my father was alive, and if so where, and then how to free him from slavery.

These were but temporary goals. What was it *I* wanted? Where was I going? What had I done to achieve it?

Mine was the day of the adventurer. Only a few years before, William, so-called the Conqueror, had led a bunch of adventurers and soldiers of fortune from Normandy into England. Possessing little beyond their courage, their judgment, and their swords, they had taken rich lands and turned them to their own use.

Another Norman family had captured Sicily and built a small empire but a rich one. He who had a sword could carve his way to wealth and power, and the kingdoms of the world were ruled by such men or their descendants.

Yesterday I arrived hungry and in rags; today I was the confidant of kings; so can a man's fortune change.

Yet power, riches, and the friendship of kings are but transitory things. Riches are a claim to distinction for those who have no other right to it. Ancestry is most important to those who have done nothing themselves, and often the ancestor from whom they claim descent is one they would not allow in the house if they met him today.

Great families were often founded by pirates, freebooters, or energetic peasants who happened to be in the right place at the right time and took advantage of it. The founder would, in most cases, look with disdain on his descendants.

To me the goal was to learn, to see, to know, to understand. Never could I glimpse a sail on an outbound ship but my heart would stumble and my throat grow tight.

Up to a point a man's life is shaped by environment, heredity, and movements and changes in the world about him; then there comes a time when it lies within his grasp to shape the clay of his life into the sort of thing he wishes to be. Only the weak blame parents, their race, their times, lack of good fortune, or the quirks of fate. Everyone has it within his power to say, this I am today, that I shall be tomorrow. The wish, however, must be implemented by deeds.

Within a few weeks my father would be free, or I should be dead.

Beyond that I had not planned, except there was an urge within me to go further into the East, to seek my destiny in the far lands of Hind or Cathay.

Women? Ah, women were the stuff of dreams, made to be loved, and he who could say the reality was less than the promise was neither lover nor dreamer.

Aziza, Sharasa, Valaba, Safia, Suzanne . . . had I loved any one the less because I had loved the others? Had not each, in her way, contributed to my education? To my appreciation? Even today did I not love each of them still? A little, anyway.

Where lay my destiny? Where beyond the Valley of the Assassins?

To Hind, perhaps? To that far land beyond the deserts? There was much to learn there, and there were dark-eyed

girls with soft lips; there were palm trees, white sand
beaches, and a soft roll of surf. There were jungle nights
with strange scents and sounds, paddles dipping and trade
winds stirring the leaves.

He who would see a far land must carry the far land
in his heart. The heat, dust, and struggle are a part of it;
these were what made the beauties worth having.

In the stillness of many a night I had taken out my
maps, those maps I carried ever close to me, safe in their
oilskin covering. I studied those maps, but I prepared
another.

I prepared a map of the fortress of Alamut, gathering
bits and pieces, a word here, a comment there, but nothing I heard boded well for what lay before me. The
villagers for miles around were their friends or members
of their sect, each one a spy. To get close without those in
the castle being informed was impossible.

The Emperor Manuel allowed two weeks to go by
with no acknowledgment of my gift. I had all but forgotten
when Odric came to my door with others of the Varangian
Guard, and with them were my lovely Arabs, the stallion
and the two other mares given me by Safia.

Wrapped in a brocaded cloak of the style worn in
Constantinople was a jeweled sword with an engraved
blade and a magnificent scabbard. The sword was of Toledo steel, an even finer blade than the one I formerly
possessed. Along with it were several purses of gold.

And that night there came an invitation to dinner
from Andronicus.

Several times I had visited the shop near the Baths of
Zeuxippus. Some said these baths were named for a famous Megarian chieftain, others from "the yoking of the
steeds," for according to tradition the Baths stood on the
very spot Hercules yoked and tamed the fiery steeds of
Diomed. The Baths were built by the Emperor Severus,
and rebuilt by Constantine. Utterly destroyed during the
revolt of Nika in 562, they were restored with added
beauty by Justinian. The Baths were situated only a little
east of the Hippodrome.

Talking with the Persian, I found he had changed his tone. He no longer tried to persuade me that what I wished to attempt was impossible, and this aroused my suspicions.

My strength had returned. The weeks of good food, exercise, and swordplay had returned my muscles to their former ability.

On the evening of the dinner given by Andronicus, I wore a magnificent tunic of a large patterned brocade of black and gold with a smaller brocade pattern. On my head a high-crowned, turbanlike hat with an upstanding brim. The hat and brim were of silk, the brim set with gems.

Phillip, in a costume of equal brilliance, came with me.

Much had been said of the dinners of Andronicus where he served the rarest food, the finest wines, and had the most seductive dancing girls. Perhaps no period in history had so many writers enamored with historical writing, and many wrote exceedingly well.

We rode in a sedan chair, entering the marble halls between armed guards. Almost the first person I saw where the guests were gathered was Bardas.

He crossed to greet me, and in the presence of a dozen people said, "Ah, Beggar, you have come far since I tossed you a coin in the bazaar!"

Eyes turned upon me, the cold eyes of strangers.

"Thank you, Bardas"—I bowed—"it is true I have come far, yet I find you where you were, licking crumbs from the fingers of your superiors."

With that I walked on, leaving him with his face tight with shock, eyes like balls of glass.

"Bravo!" Phillip whispered. "You have done what many have wished to do, put Bardas in his place!"

Running feet came from behind me, and Bardas grasped my shoulder. "By the Gods! If it is a duel of wits you wish, you shall have it!"

"I am sorry, Bardas. I could never fight an unarmed man!"

The room rang with laughter, and Bardas lifted a hand as if to strike me. I stood perfectly still, waiting, looking into his eyes. He dropped his hand and walked stiffly away.

Andronicus arose from where he was seated and gestured to a place at the head of the table. "Come!" he said, with a touch of sarcasm, "I am not a king, Kerbouchard, but I offer the seat at the head of the table! Let it never be said that Andronicus played less than the king to the Druid."

When I seated myself he said, "You were hard upon Bardas."

"He brought it upon himself. If one plans to measure blows with a stranger, one had best judge the length of his arm."

"Yes, yes, you are right. Tell me, Kerbouchard, what do you think of our city?"

"Magnificent! But I do not believe that anyone truly believes in it. It has the appearance of a city expecting disaster."

We talked of many things. He was a graceful, witty talker, gifted with occasional brilliant insights and a wealth of knowledge. His was a sharper, brighter mind than that of Manuel, but less disciplined. He held in contempt those less than himself, an attribute not possessed by Manuel, who seemed to respect all men.

It was now 1180, and Manuel had ruled successfully since 1143. These cousins, so different in every way, were fascinating to me. Manuel had all the stability and common sense that Andronicus lacked. Manuel might make mistakes, but they would never be petty. Andronicus was positive he was superior to the Emperor and was constantly outwitted for that very reason.

We ate, among other things, a dish of breast of chicken cooked and shredded, the white meat mixed with milk and sugar and cooked until thickened, served with powdered sugar and rose water.

There was also a dessert, *kazan dibi*, which was Turkish in origin.

There were a dozen meat dishes, several of fowl, fish, and fruit; some were strange fruits I had not seen before, and some were the honey-sweet tips of ripe figs.

Andronicus ended a brief dissertation on the comparative writings of Procopius and Menander, and during the pause I chose to seek information.

"What of the present? I understand the Emperor has favored the Latins of late, and there is unrest."

"It is a weakness of Manuel's. The Byzantines have no affection for the Latins. If I were emperor, I would recapture the castles to the south, particularly Anamur, Camardesium, Til Hamdoun, and Saône. If one held those castles, the rest must fall of themselves."

"I am unfamiliar with Saône."

"It was formerly a Byzantine castle, taken and improved by the Franks. It guards the southern approaches to Antioch."

"It is strongly held?"

"Its defenses, we learn, have lately improved. The Comtesse de Malcrais returned and recruited a strong band of mercenaries." He paused. "They are led by a stranger to us, named Lucca."

Lucca! But I had seen him fall on the battlefield! Still . . . I had fallen, too.

If Suzanne had recruited Lucca and survivors of the caravan, she would have a force quite capable of holding Saône against any ordinary attack.

Lucca had been a pirate, a brigand, yet he had become a successful merchant with skill at negotiation. A better lieutenant would be hard to find. Some of the caravan's men had escaped to the boats. At one time there must have been three dozen men in the water, and Lucca would be their natural leader.

"I know of Lucca," I advised. "Do not underrate him. He is a skilled fighting man, a veteran of a hundred battles."

A slave filled my glass. "Your health, Andronicus! May success be yours!"

His eyes were amused. "And if I should attack Saône?"

"My advice? Negotiate. It would be easier to make an arrangement than to capture."

He permitted himself a smile. "Your advice is good, Kerbouchard, and when the time comes am I permitted to tell the Comtesse de Malcrais it was your advice?"

"The Comtesse," I said carefully, "as well as Signor Lucca appreciates the benefits of negotiation without any word from me.

"Lucca," I added, "is one of the most dangerous and intelligent fighting men whom I have met. The cost of taking a position he holds would far outweigh its value. Especially as the Comtesse would find the Byzantine position her own, in most cases."

"Tell me, Druid"—Andronicus spoke lightly—"is it true that you can see the future? The ancient ones, it is said, could do so. Are you one of these?"

"We were trained in the method, and there is a method. It is one I have never attempted."

He was silent for several minutes, watching the others. Bardas sat across the room, looking his hatred.

"Are you not curious?"

"Who is not? But I would rather try to mold my destiny, to shape it with these"—I lifted my hands—"for we believe a man's destiny may be many things, although a way is prescribed, a man may change. It is interesting that so few do change."

"Could you read my destiny, Druid?"

Phillip was conversing with two men, not far from Bardas. Bardas said something aloud that I could not hear, but Phillip flushed.

"Bardas," I said, "is a fool. He is now trying to start trouble with my friend."

Andronicus shrugged. "Bardas is my friend."

"And Phillip is mine."

He looked at me, his eyes utterly cold. "Is it important to be the friend of Kerbouchard? Or of Andronicus?"

"To Kerbouchard," I replied coolly, "it is more important to be the friend of Kerbouchard."

His manner changed. "If there is trouble, you will not interfere. That is my order."

Rising, I stood over him. "You must excuse me then; Phillip and I are leaving."

He made no answer, and catching Phillip's eye, I indicated the door with an inclination of my head. With an expression of genuine relief he started to join me. As he did so, Bardas leaped to his feet, his face flushed with anger.

"Go, then, you bitch whelp, I—"

He sprang after us and was within reach. I backhanded him across the mouth, splitting his lips and showering him with blood. Knocked to a sitting position, he put his hand to his mouth and stared at the blood.

Andronicus had risen. He gestured to several soldiers. "Take him!" he ordered. "And throw him into the street!" He indicated Phillip. "And that one also!"

With a manner of utter disdain he started to turn away.

Suddenly, sword in hand and facing the soldiers, prepared to die rather than be thrown out, something happened to me that had never happened before.

Before me was a vision, so stark and horrible that I was shocked. In my terrible rage, this had come. Was it truly prevision? Or a wish born of anger?

My expression stopped the soldiers, even Andronicus paused. "What is it? What has happened?"

"You asked for your future. I have seen it."

He came to me, his eyes hot and eager. "What is it? What did you see? *Tell* me!"

"You wish to know? It is something I would offer no man of my own volition."

"Tell me."

"I saw a body with your face, a living body being torn by the mob. Some were beating or stabbing you with sticks; some pushed dung into your nostrils and mouth; some thrust spits between your ribs, and a woman dumped boiling water in your face. Still living, you were hung head down from a beam between two poles in the

Hippodrome, and then a spectator ran a sword into your
mouth and upward into your body!"

"Was I emperor at the time?"

"Yes," I replied, "you were emperor."

"Then it was worth it," he said, and walked away
from me.

47

How still the night! How pure the gold of the crescent moon above the dark waters of the Golden Horn! How bright were the distant stars!

Around me were lapping waters in the dark, shadowed hulls of the boats, the mutter of sleeping men.

Nothing moved, nothing stirred, only the water, only the soft wind blowing in from over Asia. Empty eyes where distant windows had been bright, staring, lidless eyes open to the night, and I, alone, wrapped in the folds of a dark cloak, waiting.

Constantinople slept; the Byzantine Empire slept beside its beautiful waters, secure, strong, playing one barbarian folk against another, moving them like pieces on a chessboard, watching with bored amusement from heavy-lidded eyes.

Tonight was to be my last in Constantinople. As in so many other places, I had been but a passerby. Arriving a beggar, I left a friend of the emperor, the enemy of his cousin.

Gold lined the belt about my waist. Gold was in the pockets of my sash; gold was concealed elsewhere about me. My horses were aboard my hired boat, my few possessions there also. Only an hour separated me from my leave-taking.

Before me and across the Black Sea lay Trebizond. Beyond lay the mountains that fringe the Caspian Sea on the south and east, and high in those remote Elburz Mountains were the Valley of the Assassins and the fortress of Alamut.

The night was cool. Lances of light lay on the dark water; the boats tugged at their hawsers. Under my dark cloak I felt for the handle of my sword. As I left the house of Andronicus Comnenus, something had been tucked into my hand.

Turning quickly, I had seen nothing but bland, watchful eyes, no one familiar, no one who might have given whatever it was to me.

Our sedan chair had awaited, but I took Phillip by the shoulder, and we fled down a dark street, swiftly skirting the Hippodrome. Neither of us was a fool, and we had made a deadly enemy of Bardas. When we finally slowed to a walk in the Street of the Spices, I warned him, "You had best leave town with me. They will kill you now."

"Where would I go? This city is my home, my life. I know no other place."

"If you prefer the view from Eyoub." I shrugged. Eyoub was the cemetery overlooking the Golden Horn. "Look," I told him, "they will be searching for us together. I shall go the way I've planned, but do you go to Castle Saône. Tell the Comtesse de Malcrais and Lucca that I sent you."

"Perhaps . . . yes, I must. I was trained in weapons and the fighting of wars but have done none of it. I was also taught the administration of estates."

A Levantine, for a price, had taken my horses aboard. At midnight we would sail. In the room at the house of Phillip I glanced at the note slipped into my hand at the house of Andronicus.

> *Go not to Alamut! It means your death.*
> *S.*

It was written in the flowing hand of Safia, in the Persian tongue.

Go not to Alamut . . . had I a choice? Was it not my destiny to go to Alamut? What had these years meant to me but a preparation for Alamut?

A warning from Safia, who knew me well, indicated

how desperately she feared what awaited me there. Safia did not fear lightly, nor did I. Hence, whatever was there to be feared was something worth fearing.

Shadows detached themselves from shadows; shadows moved toward me, and there was a vague shine of mail. If one must die, what better place than on the wharves of the Golden Horn in the light of a golden moon?

My blade was a finger of steel, lifting . . .

"No, Kerbouchard, we have come to see you safely away."

Odric stepped from the darkness, a dozen men behind him. "The Emperor ordered it, although we ourselves planned to come."

Men of the Varangian Guard, men of the north country. Odric's father, too, had been a corsair.

"You are a bold man, so our Emperor loves you. He bade me say that if you come this way again, there is a place for you at his side."

"Had he heard of tonight?"

"Of course. All Byzantines have spies, and every Byzantine is himself a spy. Everyone intrigues against everyone else. It is the sport of Byzantium; it is their game."

Aboard the boat Odric faced the Levantine shipmaster. "Do you know me?"

"I have seen you," the Levantine said sullenly.

"Deliver this man safely to Trebizond, or cut your own throat and sink your vessel. If he arrives not safely, we shall hunt you down and feed you, in small pieces, to the dogs. Do you understand?"

Tonight I was clad in a coat of mail covered by a tunic of light woolen cloth with embroidery at the edges. On my legs were hose covered by soft boots, and I wore a semicircular cloak clasped in front with a fibula. My cloak was of black, my tunic and hose were of maroon.

Our boat slipped quietly from the wharf and down the Horn to the stronger waters of the Bosphorus. The breeze was fresh and cool upon my face. Moving astern, I paused beside the Levantine. "It has a good feel," I said. "I was born to a ship's deck."

"You?" He was astonished. "I thought you some young wastrel of a nobleman."

"Lastly, I was a merchant trader." Pointing off toward the mouth of the Dnieper, I said, "We were wiped out by the Petchenegs."

"I heard of it . . . a bad business."

My horses were stabled amidships, and I went to stand with them and feed them bits of vegetables. Ayesha nuzzled my side, and the stallion nipped at my sleeve in a friendly way. Finally, I went forward and lying down with my cloak about me, I slept.

In the gray dawn I awakened. The sea was picking up. Spray blew against my face, and I liked the taste of it on my lips, bringing back memories of the far Atlantic coast and my home.

The Levantine came forward. "There is danger from the Turks," he said. "We are going further to sea."

The Byzantine Empire held Greece and as far north as the Danube, west to the Adriatic, and, under Manuel I, the coast of the Adriatic including Dalmatia. On the mainland of Asia they held the coast to a short distance below Antioch and for some distance inland. The Black Sea coast as far as Trebizond was theirs, and so also were portions of the Crimea.

Inland, Anatolia was held by the Seljuk Turkish Empire with their capital at Iconium. These Turks were a fierce group of nomadic tribes from Central Asia who migrated south and fought their way into their possessions.

The citadel of Trebizond stood on a tableland between two deep ravines that, when heavy rains fell, emptied their floods into the sea. In the foreground as we approached we could see wharves, warehouses, and resorts for seamen, shops selling supplies to ships and fishing craft. At the foot of the tableland as well as atop it were the walled homes of wealthy merchants, their walls a riot of vines.

Beyond the walls of the citadel were the towers of

Byzantine churches. It was late afternoon when we landed in a driving rain. I had changed to a *birrus*, a capelike cloak of deep red, heavier stuff, and worn for wintry or rainy weather. It possessed a hood that slipped over my helmet.

When we came ashore a ramp was run out, and I led my horses down. Several dockside loafers paused to watch, and I was uneasy, for they were magnificent animals and likely to cause comment.

The shores even on such a dismal day were crowded with heaps of merchandise, camels loading and unloading, and throngs of merchants. Mounting Ayesha and leading my other horses, I chose a narrow street leading inland. Glancing back, I saw a man standing alone in the street, watching me go.

There would be spies, and thieves, everywhere.

Aside from my sword and dagger I carried a bow and a quiver of arrows. Riding east, I passed several camel caravans bound west for Trebizond. At midnight I rode off the trail and camped in a *wadi* among some willows.

There was grass for my horses, a small area screened by a hill and the willows. Gathering fuel, I roasted mutton and ate, enjoying the stillness.

It was near this place where Xenophon's Ten Thousand, retreating after the death of Cyrus, ate of the wild honey that drove them mad. All who ate the honey had attacks of vomiting and diarrhea and were unable to stand upright. Some who ate but little seemed drunk; others were temporarily insane, and a few died. The honey was made, I learned from an Armenian, from the azalea, and contains a narcotic.

Drawing from my pack fresh clothing, discarding the Byzantine costume except for the coat of mail and the cloak, I donned a *burdah* or undercloak bound with a sash, then put on the *aba* or long outercloak. Under the sash was concealed my old leather belt, my only possession from home other than my Damascus dagger. Then I resumed the turban of the scholar, adding the *taylasan*, a

scarf thrown over the turban with one end drawn under
the chin and dropped over the left shoulder.

The *taylasan* was worn by judges and theologians,
offering a measure of security from questioning or attack,
and suited the identity I was adopting, that of ibn-Ibrahim,
a physician and scholar. It was no haphazard selection, for
the one way in which I might open the gates to Alamut
was as a scholar. Yet once inside those gates I would be
surrounded by fanatics, ready to tear me to bits at my
slightest mistake.

Hunched over my small fire, I felt the cold hand of
despair. What sort of fool was I even to hope that I might
accomplish the miracle of entering Alamut?

Again and again I reviewed all I knew and found no
help. My only hope lay in the remote possibility of an
invitation from Rashid-Ad-din Sinan himself, a man noted
for his intuitive gifts and said to be interested in alchemy.

Of this I knew nothing but bazaar gossip, and I must
stop in Tabriz and establish myself as ibn-Ibrahim in that
city. There the spies of the Old Man could observe me at
their leisure.

Once I got within the gates of Alamut, if I was so
fortunate, every second would be one of danger.

Aziza in the castle of Prince Ahmed, Suzanne in
Castle Saône, Valaba in the salons of Córdoba, did they
think of me now and then? Yet who recalls the wanderer
who appears but for a fleeting day or two and then is
gone? My passing was that of a shadow in a garden, and
who would remember? Or why should they? Would it be
always so for me? Was I but a passerby?

If one returns and stands again upon the same ground,
is it he who stands there or a stranger?

Armorica would still be Armorica; the sands of
Brignogan would still be the sands of Brignogan, but
Kerbouchard would be . . . what?

The memory of the great oar in my hands, the stench
of the filth beneath me, the arms of Aziza, the books of the
great library of Córdoba, the bite of a sword through bone
. . . or that rain-swept cliff in Spain. How much of me

remained there, in those places, and how much had brought me here, perhaps to my death?

How much of me lay on the blood-soaked turf where died the *Hansgraf* with his White Company of traders? How much of me in that muddy clearing where I had been knocked down, humbled, beaten, helpless to resist?

Was it anything more than luck that my bones did not lie back there to be picked over by wolves and vultures? A stick fell into the fire, sparks flew up.

Would I ever find a place where I belonged? Or was I destined to drift across the world like a disturbed spirit? Would I find that someone I sought? Someone more important to me than anyone or anything else?

Hah! Was I a child to dream so? I was lucky to be alive, and if I freed my father and escaped alive, I must be even luckier. And what of the walking drum?

Would I hear its beat again? And if I did, would I pick up my pack and follow?

And the *Hansgraf*? Where he was did he hear it? That drum marched us across Europe and into Asia and right to the very gates of death.

48

Who shall deny the excitement of entering a strange city for the first time? Or going ashore in a strange port?

And the beauty of Tabriz? To north, south, and east were reddish, orange-shaded hills, brilliant in contrast to the lush green of orchard and garden. Tabriz was a jewel of a city, watered by streams flowing down from the mountains.

To this city had I come, I, Mathurin Kerbouchard, now known as ibn-Ibrahim, physician, scholar, pilgrim to the holy places of Islam.

More than ten miles around were the walls of Tabriz, entered by ten gates, and outside the walls lay seven districts, each named for the stream that watered it.

My pace slowed, for I was a scholar and must proceed with dignity as befitted my position. What happened here might open the gates of Alamut.

Yet as I drew closer, it was my stallion and mares that drew attention, for no Arab lived who did not know the great breeds. The horses did not fit my role as scholar but did much to establish me as a man of wealth and importance. Wars had been fought over such mares as these, and I had three, and a stallion.

Glancing neither to the right nor left, I rode into the streets and through the great bazaar of Ghazan, one of the finest on earth. Wherever I looked were throngs of colorfully dressed people, and each trade was situated in a different corner of the bazaar. Reaching the bazaar of the jewelers, I found such a splendid collection of gems that I paused to gaze, and not only at the gems but also at the beautiful slave girls who displayed them.

Each girl had been chosen for her beauty and the symmetry of her body, and these slaves posed, turning this way and that to display their costly bangles.

Nearby was another bazaar where only perfumes were sold. Spikenard, patchouli, myrrh, frankincense, ambergris, musk, rose, and jasmine—there was no counting the fragrances. There was a street of booksellers, another for leather goods, and several streets crowded with weavers of rugs, which reminded me that I must find a prayer rug.

Riding on, I came to a hospice near the Baghdad gate. Travelers who stopped were served bread, meat, rice cooked with butter, and sweetmeats.

Everywhere were horses, camels, bullocks, and goats as well as both veiled and unveiled women. Turkish women did not veil. Frankish traders were there, whom I quickly avoided, fearing to be recognized. There were Armenians, Levantines, Greeks, Jews, Kurds, Slavs, Turks, Arabs, and Persians. There were big blond men whom I recognized as Pathans, and even merchants from Hind and Cathay, for Tabriz was truly a crossroads.

It was much changed from the time that the *Hudud-al-Alam* was compiled. The note on Tabriz in that geography said simply *Tabriz, a small borough, pleasant and prosperous, within a wall constructed by 'Ala-ibn-Ahmad*. That, of course, had been written in 982, nearly two hundred years before my arrival.

Tabriz lay in the basin of Lake Urmiah, dominated by the volcano Mount Sehend, surrounded by miles of gardens and fields. The town had once been known as Kandsag, but that was long, long ago.

My arrival at the hospice brought a stir of excitement. The Arab stable boys rushed to help me from the saddle as if I were barrel fat and helpless.

A familiar voice sounded at my elbow. "O Mighty One! I, Khatib the preacher, would serve you! I, a student of the Koran, but knowing in all the ways of evil! Trust me, O Mighty One, and you shall be guided safely!"

It was he . . . *it was Khatib*!

"*Bismillah!*" I exclaimed. "What manner of man is this who doth crawl with fleas! Thou hive of vermin, how could such a one serve me, ibn-Ibrahim, scholar and physician?"

He followed me to the door of the caravanserai, his wicked old eyes twinkling. "I knew if I waited, you must come sooner or later to this place, and surely, you have come."

"And the Comtesse?"

"Safe enough, by the will of Allah! And like to remain so, for Lucca has recruited men for her, including some thirty of those who escaped from the Cumans. She will do well enough, that one!"

"Do you know what it is that I do?"

"You are a fool to even think of it, but I am a fool who has found his master, and will help you. It has been written."

"My chances are not good."

"Who speaks of chance or chances? We have neither one nor the other, ibn-Ibrahim!" He used the name with a sly grin. "We shall be food for jackals." He shrugged his thin shoulders. "But I have lived much, and who is to say that I should die otherwise?"

"Ibn-Ibrahim, being a scholar and a physician, might be invited . . . I say *might* . . . to the fortress of Alamut."

"As Allah wills. Truly," he added, "you are the most learned of men, and there is no trick in that. I have heard wise men speak of you so, even the great Averroës. Do you have a plan?"

"Only to become known quickly as a scholar and physician. Sinan, I hear, is one to appreciate such things, and there might be an invitation. If not, I shall find another way."

Khatib shrugged. "What you wish has been done. Even before you arrived I informed all who listened that I awaited my master, who was a wise man before Allah." He grinned again, evil twinkling from his eyes. "Besides, I had no money, and men would not allow the servant of a learned man to starve in their presence."

"But the name, Khatib! Who did you tell them I was?"

"How could I know? I told them nothing as to name, just that my master was a great scholar who did not wish to become known, but who traveled in search of wisdom."

"What of the way, Khatib? Do you know it?"

"Aye . . . it is far into the mountains near Qazvin, where each village is a nest of spies. You cannot proceed one step they will not know.

"Another thing, and *beware*! There is a man named al-Zawila . . . do you know such a one?"

"No."

"He is of great power among the Isma'ili, but lately come to Alamut. Some say he is powerful as Sinan and is his strong right hand, his defender, his master of spies.

"There is a whisper, and not even walls may stop a whisper, that since his coming there has been grief and trouble for the slave named Kerbouchard. This slave had won a place for himself by diligence, but since the coming of al-Zawila he is marked for every demeaning task. It is as if al-Zawila wished to force him to anger so he could be tortured and killed!"

"Then we must move swiftly, for my father's patience is as limited as his strength is great."

We talked long, and I listened much, for Khatib knew all the gossip of the bazaars and nothing escaped him. First, I must establish myself, for what was needed was official recognition of my presence. Knowing the ways of power, I doubted I should long be kept waiting.

Al-Zawila? I knew no such name. Why, then, did he hate my father? For surely there must be hatred for such a man to even notice my father.

And but recently arrived? Could he be an enemy of mine?

I knew no such man, nor had any memory of one.

Tabriz, Khatib told me, was noted for the splendor of

its rugs as well as its books, and a rug was needed for my prayers.

Finding Khatib gave me hope, for doubts assailed me. How could I succeed where kings and emperors had failed? Yet Khatib was a man of a thousand gifts, listening well, and possessing devious ways of acquiring knowledge hidden from all.

Scarcely an hour passed before there came a fat eunuch, puffing from his exertions. "O Auspicious One! I come from the Emir! From the mighty and learned Mas'ud Khan! If you would condescend to honor him with your presence!"

"Tell your master, his wish is an honor. His nobility, his splendor, his riches and power are known to all! If he wishes this humble one to come, come I shall!"

Such are the amenities of social life, which oft makes a liar of the best of men. Never had I heard of Mas'ud Khan, nor had I any idea whether he was noble, splendid, or rich, but considering my problems, I hoped he was all three. Yet if he was an emir—and seeing the wealth of the city as well as the poverty of the poor, I had no doubt someone was squeezing the juice from the orange—rich he might well be.

Yet there were other things to consider. It was in my mind to show myself in the bazaars, for what was whispered there would echo inside the walls of Alamut. Moreover, as I was now to become a Moslem, I wished to have a prayer rug. Women and the very rich had begun to use such rugs, and as I wished to establish myself as one of the very rich and very eminent, the prayer rug was essential.

To breach the walls of Alamut with power had failed many; to enter by stealth with the network of spies was impossible. Every stranger was suspect. Hence, the solution seemed to be to herald my presence widely and hope for an invitation. Plotters and connivers were searched for in hidden places, so I would let myself be seen, heard, and talked with. Sinan was a man of varied interests, and it might be that a stranger would interest him.

The rugs woven in Tabriz were of several kinds, but the Ghiordes or Turkish knot was beginning to displace the Sehna or Persian knot in the Tabriz area. The city had long been noted for its weavers, although the industry had been damaged by Turkish invasions. Now Turks had settled in or around Tabriz and introduced their own methods of weaving. The tufted style had been suitable for a people whose rugs covered the floors of tents. The Turks invaded the country at least a hundred years before my time, but their methods of weaving had been slow to replace the Persian.

The idea of the prayer rug was new, although Moslems had marked off small areas when in the field or traveling, to keep intruders at a distance when praying. These were often marked off by sticks or stones. Despite the fact that the Moslem religion has many elements similar to Christian or Jewish practice, and all are People of the Book, the true Moslem will not pray where the footsteps of Jews or Christians have made the ground unclean.

The worshiper will, if water is unavailable, wash his hands with sand or soil, for he must bathe before praying. He will have with him his *kibleh*, a small compass to ascertain the direction of Mecca, and his *tesbeth*, or rosary.

The devout Moslem will pray five times a day, his devotions preceded by washing of the face, hands, and feet. Ears that have heard evil are touched with water. Eyes and mouth that have seen or spoken evil are washed. When washing the hands, the Moslem cups the water in his hands and lifts them, allowing the water to run down to his elbows.

It was from this habit of washing our hands before prayer that we physicians adopted the habit of bathing our hands in this manner, as it was the custom to pray before each operation.

After bathing, the worshiper would kneel upon his marked-off space or rug, prostrating himself, touching the rug with his forehead. During the years when Mohammed lived, it was the custom to pray toward Jerusalem, but following his death, the direction of Mecca was adopted.

Mats and rugs had been used by various religions
since earliest times, so the idea was not new to Arab,
Turk, or Persian.

The prayer rugs offered for sale in Tabriz were rectan-
gular rugs with an elaborate border of delicate floral design.
At the top of the rug and inside the border was a panel
some four inches wide and at least two feet long containing a stylized quotation from the Koran in Arabic. Beneath
the panel and outlining the prayer arch was the spandrel
with a field of sapphire blue worked with an intricate
design.

The Ghiordes prayer arch or niche possessed a high
central spire and well-defined shoulders. Two pillars sup-
ported the arch on the sides, and from the center of the
arch was suspended a representation of the sacred lamp of
the temple.

The coloring of the Ghiordes rugs I saw in Tabriz was
delicate but beautifully defined. The rug I purchased had
just been completed and was woven from silk with a few
designs in wool. Had the rug been woven entirely of silk
or wool, it would have been perfect, and nothing is perfect
but Allah, so the addition of a few designs in other materials indicated the humility of the weaver. The blue, light-
green, and yellow were beautiful in the extreme, and
when held in different lights the rug possessed a shimmer
like a mirage in the desert.

The pile of the rug was woven in such a way that the
nap lay in the direction of Mecca.

The rugs fascinated me, and I wandered through the
bazaars studying the various ideas and motifs expressed in
the weaving. The influence of the Chinese was quite obvious in some of the rugs. Contacts with the Chinese had
begun long before. For several hundred years ships from
Cathay had been coming to the Persian Gulf, and in
Constantinople as well as here I had seen bronze articles
as well as ceramic from China.

Rugs from Samarkand were displayed in the markets,
some worked with a pomegranate design, a Hittite symbol

of eternal life and fertility. In others the pine cone was the basic motif, a Chinese symbol of longevity, and the cypress tree, often planted in Moslem cemeteries, was often seen. In ancient times it had been believed that cypress boughs left upon the tombs of the dead would continue to mourn. The cypress had long been sacred in Persia, sacred to the fire worshipers who gave Persia its name, for the tall, slender shape of the cypress symbolized the flame.

In Córdoba I had seen many rugs from the East, fabulous in beauty and texture. It was incredible that such rugs could be woven, with hundreds of knots to the square inch. The one I finally decided upon for myself numbered five hundred and forty knots to the square inch, although this was nothing to such palace rugs as the great rug woven for the audience hall at Ctesiphon, representing a garden. Some such rugs numbered two thousand five hundred knots to the square inch, an incredible number.

The garden idea was quite common in Persian rugs, and the word paradise is Persian and means a "walled garden."

Khatib found me in the bazaar, worried by my absence, and reminding me of my meeting with the Emir. It was with rugs as with pottery and books. I have been fascinated by the ideas expressed and the symbolism woven into the texture of their work.

An hour after leaving the bazaar I appeared at the palace of the Emir, Mas'ud Khan. Upon a dais at the far end of the audience hall a low table had been spread with all manner of fruit and viands. Scarcely had I been shown into the room than Mas'ud Khan himself appeared, and my expectations were shattered.

Instead of the corpulent emir I expected, round of cheek before and behind, I found myself meeting a lean, hawk-faced man with black penetrating eyes that measured me coldly. This was no idle official, fattening upon the deeds of other men, but a warrior, lean and fierce. He carried the smell of blood and the saddle about him, and I realized I must proceed with the greatest caution.

"It is an honor to meet a scholar of such great

knowledge." He spoke smoothly, then abruptly. "You are truly a physician?"

"Truly," I replied, then added, "and you are truly the Emir?"

49

He smiled with genuine humor, albeit a wolfish humor that had more than a hint of the sardonic. "Well said!" He seated himself at a table and handed me a piece of fruit. "I think we shall be friends!"

"A scholar is always a friend to an emir," I said, "or he is not wise enough to deserve the name of scholar!"

"You must forgive my ignorance," Mas'ud Khan said, "but I believed I knew the names of the most eminent scholars. What a pity that I know so little of what you have done!"

Suspicious of me, was he? Suspicious, and therefore dangerous, for this man would act upon what he believed. Was he an Isma'ili? Perhaps an ally and friend to Sinan?

"How could you know of me? I, who am but the least of Allah's servants? My home was Córdoba, and in Córdoba one must be a great scholar indeed to be known. Yet I knew Averroës there, and John of Seville was my friend."

"What did you there? Were you a teacher?"

"A translator of books from Greek and Latin to Arabic, and sometimes from the Persian, also."

"And your plans?" Mas'ud's hard black eyes measured me.

"To study at Jundi Shapur," I said. "I have heard it is the greatest medical school in the world. Is it true the teaching there is in Sanskrit?"

"No more, but it was once so. For more than one thousand years it has been the greatest of schools, although each year it becomes more difficult to maintain the university and the hospital because Baghdad hires its teachers."

"There is a thing you could do for me, Emir. Long since, word came to me of a book of several thousand pages, the *Ayennamagh*. Can this be found?"

"Truly, you are a scholar! How few even know of this book!" Regretfully, he shook his head. "No, it cannot be had. I have never seen a copy, and if such could be found, it would be my head if it left our hands."

Yet his suspicions remained, and artfully, I guided the conversation through talk of medicine, law, and poetry to the art of war.

He had not heard of Sun Tzu and was fascinated to learn of his theories, and we passed from that to talk of Vegetius and the Roman legions. "We had them here, you know, and our Parthians defeated them. One captured legion was sold to slavery in China and marched there intact."

Artfully, I guided the talk to libraries and alchemy, knowing that in the fortress at Alamut a great library existed, and Sinan himself was interested in alchemy.

Suddenly, without warning he said, "There is a man here from your land. You must meet him."

"His name?"

"Ibn-Haram."

Had he suddenly leaned across and struck me, I could have been no more startled. Yet I believe it did not show in my face.

"Ah, yes. A good man to have for a *friend*, and a dangerous enemy. I know of him . . . he plotted long to seize power in Córdoba, even from Yusuf, his benefactor."

He was one man I must not meet, for I had no greater enemy, and he would use all the power he could muster to have me beheaded. Yet what I had said apparently caused Mas'ud Khan to think, for he was silent, musing for a long time.

"Yusuf was his benefactor, you said?"

For what it was worth, I would try. "As one scholar to another"—I spoke softly, not to be overheard—"trust him not. He is a man hungry for power, and not to be satisfied with anything less than *all* the power."

"Yusuf? He was your friend?"

"He knew nothing of me, and I knew little of him, yet toward the end of my stay I met his son, Abu-Yusuf Ya'kub. We did become friends, very good friends, I believe. We met at the house of Valaba."

"Valaba? Of her I had heard much. She is very beautiful, I think?"

"Very!" I spoke with regret. "Very beautiful, indeed."

"But thin?" He spoke sadly. "I have heard it said."

"Not for my taste, but Turks, I hear, like their women well rounded, on all sides. Is it true?"

"A Turk likes a woman with a belly," he said emphatically. "Those Persian women . . . bah! They are thin, too thin! Breasts, buttocks, and belly, all fat! That is the way a Turk likes his women! And thighs! She must have thighs! *Allah!*" He shook his head. "I cannot see what you Moors and Persians see in those women who are thin as herons!

"Would you believe it, ibn-Ibrahim? In the last three Persian towns we took, there was not a single woman taken by force? It was unbelievable! Were it not for the fact that I understand their distaste for thin women, I would believe our army had lost its manhood!"

He filled a glass and pushed it toward me. "Kumiss. If you have not tasted kumiss you have not lived." He refilled his own glass. "It is our custom," he explained, "when capturing a town to treat all captured women to a taste of Turkish victory. It has done much for the generations that follow." Then he scowled. "But if it continues, we shall be fighting our own sons."

"At least you will be assured of a good fight."

He glanced at me. "I did not know that scholars were warriors."

"And until I met you, Mas'ud Khan," I said quickly, "I did not know warriors were scholars!"

My reply pleased him. He was pleased by the compliment; I, because I had evaded what might have been a trap.

He changed the subject. "You mentioned alchemy? You can make gold?"

My smile was sardonic. "Is it so easy, then, to make gold? Many try . . . it is whispered some have succeeded. But other things are more precious than gold. Life, for example, or the means to take life.

"It is true," I added, "that I have delved into the elements of things, into all aspects and combinations of minerals, and I seek when I can the company of others who learn, for who knows when my knowledge combined with theirs might prove the answer? Each man learns a little, but the sum of their knowledge can be great."

Ibn-Haram was here! Would he know me now? Several years had passed, and I had grown older and stronger, yet that and the suffering had changed me but little. Yet I dare not risk it, for if it was revealed that I was not what I claimed, I would be in serious trouble. And ibn-Haram hated me for defeating him in the matter of Aziza.

Decision was mine. I could not afford to remain in Tabriz. "I shall pass on," I said, "I have been too long without means to study and work. I shall go to Jundi Shapur."

The idea appealed to me, for the fame of that great school, particularly in the field of medicine, was everywhere acknowledged. It was logical that I should go there, logical that I should have made this journey to get there. It accounted for my presence here.

How much power ibn-Haram possessed, I did not know. He must have overreached himself in some plot while in Spain and fled that country. Yet he was a deadly enemy who could bring disaster upon me.

Slaves came suddenly into the room, bringing three splendid silk robes, three new outfits of clothing, and a heavy purse of gold. They brought a fine saddle, bridle, and saddlebags. These gifts were magnificent indeed, but any traveling scholar, at almost any town in Islam, could expect the same. Wisdom was revered; whereas in Europe he might be burned as a heretic.

With no word of Alamut, I mounted my horse, and

followed by slaves bearing the gifts, I returned to the hospice.

Riding away, I glanced back. The eyes of Mas'ud were upon me, cold, measuring, shrewd.

Riding away, I could not throw off a premonition of danger, and my every instinct warned me to not even spend the night, but to take Khatib and fly. Yet that might draw upon me even worse danger, for it would arouse immediate suspicion.

Morning came with a babble of voices as other travelers prepared to leave. Khatib entered, and my resolve was formed on the instant. "Pack," I said. "I shall ride the new saddle, use the new bridle. Let us go at once."

We were fortunate in our time of departure, for a large caravan was leaving at the same time, and we promptly overtook and fell in with them, and riding with them, we conversed.

Among the Franks many believed that Cathay did not exist, yet here I found those who had traveled to Hind, to Cathay, and all the lands that lay between.

The region through which we traveled was fertile and prosperous, growing some of the finest pears and pomegranates I had eaten, and there were groves of olives. Stopping beside the way, many hours later, we made a lunch of cheese from Dinavar and pears of the district while seated beneath tamarisk and chinar trees.

Several of the muleteers stopped with us, and as they had shown no inclination to stop until we did, I suspected them of spying.

It was a lazy, sunny afternoon with a few scattered puffballs of cloud drifting in the sky. Lying upon the sand, I stared up at the sky and again tried to think out a solution to my problem.

Brave as I might seem to others, I knew I was no more brave than any other man. It was not willingly that I went to the fortress of Alamut, but my father was there, and we two were the last of our line. He was all that was left to me, and I could only try to be as good a son as he was a father.

No slave was ever sold from Alamut, nor allowed to leave for fear he might reveal the secrets of the fortress and its fabled gardens of paradise. If by some chance I myself was permitted to enter, my every move would be watched. Depression lay heavily upon me, for if I entered, how then could I leave? And how could I free my father? A man must be a great fool to attempt the impossible, yet my father was my father, and it was easier to risk my life than to think of him as a slave.

Al-Zawila? Who could he be? Why this hatred for my father?

"Master . . . ?"

Two men stood near me, one of them displaying a large and obviously painful boil. After lancing the boil, bathing it, and prescribing a renewal of the poultice I put on, I prepared to leave and rejoin the caravan, but already other patients were coming.

Treating several wounds and prescribing for others, including ground bone for a child reported to have convulsions, I explained to them that it was a theory of a renowned physician that such convulsions were due to lack of calcium in the system. They listened out of respect, but in their own minds, I knew, they believed it was an evil spirit that caused the trouble.

The last man wished an arrowhead extracted that had been embedded in his arm for several days. The arm was in bad condition, but when I had finished with him there seemed no reason to doubt that he would recover without further help. It was dark before we rode on, riding swiftly that we might camp with the protection of the caravan.

In Córdoba, while studying at the mosque, I had frequently practiced surgical operations under the guidance of a physician. It was the custom to practice making incisions using pumpkins, bottle gourds, melons, or cucumbers. Superficial incisions were practiced upon leather bags filled with slush, sewing was practiced on two pieces of delicate leather, scarification upon leather covered with hair.

Qazvin lay at the foot of the Elburz Mountains from

which passes led across the mountains to Tabaristan and the edge of the Caspian Sea. The town itself covered at least a mile. It was the chief fortress against the fierce infidels of the Daylam Mountains.

"Tomorrow," I whispered to Khatib, "invitation or no, we go to Alamut."

"Speak no word of that, Mighty One," Khatib warned, "for this town has many Isma'ilis."

The courtyard was crowded with horses and camels, for another large caravan had just arrived, obviously the retinue of some important person, for both camels and horses were richly caparisoned and a number of tall, finely built soldiers stood about. They were big, bearded men with handsome black eyes, immaculately clad and well armed, every man of them fit and strong. Obviously these were picked fighting men.

Yet they were unlike any men I had seen, neither Arab nor Persian nor Turk. "Khatib? Who are they?"

"Rajputs," he said, "from Hind."

The main room of the caravanserai was bustling with slaves, and we were hard put to find a corner for ourselves. Khatib personally attended to our horses, then joined me.

Suddenly a door to an inner chamber opened, and from it stepped a girl, a girl of such beauty and exquisite grace as I had never seen.

She was tall, moving as though to some unheard music, her dark eyes rimmed with darker lashes, her lips . . . her skin without blemish, her hair dark as a raven's wing.

As she came from the door, her eyes met mine across the room, and for an instant she paused, her chin lifted, her lips parting a little.

Rising, I bowed from the hips, indicating a place at the table beside me. Her eyes seemed to widen at my temerity, and then she walked through the parting crowd to a nearby table, already arranged for her.

Nor did she look at me again.

50

Our tables faced each other across the room with scarcely twenty feet separating one from the other. A dozen slaves attended her, and two Rajput soldiers stood behind her at the corners of the table. The table itself was loaded with at least two dozen dishes, superbly cooked, judging by their aroma.

On my side I had only my faithful Khatib and but three dishes.

She was unveiled, as it was not the custom of her people for women to veil themselves. She wore tight-fitting silk trousers of brilliant yellow and a bodice or *choli* of the same shade and material. Over this, suspended from her shoulders, she wore a burnt orange cloak or robe. Her sandals were delicately made of some golden material, and there were bangles on her ankles.

She wore in the center of her forehead a "fallen leaf," as it was called in Sanskrit, or *tika*. Hers was actually a tiny leaf of intricate workmanship. Her hair was combed quite flat with a triple line of pearls following the part, and the centerpiece, at the hairline, consisted of three golden flowers with large rubies at the center and a row of tear-drop pearls suspended from the lower edge.

My dishes were a *kabab karaz*, a dish of meat cooked with cherries and poured over the small, round Arab breads that I liked so much, rice with sour lemon sauce, and a bean curry.

The contrast between my three dishes and the two dozen brought to her table, as well as the crowd of servants who attended her and my lone servitor, appealed to my sense of amusement, and to that of Khatib, also. He was never one to miss the irony of any situation. He began to serve my food with an elaborate finesse and mincing manner that aped the affectations of the eunuchs who waited upon her.

Lifting the cover from the *kabab* and inhaling deeply, his ragged old brows lifting, he said, "Ah, Most Mighty One! Of this you must taste! It is ambrosia! It is nectar! It is a dream incarnate!" So saying he spooned a tiny portion to the edge of my plate and stood back, spoon in hand, to watch my appreciation.

Delicately, I tasted it, making an elaborate business of savoring, testing, tasting with frowns, rolling of the eyes, and finally a beatific smile.

"Superb, Khatib! Superb!"

He completed the serving of my humble meal with many exclamations. "Such meat! And such a pilaf! May Allah thrice be blessed!"

The face of the girl opposite was expressionless. If she noticed, it was not apparent.

"Wine, Master? It is the gift of the great Emperor of the Byzantines! Of Manuel himself! Wine?"

"Wine, Khatib!" He poured the wine, and I caught a fleeting glance from the girl across the way.

"Preacher," I said, "you are a man of august years, a traveled and learned man of great judgment and discrimination . . . tell me . . . where are the women most beautiful?"

"Where, indeed? As you realize, Magnificence, such things are a matter of taste. Now the Turks, for example, prefer their women to be"—he gestured with his hands before his chest—"to be robust here"—then his hands indicated the hips—"and here."

He filled my glass again and stepped back. "They wish their women to be fat, the Franks want their women to be strong, the Persians prefer them slender, and in Cathay they say their women have the most beautiful legs of all, but it is not their legs they appreciate, but their *feet!*"

"And the women of Hind? I hear they are short and ugly and waddle when they walk. Is this true?"

The language was Persian, and I was hoping neither of the Rajput soldiers understood. Yet she did, for I saw her stiffen suddenly, and she looked up quickly, indignantly.

"Of the women of Hind," Khatib said tactfully, "what can I say?"

"Still, every country has *some* beautiful women. Can there not be one, even *one*, in all of Hind?"

"One would believe so, Master. Usually where there are great warriors there are beautiful women, they appear together, you know."

"I respect your wisdom, O Father of Judgment, for what do I know of such things? I know nothing of women. Glorious creatures, no doubt, but my shyness keeps me from them. I shrink at their glances, I tremble at their slightest word. What could I, of all people, say to a beautiful woman?"

Khatib's wicked old eyes were amused. "What did you say to Valaba? She who was said to be the most beautiful woman in Córdoba? Or to Suzanne, the Comtesse of Malcrais?"

"What, indeed? They took advantage of my shyness, Khatib! What could I possibly do? A defenseless man? And shy? But they were beautiful, and I honor them for their deeds."

"And what of that Viking girl in Kiev?"

"She frightened me, Khatib. I was awestruck. Her long golden hair, her magnificent shoulders, her demanding ways . . . what could I do?"

"Only what you did, I suspect." Khatib helped me to more food from the covered dishes. "Eat, Master, keep up your strength! Who knows what trials lie still before you?"

Suddenly, the door of the room opened, and two soldiers entered, one stepping to either side of the door. Between them marched a pompous little man in a very large turban and a long robe: He was followed by eight slaves, each bearing a gift. To my astonishment they stopped before my table.

"O Auspicious One! O Favored of Allah! My Master, the illustrious, the great, the all-powerful Rashid Ad-din Sinan requests you accept these humble gifts from his hand!

"O Greatest of Scholars! Wisest of Men! Noble Physician and Reader of the Stars, ibn-Ibrahim! My Master requests that you visit him at the Castle of Alamut!"

Two slaves spread out a magnificent robe woven with gold thread and a second cloak trimmed with sable; the third slave brought a sword with a jeweled hilt and scabbard, a splendid blade that when drawn had written along the blade in letters of gold the Persian words, *Dushman kush!* meaning, "Killer of Enemies!"

The fourth slave carried a silken pillow on which lay three purses that chinked with the sound of gold; the fifth brought a jeweled sword belt; the sixth, a complete outfit of clothing; the seventh, a pair of fine saddlebags, handtooled and decorated with gold. The last slave brought me a robe of honor, a jeweled pen, and an inkpot.

"Tell him, Vizier," I said, "that I come on the morrow. My journey will begin when the sun rises."

Pausing briefly, I added, "Inform the mighty Rashid Ad-din Sinan that I look forward to discussing with him the secrets of many sciences, for his great wisdom is known to me."

The eunuch bowed low, backing from the room with continued bows, followed by the slaves.

The innkeeper came hurrying to my table, obviously frightened. "O Master of Wisdom! I pray forgiveness! I had no idea! I did not know who it was who honored my humble—!"

Khatib gathered the gifts, his face grave. The humor was gone from his eyes. "Master, think well of what you do. There is a saying among my people that the deer may forget the snare, but the snare does not forget the deer."

"I shall not forget, Khatib."

"He is a fool who will descend into a well on another man's rope."

The gifts were magnificent, yet I looked upon them as

did Khatib, with suspicion. They were too splendid for an unknown scholar. Was their purpose to make me forget my doubts? Did someone actually *want* me to come to Alamut? Did they think it safer to have me inside the castle, a prisoner, than possibly stirring trouble on the outside? Or did they think of me at all, except as a wandering scholar?

Yet, what choice had I? Behind the walls of Alamut my father was held prisoner, a slave. If he was ever to be free, it lay in my hands.

"In all honor, Khatib, I must go. But do you remain here, for the future is uncertain, and I go into great trouble."

"Were there no wind, would the leaves tremble? There is reason for fear, Master. When the Old Man of the Mountains sends gifts, prepare your shroud . . . a knife follows."

He paused. "But go with you I shall. How many lands have I seen, Master? How many seas? How many cities? But I have not seen the inside of Alamut."

For the moment we had forgotten our beauty from Hind, but she had not forgotten us.

Her slave stood before us, bowing. "O Eminence! My lady begs forgiveness that she was not aware of the presence of such distinguished company. She requests you to join her at her table, my lady, Sundari Devi!"

My hesitation was only brief enough as not to seem precipitate. I arose.

"Khatib, see to my presents, and see to the horses, also. It is said that in Qazvin they make most excellent bows and arrows; see that I am supplied. We shall soon," I suggested, "be crossing a desert where there are bandits.

"Also"—my voice lowered—"see that hidden within our packs there is a length of rope, strong enough to hold a climber." An instant I hesitated, then added, "I think you had best secure these items." I handed him a slip of paper. "This"—indicating an item—"you had best collect yourself from the walls of old stables or the manure of animals. Do get me a supply of this. If there is curiosity, simply say your master is an alchemist who tests all things. He is crazy, of course, but what can you do?"

Crossing the room, I stopped before her table. "I am ibn-Ibrahim."

She gestured to a place at the corner of the table to her right. "I had no idea we were in the presence of so renowned a scholar."

Bowing again, I said, "My shadow is small before the sun of your beauty."

"You are a physician?"

"That, too. Sometimes a soldier, sometimes a reader of the stars . . . many things."

She looked into my eyes and asked, "Ibn-Ibrahim, what do you read in the stars for me?"

And out of me in a voice that scarcely seemed my own, I said, and was surprised by it, "That you shall someday be my wife."

There was a moment, a moment when neither of us moved or spoke, but simply stared at one another, mutually astonished by the words. It was a moment when time seemed arrested, and then she spoke quietly, "You must look again at your stars, Wanderer, for I fear they have misled you."

"You go now to Hind?"

"To Anhilwara, to my home."

"You are a Rajput?"

"My father was, my mother is Persian. Lately, I have visited with her family in Isfahan. Now I return."

Abruptly, she changed the subject. "Did I not hear you were going to the Castle of Alamut? Is it not a fortress of the Assassins?"

"They have many castles." I gestured toward the north. "There are others in those mountains. Yes, I go at the invitation of Rashid Ad-din Sinan. We shall have much to discuss, I believe."

"Is it not true that only an Assassin may enter or leave? Are you then an Isma'ili?"

"I am many things, but I take no part in religious disagreements. The technicalities of religion have no place in the mind of Allah. It is the spirit, I think, that is important."

Pausing briefly, I added, "When I return from Alamut I shall come to Hind, to Anhilwara."

"Do you know my city?"

"Until you spoke of it, I had never heard of it."

Her eyes fell to the table while the servants filled our glasses. Did they speak Persian?

"You must not come."

"But if I wish to see you again?"

"The Moslems who have come to my city have come as enemies."

"Then I would be considered an enemy? If necessary, I could come as a Christian, a Hindu, a fire worshiper, or simply a worshiper."

"It would not do."

"What can the will do when the heart commands?"

Across the room musicians began on the *qitara* and the *kimanja,* and the soft music lingered in the room.

"The music of your beauty," I said, "stirs among the leaves of my heart."

She lifted her eyes to mine. "But I am slender, Scholar, and no such plump beauty as the Turks prefer."

"But I am not a Turk, Sundari, nor even a Persian."

"So what kind of beauty do you prefer? That of . . . what was her name? Valaba? Suzanne?"

"A man who has not known many women cannot appreciate the value of one."

Her eyes sparkled with laughter. "You do not seem so . . . helpless. When you spoke with your servant I was distressed for you. All those girls taking advantage of you! Are you not afraid I will do the same?"

"I tremble . . . with anticipation."

She laughed. "Ibn-Ibrahim, you go to Alamut, and I to Anhilwara. It is an end. We shall not meet again."

"But there is tonight?"

She looked into my eyes again as if surprised by the thought.

"Tonight I sleep; tomorrow we travel."

"And tonight," I said, "I shall walk in the garden, walk under the trees watching the fireflies scattering sparks in the night. Yet I shall not be alone, for I shall have my thoughts of you."

She arose gracefully, and looked back at me, her eyes pools of darkness where beauty lived. How like a flower were her lips! How soft her cheek! How delicate her skin!

"Good night, Scholar. Look again at your stars."

"Their message is clearer when read by two."

She started to turn away as I arose, but pausing, she said, "I go to Anhilwara, and thence to Kannauj, and in Kannauj I shall be married to a friend of the king."

So . . .

Before me lay a black gulf of desolation and emptiness.

"Tonight," I repeated, "I shall walk in the garden."

51

Moonlight's pale hand caressed the garden gate, and where shadows lay among the trees a nightingale sang, but my heart was a cavern of loneliness down which echoed the voice of Sundari.

Alone, cloaked in a mantle of shadow, I walked where jasmine filled the air. A leaf rustled, then was still.

Where was Sundari?

Now I, who had been invulnerable, was so no longer, for now I knew what love was, and knew too late. That sound! A sound like the beat of the walking drum, that was my heart beating out sadness from the emptiness within me.

Alamut waited with moonlight on its hardback peaks, but here was a season of grief. Here within the space of a single night I had found and lost what I most desired. Sadness lay upon me, but no sword could cut the thread of love, no dagger pierce the disaster that lay upon me.

Would Sundari come? Would she come to me in the moonlight when the nightingales sang? Were the Rajput soldiers her protectors or her guards? And if they found her with me . . . ?

How like years are minutes when waiting for one you love! Where was Sundari . . . where?

At each ghostly sound I swiftly turned, my arms ready to welcome, lips to kiss, but only the leaves stirred, only leaves brushing their pale green palms, brushing their pale lips.

I was a fool! She would not come. Why should she come to greet me? She was Sundari Devi, a Rajput of the royal line! A girl who could marry a king or the friend of a king!

Who was I? A scholar some called me, but only I knew the true depths of my ignorance. I, a physician, mountebank, merchant, vagabond . . . a landless man with a sword.

Who was I to expect her to love me on the instant as I loved her? I was a fool, a paltry fool, a miserable fool, a fool who marched to the sound of an empty drum he called destiny.

I, who dared think of rescuing a slave from the walls of Alamut, I had made a slave of myself to dark eyes and long dark lashes, to a slim waist and graceful hands!

Yet, why not? If slave a man must be, why not, then, be a slave to these?

Who can be called a slave who holds a sword? Should I let her be taken away to India? Or take her from her Rajput guards?

Twenty of them? Or twice twenty? The prize was worth the blood! Yet, a cool breath of sanity entered my fevered brain. If I knew anything, I knew fighting men, and those Rajputs were such. I need be a fool indeed to attempt such a thing.

A sound? A distant sound . . . was it a closing door? Or something dropping from a tree in a distant court? Alone in the shadows, breathless, I waited.

Would she come? Or was she somewhere inside preparing for bed, laughing to think of me waiting in the garden? Did her eyes promise what her heart feared to give? Or had the promise I read in her eyes existed only in my own mind?

A nighthawk swooped low; somewhere in the orchard a piece of fruit dropped from a tree.

Irritably, I paced. What a fool I was to wait! She would not come. Perhaps she had forgotten me within the moment. Or if she wished to come, how could she evade those who guarded her?

The soft wind made a shadow of movement among

the leaves. How long had I waited? Should I leave now? Bidding the dream good-bye?

The night told its beads with stars.

What was I, a boy with his first love?

The moon was low, the garden paths no longer lay white from the moon, and tomorrow I must ride to the mountains, every sense alert, I must ride through the hills to the fortress of Alamut, perhaps even to my death.

Enough! Enough of this!

Yet I did not go. I waited, and suddenly she came.

She came!

Wearing a black cloak, she came like a floating shadow, a movement of darkness from the deeper darkness, and she came to me.

"Oh? You are here! I was afraid . . . I was so . . . !"

She came into my arms, and I held her, kissing her tenderly on the lips, for she was frightened now, frightened that she had come at all.

"Must you marry him?"

"Yes"—she lifted her eyes to mine—"I must. If I do not marry him, he will come among us with his armies, and my father will be killed, his kingdom taken. Yet it is not only me he wants, he wants what we have and thinks to win it through me."

"Do you know him?"

"I have seen him. He stands at the right hand of the ruler of Kannauj."

What could I say to that? I loved her, but had I a kingdom to offer? Or wealth? Or armies to rescue her father? Had I anything but the precarious existence of a scholar and a warrior, a landless, homeless man?

A little I knew of her people's history, and the Rajputs were proud. Thirty-six noble lines had carried their swords into battle for hundreds of years before any European emblazoned heraldry upon a shield.

Had she been less than she was, or I more, I would that night have carried her away, but to what?

To wait in a hovel while I went into the fortress of Alamut from which I might never return? A man must be a greater fool than I to ask any girl to risk such a thing.

"I love you, Sundari, more than life itself, but my father is held a slave in the fortress of Alamut, and I have taken a vow to free him.

"This much I can tell you. Tomorrow I go there, and there is a chance, perhaps more than a chance, that they know why I come. Sinan has spies everywhere, even in Europe.

"If I return alive, I shall come to Hind. I shall come to Anhilwara or Kannauj or wherever you are, and I shall find a way to make you my wife. This I promise.

"Delay. Delay your marriage. Wait for me. If I come safely from Alamut, I shall ride to Hind, and to you."

"You can do nothing," she said, "nothing. And you must not come. They would only kill you. If you came with an army, you could do no better. Do you realize what forces the ruler of Kannauj can field? Eight hundred fighting elephants I have heard, and eighty thousand cavalry, all armored men . . . I do not know what else."

"I shall come," I insisted stubbornly, "and if there were three times the number of elephants and thrice the armored men, I would come."

"You must not."

Again I kissed her tenderly, and we clung to each other. How had this come upon us? From which of destiny's trees had blown this leaf?

"I shall come," I repeated, "for today he who rides before an army may tomorrow lie in its dust. I have only a sword, but a strong man need wish for no more than this: a sword in the hand, a horse between his knees, and the woman he loves at the battle's end."

"Nobly spoken."

The voice was behind me, and I turned swiftly, my hand on my sword.

"There is no need for that." He who stepped from the shadows was a Rajput, the one who captained her guard.

He was a tall, powerfully built man, every inch a fighting man. He walked toward us. "Spoken like a Rajput."

"Rachendra! You followed me!"

"That I did, and could I do less? Although believe me, I like it as little as you. But your father has given me the duty of protecting you, and I only do as ordered."

He turned to me. "I am sorry for you and for her, also, but there is no other way. I have the feeling you are twice the man she is to marry.

"Now go your way, and do not come to Hind, for you could bring nothing but trouble."

"If I live, I shall come."

He turned his head to look at me again, a powerful man with a strong face and cold eyes.

"If you do, I may have to kill you myself. This is Sundari Devi, our princess, not to be spoken of in the same breath with a wandering soldier, scholar, or whatever you call yourself. Nor with any Moslem."

Ignoring him, I said to Sundari, "Delay . . . I shall not fail."

Turning to Rachendra, I added, "As you know, I shall come, and I like you, so stay out of my way. I should not like to put a foot of steel into your belly."

He chuckled. "If I had not the Princess to care for and a long, dangerous journey before us, I would measure blades with you. But go to Alamut. You will find trouble enough."

He turned toward the caravanserai, but Sundari came to me. She put her hands on my arms and kissed me on the lips.

"Come then," she said, "and I shall wait for you if I have to put a dagger into him during our marriage." She turned to Rachendra. "You have been like an uncle to me, but if you fight him, and he fails to kill you, I shall!"

Turning abruptly, she walked past him toward the caravanserai, and the startled Rajput watched her go. "By the Gods"—he spoke softly—"there goes a *woman!*"

We faced each other, measuring ourselves against the future. He was a man of about fifty years, built not unlike my father, and like him in temperament. "You stand well," he said, "and I have no doubt you can fight, but heed this: Stay away from Sundari. Her future is written in the stars."

"In the stars? Or her father's plans?"

His features were grim. "Not her father's plans but those he dare not refuse! Stay away. I have warned you."

His face grew more kind. "I have said to stay away, but if you do stay away, you are a fool." Then he repeated what I said, " 'A sword in the hand, a horse between the knees, and the woman he loves at the battle's end.' By the Gods, that was well spoken!"

He strode away, following Sundari, and I faced away from the caravanserai and looked to the mountains. Beyond them lay Alamut. The Talaghan Range and the Alamut *Rud*—the Alamut River—and nearby the Rock of Alamut and the valleys of the Assassins. Tomorrow I would ride into those hills to fulfill my destiny.

The day broke in a crimson flood upon the storm-shattered hills, massive shoulders of granite thrown out from the fires of the earth's beginning.

"I shall go in alone, Khatib, but do you wait for me, wait with three horses saddled, for I shall come. Be it a day, a week, or ten years, I shall come!"

"Place no faith in the words of men, Kerbouchard, for all are liars when it suits their purpose. Those on the Rock are loyal to none but their own. Go prepared to die; if so, you may live."

The trail we took was a trail Khatib knew, for in the depths of his ancient mind there were memories that seemed to reach beyond any experience of his. "It was about here," he mused, "the tree is gone, but it was already old, we should find a canyon where none should be and a trail where no trail could be. Ah, we have found it!"

A trail indeed! It was but an impression of a trail, a shadow trail that turned my stomach hollow to see it.

"No tracks, so perhaps even the Assassins do not know it. There is a high valley hidden among the peaks. There I shall wait, and from there I can watch the fortress, and from the fortress there is a way . . . I will show you."

Our Arabs picked their way with dainty hooves and arched necks, blowing a little in astonishment that they could actually walk where they did.

No plow had turned the rocks of these mountains, no seeds sprouted upon this barren soil. It was a brutal land, hard-shouldered against the sky. The night left a dripping of shadows in the canyons, but we mounted, higher and ever higher, pausing only to let our horses catch their wind, to recover our courage for going further. The air of morning was cool at these heights, startlingly clear, with far-off vistas of other peaks, other castles.

"Lie to them, cheat them, draw their blood!" Khatib muttered. "You are young, and honor rides with you, but honor is important only when dealing with honorable men."

"Are these not honorable men?"

"Yes," he said grudgingly, "and good men too, often enough, Sinan among them, but they are realists. They mean to win, not one battle, but all battles.

"I think of al-Zawila. Him I do not know, but lately I heard gossip of him. He came meekly to this place but with power has become a tyrant. There is evil in him.

"Many a small man is considered good while he remains small, but let power come to him, and he becomes a raging fury. So beware of al-Zawila."

"My old Greek, who was my teacher when I was a boy in my own country," I said, "taught me this. It was a Somali saying, I believe: 'Lie to a liar, for lies are his coin; steal from a thief, for that is easy; lay a trap for the trickster and catch him at the first attempt, but beware of an honest man.' "

"Ah? Yes, yes, a good saying, a good saying."

The millenniums had rolled over these mountains; rain and wind had scoured the rocks; avalanches had wiped away trails until one rode one's imagination across the great shoulders of rock, holding the mind tight against a fall.

Our trail ran parallel to the Chala *derbend*, the Chala Pass. Against the far-off sky we could glimpse the looming majesty of the Tahkt-i-Suleiman, or Solomon's Throne, with a white cloak of thin snow about its shoulders.

We paused where a small torrent spilled over the brink into the gorge below. Tying our horses by their heel ropes and allowing them to feed upon the thin grass, we rested, eating *chapaties* and hard wild pears while looking across granite cliffs streaked with tongues of ancient lava.

When we rode on, we took our time, pausing often to let our horses catch their breath, for the altitude was high and the air thin.

Once, the beckoning finger of a tower lifted itself above the shoulder of the mountain and watched as we passed, miles away. Again we saw a tiny village clinging like an eagle's nest to a gap in the rock, the trail that led to it long since fallen into the gorge below.

"My grandsons will speak of this," Khatib said, "they will boast that their grandsire rode with Kerbouchard when single-handed he stormed the Rock of Alamut. Men will sing songs of this ride all down the ages that lie before us."

"If we survive."

"To survive? What is that? A mouse lives, a fly lives; one flees in terror, another lives in filth. They exist, they are, but do they *live*?

"To challenge the fates, that is living! To ride the storm, to live daringly, to live nobly, not wasting one's life in foolish, silly risks, or ruining the brain with too much wine, or with hashish!

"Allah be blessed that I ride with a *man*! Let cowards run for cover; let them lie, cheat, and betray to keep from gripping a sword. Let them crawl in their holes; let them pretend they are women. They are only the dregs, the useless, the misbred. Let me hold a sword and die beside a man!

"Kerbouchard, there are things worse than death. I am an old man, and often have I fled, but when I fled it was only to fight again on another front. But this! This is a mission for heroes!

"A thousand armed fanatics are within that castle! A thousand swords wait to taste our blood, and all the hills about teem with others of their kind.

"These, Master, are the virtues of a man: that he has traveled far, that he talk well, and that he can fight. That he has traveled far, for travel brings wisdom; that he speak well to speak well of what he has seen; and that he can fight, to whip the man who doubts his stories!"

"You jest, Old Man, you jest! Honor is the thing, for he who is honorable needs no praise. He is secure with the knowledge of what he is, a decent human being first, all else after."

A ridge lay athwart our path, a bridge like a great wall, and far below was the Shah Rud.

We slept the night in a clearing among trees where a cold stream ran down from the mountains, a curious little stream that crept suspiciously from the rocks, looked inquiringly this way and that, then deciding all was well, plunged gaily over the brink of a small declivity to water a few acres of grass where larkspur, lavender, and some pink tufts bloomed.

We put together a small fire of dead willows which had no business growing there, roasted mutton on skewers, and ate *chapaties* while watching the ridges and the trail. We saw the ridges turn to flame as the sun slid down the sky.

"Over there"—Khatib pointed toward the Caspian and Mazanderan—"was where the Persian hero Rustum rode his fabulous horse, Raksh, when he went to slay the White Demon. He slew armies with his single sword and fought for two days with Asfandiyar. He fatally wounded Asfandiyar with an arrow provided by the bird, Simugh."

"I have read of it in the *Shahnamah*."

"Ah? I had forgotten you knew Firdausi. Over there," he continued, "is where the bird Simurgh carried the baby Zal to his nest to protect it. Zal was the father of Rustum."

"I can believe it."

"There is mystery, too. There are treasures here. Over there is a mound that covers an ancient city. I have myself picked up shards of ancient pottery and once a marble hand. Allah, how beautiful it was! I carried it with me for years and valued it greatly. At lonely times I took it from my sash and looked upon it, feeding my soul with its beauty. I was never alone when I had the hand."

"What became of it?"

"A prince took it from me, saying it was too beautiful for one such as I. Do not the poor also love beauty?"

He glanced at me suddenly. "It is whispered, Kerbouchard, that you have second sight. Is it true?"

"What is second sight? A gift? A training? Or is it simply that suddenly within the brain a thousand impressions, ideas, sights, sounds, and smells coincide to provide an impression of what is to be?

"The mind gathers its grain in all fields, storing it against a time of need, then suddenly it bursts into awareness, which men call inspiration or second sight or a gift."

Khatib raked the coals together and banked them against a cold dawn. The chill had grown, and the gorges lay in darkness while the ridges were threads of scarlet in a tapestry of shadow, clinging to the last of the sun's beauty, reluctant to yield their transient beauty to the night.

"The mind is a basket," Khatib said, "if you put nothing in, you get nothing out."

"It is a time for sleep," I said, "not for philosophy."

Khatib huddled in his burnoose. "I bless Allah that I ride with you, Kerbouchard. You are indeed a hero, the equal of Rustum."

"If you think that, watch me on Alamut, for I shall have fear for a companion."

"Aye, and he is brave, indeed, who fears but does what must be done despite it. You will do what you must, with reason to live, for there is always Sundari."

Ah . . . Sundari, where now was Sundari?

52

The mountain of Alamut, they say, resembles a kneeling camel with its neck stretched out on the ground. Deep ravines cut the rock on which the castle was situated from the surrounding mountains, leaving the castle itself virtually impregnable.

The entrance to the valley that was the approach to Alamut was hidden by a fold of the mountain in such a manner that a traveler might easily pass by without seeing the opening at all.

Riding into this valley, we came to a lovely meadow and drew up under the willows. This was the meadow of *Bagh Dasht*, the Garden of the Desert, and a truly beautiful spot, with the great wall of the Rock of Alamut rising above it.

We tied our horses with their heel ropes, squatted in the shade of the poplars along the stream, and ate our small meal in silence.

No doubt we had been observed, but they must be puzzled as to how we had reached this point. The trail over which we had come had long been abandoned, forgotten before the Castle was built. Had the Isma'ili known of its existence, there would have been a watchtower there, or they would have destroyed it entirely.

These mountains were crisscrossed with ancient trails, old before the time of Alexander the Great. At a far distant time caravans had wended their way from Persia to the Merv Oasis and on to Turkestan and Cathay itself. The Assassins had been in the Elburz Mountains scarecely one hundred years, mere visitors by mountain standards.

Khatib knew what he must do, no simple task, his success depending on what he knew of the mountains.

"They will not catch me, Kerbouchard," he said. "My mother came from Daylam, and her people live yonder." A nod indicated the direction. "When you shall go I shall disappear, and the hour will be sundown.

"In three nights I shall be here, at this point." He drew a trail in the dust. "I shall come here each night after that, and wait one hour after midnight. If you wish to come to me, you will know where I will be."

In my pack I hid the strong but slender rope for which I had asked Khatib, and in my saddlebags were the white crystals taken from the manure and the walls of stables. The other things needed were there also.

Along the stream where I had walked I gathered various herbs and some bark. This it had long been my custom to do, for from these came medicines used in my practice. Following the profession of physician as little as I had, it was rare that these were necessary, but a few remedies were always at hand.

There was a story remembered from Córdoba told me when I was myself studying medicine. It was a tale told of Jivaka, the personal physician of Bimbisara, of Magadha.

Jivaka, who became the greatest medical expert of his time, was sent by the emperor to attend Buddha during an illness. Jivaka was a foundling, the child of a courtesan of Rajagriha, thrown out on a dust heap to die. Found by Prince Abhaya, the son of Bimbisara, Jivaka studied medicine at Taxila, the greatest university in the world at the time. Before being allowed to graduate he was told to go out and find a plant within several miles of Taxila that was of no use to a physician. After a long search, Jivaka returned, saying he could find no plant without medicinal value. He was then graduated and given a little money with which to begin his practice.

Khatib, according to plan, picketed the horses out of sight among the willows, then lay down under his burnoose. The position he chose was at the edge of the shade, and when I glanced around a few minutes later, the burnoose still lay there but Khatib was gone. With him had gone our horses.

Idly, I wandered along the stream gathering herbs in full view of the walls of Alamut, but when the shadows grew longer I gathered the burnoose from the ground and started toward the gate and my rendezvous with destiny.

From now on I must live from minute to minute, prepared to move quickly as opportunity offered. My mouth was dry, my stomach hollow. I was going into the very jaws of the enemy. And my father? What of him? Would he be fit for travel? Would I see him soon?

The Castle of Alamut had been built three hundred years before, and I had studied the history of Sallami in which he described the building of the Castle, and how each entry and exit had been built with double gates, massive oaken gates with straps of iron. Having entered the first gate, one crossed a small court to the second, vulnerable to attack from above. The second gate was as strong as the first.

The rooms of the Castle had been carved from solid rock. Long galleries had been constructed, and beneath them were tanks in which were stored wine, vinegar, and honey. A moat led halfway around the Castle, and the river guided into it. Beneath the Castle great tanks had been carved from the rock for the storage of water against a time of siege.

As I went up to the gates, they swung inward, and I went through and heard them clang shut behind me. A chill went up my spine. There would be no turning back now.

A dozen soldiers were there, lean, well-built men armed with pikes and swords. An officer came up to me.

"Where is your slave?"

"Who?" I appeared puzzled. It was still not quite dark, and Khatib would need every second.

"Your servant. The man who was with you?"

"Oh? A good man with horses, a likely man."

"Where is he?" The officer was almost shouting.

"You are unduly excited about a mere hireling, a man of no consequence. Nor do I like your tone."

"*Where is he?*" The officer grasped my arm.

Jerking my arm free, I stepped back and put my hand on my sword. "If you have not learned how to address a visitor," I said, "you can be taught."

In an instant I was surrounded by leveled pikes, but before another move could be made, a voice said, "Bring ibn-Ibrahim to my quarters, Abdul."

Abruptly, the officer turned away, his face taut with fury. Pikemen fell in about me. If I needed no more, this assured me I was a prisoner.

My venture attempted, and lost already. Or had I? No man is lost while yet he lives.

That voice!

It struck me suddenly. *I knew that voice!* Who could it be? Not Sinan, for I had never known him.

The room to which I was shown was long. At one end was a low table. Two guards stood at the door, one stood at either end of the table.

There had been no move to deprive me of my weapons, nor was I sure how I would have reacted had such a move been made.

As I moved, my eyes and ears were busy. Somewhere near was my father, and somewhere a secret tunnel that admitted one to a mysterious valley in the mountains. Or so I had heard.

Darkness had fallen. As I was seating myself, I heard the gate clang shut and the sound of horses' hooves on the paved court.

Had they found Khatib? Not if I knew him. Given the start he had, he would be hidden by now, and not far away.

Yet every time he returned to the meadow he would be in danger.

Despair welled up within me. What *could* I do? Wherever my eyes turned there were guards, lean and savage men, fanatically devoted to the Old Man of the Mountain.

The door opened, and a man stepped in, standing in a
shadow. He paused, taking my measure.

"It has been a long time, Kerbouchard."

So much for my assumed identity. With that sentence,
ibn-Ibrahim died.

He stepped into the light then, and I took a half-step
and stopped, frozen in astonishment.

Mahmoud!

Yet a Mahmoud who had changed. He had grown
heavier; his features had coarsened, his eyes were harder.

"Yes," I agreed, "it has been a long time."

He gestured to a seat, and I crossed my legs and sat
on a cushion, careful to arrange my sword so the hilt was
ready for my grasp. He noticed it, and smiled.

"The sword is of no use, Kerbouchard. I have a
thousand armed men. You can make no move unless I
wish it."

"I understood you were in the service of Prince
Ahmed?"

"That fool! He dismissed me."

"What did you do? Try to approach Aziza?"

His face mottled with anger, and I knew what I
surmised was true. Mahmoud had believed her flirting
with him when she was recognizing me, in Córdoba.

He had been a vain, weak man then. He was older
now, infinitely stronger, yet a vain man still, perhaps a
weak man still.

"It does not matter," he said smugly, "they are dead."

"Dead?"

His teeth bared in what was intended for a smile, but
there was too much hatred in it. "I had them killed.
Prince Ahmed first . . . it was done in the street with a
poisoned dagger."

That Mahmoud was malicious I well knew, that he
would stoop to this I would not have believed. It was an
indication that I had much to learn about human nature.
Or inhuman nature. Judging the change in Mahmoud and
my own position, I had best revise my thinking, and
suddenly.

Caution . . . I must be very cautious.

"You can order a man's death? Or did you give Sinan a reason for having him killed?"

"Al-Zawila can order anyone killed"—he looked at me coolly—"anyone at all."

"Who is al-Zawila?"

He smiled condescendingly. "I am al-Zawila."

Mahmoud . . . *al-Zawila*!

My eyes, I hoped, showed nothing.

"You have heard of me?"

"Nothing that matters," I replied, "just a mention of the name here and there. When Alamut is mentioned, your name comes up."

He was pleased, I could see that. The man had always been vain. It was something to remember.

"Do you know why you are here?"

"I was told Sinan wished to talk with me." Pausing, I wondered. Did Sinan even know I was here? Certainly, within hearing there must be spies. "I am an alchemist, a physician. I hoped to talk to him, for his interests are widely known."

Mahmoud's smile was not pleasant. "He cannot be disturbed by such as you. He does not know you are here. In fact, I brought you here for a particular reason, and because you are a physician and a surgeon.

"After all"—he smiled warmly—"we can be friends, can we not? We had a good many talks, you and I, and I miss them."

For a moment I almost believed him. We had had long talks, many of them, of all the things young men with ideas talk about. His trouble had always been that he wished to know, but he did not want to go through the struggle of learning.

"You could be valuable here. As for Sinan, he is busy with other things."

"I would like that," I said, "this is an interesting place."

"It is the strongest fortress on earth," he boasted.

"Nobody could capture it. Many have tried, and there was one who led his troops to destroy Alamut, but one morning he awoke to find a dagger thrust into the earth beside his bed. A note pinned by the dagger reminded him it could as easily have been in his heart. That man led his army back where they had come from."

"I should like to meet Sinan."

He dismissed the idea with a gesture. "He is much too busy. You are my concern, and mine only." He smiled in a friendly fashion. "You can be of help to me, Kerbouchard. I sent for you because I knew with what respect some of the best physicians in Córdoba held your knowledge of medicine."

"Do you need a physician?"

"Not I . . . another. A favorite slave. You would not refuse me, I am sure?"

"There is the oath of Hippocrates. I would never refuse anyone aid."

"Good!" He got to his feet abruptly, for we had eaten as we talked. "You have ridden far. We will talk in the morning."

I was shown to my sleeping quarters, and my saddlebags and pack were there before me.

The door closed, and I heard the bolt of the massive lock click home. Feet grated on the stone of the passage outside. Locked in, and a guard posted.

Quickly, I went to my pack and opened it. The rope was gone!

So then, I was trapped.

The room in which my pallet lay opened upon an inner court. There was no window to the outside wall of the fortress, and had there been, it would have been to no avail, for we were too high above the ground. Nor would there be any scaling of the rock face as I had done in Spain. Mahmoud must know of that, for it was he who betrayed me into prison.

The change in Mahmoud worried me. He was sure of himself now, for he had a handle on power. He was stronger because of it, and more dangerous. Whatever was in his mind for me could be nothing but evil. At every moment I must be on guard against him.

First, however, I must find my father and where he was kept. Also, I must discover the routine of the changes of the guards and if there was another way of escape from Alamut. Somehow I must let my father know that I was here, for he would know the situation here better than I, and he would have been thinking of escape.

Al-Zawila had been torturing my father, and now I knew why. My father had suffered because of Mahmoud's hatred of me.

Carefully, I examined my position. Sinan apparently knew nothing of my presence. Suppose Sinan could be made to know? Might not Sinan be interested in my knowledge of alchemy? All alchemists, everywhere, had interests in common and often shared ideas or chemical methods.

Al-Zawila, I suddenly recalled, was a place on the coast of Africa. Mahmoud must have come from there. That knowledge would not help, but it made the picture a little clearer. He was, I suspected, a Berber. The Berber relationship with the Arab had been tentative, at best. I must think, think!

The guards here? Berber? Probably not. This was Persia, so the guards were likely to be Persian, Arab, or some other Central Asiatic people.

Nothing could be lost by informing Sinan of my presence, and it was a rare ruler indeed who liked things done without his knowledge. Mahmoud al-Zawila was not serving his master now, but himself.

The favorite slave who needed treatment? Was there such? Or was it a mere trick? Once I had treated the slave, if such there was, then I could be eliminated or enslaved myself.

Blowing out my candle, I went to the window and looked down into the court. A flaring torch showed me a quadrangle of pavement and the castle around it. There were gate towers, and a movement there warned me that there would be guards in the towers, perhaps walking the wall.

Torchlight reflected on the armor of a man standing guard at a door. Such a guard might be posted outside the apartments of Sinan. Of course, it might be a storehouse, an armory, or the entrance to a treasure room.

Somewhere among this hive of rooms and passages was the entrance to that secret valley of which rumor whispered.

Such was the fear of the Old Man's Assassins that kings of the East paid tribute, and those who incurred his displeasure died.

Nor was there any place of safety to which such a one might flee, neither a mosque, the center of an army, nor the presence of a priest or king could save the victim from the poisoned daggers of the Assassins. Doped with hashish and promises of paradise if they died in the Old Man's service, they were absolutely fearless and heedless of their lives. Many died, but rarely before murdering the man they had been sent to kill.

Some of the most notable who had been slain were Nizam-ul-Mulk, minister of Malik Shah, the sovereign of Persia, then his two sons, in 1092; the Prince of Homs, killed at prayer in the leading mosque of that city, in 1102; Maudud, Prince of Mosul, in the chief mosque of that city, 1113; Abul Muzafar 'Ali, Wazir of Sanjar Shah, and Chakar Beg, granduncle of Sanjar Shah, 1114; the Prince of Maragha, at Baghdad in the presence of the Sultan of Persia; the Wazir of Egypt, at Cairo in 1121; Prince of Mosul and Aleppo, in a mosque, 1126; Moyinuddin, Wazir of Sanja Shah, 1127; the Caliph of Egypt, 1129; Prince of Damascus, 1134; Caliph Mostarshid, Caliph Rashid, and Daud, Seljuk Prince of Azerbaijan, 1135–38; Count Raymond of Tripoli, 1149; numerous attempts to murder the great Saracen ruler, Saladin, in 1174 and 1176.

My decision was made suddenly. I spoke into the silence beyond my window, into that stone-walled court where sound would carry.

In a carefully modulated tone, I said, "I want to see Sinan. I wish to speak to Rashid Ad-din Sinan."

A voice from below commanded, "Get back inside! Be still!"

Again I spoke, and somewhat louder. "Do you dare deny me the right to see Rashid Ad-din Sinan?"

53

$\mathbf{M}$y voice was clear and strong, a challenge that sounded loud in the echoing court. No guard dared protest, for if Sinan discovered he had been deliberately kept in ignorance, heads would roll.

My theory was simple. Mahmoud was a man these guards might fear and such men have enemies. He was a latecomer to Alamut, and no doubt, there were some who resented his officiousness. Knowing Mahmoud, he would have been imperious and often disagreeable. Such power as Sinan's lived through spies, and someone would report what was happening if he did not hear it himself.

What I needed was time, to learn what lay about me, where my father was, and some means of escape.

Now I could force the issue, force Mahmoud to explain to Sinan, force him to move in directions he had not planned. If an enemy can be pushed into moving in haste, he may be pushed into mistakes and indiscretions. It was an old policy: Never let an enemy get set; keep him moving.

Countermeasures, whether in diplomacy or war, are never so good as direct measures. Attack, always attack should be the policy of all men, all nations, when facing an enemy. Attack here, there, somewhere else; always keep the enemy on the defensive and in a state of uncertainty as to where the next blow may fall.

Word of my presence would reach Sinan, and Mahmoud must be clever indeed if his explanations would satisfy Sinan.

Sinan, in control of a set of fanatic believers, must

432

know at all times what is happening. He must be a skilled musician of men ready to play on all the strings.

Mahmoud had planned and acted without him, and I did not believe Sinan would appreciate the fact. Mahmoud was skillful at working himself into positions of importance, but his own conniving methods were sure to defeat him eventually. And I must see that eventually was now.

The dried leaves of autumn are lightly blown away, still more easily is the fortune of man destroyed. My fortune, or his?

And then I did what all men must . . . I slept.

Dawn came with lemon-yellow light upon my wall, and I went swiftly to the window and peered into the court. Shadows were still deep there, so I bathed, dressed carefully, and rewound my turban. From my saddlebags I took the materials Khatib had gathered for me, the charcoal, sulphur, and the white crystals from the stable walls. These I mixed in their proper proportions and placed in a white bag inside a saddlebag. The mixture filled the saddlebag when completed.

From the herbs gathered, I prepared several preparations, crushing dried leaves into powder and tucking them away in small papers in the folds of my turban.

This could be my last day on earth.

That I must face. If I escaped and rescued my father, it would be nothing less than a miracle. In this place a weapon might help but could not bring victory.

What had I said that night in Constantinople?

My mind is my sword.

And so it must be.

There was a rush of feet in the passage, and my door was thrust open. In the doorway stood Mahmoud, his eyes hot with hatred. "What have you done? If you think to escape me—"

Smiling, I remembered a saying: *Whom the gods would destroy, they first make mad.*

My smile infuriated him, as I was sure it would, so I added, "Escape *you*? You misunderstand the situation, Mahmoud. It is you who shall not escape me."

His fury astonished me, and I learned something else about Mahmoud. As he had grown older and stronger he had also become impatient of restraint, impatient to a degree that approached imbalance.

"What is the reason for this outburst?"

"Sinan wishes to see you!"

Could I shake his confidence? "Mahmoud, when will you learn to consider not only what you are doing but what others may be doing also?

"Sinan is a master of intrigue, you are only the student. You may be sure he knows more of what you are planning than you suspect. If you believe you will ever replace Sinan, you are mistaken."

Of course, he had been thinking of that, for there was no loyalty in Mahmoud. No matter who his master might be, he would begin at once to try to supplant him. He loved authority, hated to bow to it, yet he was a man who might kill viciously and suddenly, from sheer frustration. I walked a thin line between his ambition and death.

Rashid Ad-din Sinan was a man noted for the majesty with which he surrounded his position. He never allowed anyone to be present when he was eating. He listened much, spoke little, and then only after careful consideration of the problem. He conducted himself carefully when appearing, ruling more by personality than fear.

Assassination was used by the Isma'ilis as a means of war, waged in this manner because they lacked a large army. It was carried out with deadly efficiency. Yet Sinan was a diplomat also, managing the affairs of his sect with skill.

He was also noted for wonders he was said to perform, yet how much was due to second sight, mental communication, or clairvoyance was a question. The same effects could be produced simply by possessing secret information.

Upon one occasion he was foretold the deaths of a number of his enemies following a dispute on the subject of religion. He told each one the day and place of his death, and all died approximately as he foretold.

Of those forty deaths none was by dagger, so he was feared even the more.

My eyes were busy as I was shown into a long room where Sinan was seated upon a dais. As we approached, he kept his eyes on us, studying us.

Some fifteen feet from him we were stopped by a guard. Ignoring Mahmoud, he studied me with attention.

"Ibn-Ibrahim or Kerbouchard, why do you use a name not your own?"

The Isma'ilis were considered heretic by old-line Moslems, and there had been many freethinkers among them, so I decided upon frankness.

"To travel with greater facility, and to avoid discussions. I cannot claim to be a Christian, nor yet a true Moslem, although I have studied the Koran."

"What are you then?"

"An inquirer, Your Excellency, a seeker after knowledge. I am something of a physician, a geographer, and when opportunity offers for experiment, something of an alchemist."

"You knew Averroës?"

"He was my good friend. John of Seville, also."

"And why did you come to Alamut?"

Mahmoud started to speak, but my voice overrode his. "I was invited to come. I understood the invitation was from you. I accepted quickly, for I had heard of your great knowledge of alchemy, but when I arrived I discovered that Mahmoud al-Zawila had invited me. He is an old enemy from Córdoba."

Sinan gestured Mahmoud to silence. "What was the nature of the enmity?"

"Your pardon, Magnificence. I did not say I considered him an enemy. It is he who holds enmity against me. Not," I added, "that I am inclined to forgiveness.

"We were friends as students in Córdoba until I fled the city with a girl. When we returned we were seized, betrayed to Prince Ahmed by Mahmoud."

"Prince Ahmed, you say? And Aziza?" Sinan's expression had changed. His eyes were suddenly cold and attentive. He glanced at Mahmoud, then back to me. "I have heard the names."

Mahmoud was deathly pale. As skillfully as it could be done, I was scuttling his ship, but only by telling the truth. Mahmoud might succeed in having me killed, but now he must be wary of his own life.

"I should believe," Sinan suggested, "Prince Ahmed would reward such service."

"He did, Magnificence. He gave Mahmoud a position at his side."

"Ah?" Sinan's fingers tapped upon his knee.

What I had said might warn him of Mahmoud, might even destroy Mahmoud, but there remained my own safety, and I had an idea the interview was about to end.

"Your Excellency, you are considered among the greatest of alchemists. I hoped to study at your feet, and"—I paused just long enough—"to exchange ideas. Some discoveries of mine have been curious indeed, and of a sort that might interest you."

He arose and was taller than I had thought. Also, he was two steps higher, an interesting position strategically, for we must look up to him.

This man thinks of everything, I thought. He keeps himself ever in a commanding position. It might be nonsense, but it was shrewd nonsense, and effective.

"You will return to your quarters, Kerbouchard, and I shall send some books from my library. Later, you may visit my place of experiment."

He gave a gesture of dismissal, and we turned about and walked from his presence.

We had reached the door before Sinan spoke again. "Al-Zawila, you will answer for the presence of Kerbouchard."

Mahmoud did not speak until outside my door. His face was still pale, but he was in control of himself. "You believe you have defeated me, but know this: Once within these walls, only one of us may leave, only an Isma'ili, and I shall see that if you do leave, you will not be the same man as when you arrived."

He was speaking in Arabic, which he evidently knew the guards did not understand. They were Persians from Daylam.

"He will not move against me, and if he does, we shall see who is master here." He smiled. "No, I shall not submit you to torture . . . not yet. There is first the patient you must attend."

Only a few minutes later a slave appeared at my door with a book. It was the *Ayennamagh*, the book requested from Mas'ud Khan, in Tabriz. Was it coincidence? Or did the lord of Alamut's ears reach so far? No doubt Mas'ud Khan was his man. Yet such a small detail? I was impressed.

The *Ayennamagh* was a book written or compiled during the years of the Sassanian Empire of Persia, translated into Arabic by ibn-al-Muqaffa. It was a compilation of history, court annals, government regulations, and laws, containing discussions of strategy in war as well as politics, archery, and divination.

Yet, no matter how interesting the book, I could not keep my attention on it.

Restlessly, I paced the room. I was no nearer to discovering the whereabouts of my father, and bribery had no chance of success here.

Some things I had noticed in my walk from my quarters to those of Sinan. From the top of my window to the roof was no more than four feet, if as much, and my window was long and narrow. A man might, just *might*, stand on my window's ledge and, holding himself inside with one hand, might reach up and grasp the edge of the roof with the other.

He would have to do it without being seen, and would risk a fall to the stone-paved court below. There was always the chance that he could not reach the roof's edge, nor pull himself up if he did.

Obviously, for reasons of defense there would be some connection between the roof and other roofs as well as the walls.

Below me, in the Castle of Alamut, a struggle for power was taking place in which I had no part, yet which very well might mean life or death for me. Nor dared I make any move without first ascertaining where my father was. As yet I had seen no slaves or any women.

The fortress gave the appearance of being inhabited by men only, and if my father was here, being a slave, he would be at work.

Had they tortured him? Had they broken his spirit?

The spirit of a strong man does not easily break, but he must be inwardly strong, secure in his beliefs and in what he is.

Although my father had often been away at sea, his image had been ever before me, and my mother had led me to assume responsibilities from my earliest youth. There is no miraculous change that takes place in a boy that makes him a man. He becomes a man by being a man, acting like a man.

Now was the time to show what I was made of. No help would be coming from the outside. I was alone.

So it ever is in moments of trial or decision. One is born alone, one dies alone, and usually faces the trials and tribulations alone.

Returning to my book, I turned its pages, reading here and there to acquire as much as possible in the short period of time I would have, struggling to grasp its message while half my faculties were turned to other problems.

Even had he wished, Sinan could not save me. Much of the strength of Alamut was that no one outside could assess its strength, and that meant no one must escape.

Slowly, the day dragged by. My thoughts sought out every possible escape route, every stratagem, every ruse. Nothing happened. By afternoon I could stand it no longer. I must move! I must do something. It had seemed such a simple thing to find my father once inside, but I had seen not one slave, and my food was brought me by a warrior.

And then the door opened . . .

Two guards waited. "The Imam will see you now."

The Imam . . . that would be Sinan. Picking up my bags, I followed them.

The guards escorted me into a branch of the castle where I had not been. On every side, the walls of the rock fell sheer away. Where then was the mysterious valley?

We paused at last before a door. The passage we had followed continued on, perhaps thirty feet further.

The guard tapped lightly at the door, obviously of oak and bound with straps of iron.

My eyes fell to the floor at my feet, and for an instant my breath caught. On the stone floor, mixed with a little black loam, was a fragment of a leaf, a pomegranate leaf!

Nothing grew upon the Rock of Alamut. Nor had I seen a pomegranate within miles, or any fruit that I could remember except for wild pears.

My eyes turned to the door at the end of the passage. Was that it? Had I found the entrance to the fabled Valley of the Assassins?

There were many valleys in the mountains, but there might be no real valley of that name. On the other hand, what lay beyond that door? And where was my father?

A key turned in the door before us, and the door opened. Beside the door stood a huge, powerfully muscled man with a massive sword. He was naked to the waist, and his muscles shone with oil. He stepped aside for us to pass, but his cold little eyes probed as if to read my heart.

Across the room near another door stood the twin of this guard, except that if anything he was larger and uglier.

Seated on a cushion among a pile of books was Rashid Ad-din Sinan, the Old Man of the Mountains.

Around the room were vats, retorts, and furnaces, some of the finest alchemical working materials that I had seen.

"Come! We will talk, Kerbouchard! We will see what kind of alchemist you are!"

54

Where was Sundari now?

Night lay upon the castle, and the wind held a promise of rain. Far off, like muted trumpets, thunder rolled down empty gorges. I lay upon my pallet, staring into darkness, my sword at hand, my bags close by.

The time was near.

The night held a warning, a threat of waiting danger. My ears strained to interpret the warning but found nothing. Nothing moved, all was still.

Today, I had spent hours with Sinan, working with retorts, furnaces, and bowls, quieting any doubts that I was not what I said. We talked of acids and powders, of the Chinese "art of the yellow and white," their term for alchemy. Most of all I tried to build his hopes of what he might get from me.

I wanted to give him an excuse to keep me alive.

Quickly, I discovered that I knew more than he, for he was the victim of his own isolation and knew little that had happened in alchemy since Jabir ibn-Hayyam, known to the Franks as Geber.

He possessed the most complete library of the works of Jabir that I had seen, and Jabir's methods had been sound, his knowledge of alchemical relationships beyond the usual. Aside from his search for a means of making gold, he had studied the manufacture of bronze, steel, and the refinements of metals. He introduced new methods to the dyeing processes. He knew how to produce concentrated acetic acid by the distillation of vinegar, the use of manganese dioxide in glass manufacture, and much else.

Several experiments of which Sinan had only heard, I reproduced for him . . . or perhaps he was but testing my knowledge. Despite my restlessness, I enjoyed knowing him and enjoyed the work. I possess a deep respect for men of knowledge and of inquiring mind, and I am only impatient with those who allow themselves to vegetate.

At last I had been escorted back to my quarters, and I lay down, thinking of the door.

Twice that day, eunuchs had come into the workroom, and where eunuchs were there were usually women.

And where was Sundari? Far and away upon the road to Hind, going to the land of her marriage. And here was I, virtually a prisoner.

A stealthy step in the outer hall, a rattle of keys. Rising to my feet, in one swift movement I drew my sword.

The door opened, and Mahmoud was there with two guards who were not those I remembered. "You will not need that"—he indicated the sword—"but bring it if you wish." He smiled in a way I did not like. "Bring your kit. Tonight we go on an errand of mercy."

Sheathing my blade, I took up my bags and followed. We walked swiftly and silently along the passage, across the court where a few drops of rain were falling, and past the workroom where I had spent much of the day, and down the passage to that door, which I believed might lead to the hidden valley.

A key rattled, the door swung wide, and a dark passage loomed beyond, sloping steeply downward. We walked for several minutes preceded by a guard bearing a torch. Then he paused before another door. It swung open, and I stepped inside.

The room was brightly lit, and six guards stood about with drawn blades. Behind me the door closed with a clang, and a key turned in the lock. Glancing back, I saw that the guard who had followed us stood before the closed door with a drawn blade. With Mahmoud and a guard now lighting more lamps, there were nine. It was too many.

On a table in the center of the room a figure lay, covered with a white spread. Around the room were implements, running water in a tank, and other things that told me this was a room used for surgical operations. The drawn swords I could not understand.

Nor could I understand the fierce triumph in the eyes of Mahmoud.

"Tonight you will perform the operation for which you were brought here. The man upon that table is needed in the Valley, but in his present condition he is no longer of use to us. Your operation will save his life." He was smiling now. "Take your sharpest knife," he said, "and make this man a eunuch. Castrate him."

With a flip of his hand he swung away the sheet, and the man tied upon the table was my father.

Cold . . . I was icy cold. My eyes did not again go to the man on the table; they could not bear to meet those of my father.

Slowly, I glanced around the room. Mahmoud stood back, smiling with triumph. Around stood eight men with drawn blades, and there was no doubt they intended to see I did what was ordered.

Time seemed frozen in an awful stillness, and in the hollow of my skull, where no feeling seemed to exist, my brain struggled for escape, for a way out.

He was bound with four stout cords, and had been tied so for some time. Even if cut free, he would be stiff from being so long immobile.

Mahmoud was amused. "Come, come!" He smiled at me. "You are a physician, and you came prepared. However, if you do not perform the operation, one of my men will do it in your place, while you watch. But I am afraid he will not be so skillful as you."

My eyes swept the room, mentally placing each man. It was a large room, but there was a chance. The fire under the water tank crackled in the silence. "Is the water hot?" I asked. "Is it boiling?"

He glanced into the tank. Now I went up to the table for the first time and looked down into the eyes of my father. The eyes that met mine were the ones I knew, the strength was there. "Be ready." I spoke softly in our Breton tongue.

At a table nearby I took out the knives necessary and laid them on the table. My hands were damp with sweat, but now my mind was working with icy clarity. We both might die here, but there was a chance, a slim chance.

I took several dried plants from my bags and put them on the table.

Once I glanced at the tank, which now stood on a table. There would be water enough.

Taking a scalpel, I stepped to the table where my father lay and concealing the movement with my cloak, I slit the rope near his wrists with the razor-sharp scalpel.

A guard stepped closer, and Mahmoud circled to see what I was doing, his eyes hot with eagerness. In that instant, as several of the other guards crowded closer, I hooked my toe behind the leg of the table on which sat the boiling water, and jerking back with the toe I suddenly threw my weight behind the tank.

The tank and table went over with a crash spilling boiling water across the legs of the three nearest guards. Screaming with agony, they sprang back, one of them falling to the floor, entangling the others. Turning swiftly, I slashed another of the cords that bound my father, then I thrust the scalpel into his hands and drew my sword.

The first came too quickly and stopped his rush too late; my point took him in the throat with a sharp twist to the side, and he staggered back, blood covering his chest. Then the outer door burst open, and a dozen men rushed into the room. In an instant it was filled with fighting as the men of Mahmoud turned to meet these, evidently the men of Sinan.

Catching up my bags, I ran after my father who was already at the unguarded door. He stumbled on legs still numb from the binding, but he pointed with a blade caught up from a fallen guard. We rushed down the long passage, deeper and deeper into the mountain. Then he stopped suddenly, listening. We heard no sound.

We walked on a dozen steps, catching our breath for what might lay before us. "I have been waiting for you." He spoke quietly. "Al-Zawila has tormented me for days with what he would do when you came."

"Did he tell you about Mother?"

"Do you think he would miss that? The man's a devil, Mat."

Mat! I had not been called that in many a year. It was good to hear, and whatever lay before us, we had this moment. We were together again.

"She was a fine woman, your mother. Better than I deserved. There was wildness in me, and she knew it when we married, but never did she try to hold me back until that last trip. She warned me not to go. She had the gift. Do you have it?"

"I suppose so, but it is less a gift than a method. I have never tried to use it, but sometimes when the season is right it comes without warning."

"In that sense I was not one of you, only by marriage, and that did not count with the Old Ones."

We walked on together, two strong men, each with a blade, father and son. The world would be mine now, for my father was with me.

"You taught me well," I said; "the years have proved it."

"I tried."

Behind us, we heard them coming. "Only a little further," he said, and we ran.

"Do you know the Valley?"

"Aye, they had me slaving there, working on the conduits. They are a marvel, I will say that for them, and nobody today knows them well unless it be Sinan, from the maps."

The passage divided into three. He pointed ahead. "There lies the entrance, but the devil himself could not force it. Luckily, there is another way."

We took the left branch and ran on. The hard work they had him doing had left him fit. He had always been enormously strong, and he was heavier than I, no broader in the shoulder but heavier in the chest and thigh.

"Who killed your mother?"

"It was Tournemine, after he heard you were killed."

"Ah . . . well, we shall go back, Mat. We've that to do, you and I."

"It is done." I told him of it as we walked on, and of what I had done with the body, casting it with all its evil into the sulphurous bog of the Yeun Elez.

He glanced around at me. "Now that was a thing! I should not have thought of it."

The passage narrowed, and we heard running water. Our passage became a bridge, and below it ran dark, swift water. Our torches had burned down, and he led me to a small pile of them.

He glanced at me as we lighted torches. "Can you stand a tight place? That's the aqueduct that takes water to the Valley."

The water was waist high. We lowered ourselves into it and once in the tunnel we put out our torch. We moved forward, my father taking the lead. It was a long distance to travel in abysmal darkness, with no ray of light. Emerging suddenly, we heard water falling ahead of us. My father turned suddenly and grabbed the top of the wall and pulled himself up and over. I followed.

Rain fell gently in the Valley of the Assassins. We could feel it, and hear the gentle patter on the leaves. In the distance, lightning flared. We leaned against the outer wall of the flume, shaking with cold.

"Won't they come here?"

"Yes, at last. But the gardens are empty at night. Come, I know a place."

In a corner of the garden, on a shelf of rock, we waited. It would not be long until daybreak.

"This was where we stored materials," my father explained. "These are sections of conduit pipe for new fountains and for repairs."

We huddled shoulder to shoulder, sharing my cloak, and the thought came to me slowly, and only shaped itself when the first light appeared. Standing up, I looked about. Most of the pipe sections were too large and of fire-baked clay. The smaller pipes were of lead.

Such piping was far from new and had been used all over the Arab world in the houses of the wealthy, as it had been used in Rome as well. Looking about, I chose several short lengths of pipe, obviously left over from construction.

Taking several of these I began whittling wooden plugs to fit each end, then tamped them full of the prepared dust from my saddlebags.

"Now what are you doing?" My father was curious. "Is this charcoal?"

"Some of it." I completed filling every bit of space with fragments of lead lying about, pebbles, and some bent and discarded nails. From each pipe I led a piece of string rolled in melted fat from meat that had been served me and that I had carefully hoarded for the purpose. These strings I rolled in the dust packed into the short lengths of pipe. When completed I had three pieces of the prepared pipe.

"What do you plan?" My father had watched my every move. "You seem to know what you are about."

"A vain hope. Something learned from an old book. It is something they have done successfully in China."

"They are a canny folk. I have known men from Cathay."

Strangely, there was nothing to talk about. There was an odd constraint between us. Why is it much easier to talk to a stranger than one from one's own family.

He slept, finally, but I did not. Soon searchers would be looking for us, and tonight Khatib, if still alive and free, would come to the meadow by the Shah Rud. We must be there to meet him.

Day came to a clouded land. The peaks were lost in a cottony gray billowing of cloud. No birds sang today in the Valley of the Assassins.

How long before they found us?

My father slept, his great muscles relaxed, his strong, hard-boned face strangely gentle in the quietness of sleep.

He looked older than I expected, and there were raw scars of burns on his shoulders, as if he had been touched with red-hot iron. The work of Mahmoud, no doubt.

Mahmoud? Where was *he*? In the fierceness of the fight he must have fled. Had he escaped Alamut? Or was he now in command? Those must have been the men of Sinan who rushed in to attack his guards.

Thunder grumbled sullenly, warning that the storm was not over. The trees in the garden were strangely green in the vague light. Peering around the piles of pipe and building materials that screened us, I could see pomegranate and walnut trees from where we lay. Fountains were playing; did some of them actually run with milk and wine?

The Valley was longer than expected, concealed artfully in hills. Knowing something of mountains I could see there would be no way of looking into the valley from above, for the walls bellied out in such a way that if one tried to walk down to look over one would fall. An observer could only see across the canyon, not into it.

Slipping out, I gathered pears from nearby trees, not the hard wild pears, but great luscious fruit as large as my two fists.

Yet, from all I could see we were trapped. I could see no way out except back through the fortress of Alamut.

55

It was a lowering, sullen day. Many times I had pictured the Valley of the Assassins, and always I saw it in sunlight and the dappled shadow of leaves.

Beyond the roof of a pavilion I glimpsed a palace, white and lovely despite the grayness of the day. I ate of a pear and considered the situation without favor.

To return through the fortress was madness, but I saw no alternative.

Rain would restrict movement in the garden, and in this corner where a new palace was to be built there was unlikely to be anyone. How long before they suspected we had escaped through the aqueduct?

It was an unlikely route, and I suspect my father had gone to some difficulty in exploring the way. It was even possible the present rulers of the castle knew nothing of the aqueduct. No doubt it was hundreds of years old.

Somehow, before the day was over, we must plan our escape, and be prepared to move when darkness fell. Until then we must not be found.

My sections of pipe with the prepared dust were not to be trusted. I knew them only from study and not experiment, and I had become a disciple of the trial and error method of the Arabs.

Studying that part of the mountain visible to me, I thought it appeared impossible to climb out. Nor had I any desire to repeat my escape from the castle in Spain, nor to subject my father to such an ordeal.

Once, I heard laughter. Gay laughter, of a young woman or girl, and I heard music. Undoubtedly, the sounds came from a window. No one would be out in this weather.

Shivering, with no fire because of the smoke smell, I waited. My father slept, and no doubt needed it. It was midday when he opened his eyes, immediately alert.

In whispers I explained the situation, and then he began to fill me in. He had only worked in the Valley under the lash of an overseer, yet he had located the various buildings. "There is another aqueduct under the mountain that has steps inside, under the water, but in such a rain as this it is probably running full and with force. It is all enclosed, and I have no idea where it emerges."

While he ate a pear and finished the *chapaties* and fragments of meat, I studied the situation.

Suppose I were Hasan ibn-al-Sabbah? Suppose, being the first of the Assassins, I took over the fortress of Alamut? Whoever the builders were, and it was built about 830 in our time, he would want an escape route. Any man who locks himself inside a fortress must consider the possibility of the fortress being taken. What then? Obviously, a secret escape route, and I had some familiarity with secret passages.

Such an escape must be easily available, and more than one entrance necessary, in the event he was cut off from other parts of the castle. Surely, there must be an escape from the Valley of the Assassins.

The same problem existed here as at the Castle of Othman, so long ago. Any passage must have a place where the escaper could emerge unseen.

Where was Mahmoud? I feared the man. The weak can be terrible when they wish to appear strong, and he was such a man, darkly vengeful and unforgetting. If dying, he would strike out wickedly in all directions to injure all he could to his last breath.

My father gestured toward the filled pipes. "You learned from a book? You read well, then?"

"Latin," I said, "Greek, Arabic, Persian, and some

Sanskrit. In the Frankish tongue I cannot read, but I know of nothing written in that language as yet."

"You are a physician, as they said?"

"It is something I have learned, and practiced a little, not a profession. All knowledge is related, and I have learned what I could. Much of the sea and the stars, much of history, as well as the structure of land, and something of alchemy."

"You have been busy," he said dryly.

Outside, there was a stir of footsteps. A girl or woman wrapped in a burnoose came along a path under the trees, and when close to us she threw back the hood of her burnoose and turned her face up to the soft rain. She stood there a moment, as blond as some of our Frankish girls, lovely as a flower.

We needed help and here it was. The generosity of women was something I had come to trust, the younger ones most of all, for they are less calculating, more romantic. Any girl who turned her face to the rain was a romantic, even if she was in the Valley of the Assassins.

We were alone, and unobserved. "Feels good, doesn't it?"

She turned sharply.

"I am the one who should be afraid," I said. "I am hiding from them."

"You hide from Shama?"

"Who is he?"

"You do not know Shama? He is Chief Eunuch. He brought me here."

"We hide from them all." Trusting this far, I must trust completely. "My father has been a slave here. I am helping him to escape, and trying to escape myself."

"I wish you would help me. I wish to escape, too!"

"We can help each other." I drew her back under the edge of the trees. "We must find a way out. Not the one through the fortress."

"The gardener takes the leaves beyond the wall for burning. It is a small gate, very strong, hidden in a corner of the wall."

"Could you take us there? After sundown?"

"We are not allowed in the garden after sundown. Shama himself locks all the doors. That is when the gardeners work and when the chief gardener takes leaves and dead grass outside the wall."

"He is alone?"

"Two guards are with him. They are huge men, as he is, and very cruel. Everyone warns me I must never be near them. They have killed one girl and several slaves who came too close to that gate."

Obviously, the gate was important. Why had I not considered the obvious—that in every garden there is debris to be disposed of?

"The eunuch has the key?"

"The only one. It is a very strong lock and a heavy door."

"Good. Do not be locked in tonight. Get as near to the gate as you can, and wait there."

"They will kill you!" Her wide blue eyes searched my face. She was young, this one. Too young and tender for such a place as this.

"Possibly. We will avoid fighting if we can, and if we cannot, then we will fight."

She looked at my turban. "You are a *khwaja*, a member of the learned class? A wearer of the turban?"

"A physician at times, a student always, but only a beginner where women are concerned. Will you teach me?"

She flushed and said primly, "I doubt if you have much to learn. Go then; if I can, I shall meet you."

Briefly, once more in our shelter, I explained the situation to my father. He looked at me with ironic amusement. "I see you have not neglected your lessons. I suppose when we go, she goes with us?"

"My father taught me to obtain some profit from each situation," I said, "and she *is* lovely!"

The day moved upon leaden feet with no shadows to mark the hours. We shivered and were cold, but colder when six soldiers passed by, swords in their hands, searching. Sometimes the obvious is missed, and they did not investigate our shelter.

The rain helped, for a soldier is ever a soldier, and they wished to return to warm quarters and the games they had left rather than search for men they did not expect to find here, anyway.

Yet the first was a lucky man. Had he bent to look behind the stacked pipes, never guessing there was space behind there, he might have tasted a foot of steel in his throat, a most unappetizing piece of business.

The rain continued, and the thunder in the hollow gorges, growling and rumbling, a sullen brute of thunder, irritable over Allah knows what.

"Three men at the gate?" my father asked. "Three men. Well, I shall have two of them."

"Two? I did not know you for a greedy man. The least you could do for a growing boy was to let him have the best of it. Two for me, I say."

"You are a scholar, I the warrior," my father said dryly. "Each to his trade."

"You have much to learn of the cub you sired. I have had more to do with the giving of wounds than the healing of them. Do you look to your man, and I to mine, then we shall see who is better at his trade."

He looked at me with hard, level eyes, amused eyes. Then he stretched out and slept, and I admired him for it, for a good fighting man will eat when there is food, and sleep when there is time, for he never knows when opportunity will come again.

"She is a beautiful girl," I said as he closed his eyes.

"You think of women at a time like this?"

"Any time is a time for thinking of women," I said, "and when they thrust the blade that takes my life I shall be thinking of women, or of a woman. If not, then death has come too late."

The clouds grew heavier, blacker, and thunder rolled its drums to warn of the assault to come. I had a feeling it would be a bad night, a worse night than I had seen.

Yet I wiped the moisture from my blade and looked again at the golden words that said, *Killer of enemies*!

"Do you live up to your name this night," I said, "or I shall have no more enemies and no more use for you!"

So saying, I drew my cloak about my ears and went to sleep.

56

The hand of my father touched my shoulder, and my eyes opened as my hand grasped the blade. "It is time," he said, "and the storm grows."

Rising from where I had been seated, I brushed my robe and gathered it about me.

"There was a time," my father said, "when at the sack of a coastal city we who attacked threw our scabbards away, vowing never to sheathe our swords short of victory."

"A noble sentiment, so consider mine thrown away; only as it is studded with gems, I shall keep it. Who knows when a ruby will be needed?"

We walked shoulder to shoulder, our blades drawn. When one has lost his freedom it is always a long walk back.

We stopped in the deeper shadows of a tree, looking to the torches that spat and sputtered in the rain. A huge man stood there, wide as the two of us together. "It will take more than a foot of sword to scuttle that ship," my father whispered. "Let me have him."

"You have too much appetite," I said, "but do you take him if you reach him first."

The huge man was striding about, bawling his displeasure. His was a brutal, bullying manner, and I had never seen a man it would give me more pleasure to bleed.

"Lazy!" he shouted. "Starve a slave and he sleeps; feed him and he fornicates!"

They were coming with baskets on their heads, a line of them moving toward the gate. Seeing no guards, I judged they would be outside, as there was a torch there, also.

A stir of movement in the shadows near the building. It was the girl whose advice had given us this chance, but the big eunuch saw the movement also.

"You, there! Come out from there! Allah, the Holy, the Compassionate, what have we here?"

A guard stepped through the gate. "Give her to us. She would be of no use to you, Laban."

"Speak for yourself, soldier, and find your own women. In my case the operation was not complete, and I shall—!"

Stepping into the open, I said, "Then I shall complete the operation, Fat One, and open your belly to the rain!"

My father sprang past me, and the big eunuch screamed as he took the steel. Striking aside the blade of the soldier, I lunged, too swiftly! He caught me with but the tip of his point, and it drew blood, but my blade backhanded, and the razor-edge of it half severed his arm. He stumbled back, and seeing their chance the slaves dropped their burdens and rushed the gate.

The soldier I had slashed came at me, but my point pinned him, and my father was at the gate. "Too slow!" he shouted. "Come, take a lesson at this!"

Yet at the moment he would have passed through, the big guard swung it shut. The lock clicked shut. From far away there was a shout and a sound of running men.

The key was gone.

Our chances had gone with it, unless . . .

"Stand back!" I said, and I jammed one of my sections of lead pipe behind the handle of the gate and close against the socket that held the bolt. Another I hung from a string to a hinge, then lighted both fuses.

"Back!" I shouted. "Stand back!"

"What is it?" My father grasped my arm. "What do you do?"

"The Chinese call it *huo yao*, the fire chemical," I said.

The running feet were closer; outside, a guard pounded against the gate.

The strings hissed as the fire crept. My heart was pounding. Was it too wet? Was the book mistaken? Half frightened by the forces I might be loosing, I stepped back, moving my father and the girl with me.

Was it true? That which I read so long ago in Córdoba? That thunder, lightning, and destruction were hidden in that dust?

Armed men were running upon us, light from the torches reflected from their naked blades. Now they were coming through the garden, among the trees . . .

The night ripped apart with a shattering blast, and a tremendous flame shot up, then another. Something whizzed past my head with an angry snarl, and we were surrounded by a choking, billowing smoke.

Behind us, men stopped running, astonished by the blast of sound, the smoke, and the huge flashes of light. Through the smoke we could see the shattered gate, hanging only in fragments from the bottom hinge.

My father was first through the opening, and we were close behind. The outer guard's head was blown away, an arm gone at the shoulder; that much I glimpsed as we fled, leaping and bounding down the storm-swept rocks of the mountainside, for as if envious of our blast, the storm broke in all its fury.

Lightning hurled its flaming lances against the mountainside, ripping apart the curtain of the sky with writhing fire-snakes that raced with incredible speed along the naked peaks of the mountains.

We ran shouting into the night, crazy with our joy at being free, and around and before us ran the slaves, free also.

We fell, we scrambled up, charging on, our madness unabated. The meadow was just below, and with Allah to be blessed, Khatib came riding from the shadows. Towering above us were the massive walls of Alamut, and then suddenly, as if from the ground, a dozen soldiers.

My father, berserk with freedom, the storm, and the feel of a sword in his hand at last, sprang to meet them, sweeping the head from the shoulders of the nearest, and then the slaves were upon them. One leaped to the shoulders of a soldier and began tearing at his eyes with long, raking fingers.

I saw only flashing blades weirdly lit by flashes of lightning while the thunder rolled massive drums against the walls of Alamut.

Blood soaked my shirt beneath the mail, blood from my neck wound. Sword in one hand, the girl in the other, we plunged on, and then the horses were there, and Khatib was shouting at us. We sprang to the saddle, my father on the stallion, and I upon Ayesha. The girl sprang barebacked upon the other mare.

We rode, running before the storm, following where Khatib led.

The hammer of the storm beat upon the anvil of the mountain; rain lashed our faces, pounded upon our backs. We switched this way and that across the meadow, dodging soldiers who would stop us and slaves cheering us on, and then we were in a canyon, out upon a narrow ledge that clung to the mountain only by imagination, riding through a cascade that poured down the mountain above us.

Suddenly, livid and white in a brilliant flash of lightning, the Throne of Solomon!

When the sun of morning broke through the shattered storm, we were riding along a barren slope of rock, then a trail made by *djinns*, and then we came to a city where no city could be.

Khatib chuckled at my astonishment. "It was built as a refuge before Darius, perhaps by Daylamites . . . perhaps by *whom*?"

An ancient town with an ancient shrine on a mountain where men no longer ride. Then Khatib pointed his bony finger at tracks in the earth, fresh tracks. "No! It cannot be!"

We rode across the small valley, we four, and up to the broken wall. No gate remained, only a hollow arch,

and towers beside from which stones had fallen. Our
horses picked their way with dainty feet among the stones.

Under the wide and empty sky from which the clouds
fled like scattered sheep lay the empty streets, the roofless
halls, the hoofbeats of our horses echoing hollowly. Beyond
the frame of an arch lay a temple poised against a tawny
slope, a solitary pillar like an arresting finger against the
sky. Then there was a rattle of other hooves, and we drew
up.

We waited.

A dozen mounted men and Mahmoud.

Of her own will, Ayesha stepped out toward them,
her head up, nostrils distended.

"*Mahmoud!*" My challenge rang against the echoing
walls. "Mahmoud! You and I . . . alone . . . *now*!"

"I shall kill you, Scholar! I was always the better
man!"

Ayesha stepped toward them; she knew her business,
that young lady did, just as she had on that day, long
since, against Prince Yury.

He charged upon me, cloak billowing behind. He had
always been a good man with a blade. I parried his blow,
but he would not be put off and had at me again. He lifted
his blade, and mine was too low. He started the downward swing, and death rode its edge.

"I am Kerbouchard," I shouted, speaking out of our
past, "a student and a drinker of wine!"

Involuntarily, his muscles seemed to catch, gripped
by memory, by surprise. My own blade came up, and his
struck, but the force was gone, and his blade slid harm-
lessly off mine.

My thrust followed through; our eyes locked, and
then his falling body wrenched the sword from my hand,
and he struck the pavement on his back, looking up at me.
Stepping down from my saddle, I lay hold of my sword.

"When you withdraw that blade," he said, "I shall
die."

"Yes, Mahmoud."

"You always bested me. I was a fool to speak to you

that day in the garden by the Guadalquivir. 'A student and a drinker of wine.' I remembered the words."

He stared up at me. "How often I remembered them! I hated you!"

My hand tightened upon the sword hilt. "Draw it," he said, "draw it, and be damned!"

I drew the sword.

57

We paused upon the high road where the sun lay with a white hot hand, and our four horses were restive in the heat.

Behind us, a few miles off, lay Hamadhan, a fair white city in a fertile lovely plain. It was said that long ago, under another name, it had been the capital of the Medes; at the moment I did not care.

Khatib and I faced my father, beside him, Zubadiyah.

"It is here then?" my father asked. "Is it here that we part?"

Two weeks had gone by since the death of Mahmoud on a shoulder of the Throne of Solomon, two weeks in which we had ridden down the mountain and to Hamadhan. From here my father would ride to Basra, on the Persian Gulf.

"And then?" I asked.

"A ship of my own, the broad sea. Men of my own kind."

"You will find them here?"

His hard brown face broke into a smile, revealing white, strong teeth. "Where there is a sea," he said, "there are corsairs. Pirates, if you will."

When Mahmoud died upon the mountain we stood shoulder to shoulder, we two Kerbouchards, prepared to meet the others, but they lacked the will to face our steel, too many had died.

"My way lies to Hind," I said, "to Rajastan."

"And mine to the sea again." He looked at me, understanding what I must do. "For two weeks I have had a son."

"We shall meet again. Wherever you go, in time I shall find you again."

We divided the purses of gold that had come from Mas'ud Khan and from Sinan. To my father I gave two mares. Zubadiyah would ride one to Basra. Her mother had been a Circassian, but her home lay near the Gulf.

We clasped forearms in the Roman fashion, and for an instant each stared into the eyes of the other. "You have the eyes of your mother," he said roughly—and then he smiled—"but my fist with a sword!"

"My destiny lies there"—I moved my head toward Hind—"you understand?"

"Go," he said, "it is the way of sons, and better so. A knife is sharpened on stone, steel is tempered by fire, but men must be sharpened by men."

We rode away then, and when a long way off, I looked back; they sat there yet, gazing after us.

Ayesha was impatient, bobbing her head and tasting the bit. She was ever the mare who loved the road.

Khatib waited, facing east.

"Sundari," I whispered, "Sundari, I come! I come . . . !"

THE END

Author's Note

I have always been fascinated by the period of history dealt with in *The Walking Drum* and have so enjoyed the writing and researching of this story that I am planning to continue Kerbouchard's tale in at least two more adventures during the next few years, the first of which will follow Kerbouchard to Hind (India) in search of Sundari.

The place names, titles of books, authors, and dates are factual, the descriptions of places and people are based upon the best contemporary and historical sources, as well as personal observation. On occasion I have referred to places by names now in use for purposes of clarity.

Unhappily, history as presented in our schools virtually ignores two thirds of the world, confining itself to limited areas around the Mediterranean, to western Europe, and North America. Of China, India, and the Moslem world almost nothing is said, yet their contribution to our civilization was enormous, and they are now powers with which we must deal both today and tomorrow, and which it would be well for us to understand.

One of the best means of introduction to any history is the historical novel.

ABU-YUSUF YA'KUB: Succeeded his father in 1184 and ruled for about fifteen years.

ALAMUT: Only ruins are left in a remote corner of the Elburz Mountains in Iran. The fortress was destroyed by the Mongols under Hulegu who found it commanded by a weak ruler. After its surrender the fortress was destroyed with a thoroughness typical of the Mongols. The details of the destruction are provided by 'Ata-Malik Juvaini in his *History of the World Conqueror*, translated from the Persian by John Andrew Boyle. Juvaini was a companion of Genghis Khan, and was with Hulegu at the time Alamut was taken.

ANDRONICUS (Comnenus): Became emperor two years after the death of Manuel. As foreseen by Kerbouchard in this story, the mob turned on him, and he died as told here. No monarch in history died more horribly.

ASSASSINS: Members of an Isma'ili sect, now an important and honorable sect with many members in Pakistan and headed by the Aga Khan, successor to the Old Man of the Mountain.

BLANDY: The ruin of this castle with its interesting crypt and secret passage is just over a mile from Champeaux, not far off the route from Paris to Fontainebleau.

BRIGNOGAN: A small seaside resort with white sands and fantastically shaped rocks on the north coast of Brittany not far from the end of the peninsula.

CELTS: Their place of origin is uncertain. Perhaps eastern Europe, southern Russia, or even Central Asia. A Celtic language probably existed by 1000 B.C. Celts fought as mercenaries in the armies of Egypt, Carthage, and Greece. A relationship with the Aryan peoples of northern India is indicated, and the tradition of oral learning was common to both. There are ritualistic and ceremonial similarities.

CHAMPEAUX: The old church, built in A.D. 550, is especially interesting.

DRUIDS: The Druids were the priests, judges, magicians, and philosophers of the Celts, who carried in their memories the history, ritual, traditions, and genealogies of their people. The earliest recorded mention is by Sotion of Alexandria, a Greek of about 200 B.C. An ancient order, they very likely had roots among pre-Celtic peoples of western France and the Mediterranean. They taught the immortality of the soul, that it passed into other bodies, but there seems to be no connection with the doctrines of Pythagoras. There was some variation in Druidic custom in Brittany, England, Wales, and Ireland. There is an affinity with the Brahmins of India. Julius Caesar and Tacitus both offer comments on the Druids. There is some indication of communication between these peoples and the Minoan civilization of Crete.

THE FLAT WORLD: The Chinese, Hindus, Arabs, and Greeks long knew it was nothing of the kind. So did many people in western Europe. The story of belief in a flat world has been endlessly repeated by those who would magnify the voyage of Columbus out of all proportion. As a matter of fact, if one studies maritime navigation before and after it will be seen that Columbus had rather an easy time of it. His ships were small by our standards, but oceans have been crossed by many much smaller craft both before and after his time.

Traveling the routes he followed in his earlier years, visiting or residing in Genoa, Lisbon, etc., Columbus would have had to be both deaf and blind not to have heard of Atlantic voyages. Columbus and his brother made their livings, for a time, copying charts.

Ancient sea voyaging was much more extensive than has been suspected, and there was probably no land on earth that had not been visited before recorded history. Evidences of man have been found on even the most remote islands.

The secret of making a discovery then, as now, was to make it at the right time with proper attention to publicity.

GEESE: The discovery of land by following the flight of birds is as old as mankind. The annual migration of geese from Ireland to their nesting places in Iceland, Greenland, or Labrador would have indicated land in those directions. It is roughly but 600 miles from the west coast of Ireland to Iceland, less than 200 miles to the nearest point on Greenland, and only about 600 or a bit less to Labrador.

The distances were nowhere so great as those sailed by small craft in the South Pacific or Indian oceans. Many South Pacific islands were discovered by following the flight of birds.

GUNPOWDER INVENTION: Despite arguments for Roger Bacon, Black Berthold, and others, gunpowder had been used in China before A.D. 1000 (*Science in Traditional China*, by Joseph Needham). Grenades and explosive bombs hurled by catapults had been used, and it is probable that gunpowder had been used in fireworks as early as the T'ang dynasty.

HIND: India

HUELGOAT, YEUN ELEZ, etc: Very much as described. A wild, beautiful setting, strangely eerie, especially on a moonlit or stormy night.

IRISH IN ICELAND: Recorded in the Norse sagas. When the first Norsemen arrived in Iceland, they found Irish priests waiting on the beach. The Irish had made many voyages into the western seas before the Vikings.

MANUEL I (Comnenus): Emperor of the Eastern Roman Empire at Constantinople, was in the last few months of his reign at the time of this story, and died in the same year. A man of enormous physical strength, a fine soldier, and a competent ruler, he waged some wars that were wasted effort and failed to strengthen his overall position.

MEN MARZ: The Miracle Stone, probably erected in Neolithic times. About twenty-five feet high. An object of veneration for several thousand years.

MOORISH SPAIN: Arabs from North Africa, called Moors, had intermarried somewhat with the Berbers, a white people who occupied most of North Africa, and conquered Spain 710–712. They held all of Spain and a part of France for a time, and more than half of Spain for the best part of

750 years, leaving an indelible stamp upon the land. Cultural diffusion from there and from Sicily, also held for a time by the Arabs, had much to do with the beginning of the Renaissance in Europe.

MOSLEM LIBRARIES: Literally thousands of manuscripts lie untranslated and unknown in mosque libraries. Many are of religious character, but undoubtedly others could add important chapters to the histories of science and exploration.

It is possible that archives in private libraries, mosques, and monasteries in China, India, Japan, Tibet, and the Arab countries contain as many books awaiting discovery as ever have been translated into any European tongue.

PETCHENEGS: Pre-Mongol invaders from the steppes of Asia, who lived, fought, and looked much like the Mongols who were to conquer much of Asia and Russia in the century following this story.

PRE-COLUMBIAN VOYAGES: Breton, Norman, and Basque fishermen, as well as others from Bristol and Iceland, had apparently been fishing off the banks of Newfoundland for many years before Columbus.

Settlers from Greenland came regularly to the coast of Canada to cut timber for building houses or ships, and there is some evidence of temporary settlements at various points along the coast as well as on the rivers. The Maine islands were visited and temporarily occupied at a very early time.

Alexandre Aufredi, for example, sent ten ships on a voyage into the west from La Rochelle. The ships were gone for several years, but at last when hope had been given up, they returned. The details of the voyage are lost.

There was never any need to "discover" America. The Chukchi Indians of Siberia had been crossing the Bering Strait for centuries.

Vitus Bering had a chart showing the west coast of Alaska and Canada as far down as Vancouver Island before any known explorer visited the area. Magellan had a chart of the Strait before beginning his voyage. Seafaring and exploration are far older than any recorded history.

PROVINS: A walled town with a maze of catacombs, cellars, and tunnels beneath it. The tunnel from Champeaux to Melun and Provins was reported to have been built in the seventh, eighth, and ninth centuries.

RUE DU FOUARRE: Site of one of the first schools of Paris, this lies behind the Church of St. Julien le Pauvre on the Left Bank, not far from Notre Dame itself. It was named for the bundles of straw on which students sat for lectures. Dante visited there in 1304.

SAÔNE: This Crusader castle stands in remote, rocky, and brush-covered hills not far south of the ancient city of Antioch, the modern Antakya. It is approximately opposite (but some distance inland) from the isle of Cyprus. It is still an impressive ruin, but off the beaten track and rarely visited.

TOLENTE: One does not think of lost cities when thinking of Brittany, yet there were several. Tolente was destroyed by the Norsemen in 875, and was reportedly the site of a school of necromancers. The supposed site is now occupied by the village of Plouguerneau.

TOURNEMINE: A lawless family of unknown, perhaps British, origin, known for the Castle of Hunaudaye in the forest by that name, situated a bit south of the road from Plancoet to Lamballe. It is a massive and picturesque ruin, said to have been built in 1378 by Pierre de Tournemine, possibly on the site of an earlier castle built in 1220. The last of the Tournemines is reported to have killed his father, wife, and brother, and according to legend was carried off by their ghosts. There is some suggestion that a still earlier timbered fortress occupied the site before 1220.

VENETI: The first seafaring people of western Europe, *of whom we know*, from whom the Irish may have received their impetus. Brittany was their home. The best description of their oak-hulled ships with leathern sails is found in Caesar's *Commentaries*. The ships of the Veneti were of heavier construction than necessary for coastwise voyages, and they had many such ships. Nobody knows where or with whom they traded aside from voyages for tin to the Scilly Isles or Cornwall.

ABOUT LOUIS L'AMOUR

"I think of myself in the oral tradition—as a troubador, a village taleteller, the man in the shadows of the campfire. That's the way I'd like to be remembered—as a storyteller. A good storyteller."

It is doubtful that any author could be as at home in the world re-created in his novels as Louis Dearborn L'Amour. Not only could he physically fill the boots of the rugged characters he writes about, but he has literally "walked the land my characters walk." His personal experiences, as well as his lifelong devotion to historical research, have combined to give Mr. L'Amour the unique knowledge and understanding of the people, events, and challenge of the American frontier that have become the hallmarks of his popularity.

Of French-Irish descent, Mr. L'Amour can trace his own family in North America back to the early 1600s and follow their steady progression westward, "always on the frontier." As a boy growing up in Jamestown, North Dakota, he absorbed all he could about his family's frontier heritage, including the story of his great-grandfather who was scalped by Sioux warriors.

Spurred by an eager curiosity and desire to broaden his horizons, Mr. L'Amour left home at the age of fifteen and enjoyed a wide variety of jobs including seaman, lumberjack, elephant handler, skinner of dead cattle, assessment miner, and officer on tank destroyers during World War II. During his "yondering days" he also circled the world on a freighter, sailed a dhow on the Red Sea, was shipwrecked in the West Indies and stranded in the Mojave Desert. He has won fifty-one of fifty-nine fights as a professional boxer and worked as a journalist and lecturer. A voracious reader and collector of rare books, Mr. L'Amour's personal library of some 10,000 volumes covers a broad range of scholarly disciplines including many personal papers, maps and diaries of the pioneers.

Mr. L'Amour "wanted to write almost from the time I could walk." After developing a widespread following for his many adventure stories written for the fiction magazines, Mr. L'Amour published his first full-length novel, *Hondo*, in 1953. Mr. L'Amour is now one of the four bestselling living novelists in the world. Every one of his more than 85 novels is constantly in print and every one has sold more than one million copies, giving him more million-copy bestsellers than any other living author. His books have been translated into more than a dozen languages, and more than thirty of his novels and stories have been made into feature films and television movies.

The recipient of many great honors and awards, in 1983 Mr. L'Amour became the first novelist ever to be awarded a Special National Gold Medal by the United States Congress in honor of his life's work. In 1984 he was also awarded the Medal of Freedom by President Ronald Reagan.

Mr. L'Amour lives in Los Angeles with his wife, Kathy, and their two children, Beau and Angelique.

A MESSAGE FROM LOUIS L'AMOUR

I had a wonderful time writing the story of Kerbouchard in *The Walking Drum*, and I have completed much of the research for the second volume of what I plan to be the three main adventures in his saga. Many of my readers have been kind enough to take the time to write to me after reading the hardcover edition of *The Walking Drum* to tell me how much they enjoyed this story and to let me know how eager they are to find out what happens when Kerbouchard follows Sundari to Hind, or India as we now know it.

Well, nobody is more eager than I am to find out what's going to happen next to Kerbouchard, but I had another character who had been waiting patiently for me to tell *his* story, one who also had been generating a lot of queries from readers, and I felt it was time to turn my attention to him. And so I wrote my newest historical novel, the saga of *Jubal Sackett*.

Jubal Sackett is the eighteenth novel I have written featuring members of a single family, The Sacketts. Its publication in 1985 will mark the twenty-fifth anniversary of the first Sackett novel, *The Daybreakers*. I mentioned above the great experience I had writing about Kerbouchard, and I thoroughly enjoy the creation and research of all of my novels and stories. I really don't have any favorites other than the book on which I'm currently at work. However, the Sackett novels—well, they do seem to have a special attraction for me and for many of my readers. My wife, Kathy, still enjoys reminding me of how exhilarated I was when I was writing that first Sackett novel, how I would come bounding up the stairs to read her practically every page fresh from my typewriter.

The idea for the Sackett family actually started in the town square of Tucumcari, New Mexico, during my own "yondering" days. I got into a fight there. It wasn't a fight in the ring—I was a stranger in town, and a stranger in some of those towns is the butt of anybody's jokes. I got into a fight with a fellow, and I was whipping him, when some of his friends tried to step in and help him, and then two fellows stopped them.

When it was all over, I became quite friendly with these two gentlemen, and I learned they were cousins. We rode across the country together, and while we were camped out one night, we got to talking about the fight. One of them said, "We never have any fights."

I said, "Well, you're lucky."

He said, "No, we're not lucky. I have thirteen boys in my family, and he's got sixteen in his." I figured, boy, that's the way to go. I began thinking of writing a story about a family like that, where whenever one member was in trouble, all the others always came to help.

As they developed over the years the Sackett men and women all had one thing in common. There is no back-up in a Sackett. The Sacketts have all been "up the creek and over the mountain." In the various Sackett characters I have tried to express much of the spirit and qualities that helped our nation to be built and to thrive. Much of the Sackett curiosity, energy, willingness to face danger, and fierce independence—yet absolute readiness to take responsibility for aiding others in a jam—was typical of the men and women who made this country work.

I am extremely proud and grateful that so many readers have followed the Sackett family stories over these past twenty-five years. I set out, back in 1960, to do something different, to create a family of characters through whose eyes readers could experience much of the sweep of the settling of our continent. Eventually, I came to expand this idea to include two other families, the Talons and the Chantrys, whose adventures would, I hoped, enhance readers' understanding of the different types of people who helped to establish our nation.

After writing a number of novels with Sackett brothers and cousins as they struggled to make a place for themselves in the post–Civil War West, I began getting some wonderful letters from my readers. As always, they proved to be not only thoughtful but encouraging to my own creative instincts.

I began to realize that readers were beginning to respond to the lore and family history that I was trying to develop in the Sackett novels. People were writing to ask me about the early pioneers, about how men and women made those first momentous decisions to come to the frontier, and about what it took to stay. I knew I had to go back in time to tell the story of the first Sacketts and how they came to settle in America.

Beginning with *Sackett's Land*, which describes the flight of the patriarch, Barnabas Sackett, from the tyranny of England in 1599 as he seeks the opportunity of the largely unknown lands of the New World, I started to fill in the early generations of the Sacketts. Subsequent novels move back and forth in time, but I found myself drawn more and more to the early Sacketts. *To the Far Blue Mountains* continues the story of Barnabas, his wife, Abigail, and their three oldest sons, Kin-Ring, Yance, and Jubal, as they carve out a home on the eastern frontier. *The Warrior's Path* is a story of Kin-Ring and Yance, but I've long wanted to set down the saga of Jubal Sackett.

Jubal Sackett is that story, and it is the longest of the Sackett novels. Like the other Sackett novels, it stands on its own; one need not have read any of the previous Sackett stories to enjoy it, but I hope Sackett fans will be satisfied with a character whose brief appearances seem to have won him a number of admirers.

I found Jubal so intriguing as a character because he was one of that rare breed of men whose urge to be on his own, to explore, to experience, really opened up this continent. At the novel's beginning he has "gone over the mountain," left his home and family in the mountains of what is now Tennessee. He has answered the call of the lonely, wild places and is beginning his trek westward, ever westward, into an empty, largely unknown land.

Through Jubal's adventures I have tried to get readers to know very directly what it must have been like, to be one of the first white men to see this vast land that is now ours—its nameless rivers, swamps, mountains, forests, and plains beyond what Jubal knew only as the Great River—all unspoiled. It was a chance for me to write in great detail about the various Indian tribes Jubal would meet on such a journey, who, even then, were "old upon this land," and from whom he learns a great deal—from the fascinatingly intricate society of the

Natchee tribe to the terrors of the Plains, the Comanche. It is the hunt for a missing Natchee woman, by the way, that involves Jubal in the great love of his life, as well as some of his greatest dangers.

I hope you enjoy *Jubal Sackett*. It has certainly been as much fun for me in the writing as any of the other Sackett novels, and I think you will find it has lots of facts and feelings about the early days of this country, lots of detail about life among the seventeenth-century Indian tribes, and lots of adventure. I'm also proud to tell you that in celebration of the twenty-fifth anniversary of The Sacketts, Bantam Books will begin publishing all of the other seventeen existing novels with a whole new "family" look, with brand-new, handsome, and historically authentic cover paintings, as well as maps in most of the books. It's one very visible way of saluting the Sackett family at this milestone point, and I certainly want to join in saluting all of you readers who have helped them—and me—to reach this happy occasion.

Louis L'Amour

Louis L'Amour
Los Angeles, California

Here is a special preview of
the opening pages of Louis L'Amour's
newest historical novel

JUBAL
SACKETT

A cold wind blew off Hanging Dog Mountain and I had no
fire, nor dared I strike so much as a spark that might betray
my hiding place. Somewhere near an enemy lurked, waiting.

Yesterday morning, watching my back-trail, I saw a deer
startle, cross a meadow in great bounds, and disappear into
the forest. Later, shortly after high sun, two birds flew up
suddenly. Something was following me.

Warm in my blanket, I huddled below a low earthen bank,
concealed by brush and a fallen tree. The wind swept by
above me, worrying my mind because its sound might cover
the approach of an enemy creeping closer. Then he could lie
in wait to kill me when I arose from my hiding place.

I, Jubal Sackett, was but a day's journey from our home on
Shooting Creek in the foothills of the Nantahalas, close upon
Chunky Gal Mountain.

All the enemies of whom I knew were far from here, yet
any stranger was a potential enemy, and he is a wise traveler
who is forever alert.

Our white enemies were beyond the sea, and our only red
enemies were the Seneca, living far away to the north beyond
Hudson's River. No Seneca was apt to be found alone so far

from others of his kind. The Seneca were a fine, fierce lot of fighting men of the Iroquois League, who had become our enemies because we were friends of the Catawba, who were their enemies.

Whoever followed me was a good reader of sign, for I left little evidence of my passing. Such an enemy is one to guard against, for skilled tracking is evidence of a great hunter and a great warrior. And I did not wish to leave my scalp in the lodge of some unknown enemy, when my life had scarcely begun.

I thought about how I came to be here. What was this strange urge that was driving me westward, ever westward, into an empty land?

Behind me were family, home, and all that I might have become; before me were nameless rivers, swamps, mountains, forests, and, beyond the great river, the plains, those vast grasslands of which we had only heard, and of which we knew nothing.

About me and before me lay a haunted land whose boundaries we did not know. What little we had heard was from the tales of Indians, and we knew they shied from this land, hunting here but always moving and returning to their homes far away. When the night winds prowled, they huddled close to their fires and peered uneasily into the night. There was game here in plenty, and when the need was great they came to hunt. We did not know what mysteries lay here or why it was shunned, but the Indians spoke of it as a dark and bloody ground.

Why, in such a land of meadows, forests, and streams were there no habitations? Once it was not so, for there were earth-mounds, and friendly Indians had told us of a stone fort built they knew not when nor by whom.

Who were those who vanished? Why did they come, build, and then disappear? What happened upon this ground? What dark and shameful deed? What horror so great that generations of Indians feared the land?

There was a legend of white men, bearded men who came to live along the rivers in a time long past. All were killed. Some said it was done by the Cherokee, some by the Shawnee, but it was an old memory and old memories have a way of escaping their origin, carried by word of mouth or by intermarriage from one tribe to the next.

There were rumors, also, of a dark-skinned people who lived in secluded valleys, a people who were neither Indian nor African, but of a different cast of feature, who held themselves aloof and kept strange customs and a different style of living. But we knew nothing beyond the rumor, for their valleys lay far from ours.

I did not come to solve mysteries, but to seek out the land.

My father, Barnabas, was the first of our name to come to this place beyond the ocean from the England of his birth. Of Barnabas I was the third son, Kin-Ring and Yance born before me. My older brothers had found homes among the hills. My younger brother Brian and my one sister, Noelle, had returned to England with our mother, my brother to read for the law, my sister to be reared in a gentler land than this. I did not believe I would see them again, nor hear of them unless it would be by some distant whisper on the wind. Nor shall I again see my father.

I have been called the Strange One, like the others but different. I love my brothers and they love me, but my way is a lonely way, and I chose to go into a land from which I believed I would not return.

Of them all my father understood me best, for with all his great strength and magnificent fighting ability there was much in him of the poet and mystic, as there is in me.

Our last evening together I shall not forget, for each of us knew it was to be the last time. Lila, who prepared our supper, also knew. Lila is Welsh and the wife of my father's old friend, Jeremy Ring, and had been a maid to my mother ere they departed from England.

My father, Lila, and I had the Gift. Some call it Second Sight, but we three often had previsions of what was to be, sometimes with stark clarity, often only in fleeting glimpses as through the fog or shadows. All our family had the Gift to some degree, but I most of all, yet I had never sought to use it, nor wished to see what was to be.

I knew how my father would die and almost when, and he knew also when we talked that last time. He accepted the nearness of death as he accepted life, and he would die as he would have wished, weapon in hand, trying his strength against others.

We parted that night knowing it was for the last time, with a strong handclasp and a look into each other's eyes. It was enough. I would keep his memory always, and he would know that somewhere far to the westward his blood would seek the lonely trails to open the land for those who would follow.

A faint patter of rain had awakened me, and now I eased from under my blanket and prepared a neat pack. Daylight, or as much as I was likely to see, was not far off. It had been snug and dry where I slept but with only a few inches of overhang to shelter my bed from the rain. I had shouldered my pack and girded my weapons before the thought came to me.

I smoothed the earth where I slept and took up a twig and drew four crosses in the earth.

The red man was forever curious, and to most of whom we call Indians four was a magic number. He who followed would come upon this mark and wonder. He might even worry a little and be wary of seeking me out, for the Indian is ever a believer in medicine or, as some say, magic.

So it was that in the last hour of darkness I went down the mountain through the laurel sticks, crossed a small stream, and skirted a meadow to come to the trace I sought.

Nearly one hundred years before, De Soto had come this way, his marchings and his cruelties leaving no more mark than the stirring of leaves as he passed. A few old Indians had vague recollections of De Soto, but they merely shrugged at our questions. We who wandered the land knew this was no "new world." The term was merely a conceit in the minds of those who had not known of it before.

The trace when I came upon it was a track left by the woods buffalo, who were fewer in number but larger in size than the buffalo of the Great Plains. The buffalo was the greatest of all trail-makers. Long ago the buffalo had discovered all the salt licks, mountain passes, and watering holes. We latecomers had only to follow the way they had gone, for there were no better trails anywhere.

When I came upon the track, I began to run. We who lived in the forest regularly ran or walked from place to place as did the Indians. It was by far the best way to cover distance where few horses and fewer roads were to be found.

My brothers ran well but were heavier than I and not so agile. Although very strong, I was twenty pounds lighter than Kin-Ring and thirty lighter than Yance.

Our strength was born of our daily lives. Our cabins and our palisades were built of logs cut and dragged from the forest. The logs for the palisade stood upright in ditches built for the purpose. Only in the past few years had we managed to obtain horses from the Spanish in Florida, who broke their own law in selling them to us when they departed for their home across the sea.

Every task demanded strength, for logs used in building the cabins were from eight to twenty inches thick and twenty to thirty feet in length. There are "slights" and skills known to workingmen that enable them to handle heavy weights, but in the final event it comes down to sheer muscle. So my brothers and I had grown to uncommon strength, indulging in wrestling, tossing the caber, and lifting large stones in contests one with the other.

Our Catawba friends marveled at our strength, for quick and agile as they were, and very strong, nothing in their lives called for the lifting of heavy weights. Unaccustomed to lifting, their muscles were longer and leaner. They were excellent wrestlers, however.

At an easy trot I moved through the forest, my moccasins making no sound on the damp leaves underfoot. Emerging upon a hilltop not unlike the "balds" found in the higher mountains, I drew back against the wall of trees, letting my soiled buckskins merge with the tree trunks and brush, scanning the vast stretch of land that lay before me.

For the moment the rain had ceased, although far off against a mountainside I could see a rainstorm drawing its gray veil across the distant hills. Never had I seen a land so lovely.

Carefully, I studied my back-trail or that portion of it visible from where I stood. There was nothing in sight. Had I escaped my unknown pursuer? Not for a moment did I believe that.

Somewhere before me lay the river called Tenasee and the long, narrow valley of which we had heard. My father had put this task upon me, to find a new land to which we could move if necessary.

My father was a fugitive from England, sought because it was mistakenly believed he had recovered King John's lost treasure from The Wash. Also, we had settled upon our land with no grant from the King or Governor, although we had proved useful to the powers that were in Virginia and they had not been inclined to cause trouble. Yet, a new governor might be appointed at any time, and my father warned us that we must seek a new land, further west, and make our plans in case something went wrong. We could then, at a moment's notice, pick up and move west beyond the reach of the King or his minions.

"See to it, Jubal," my father had said. "Find us a westward way. The King does not realize the size of this country nor how that size will affect its governing. In the old country land was held by the king, given to his great lords for their services to him, and it was farmed by serfs. There one must cling to one's place or become a landless man. Here there is land for all and no man need work for another."

He had paused then and looked into my eyes. "Do remember your brothers, Jubal, and all who bear our name. 'Tis a wide and a lonely land, but if we stand together we have naught to fear."

"I shall not forget."

"And pass the word, Jubal. Let your sons remember, and your daughters.

"My envy for you is great, Jubal, for I, too, would see the lands where you will walk. I wish I might feel their rain, accept the shade of their trees, and smell the fragrance of those distant pines." After a moment he added, "I, too, shall go west, Jubal."

"I know."

"Where the chips fall, there let them lie."

"It shall be so."

For too long I had stood staring across that vast and lovely land thinking of my father and the long way he had come from his birth in the fens of England to his arrival here, among the first of those who came to this land.

The far-off veil of rain diminished, then faded. A shaft of sunlight fell through a hole in the clouds revealing the long, loaflike mountains.

Chilhowee . . . from there I would turn north. I did so abruptly . . . and it saved my life.

A hard-thrown spear thudded into the tree where I had been standing, its shaft vibrating with the force of the throw.

Dropping to the earth, I rolled swiftly over and over,

coming up near a fallen tree, bow bent, and arrow ready . . . waiting.

My position was a good one, and above all, I had his spear before my eyes. It was a very good spear, handsomely crafted, and he would not wish to lose it. Therefore, I had only to wait, and when he came for it I should have one enemy less.

It had never been my way to seek trouble, but if one is attacked by a man whose time has come, who would stand in the way of fate?

My back was well covered by a gigantic up-rearing of roots and earth from a fallen tree, and scattered near were many pinecones on which no one could step without making a sound. Nevertheless, I could take nothing for granted. My bow bent slightly, I waited.

For a long time there was no sound. The Indian is a great hunter and as such he has patience, yet my life in the wilderness had taught me patience also. One learns to adapt to the land in which one lives.

My ears were tuned for the slightest sound, my entire body alert to move or adjust. Nothing happened, and the slow minutes plodded by on lagging feet. The low-hanging branches held shadows away from the sun, and the tree trunks were dark columns with only small spaces between. It needed a quick eye to catch any movement among them.

A thrush flitted from a branch to another, then took off down a long lane of the forest toward the trace I had followed. Somewhere a squirrel chattered irritably, but I heard no human sound—even a moccasin whispers lightly when it moves.

Glancing about, I managed to keep a corner of an eye upon the spear. Suddenly, there was a faint sound. My head turned. Quickly I glanced back. The spear was gone!

Exasperated, I swore softly to myself. I had been a fool! That sound that had diverted me . . . he had thrown a stick or a chip, and like a child I had taken the bait.

Moreover, now he had his spear in hand once more, and it was, perhaps, his favorite weapon. Certainly he had thrown it with skill, and only my unexpected movement had saved my life. Would I be so lucky again?

Undoubtedly on recovering his spear he had moved, but in

what direction? He wanted to kill me, so he would be waiting in ambush somewhere. At the same time, it was best for me to move, for he would soon discover where I lay, if he had not already done so. A moment longer, I waited.

There was, alongside the great fallen tree, a narrow way that was free of the scattered pinecones, and the branches of the dead tree did not begin for at least thirty feet.

Swiftly, silently, I moved, keeping low alongside the tree, then ducking under it among the hanging bark. Waiting, I heard no sound, and I plotted my next move. A swift move again and I was among the standing trees, flitting away, an impossible target for a spear . . . if he saw me.

Months before, I had come this far west, exploring a route to the Great River of which we had heard, and I knew the trace I planned to follow made a great arc not far ahead, so, moving through the thick of the forest, I headed for that trace. Hours later, when I reached it, I found no tracks upon the path. Apparently, I was before him. Again I settled down to running.

What manner of man was he who followed me? A wandering hunter, seeking a scalp? Few Indians traveled alone. Usually there were small parties of them when they went either hunting or seeking war. Yet this man was alone. A strong warrior, no doubt, sure of his skills, and a man to be reckoned with.

On and on I ran, running easily, smoothly. Several times I glimpsed the tracks of buffalo and once a deer. Later, as the afternoon drew on, I stopped for a drink at a small creek. Near the water's edge there were the tracks of a large bear. They were fresh tracks made within minutes of my arrival.

After a careful look around I made four small crosses inside the bear track.

Now I no longer ran but walked, alert for means of obscuring my trail. I walked upstream in the water for a short distance, pausing to make sure the swift current was wiping out my tracks in the streambed. Then I followed a smaller stream for a hundred steps, followed a log from which the bark had fallen away, and then stepped off on a rocky ledge and followed it to the end, careful to disturb none of the leaves or gravel scattered upon it. Then deliberately I changed direction and went back toward my last night's camp, now far away.

There was a path high among the rocks of which I knew, and when I reached it I found no fresh tracks. This path ran along the way in which I wished to go. As I walked I thought of Pa and how he would have enjoyed this, but so would Kin-Ring and Yance, although Yance would have been inclined to try to ambush my pursuer and have it out with him.

I had no wish to kill the man even though he had tried to kill me. If it became necessary, of course . . .

Night was coming and I was alone. It was time for rest and food.

I chose three ancient oaks beside a small stream, one leaning far out. A grassy bank and driftwood scattered along the stream.

A fire, meat broiling over a flame, a time of eating, of listening to the rustle of water and the subdued crackle of flames, then sleep. This is what I wished for but could not quite have, for a man had followed me and might find me again.

He had come shrewdly upon me, and I did not doubt he would work out the trail I left for him. Many another might have lost it, but not this one, I thought. Yet I would wait, for I had an idea.

My fire was the work of a moment. A handful of crushed bark, a few slivers of pitch pine from an old stump that I had carried with me, then a blow with flint and steel, a spark, then a small tendril of smoke, a puff or two from the lungs and a flame. It is not always so easy. To light a fire properly one must prepare it well. Fire is man's first and faithful friend, and ever a potential enemy.

He who followed might come to my fire, and something told me he would. He was curious, as all wild things are inclined to be, and I believed he wished to know what manner of man I was.

Where I was pointed no white man had gone, although Indians had told me that far to the westward there were men who spoke like those of Florida and who wore iron headdresses. Westward lay the Great River, which some said was discovered by De Soto but we who knew of such things knew it had been discovered twenty years earlier by Alvarez de Pineda. Who else might have seen the river we did not know, but there were rumors of others who came, of much fighting and dying.

My fire blazed up, a small, hot blaze but larger than usual. Deliberately I was inviting my enemy in. By now he knew it was not my custom to build large or very bright fires, and he would recognize the invitation. As he was curious about me, so I was curious about him. Who was this stranger who wandered alone where all went in company?

He had tried to kill me, but that was expected where any stranger was a potential enemy. Drawing back into the shadows with a great tree at my back, I waited. My longbow was placed near in plain sight, but a pistol lay in my lap. My visitor would be friendly, I hoped, but if his destiny was to die, I would not stand in his way.

Chewing on a bit of dried venison, I listened and waited. Then, suddenly, he was there at the edge of the firelight, a man as tall as I but leaner.

He was an Indian of a kind I knew not.

The dangers that Jubal Sackett faces are only beginning. Drawing upon his skill with weapons, his courage and wits, and his intense spirit for the land, he continues his journey across the untamed and virtually uncharted American wilderness. He has a restless urge to seek adventure, to explore fresh territory, and to meet new Indian tribes. One of those tribes is the Natchee, who call themselves "Children of the Sun." It is Jubal's search for the missing daughter of the Great Sun, a beautiful but very strong-willed woman, that will sweep him up in his greatest love—and his greatest challenges.

Read Jubal Sackett, *now on sale in paperback.*

Special Offer
Buy a Bantam Book
for only 50¢.

Now you can have Bantam's catalog filled with hundreds
of titles plus take advantage of our unique and exciting
bonus book offer. A special offer which gives you the
opportunity to purchase a Bantam book for only 50¢.
Here's how!

By ordering any five books at the regular price per
order, you can also choose any other single book
listed (up to a $5.95 value) for just 50¢. Some
restrictions do apply, but for further details why not
send for Bantam's catalog of titles today!

Just send us your name and address and we will send
you a catalog!